Losing NUKA

Kayla Howarth

Illustration : Erica petit Illustration

http://andromnesia.com

Edited by Xterraweb Edits

http://editing.xterraweb.com/

ISBN: 1530115248

ISBN-13: 978-1530115242

DEDICATION

For my fans of The Institute Series.
Without you, I wouldn't be living my dream. Here's hoping the spin-off lives up to its predecessor.

ACKNOWLEDGMENTS

To my betas: Hannah, Lisa, Linda, Kimberly, The Michelles, Bethany. I'm sure I'm forgetting people, and that makes me a horrible person. But you all know that already.

To Erica Petit for the awesome cover.

To Kelly Hartigan for editing my comma deficient mess. Not to mention the numerous dangling participles (I swear those bastards write themselves and have nothing to do with me.)

I always thank my husband for supporting me, so this isn't new. But thanks anyway, hubby! Thank you for living in a messy messy house so I have time to write.

-1-

SAY MY NAME

The warm glow emitting from inside my childhood home casts an illusion of perfection. The light blue panelling is almost grey in the early evening dusk, but it still has that homely presence about it. The tyre swing in the front yard sits immobile, dangling from the large tree branch. Children's bikes lie on the front lawn. A basketball hoop sits above the garage. It's obvious the kids who grew up here never wanted for anything. They've been raised in a loving and nurturing environment.

But that's the thing about illusions—they're misleading. Who would've thought a simple two-storey house could hold so many lies?

I try to summon the courage to make my feet start moving towards the front door, but it doesn't work. Locked in a trance, I stare at my home of the past … I start counting … *six, seven …* eight years.

How can I look Mum and Dad in the eye and accuse them of

lying to me for *twelve* years—ever since they adopted me when my biological dad died? I was only six at the time and can barely remember him. To me, my parents have always been Lia and Jayce. I never knew my birth mother. I never even knew her name … until now.

Cadence Edwards.

Turns out *her* name isn't the only thing Mum and Dad have been hiding from me. How could they have kept something this big from me? And what else have they been hiding?

Sure, they'll probably use some excuses like "We were waiting for the right time," or "We were waiting for you to bring it up." But I personally would've preferred them to blurt out, "By the way, Nuka isn't your real name. Just so you know" while we were doing the dishes one night.

"Sorry. No record of a Nuka James born on that date. Or any other date for that matter." The guy behind the counter at Births, Deaths, and Marriages delivered his words like they couldn't possibly have life-altering consequences. *Boom*, everything you thought you ever knew was a lie.

Okay, so maybe that's being dramatic—it's just a name. It doesn't mean anything, right? Isn't there that old saying, "what's in a name?" Does a name have any reflection on the person you become?

Would a different name have led me to lead a different life? Would I still be living with my adopted family and going to uni? Would my birth name have an impact on the way I behaved? Would I be more of a girly girl if I were named anything but Nuka? Would I be a tomboy?

People say there's nothing in a name, but the list of what-ifs is endless.

I've been trying to rationalise why they would've changed my name, but I've gotten nowhere. What possible reason could my family have for lying to me for so long?

Now here I am, hours after the biggest bombshell had been

dropped, still trying to make sense of the information I *did* manage to find at BDM. I guess there's only one way to do that, and it involves going inside.

Sighing and standing up straight, I make my way to the front entrance with feigned confidence. Something I completely lose the minute I step over the threshold.

"We were about to start dinner without you," Mum says as I dump my backpack on the ground near the hallway.

"Sorry. Study group went a little long." I walk into the dining room, nervously running my fingers through my blonde hair. It's a reflexive habit I have when I lie.

"You were probably too busy making out with Declan," Will, my annoying little brother, says. He's twelve with the attitude of a sixteen-year-old. He's a smartass and know-it-all.

"Declan and I are just friends." I slap him on the back of his head as I take the seat next to him at the table.

"What's *making out*?" my sister asks, making the table laugh.

"You won't have to worry about that for a few more years yet, Illy," Dad says, reaching across the table to pat her on the head.

"Is it like sex? Because that's totally gross, Nuka," Illyana replies.

I bite my lip and try to stifle a laugh because both Mum and Dad are scowling.

"How do you know about … *sex*, Illyana?" Mum fumbles over the words.

"Please. I'm eight, not six."

This time I do laugh. Will does too.

"All right," Dad says in his most authoritative tone, "which one of you has been talking to Illy about sex?" He points his fork, waving it between Will and me.

"It wasn't me," I say, holding up my hands in surrender. Will's suspiciously quiet though.

"Will told me." Illy rats him out in an ever-so-casual tone, not even lifting her head from her plate. "It's when two people lie down and kiss, and the boy grabs the girl's boobs, and—"

"That's enough, Illyana," Mum says sternly, but I get the feeling she's now trying not to laugh with us.

The rest of dinner is quiet … well, as quiet as a table of five people can be. There's small talk about school, but I don't participate. Will and Illyana do enough talking for the three of us. Will leaves the table first, dumping his plate in the sink and going upstairs to his room. Illyana is next to leave. I'm still pushing my peas around my plate when Dad gets up and starts doing the dishes.

"What's wrong?" Mum asks, leaning over the table and grabbing my hand.

Looking into her brown eyes, I'm reminded of how young she is. Yes, she's my parental figure, but the truth is, she's only fourteen years older than me. She's more like an older sister than a mother. She was only twenty when she took six-year-old me in.

It took a long time for me to call Mum and Dad, "Mum and Dad." They were Lia and Jayce for a long time. When Will was five, he started calling them Lia and Jayce too. I asked them if they wanted me to call them Mum and Dad instead, not to confuse Will, but I was just looking for an excuse. I'd wanted to call them Mum and Dad for a long time but was worried they never truly saw me like that—like their actual daughter. Hearing them say they'd love for that to happen was still one of my happiest memories of living with them. They made me feel like I belonged. It makes their betrayal so much worse.

"Nothing's wrong," I reply, but even I can hear the upset tone in my voice.

"Did you and Declan have a fight?"

"We're just friends."

"Friends can't fight?"

I shake my head. "This isn't about him."

"Is it about uni? Are the classes too hard? I'm sure you just need time to get into a routine."

I shake my head again.

She stands and comes to sit in the chair next to me, grasping my hand on the table again. "Then what's this about?"

I can't bring myself to look at her. "What's my real name?" I whisper. *So much for being confident.*

She lets go of my hand, suddenly sinking back in her chair. "What did you just ask?" Her tone is rigid, but I can also hear a hint of fear in her voice.

"My real name. What is it?" I say louder but still have my eyes planted firmly on the table in front of me. That is, until a loud crashing sound comes from the kitchen as Dad drops a plate in the sink. He must've heard me that time too.

"It's Nuka." Mum's voice breaks.

Dad appears in the doorway, leaning against the doorframe that leads to the kitchen.

"I wasn't really studying this afternoon," I admit. "I tried to get a copy of my birth certificate, but they had no record of me. How could I be here if I technically don't exist?"

Mum sighs. "We knew you'd want to find out about your birth parents sooner or later. We just hoped you'd come to us first."

Dad comes and sits on the other side of me.

My stare is glued to the plate in front of me. "I didn't want to hurt your feelings. I'm glad you're my parents, but …"

"You want to know who you come from," Dad finishes for me. I silently nod. "We completely understand you wanting that," he says reassuringly in his soothing psychologist voice.

"Why couldn't they find my name?" I ask.

Out of the corner of my eye, I see them glance at each other then back at me.

"Your birth mother …" Mum hesitates. "She gave you up, turned you over to the Institute behind your father's back. He was against sending you there, even though you're Immune."

I roll my eyes at her using that term. It's so politically correct, it's so … *blergh*. Everyone still calls us Defective, whether we like it or not.

"So, you're saying she didn't want me?" My eyes start to fill with tears. I always thought that's what happened, but a big part of me was hoping that it wasn't her choice to give me up. I hoped she was forced to abandon me, to obey the law at the time, which stated all Defectives must live and receive treatment at the Institute—a glorified prison in the middle of nowhere, far away from "normal" people.

"You have to understand what it was like back then. The entire country was scared of Immunes because of what we can do. Because of our abilities, they didn't see us as normal. They thought they had to segregate us to keep everyone else safe. Thanks to your biological father, everyone now knows that's not true. He spent the last few years of his life convincing the world we're just like everyone else."

My dad took over as the director of the Institute when I was five, and he set everyone free. He found loopholes in the stupid law and used them to liberate us.

"Then why do we still have separate schools? Why is there a normal school and a Defective school? Why are there so many Institute Estates in the outer suburbs so Defectives can live in communities with other Defectives? You say it's different now, but it's not really."

"There will always be hate and discrimination against those who are different. Especially when even Immunes don't have enough pride to refuse using the word Defective." She gives me a stern look. I roll my eyes again. "It's a sad thing for the world to endure, but it seems to be human nature. I shouldn't have to explain all of this, Nuka. I know you didn't do great in History at high school, but come on—I'd like to think you at least listened to my public ramblings over the years."

She's right. With her being the most famous Immune activist in the country, I've had to listen to numerous speeches of hers. Not to mention the constant ramblings at home, too.

"I know," I say dejectedly. "I just don't understand it still."

Mum purses her lips. "Many of us don't."

"It still doesn't explain why they couldn't find me in the system," I say, getting back on topic.

"Your dad changed your name to Nuka after your mother sent you to the Institute, and then he sealed the files. You've always been known as Nuka to me, and we didn't actually learn it wasn't your real name until we tried to adopt you legally—long after your dad was gone."

"What do you mean, 'tried'?"

"Your father left you to me in his will. I know that sounds like you were some sort of possession, but what I mean is, he wanted me to look after you. I was worried your mother was going to try to come back and claim you, and I wasn't going to let that happen. We looked into adopting you properly around the time Illy was born, around the time we moved into this house, but we needed your birth mum's permission. So we dropped the whole thing. We knew opening that can of worms wouldn't have ended well."

"So I'm not yours?"

"Of course, you're ours," Dad says firmly. "We raised you, you're our daughter. We're your legal guardians."

"Just not my legal parents," I state.

"It's only a title," Mum says, trying to reassure me.

"So you never told my birth mother that Dad died?"

"She would've seen it on the news. He was a promising presidential candidate when he was…"

"Murdered," I say without emotion. "You can say it. I do remember what happened to him."

"If she wanted you, she would've come for you then."

"How do you know she didn't? She could've come but didn't

know where to find us."

Mum and Dad look at each other again before Mum sighs and looks away. "Your father didn't want that."

"She had a right to claim me, and you kept me from her."

"She could've come, but she didn't," she says.

Dad remains silent next to me.

"You don't know that. Not for certain. What if I was never meant to be yours? What if my real mother was looking for me but was looking for my birth name? She wouldn't have been able to find me."

"Nuka," Mum says, her condescending tone fuelling my sudden anger. "She wouldn't have given you up in the first place if that was the case."

"I still think I have the right to find that out for myself."

"I suppose that's true, you do have that right, but as your parent and the person who raised you for a lot longer than that woman ever did, I don't want to see you making a mistake you could never recover from."

"You kept my mother from me," I say, proud of myself that my voice doesn't waver.

"*I* am your mother," she practically growls. "*She* abandoned you."

"Did she, though? I should at least be able to find out the truth. And not from the woman who got stuck with me because my dad died. The same woman who has lied to me for years. You never adopted me willingly, you inherited me."

"That's not true, Nuk—"

"Will you at least help me try and find my birth mother? If for nothing else, then just to get some answers? I need to know why my dad changed my name, I need to know why she gave me up. And, if she hasn't come looking for me, I want to know why."

"That's all perfectly natural to want those things," Dad says. "But you also have to be strong enough to handle the consequences of your search. How will you feel if you do find this woman and she shuts the door in your face? What will happen if she rejects you again? We don't want to see you go through something like that. She's abandoned you once before, what's to stop her from doing it again?"

"Says you two. How do I know you're telling me the truth? You've been lying to me my entire life. And not only me, but William as well. BDM couldn't give me my birth certificate, so I asked for all the info I could get on my dad. I found it interesting that *you* were engaged to my dad at one point." I give Mum a pointed glare. "They gave me your marriage license application form, but what else is interesting is it was for *after* Will was born. So I'm guessing Will doesn't belong to Daddy Jayce? Is Will my *actual* brother?"

Mum winces as if she's in pain. "No. It wasn't like that between your dad and me. We were just friends."

"Dad isn't my real dad?" Will's tiny voice echoes through the suddenly silent house.

Crap! I didn't mean for him to hear that. I hadn't completely decided whether or not to bring that up at all, but I want to know the truth. If Will is my biological brother, that means they've been lying to both of us.

"I really wish you had come to us first," Mum mumbles to me as she turns to Will. "William, sweetheart—"

"I'll talk to Will, you finish with Nuka," Dad says, standing to guide my brother back to his room. He turns back just before they disappear upstairs. "We knew this day was coming sooner or later," he says to Mum.

"Will is not your biological brother," Mum says quietly, turning to face me. "His father died long before your dad and I ever … well, we weren't even together. If you must know, I've only been with two men in my life—Will's dad and Jayce."

I wince, not really being comforted by her words. I did *not* need to know that about my mum.

"Your father and I, we had an agreement. We were friends who agreed to marry on the grounds that it would be good for his presidential campaign, but he was killed not long after our engagement. I didn't even know he had already applied for a marriage license. When he died, he wanted me to take you, and I did. I've always looked at you like a daughter, and I didn't want to lose you. That's why we never sought out your birth mother. We knew you'd want to know about your past one day, but we didn't want to be the ones to bring it up. In hindsight, we probably should have, but there's never really the right time to have this kind of conversation."

Mum's tone is downright disappointed. This is why I didn't come to her first. I'd feel guilty if I wasn't so mad. It's like a fire has ignited in the pit of my belly, full of rage and anger. A part of me knows it's irrational, but there's a bigger part of me that wants answers. And it's clear they aren't willing to give them to me.

"What's my real name?" I ask again.

She doesn't respond.

I don't want to be in this house anymore. I stand up, preparing to leave.

"Where are you going?"

"What do you care?" I yell.

"Really, Nuka? Going to play the teenager card? Going to yell irrationally and run away? You're a bit old for that now, aren't you? I thought we lucked out with you, that we weren't going to go through this phase."

It's not like Mum to lose her cool—be sarcastic, yes, but not yell. It rattles me further. "Well, I thought you'd always be honest with me. There's so much that you haven't told me, *and* Will, *and* I'm assuming Illy as well."

Storming to the hallway and grabbing my backpack off the ground, I head for the door when Mum's pleading makes me pause.

"Please don't leave like this." Her voice is quiet and full of pain.

"Tell me what my name is."

"We don't know," Mum says.

Forcing myself to turn and look at her, I have to quickly glance away again. She looks so distraught, but I don't see how she could be telling the truth. She's a sergeant on the police force, not to mention a well-known public figure in the political world. She's one of those insane do-gooder types. Always helping, never taking any of the credit. If she wanted to, she could take this Immune advocacy platform and use it to become one of the most powerful people in the country. Instead, she chooses to stay on the force and train new recruits in the Special Ops department. She says it would be hypocritical of her to preach about Immunes living a normal life if she didn't have normalcy in her own life … or some crap like that.

Still, I don't believe for one second that she hasn't worked out a way to find out what my real name is.

"Honestly. Your records were sealed, even from us," she says.

"I wish I could believe you," I say as I walk out.

-2-

THREE YEARS LATER

"I'm going to do it. I'm going to knock. Just watch me go," I say, remaining completely still in the passenger seat of Declan's car. I think I'm trying to convince myself more than my best friend that I'm actually going to go through with this.

The small, white fibro house with perfectly manicured gardens mocks me. It's daring me to go and knock, but my nerves aren't allowing me to move. I'm frozen.

I've been waiting three years for this moment. I'm about to meet the woman who gave birth to me twenty-one years ago.

"*Are* you going to go knock?" Declan asks. I think he's getting a little impatient.

I don't reply and we continue to sit in silence for another fifteen minutes while the house continues to taunt me, like we're playing some messed-up staring contest … and the house is winning.

"Nuke, we don't have to do this today," he says.

"Yeah, I do," I say, finally summoning the courage to open the door. It clicks open, the fresh cool breeze hitting me.

Declan gently grabs my arm before I get out. "Do you want me to come with you?"

"No. I have to do this alone."

He smirks. "I knew you'd say that. I'll be here if you need me."

I get out of the car, taking a deep breath as I step towards the house, but I don't get far. A police car pulls up next to us with its lights on.

Crap.

Two officers climb out of their car; one I recognise as one of Lia's colleagues. He's a regular at all the barbecues my adoptive mum's hosted over the years. He's practically an honorary uncle to me.

"Hey, Kai," I say casually.

"Nuka," he says in a more serious tone than I was using. "Declan." He nods to Dec as he gets out of the car. "Haven't seen you two at your mum's gatherings lately. Where've you been?"

Ignoring his question, I ask one of my own. "Patrol's a bit beneath you, isn't it?" He's one of Lia's taskforce agents.

"Everyone has to pull patrol duty every now and then. It keeps us on our toes."

I narrow my eyes at his lie, and he picks up on my scepticism.

"I heard Declan's name when they ran the plates. I came as a favour."

"To my mother?"

"No, Nuka. To you. What are you doing here?"

"How do you all know each other?" Kai's younger partner asks.

"She's the sergeant's daughter," Kai replies.

The partner's eyebrows shoot up in surprise. "She must've been young when she had her?" This is something I've heard nearly my entire life.

"That's a long story," Kai says before facing me. "What are you doing here?" he asks again.

"That's a long story," I repeat his words.

"What's going on? Why did they run my plates?" Declan asks. "I don't think we have time for a classic Kai-slash-Nuka argument. As entertaining as they are." Declan's joking manner dissipates as he gives me a stern look, one that tells me to stop being difficult.

I sigh, turning to Kai to tell him the truth. "A PI found my birth mother. He tracked her last address to here, and I've been sitting in my car trying to build up the courage to go knock. What are *you* doing here?"

Kai's stance relaxes a little. "I'm so sorry, Nuka. Your birth mother doesn't live here."

"What?" I croak.

"We got a call from the resident. She made an official complaint about a strange car with 'suspicious younglings' sitting outside her house. Her words, not mine. Unless your birth mother is a seventy-six-year-old woman named Elizabeth, you've got your information wrong."

My shoulders slump forward in disappointment.

"I'm really sorry," Kai says. "I'll come with you to explain yourself to Ms. Sean. I'm sure she'll back down if you tell her the truth. Otherwise, I'll have to take you down to the station."

I nod, and Kai starts escorting me along the short pathway and up the three patio stairs to the front door. Declan and the partner stay with the cars. Kai knocks for me, and a tiny lady with short, curly grey hair answers the door.

"Hello, Ms. Sean. This is Nuka James. She's the one who has been sitting outside your house."

She looks at me, her face turning into a scowl. "What do you want?"

"I … Umm …"

"I'm afraid there has been a misunderstanding," Kai talks for me. "Nuka was given wrong information about the possible whereabouts of her birth mother, whom she has been trying to locate for a long time."

The woman's face turns from a look of anger to one of sympathy. "Oh, honey. I'm sorry to hear that, but as you can see, I'm the only one here, and I'm a little old to be your mother."

"Thanks anyway," I manage to say. "I'm sorry to have upset you."

"That's okay, dear. All is forgiven. I'm sorry I couldn't help."

I turn to walk away but wonder if she knew about the people who lived here before her. "You wouldn't happen to know if a Cadence Edwards used to live here, would you? Or a Cade Edmunds?" I ask over my shoulder.

Three years ago, I found out through Births, Deaths, and Marriages that my mother's name was Cadence Edwards. After searching for any information I could find on her, it seemed she mysteriously disappeared around the same time she gave me up. The PI Declan recently hired uncovered that she changed her name and now goes by Cade Edmunds.

The old woman thinks for a moment before a look of recognition crosses her face. "There used to be an Edmunds living next door. I haven't seen them for a while, but the house has never been put on the market. I think they rent it out now."

"Maybe the PI got the wrong address," Kai says.

The house next door is almost the complete opposite of this one. It's cement rendered and a dark charcoal colour. A modern wooden archway sits over brick stairs leading up to the wooden floorboard porch. It's even more daunting than this house, but I don't know if it's because it's my new target or if it's just really intimidating to look at.

I mutter a quick thank you as I make my way down the footpath and rush over to the next house. Urgently bounding up the steps, I don't hesitate to knock on the door this time, adrenaline urging me forward.

A young blond guy in his twenties answers the door. "Can I help you?" he asks, his blue eyes shining at me through thick-rimmed glasses.

"Uh—"

"Nuka, you can't just go knocking on everyone's door in hopes of finding her." Kai finally catches up to me.

"Who are you looking for?" the guy asks, giving Kai the evil eye.

"Cade Edmunds," I state in a flustered rush, worried Kai's going to drag me away any minute.

The guy shakes his head casually. "Sorry. I've never heard that name before."

"Are you sure? She's not like your landlord or something?"

"Nah, a cranky balding guy is my landlord. Sorry again," he says and goes to shut the door.

"What about Cadence Edwards?" I practically yell, putting my foot across the threshold to stop the door from shutting completely.

His eyes travel down to my foot in the doorway and then back up to meet mine. "Again, no. Sorry." His casual tone doesn't match his look of contempt.

"Sorry to have bothered you," Kai says before grabbing my arm and dragging me back down the steps of the porch. "I know you want to find her, Nuka, but you can't bother everyone on the street. My advice would be to go back to your PI, tell him he gave you bogus information, and ask for a refund."

He leads me over to Declan's car before finally letting go of my arm.

"What happened?" Declan asks.

I just shake my head at him. Looking at Kai with pleading eyes, I beg, "Please don't tell my mum about this?"

Kai glances over at his partner before nodding to me. "Get out of here now, and I won't say a thing."

"Deal," I say, turning and climbing into the car.

Declan gets back in the driver's seat. "What happened?" he asks again. He puts the keys in the ignition but doesn't turn the car on just yet.

Tears break me as I put my head forward on the dashboard. Declan rubs my back in a soothing way.

"It was a dead end," I whisper. "The old lady said that an Edmunds used to live next door, but when I asked the guy who lives there now, he had no idea who I was talking about."

"Hey, it's okay. We'll just make another appointment with the PI and give him more money. Although, you might have to fund this one. He's not cheap. But I'm sure he'll find her. He was able to find this information pretty quickly."

I nod and lift my head off the dash. "Okay."

Declan surprised me for my birthday by hiring the PI. I've spent the last three years trying to find out everything I could about my bio parents. There's an abundance of information on my dad. Kind of helps that he was an assassinated presidential candidate. At the age of thirty, he was killed on the campaign trail by an activist group against Defectives. The activists were not expecting what followed. The death of my father united the nation. It was the first major step in equality between Defectives and normals. Even though we still aren't quite there yet, it was his legacy that has got us to where we are today. We're no longer imprisoned for who we are, and we're free to do whatever we want.

So, naturally, there are countless news articles on him, but no dirt. The media seemed to think he was perfection wrapped in flawlessness. I'm not that naïve, everyone has dirt, but even Lia wouldn't tell me anything I couldn't read in a history book or archived news articles. In fact, she more or less refused to talk about him at all when I'd ask.

There's nothing on my birth mother, anywhere. All the information I could find on Cadence at the city library was from before I was born. The computers at the library aren't exactly the best search tools, though. I tried to sneak Lia's work tablet once, but it's password secured. Back in the old days, everyone had access to online information, everyone had their own tablet or online device, but when the pandemic hit and millions of lives were lost, the country became self-sufficient from the rest of the world. Now it's only important government employees or people with a ton of money who have them.

Everything used to be imported from overseas. Now everything has to be made here, and the costs are ridiculous. The country struggled for decades after the worst pandemic in history broke out. It caused a time-machine effect, taking us back to a time of fewer technologies. We've since advanced in some areas like medicine and essential living needs—lab-created food for sustainability, lab-made medicines for cheap healthcare—but cars, electronics … any luxury items became nearly obsolete. It's taken a long time, but we're slowly getting back to how things used to be. Cars no longer cost more than real estate like they used to twenty years ago, and tablet devices are available to buy, *if* you have the money to afford it. *Maybe I could get myself one now with my trust fund,* I ponder.

My trust fund kicked in yesterday on my twenty-first birthday, and if I'm smart with it, I'll never have to take a depressing waitressing job ever again.

"You still want to go apartment hunting?" Declan asks as we start to drive.

"Nah. Not today, not now. I'm not really in the right mood for apartment hunting."

"Maybe I can talk to Mum and Dad about you moving in? You're practically crashing in my bed every night anyway."

"You know they won't allow that. They hate me," I say, pointing to my Defective mark in the crook of my elbow, "because of this."

It was put there when I was five, right after Defectives were released from the Institute. The government decided we needed to be tracked, seeing as we were no longer confined. The mark appeared when the tracker was inserted. While the government no longer tracks us because of the Immune Rights Laws that were brought in by my Uncle Tate and his political party about five years ago, we're still branded with the mark: a small, black backwards "S" shape.

Everyone now has a blood test at birth, and if it comes back positive, they get the mark. Immune Genetics Laboratory has been studying Defectives for decades. They found a connection between Defectives and the immunity to Cataclysm Fever, the disease that eradicated the majority of the population almost seventy years ago. Those who are born naturally immune to the disease are Defective. Those who aren't are given the vaccine and are deemed as "normal." Hence the term "Immune," but to most people we're still Defective. We're still broken.

It was never worked out why some people are born immune and some aren't or why the natural immunity also causes supernatural abilities, but the most logical theory out there is that we evolved—adapted to our new environment to ensure we'd survive the Fever.

What all that has to do with our abilities, I don't know. It also doesn't explain why the abilities are all different. I mean, I've met a few people with a heating ability like mine, but all of my "family" have different abilities. Uncle Drew is an Empath—able to sense what you're feeling, Uncle Tate is a Telepath—can hear what you're thinking, Uncle Shilah gets visions of the future, Nanna can tamper with your memories, and Great Aunt Kenna can alter her appearance. My brother, William, is proven to be Defective but doesn't have an ability at all. Then there's Lia and Illy—they both have rare double abilities. It doesn't make any scientific sense, and yet it still happens.

"That's not true," Declan says, bringing me out of yet another long internal struggle with the science of Defectives. I don't even know why I bother thinking about trying to make sense of it anymore. "My parents don't like you because you're a smartass. It has nothing to do with the fact you're a walking microwave." He loves making that joke.

"You know what's funny? I used to think it was such a coincidence that my name reflected my ability, but my bio dad changed my name. He named me Nuka, because I can nuke things."

"Lucky your ability isn't to control lightning. He might've called you Striker."

I nudge Declan with my elbow. "Shut up."

"Make me … *Striker.*"

"No. That's not becoming a thing."

"How about we forget this Cade business, just for a few days. You've been obsessing over this woman for three years. You need a break. So let's go for coffee and put a ban on speaking Cade's name for the next twenty-four hours, at least."

"You know I hate coffee." I grimace.

"But *I* don't," he says, giving me a cheeky grin.

"Fine. I don't really want to go back to your place and deal with your parents anyway. We'll do coffee now and apartment hunting tomorrow."

After arriving at Declan's favourite coffee place a short time later, he grabs a table outside while I go in and order.

The barista hands me the two drinks, and as I turn to walk away, they're almost knocked out of my hands by some big lug not watching where he's going. I quickly twist so he doesn't bump my hands, but some of Declan's scalding hot coffee spills on my wrist.

"Ugh, son-of-a—"

"Whoa," the giant says. His voice is soft, and his gentle hand on the small of my back startles me, making me forget what I was going to say. His voice is warm and inviting for someone who is so big and … muscly. A smiling face stares down at me when I finally make eye contact. "That was close. Are you okay?" His brown eyes hold my gaze for a moment before he catches sight of my hand. "Ah shit, sorry." He runs his hand over his hair. "Let me buy you another one."

A small blush floods my cheeks, although I don't know why. "Uh … nah, don't worry about it." I fumble for words. "It was only a little spill, and it wasn't even my drink." I try flashing a polite smile, but I don't know if I'm pulling it off. My hand really friggin' hurts.

He glances in Declan's direction. "Oh, boyfriend's drink?"

"Yeah … I mean, no. He's not my boyfriend, but it is his drink."

His lip curls up into a smile. "Lucky for me then."

"Yeah … uh, lucky." *What does that even mean?*

We stand there looking at each other for a few moments before he finally breaks his gaze. "I should probably let you pass so you can get back," he says, stepping aside.

"Yeah, probably."

"Sorry again," he says as I walk by him.

"No worries," I call over my shoulder, making my way outside to my table.

"What was that all about?" Declan asks when I sit down.

"Nothing. I just almost spilled your coffee everywhere is all."

"Oh."

Declan starts talking to me about something-or-other, but I'm still focussed on the brown-eyed, dark-haired guy standing inside the coffee shop, waiting for his coffee. They hand it to him, and on his way out, he looks over and smiles at me, nodding goodbye. I smile back but don't attempt a nod in reply. I've never been able to pull that move off. I always look like I have a nervous tic.

"Hello. Earth to Nuke," Declan says, waving his hand in front of my face.

"Sorry, what?"

"Are you going to go see your parents anytime soon?"

I shrug. "I don't really have to anymore."

Declan tilts his head to the side disappointedly. His sky blue eyes bore into my purple ones. My stupid purple eyes.

I was born with hazel eyes, but they started turning around the time I hit puberty. Lia and Jayce took me to numerous doctors, none of which helped explain why my eyes were changing colour. The best explanation they could come up with was because of the higher levels of radiation coursing through my body due to my ability to heat things, my eyes had some sort of reaction to the radiation. They assure me I'm completely healthy, though, and the radiation hasn't caused any other changes in me. I do have to go for regular checks, however, and will have to for the rest of my life. Apparently, I'm at high risk for developing cancer, but it's not like that's not curable these days—depending on which type it is.

"They're your family, Nuke."

"They stopped being that when I turned eighteen."

"Really? Because they won't help you find the woman who gave birth to you? Haven't you ever wondered why they wouldn't help? That maybe they're protecting you?"

"I just want to know why I am the way I am. Answers—that's all I want. I know that sounds totally cliché, a girl not knowing who she is. Trust me, if it wasn't me going through this and I didn't actually know how this felt, I'd want to punch myself in the face. But, what if … what if I'm not living the life I was meant to? I feel like an outsider with Lia and Jayce, like I don't belong. It may be unfair on them, but it feels like they're not really mine, like I don't have a real family."

Declan leans forward, placing his hand on top of mine on the table. "That's not true. You have me, and I will *always* be your family."

I nod absentmindedly.

"I mean it, Nuke. You're everything to me."

His reassuring words give me an idea. "We should get a place together."

Declan sighs. "You know I wouldn't be able to afford my half. It's why I still live with my parents, and not in the dorms like a normal uni student. Not all of us were blessed with rich bio dads."

"But I can use my money for it. You won't have to pay for anything."

"I'm not taking money from you, Nuke. And you already know how I feel about you buying an apartment, but you're so stubborn I know you're not going to listen. You shouldn't buy an apartment with it, you should do something smart with it."

"How old are you? Twenty-one or fifty?"

"Just be careful. I know it's got to be a lot of money."

"I'm not going to blow it on something stupid."

"So you're really not going to go home anytime soon?"

I shake my head.

"You'll have to see them soon to get the remainder of your stuff, right? Why don't you go tonight? Make peace now that you're officially moving out … not that you've really lived there for a long time anyway."

"Why are you pushing for me to go back there all of a sudden?"

"They … You …" Declan stutters.

"Spit it out, Dec."

He breathes in deep, letting go of a whole lot of words at once. "You disappear every other week, you don't call them, you don't let them know you're okay, and yet they still support you when you come home. That's got to count for something. Don't shut them out completely just because you're financially free of them now." He sits back in his chair, letting go of my hand I forgot he was holding. His guilty expression gives everything away.

"They asked you to get me there, didn't they?"

"They want to see you for your birthday," he says quietly.

"Unbelievable," I mutter. "I'm not going. I can't … I can't face them. Not yet. Maybe one day I'll be able to look at them and not wonder what else they're hiding from me, but right now? I just … can't do it."

"They miss you, Nuke. It's been three years."

"I don't care." *Liar!* I wish I were telling the truth.

-3-

MY BEST FRIEND

"Come on, Striker," Declan yells through the bathroom door. "Birthday celebrations are going to start in five minutes."

"Yeah, because nothing says fun like needing to stick to a schedule," I yell back. "And that name's still not becoming a thing!"

I'm looking forward to this. I need a night out to relax. Declan's right, I've been obsessing over finding Cade for three years, and I'm completely exhausted.

I check myself over one more time in the mirror. My blonde hair is styled into long curls and flows down my back. My black halter top sits perfectly thanks to some strategically placed double-sided tape so I'm showing off just enough side boob, and my tight dark short-shorts and five-inch heels make my butt look awesome. I'm ready. The only thing I'm missing are my contacts. Declan friggin' hid them on me, claiming I had to look like "myself" on my birthday. Even though, technically, my birthday was days ago now.

He likes my purple eyes, but he doesn't have to answer all the questions I get about them. The irony isn't lost on me that I have to wear coloured contact lenses to escape being asked if I wear contacts.

Declan's ready and waiting for me when I get out of the bathroom. He's dressed in dark jeans and a black shirt, his dark hair purposefully styled to make it look like he just rolled out of bed. His mouth drops open when he catches sight of me.

"What's with the face?"

"You're going to make tonight torture for me, aren't you?" he says in a flirty tone … at least, I think it was flirty. *Is Declan flirting with me?*

I raise my eyebrow at him, staring silently at my best friend, the person who's been there for me ever since I met him at the playground up the street eleven years ago. I shake my head. There's no way Declan looks at me that way.

When I met him, we'd just moved into the neighbourhood, and Lia was heavily pregnant with Illy. Jayce asked me to take Will out so he could unpack without the help of an overactive four-year-old. Declan was at the skate park next to the playground, and I couldn't keep my eyes off him. I was in awe of him from the moment we met. He's the best person I know, inside and out.

But it's pretty safe to say, if nothing has happened between us in eleven years of friendship—not even a kiss—nothing ever will.

"You're going to be all over me *all* night because every single guy in the club is going to be hitting on you, and you're going to be all 'Declan, save me,'" he imitates me in a high-pitched voice.

"Is that your way of telling me I look good?"

He takes a step back, rubbing his stubbled chin as he mockingly assesses me. "You'll do. Let's go. We're already late."

We get a taxi into the city, and as I go to pay for it, Declan pushes my hand away. "You don't pay for anything tonight," he says with a smile.

I loop my arm through his as we enter the newest club in the city and have to navigate our way through a massive throng of people. *This place is packed!* Declan grabs my hand and holds it tight, leading me to a cordoned-off area with balloons.

"Surprise," he whispers in my ear.

It isn't until I hear my name being yelled that I recognise the group of people occupying the area as our old high school friends. I run towards the group and start hugging everyone. I haven't seen most of them since school.

Thanks to Lia's stance against segregating Defectives, I went to a normal high school. She said we should set the standard that we won't cower and won't remove ourselves from society. So that means none of my friends here are Defective like me.

Declan's arms wrap around me from behind as he places a drink in front of me. I thank him with an appreciative smile. The rest of the group stare at us, their expressions full of hope and suspicion.

"Please tell me you two have finally got your act together?" one of the girls asks in a high-pitched, excited tone.

"No, Gabs. Still just friends," I say.

All of their faces drop in disappointment, but this is typical. Even in high school, everyone was pushing for Declan and me to get together.

Eventually, as the night goes on, we all disperse from our little hideaway in the corner of the club for the bar, the dancefloor, or the bathrooms from having drunk so much. The drinks are coming freely, and before long, I find myself on the dancefloor with Gabby, both of us laughing and practically falling over one another.

My eyes find Declan at the bar, being approached by a girl.

Declan's not one to be rude, and I can see him politely flirting back, but surely he can't actually be interested in *her*.

I know I have no right as the best friend to pass judgement, but seriously, he has the worst taste in girlfriends.

An arm wraps around me, some guy grinding against me. I try to pull away, but he grips me tighter. With a strong elbow to the ribs, I make him take a step back, and just before I get the chance to turn around and punch him in the throat like Lia taught me, a hard body slams into me from the side, moving me away from him. Declan's eyes find mine, his arms wrap around me, and our faces come so close they almost touch.

"You looked like you needed some help," he says, smiling.

"You know, I could've handled that myself." I smile back.

"Yeah, and got us kicked out in the process."

We start moving to the beat, our arms still around each other. It's not exactly a slow song, but we're making it one.

"So, having fun?" I ask. "The girl at the bar is probably missing you."

He pulls his head back, confusion marring his features. "If I didn't know you better, I'd say I detect a hint of jealousy, Miss James," he teases.

I hang my head in sudden embarrassment.

He brings his hand up to my face, brushing my fringe behind my ear. He leaves his hand cradling my head, and part of me doesn't want him to move his hand away. The other part is screaming at me, *"What the frick is happening right now?"*

Swallowing hard, I look up into his eyes only to see they're no longer trained on me.

"Shit," he swears, dropping his hand from my face.

"What?" I follow his gaze and there *she* is. Standing at the edge of the dancefloor giving us an evil stare is Cassia, the wicked witch of an ex. With her long legs and fake blonde hair … ugh. "You're not going to go talk to her, are you?"

"You know it'll only be worse if I don't, Nuke." He pulls

completely away from me and walks off the dancefloor, leaving me alone.

Gabby's no longer on the dancefloor anymore either. Storming off in a huff, I head for the bar. Maybe drinking more will help. *Yeah, because alcohol is so known for making things better.* I probably shouldn't have any more, but oh well, it's my birthday and I can do what I want to. *Real mature.* I tell my inner voice to shut up.

I lean over the bar, trying to get the bartender's attention by making my cleavage more noticeable. It's despicably un-feminist of me, but it works and I want a drink. At least, it usually works. This guy isn't giving me any attention. *I need bigger boobs.*

Some guy approaches on my left, raising his hand to the bartender who promptly places two beers down. I turn to ask how he managed to do that when I'm met with a familiar face. Coffee Guy is standing beside me.

He smiles at me, handing me one of the beers he just bought.

"Thanks," I manage to say, although it comes out quieter than I would've liked.

"I thought you said he wasn't your boyfriend?" He nods towards Declan who's now sitting in a booth with the witch, getting into an overly heated discussion. Her arms are flailing about, and he's wearing a permanent scowl.

"He's not," I say, turning back to Coffee Guy.

"Didn't look that way on the dancefloor."

"Have you been watching me?"

He leans in and says in my ear, "I haven't been able to stop watching you since I got here."

I feel myself start to blush, so I take a swig of beer, hoping to cover my schoolgirl-like crush that threatens to take over me. He's got to be at least twenty-five. I'm sure he's used to women who can take a compliment.

"So what's the story?" he asks, leaning on the bar and taking a drink.

Following his lead, I lean against the bar next to him. "There is no story. We've been friends since we were ten."

"Oh, I bet there's a story there. If I had to guess, I'd say that's an ex-girlfriend who broke up with him because of how close he was to you. She thought he was cheating with you and so she cheated on him as revenge, only, you guys weren't hooking up—even though you want to—and now she feels guilty for not trusting him."

I gape at him. "Damn, you're good. Apart from the wanting to part. We're just friends."

"Mmhmm."

"What's that supposed to mean? And how did you know all that anyway?"

"It's completely obvious," he says, smirking.

I grimace at him, unconvinced.

"Okay, fine," he says rolling up his sleeve and uncovering his Defective mark. "We match." He lightly runs his finger down my arm and over my mark. "I can hear everything they're saying."

"Oh. I was beginning to think I was the only Defective person in here."

"You dare say the D word?" he asks, more amused than shocked like most people are at that word.

"What can I say, I like the D."

He almost chokes on his beer.

My eyes widen. "I didn't mean *that*." *Oh my God, I could die.* "I just mean that everybody else says it. Maybe not in public, but they do."

He takes another swig of his drink, trying to hide his smile.

"So you can really hear them from all the way over here?" I ask.

He nods.

"Can you hear every single conversation going on in here right now? Wouldn't that give you a headache?"

"I've learnt to turn the volume down over the years. I can focus on who I want to listen in on."

"That seems a bit rude. Weren't you ever taught that eavesdropping isn't nice?"

He laughs. "Maybe. But without doing it, I wouldn't have learnt your name, Nuka."

"You could've just asked me like a normal human being."

"I could've," he agrees but then shrugs. "But where's the fun in that?"

"Well, that's just a little unfair. Now you know my name, but I don't know yours."

"Brett," he answers quickly. We smile at each other, and I can't seem to tear my gaze away from him, but then his smile suddenly drops. "I'm sorry to say, but your boy is about to abandon you here."

"What?" I turn to face Declan who's glaring at me from across the room. Cassia climbs out of the booth and stands there waiting as Declan climbs out too. He shakes his head subtly and breaks his gaze with me, walking towards the exit with Cassia.

"You know what'd really make him jealous?" Brett says in my ear.

"What?"

"If you come home with me," he whispers in a husky voice.

I down the rest of my beer. "Let's go."

Brett grabs my hand and starts leading me out of the club.

We don't get far through the crowd on the way to the exit when I start doubting my decision.

What am I doing? I'm not the kind of person to just go home with some random guy.

I wonder if he'd still want me after I told him I'm not exactly experienced. I'm not a V-card-holding, wait-for-marriage type of girl, but the one and only guy I've been with was in high school, and it was a one-time event. One I haven't had the courage to try again. Thankfully, Cameron wasn't here for our little high school reunion tonight. I don't think I could face him.

It's something I don't like to be reminded of. The whole experience was awkward and fumbly. It was more painful than I was expecting, and well, my ability kind of made me react a little defensively. I didn't mean to burn him, but it was reflex. Having to call an ambulance for second-degree burns to the guy's special place is not something I want to have to do again.

Brett and I make it out into the alley behind the club before I really begin to hesitate and stop walking.

"What's wrong?" he asks, turning back to face me.

"Uh … maybe this isn't such a great idea."

He closes the distance between us, his arms wrapping around my waist. "Are you sure about that?" His lips are teasingly close to mine, his scent filling my senses.

My legs wobble beneath me as a lusty dizziness takes over my body. "No."

He smiles and starts pulling me down the alleyway, our bodies still firmly up against each other. We stumble into the shadows, and he pushes me against the wall of the building. His body blankets mine and he's staring at me with lustful eyes. He smirks when he sees the hesitant excitement in mine.

His lips come down on mine, his mouth hungry for more. And he clearly knows what he's doing as his tongue dances with mine, sending shivers all over.

His hands start in my hair before running down my arms to my fingertips. I struggle to find my breath as he starts raising my hands above my head, pushing his body harder against mine. His grip almost becomes painful as he pins my hands against the wall, his mouth never leaving mine.

Loud footsteps approach from the right. Pulling my head away to the sound, breaking our lips apart, I'm suddenly staring down the barrel of a gun. I recognise the blond guy with thick-rimmed glasses from yesterday as the one holding it to my head.

My eyes go back to Brett, the lustful look from before is gone and it's replaced with one of anger. His voice comes out gruff and demanding. "What do you want with Cade?"

-4-

SECURITY

"What?" I choke out.

"What do you want with Cade?" Brett asks again through gritted teeth. "My friend here won't hesitate to shoot you if you don't answer."

He still holds my hands above my head, his body still against mine, locking me in place. Narrowing my eyes, I focus on burning him with my ability. It causes him to wince, but he doesn't let go. I try to struggle free, but he's too strong.

"Keep struggling and I'll shoot you right now," Blondie says.

"Why are you looking for Cade?" Brett asks again with more aggression in his voice. He has to be in a lot of pain now, but he still isn't loosening his grip. *How strong is he?*

"She's my mother, you asshat!" I yell.

This causes him to quickly let go and take a step back. "She's *what*?"

Blondie starts laughing so hard, he's having trouble keeping the gun focussed on me. I take the opportunity to turn and kick it out of his hand, implementing my years of self-defence training Lia forced me to learn.

Even in my inebriated state, and the giant heels I'm wearing, I manage to make the gun go flying. I take another step forward and punch him in the nose, and he stumbles back. Moving closer and grabbing a hold of his shoulders, I knee him in the groin, making him double over in pain. I'm about to punch him again when Brett slams into me. I crash into the building and hit my head against the wall.

As I sink to the ground, a red flash disrupts my line of vision, intense pain radiating behind my eyes. I squeeze them shut to try to prevent the agonising pain spreading to the rest of my head.

When I open my eyes again, the two men tower over me, this time with Brett pointing the gun at me.

"You just made out with the boss's daughter." Blondie is still laughing, even though he's still hunched over supporting his nether regions. "Mr. Stickler-for-the-rules just broke the biggest one."

"Boss?" I ask, rubbing the back of my head where an egg is definitely beginning to form.

"You know how pissed she gets if anyone looks at Sasha the wrong way," Blondie says.

"Drake, I don't want to hear it," Brett scolds.

"Sasha?" I ask.

"You can't be her daughter," Brett says with a tiny hint of doubt. He looks down at the palm of his left hand, which is beginning to blister where I burnt him. "Oh shit," he says, his eyes widening in realisation. He lets both arms rest by his side, no longer pointing the gun at me. "You really are her."

"You know about me?"

He nods.

"Why didn't you say who you were yesterday?" Blondie—Drake as Brett called him—asks as he holds out a hand to help me up.

"I did," I say, ignoring his helping hand and getting to my feet by myself.

He shakes his head. "No you didn't."

Didn't I? I think back, my shoulders slouching when I realise it wasn't him we told why we were looking for Cade, it was the neighbour.

"So you followed me to the coffee shop?" I ask Brett. *Our whole meet-cute was a set up?*

"Why do you have purple eyes?" he asks, ignoring my question and successfully pissing me off with his own.

"Why do you have brown eyes? Who asks someone why their eyes are a certain colour?"

"Cade told us you have blue eyes."

"Well, mother of the year strikes again. Before my eyes started turning purple, they were actually hazel if you must know. Blue on the outside with brown in the middle. But she'd know that had she not abandoned me."

"You think that's what happened?" Drake asks. "If she did that, then why has she been looking for you?"

"She what?"

"We've been told to keep an eye out for you. We didn't know you go by Nuka. I'm guessing Cade didn't know that either," Brett says.

"You know what my real name is?" I ask, hope filling my voice.

"Uh … maybe we should let Cade fill her in?" Drake asks Brett. "I don't want to piss her off by telling the story wrong or something."

Brett nods. "Let's go."

"Go where?" I ask.

"To see your mother."

"Wait. How do I know I can trust you?"

"You don't, but if you want to find your mother, then you

will," Brett answers simply.

Just how desperate am I to meet this woman? "Yeah, I'm not getting into a car with the two guys who just tried to attack me. As much as I want to see my mother, I'm not a complete moron." *And yet, I'm in an alley in the middle of the night with two complete strangers. I have to admit, I'm at least part moron.*

"That's really not the answer I was hoping for, Nuka."

"I'm sorry to disappoint you, *Brett*."

Drake looks at Brett, surprise etched on his face. "Told her your real name, hey?"

"Shut up," Brett replies, handing Drake the gun before lunging for me. He grabs me around my waist and throws me over his shoulder as easy as he would a rag doll. "I didn't want it to come down to this ..."

I barely hear him over my screams. Brett's carrying me farther into the alley now, my butt up in the air.

They're going to take me, and I need to stop them. I scream louder and kick my legs, but it doesn't seem to do anything.

"Is there any way to shut her up?" Drake yells over my screeching.

"Let's just get her to the car," Brett yells back.

Realising it's futile, I stop screaming and try another tactic. Lifting Brett's shirt, I press my hands into his skin and start burning him. The muscles in his back stiffen at the pain, but he manages to push through it. I contemplate using my entire body to try to burn him, but it'll take too long for all of me to heat up to the kind of temperature that will do any damage. I decide to focus on my hands and push all of my energy through them.

"Friggin' hell, Nuka. I'm helping you here," he says, clearly starting to struggle.

"The way I see it, you're kidnapping me."

"Your mother would never forgive us if we let you get away. I need this job, Nuka, I have nothing else. You know what it's like for *us* in this world."

This brings me up short. I take my hands off him and stop struggling, letting out a loud sigh. "You must have some pretty mad skills to do what you just did."

He adjusts me over his shoulder to get more comfortable. "What did I just do?"

"Pulled the Defective card, made me feel guilty when I'm the one being abducted."

He lets out a laugh. "I'm not abducting you, I promise. Your mum has been searching for you. She'd hate to know that we screwed up and almost lost you."

"Okay," I reply, no longer having any fight in me.

"If I put you down now, are you going to run?" he asks.

"I guess not."

He puts me down and stretches out his back, wincing from the burns I put there.

"Come on, keep moving," Drake says impatiently.

We cross a street and make our way down another alley where an older, black three-door sports car is waiting.

I whistle. "Nice car. It's got to be at least seventy years old, right?" All the modern cars are the same. After the pandemic, cars stopped being looked at as a trend to keep up with and were more of a necessity for getting from point A to B. There are five basic models to choose from, and sports car is not one of them.

"Eighty actually," Brett says, the pride in his voice obvious.

Drake opens the passenger door and pushes the front seat forward. He holds out his hand for me, gesturing for me to climb in the back.

"Nah, I call shotgun," I say.

"Your legs are shorter than mine."

"You just attacked me and held a gun to my head. You think my mother is going to be pissed at Brett for making out with me, what will she think if she found out what you did?"

Brett starts laughing as he gets into the driver's seat. Drake swears under his breath and climbs in the back. I can't stop the smirk from finding my face.

Brett stares at me with an expression I can't decipher while I climb in the front seat. I can't tell if it's amusement or resentment. Perhaps it's a little of both.

"You're going to be worse than Sasha, aren't you?" he says with an exasperated smile.

"Who's Sasha?"

His smile drops from his face slightly. "She's your sister."

"I have a sister?" *I have a sister.*

Brett starts the car. "I'll let Cade fill you in on everything," he says, driving off.

"So who are you guys anyway? What exactly is your job?" I ask.

"We're security," Drake says. "And I'm Simon, by the way."

"Simon? I thought your name was Drake."

"Last name. You can call me Drake if you want, everyone else does."

"Why does my mother need her own security team?"

"We're home security, assigned to your sister mostly, and I guess you now," Brett answers.

"I don't need any security looking out for me."

Brett raises an eyebrow at me. "Really? Because I think you just willingly followed a guy into a darkened alley."

I try to think of something to defend my actions, but I can't. Following him was not my brightest moment. Neither was voluntarily getting into this car with him, but I'm not going to say *that* aloud.

"You must be pretty strong," I say, changing the subject from my poor choices. "I'm sorry about your hands and your back."

Brett shrugs. "All part of the job."

"You get attacked often?"

He doesn't answer me.

What the hell is my mother involved in?

***

"How much longer?" I complain. It feels like we've been in this car forever.

"Now you even sound like Sasha," Drake says with a laugh.

"What's she like?"

"Sasha or your mother?" Drake asks.

"I was meaning Sasha, but I wouldn't mind knowing about my mum, too."

"Sasha's a pain in the butt," Brett mumbles under his breath. Drake laughs. "Your mum's not too bad … as long as you're on her good side."

"How old's Sasha?"

"Sixteen," Drake answers. Five years. I was five when Sasha was born. "Doesn't help that Sasha thinks she's older than what she is. She doesn't exactly appreciate Mummy's rules either. She's certainly a handful."

"She kind of sounds like a spoiled brat," I say.

Both of the guys laugh now. "Yeah, I can already tell you two are related," Brett says.

"Excuse me?"

He lifts one of his hands off the steering wheel, showing me the blisters on his hands.

I shrug. "That was your own fault."

"Yup, just like Sasha," Brett says, putting his hand back on the wheel, a small hiss escaping his lips at the pain.

Before long, we're pulling up to a gigantic stonewall fence with a wrought iron gate in a fancy suburb I've never been to.

"Where are we?" I ask.

"This is the main residence," Brett replies.

"Main residence? How many are there?"

Brett looks in the rear-view mirror at Drake. "A few," Drake says.

Brett reaches through his window and presses a code into a keypad that sits in a box coming out of the garden next to the driveway. The gate begins to open, and it suddenly feels like someone has punched me in the stomach; it's churning so much. Sweat starts beading down my forehead.

"Is it really hot in here? I feel really hot," I say, trying not to freak out.

"Don't worry, she'll be happy to see you," Brett says, but it does nothing to reassure me.

"At 2:30 in the morning?" I ask, noting the time on the dashboard clock.

Brett lets out a small laugh. "You're cute when you're nervous."

"Careful there, bro," Drake mocks.

Brett rolls his eyes as we arrive in front of the biggest house I've ever seen. He kills the engine and climbs out of the car, reaching my door before I've even had the chance to take my eyes off the brick monstrosity before me.

He gives me his hand to help me out. I take it in mine, still staring at the giant Victorian mansion. Drake moves the car seat forwards and climbs out behind me. He starts pushing me, my feet stumbling to the front door as I'm wedged in between the guys.

"Can't I come back another day when I don't smell like nightclub and alcohol? I think I'm starting to sweat the stuff—it's gross."

"She's not going to care about that," Drake says. "You'll practically smell like the rest of the family." He laughs as if he's joking, but I get the feeling he's not.

Brett takes his keys out of his pocket and opens the arched wooden door. The foyer is completely white, so white it's almost blinding. Or maybe I'm already starting to feel the effects of a hangover kicking in.

I shouldn't be doing this now, this is crazy.

Is this really happening? I wish Declan were here.

Taking a deep breath in, I tell myself to calm down.

"Come into the informal living room," Brett says. "I'll go wake her up."

The foyer leads off into three directions. There's a staircase to my left and another to my right, each leading upstairs to two different hallways. Brett walks down the three steps in front of us to the split-level. I follow and we continue into a living area on the left and a small kitchen on the right. By the size of this house, I'm guessing this is one of many kitchens here.

"Take a seat," Brett says. I wander over to the plush cream L-shape leather couch and sit on the very edge. I think it's obvious I'm not too comfortable because Brett shakes his head and laughs at me before walking off. "I'll be back down soon."

My leg starts bouncing uncontrollably.

"Calm down," Drake says, sitting on the other side of the couch from me. "I know this is probably hard for you—"

"Hard? I'm about to meet the person who turned me over to the Institute when I was just one year old. She abandoned me, what's to stop her from doing it again? How can you be so sure she even wants to see me? How—"

"She's been looking for you, Nuka. Why would she do that if she didn't want to see you?"

I shrug. I don't have an answer for that. "So do you guys live here too?"

"Brett does. I'm out at the house you were at yesterday. It doesn't get used very much by the family anymore, and someone needs to look after it."

I nod as Brett re-enters the room. He goes to the fridge and pulls out two bottles of water. He brings one over to me, taking the other for him.

"Drink up, it might sober you up a little."

"I think I'm completely sober now." Fear, anxiety, and nerves have pretty much ensured my sobriety. Looking at the water reminds me of how much I've had to drink tonight, which reminds me my bladder has been screaming at me to be emptied.

"Can I use a bathroom real quick? I kind of drank a lot."

"Kind of?" Brett scoffs. "You were downing them like there was no tomorrow."

"You know, at first I thought it was charming that you were watching me tonight, now I'm realising it was just plain creepy."

Both of them laugh. "You'll have to get used to one of us watching you from now on," Drake says.

"What do you mean—"

"Come on, I'll show you where the bathroom is," Brett says.

I follow him through the kitchen, down more steps into a laundry area, and he points to a door on the other side of a row of washing machines.

After peeing forever, I catch a glance at myself in the mirror and realise how bad I look. My mascara has run from sweating, my skin is a weird pasty colour, and my eyes are bloodshot from the alcohol. I really wish the guys had let me go home and meet my mum another day. I'm not exactly going to make the best first impression.

After splashing water on my face, I start to fix up what I can of my makeup. I run my fingers through my hair and head back out to the living room. My heart thunders as loud as my heels clacking on the tile floors when I hear a woman's voice has joined the two guys'.

My eyes find her golden hair immediately when I enter the room. Brett notices me first and gives me a reassuring smile. My mother follows his gaze, and the room goes suddenly quiet. Eerily quiet.

She's wearing a gold silk bathrobe that's tied around her tiny waist. Her blonde hair that matches mine flows down her back.

I'm surprised at how young she looks. She has to be in her early forties, but she looks at least ten years younger.

I approach the room cautiously, trying hard not to stare at the ground, but my eyes keep finding their way there as I drop them from her gaze.

She slowly walks up to me, her hands finding my shoulders as her eyes search mine for recognition.

"Lavender? Is it really you?"

-5-

MY SISTER

"Lavender? My name is Lavender?" My eyes widen when I realise how judgemental I sound; Cade seems angry at my reaction. "Sorry. I just didn't expect my name to be so …"

"Feminine?" Brett finishes for me.

"Exactly. My dad changed my name to Nuka," I tell her.

"So Brett was saying," she replies, her voice thick with suspicion and disapproval. She removes her hands from my shoulders. "Why are your eyes purple?"

Brett starts laughing, I assume at the fact she asked the same question as him.

I glare at him while answering her, "It's … uh … it has to do with my ability."

"Right, you can heat things? You were always unnaturally hot as a baby."

"My best friend always jokes about me being a walking microwave. The radiation levels in my body are higher than any normal human could withstand, but because of my ability, it doesn't harm me. It did, however, cause my eyes to turn purple when I was a teenager." *You're rambling, Nuka. Shut your mouth.*

"I see," she says curtly.

The four of us stand silently. My eyes keep diverting between Brett and my mother until the front door opens, startling me out of my imaginary tennis match. The sound of the door is soft and quiet, but so are we so we all hear it.

There, trying to close the door as quietly as possible before tiptoeing her way to the left staircase, is someone I can only assume is Sasha. She's young, has the same colour hair as me—although she has a pink and blue thin stripe running down the right side of hers—she's in a sequined mini skirt and a top that doesn't leave much to the imagination. She's also carrying her giant high heels to avoid making noise on the tiles. I have no doubt in my mind this is my sister.

Drake swears under his breath.

"Who was on Sasha duty tonight?" my mother asks.

"We were kind of held up in your other pressing matter," Drake says, running one of his hands through his hair, while gesturing to me with the other.

"And she didn't have a scheduled outing planned," Brett adds.

"Sasha, you get your butt in here, young lady," our mother yells at her.

Now it's Sasha's turn to swear. She walks into the room—more like stumbles really—her head held low.

"You know you're not allowed out without one of your guards with you," my mother says in a surprisingly calm tone.

"I know," Sasha says, her head still down.

"Where were you?" our mother asks.

"At a friend's house," Sasha answers.

Wearing that? Yeah, right.

"Okay, well, you should go to bed now. We'll talk tomorrow."

That's her punishment?

Sasha nods, and as she turns to walk away, I don't miss the smirk on her face. She doesn't acknowledge me as her eyes finds mine but more stares at me like she's saying, "Yep, I rule this house."

The guys were right—she is a spoiled brat.

"So that was my sister," I say as she heads up the stairs and disappears.

My mother turns towards me. "Sorry. I should've introduced you, but I didn't want to reward her after her behaviour. You can get to know each other at a more reasonable hour."

"Uh … okay."

"Can I get one of the boys to drive you home?" she asks.

That's it? She's met me, now she's sending me on my way?

"I don't really have a home," I mumble as I look down at my feet. And I can't really go back to Dec's tonight—he's probably with Cassia, no doubt. When I look up again, all three of them are looking at me blankly.

"You don't?" my mother asks.

"That would explain why we followed you for most of today looking for apartments," Drake says.

"You followed me then, too?" I ask, a little pissed off.

"They were just doing their job. I asked them to do it. I was wondering why a young woman and a cop were looking for me. Part of me was hoping it was you, but the purple eyes threw everyone off. I thought it couldn't have been you." She purses her lips in thought. "You can … I mean … we can put you up here if you need it. I'm sure it will be fine with Jonas. Uh … my husband."

"Thank you, but I don't want to impose." *Not that I really have another option right now.*

"It's no trouble. Brett, can you take her to one of the rooms in your wing, also find one of the maid's supply rooms and get her some toiletries and things?"

Brett nods at her.

"Drake, you're off the clock now, but I still expect you to be back here at 7:00 AM for your day shift. You're welcome to stay too, save having to drive all the way back to that shack you live in."

She refers to that giant house I was at yesterday as a shack? How much money does this woman have?

"I'm going to go back to bed." My mother leaves the room and heads up the right staircase without even so much as a goodnight.

"That's it?" I ask myself more than the guys. I turn to them. "Why do I get the impression that could've gone a lot better?"

"What, were you expecting long-lost reunions of hugs and apologies? Hate to say it, but you'll be waiting forever if you want her to be that type of mother," Brett says. "But I guess you're staying here now, so come on, I'll show you where to go."

I say goodnight to Drake as Brett leads me through to the other side of the living room to a hallway. I can't get over how massive this house is.

"I don't think she likes me," I say, practically whispering.

Brett stops walking and turns to face me. "She's probably tired from us waking her up, and Sasha didn't help things. She probably just needs to get over the shock of her long-lost daughter suddenly being here. She'll be more civilised in the morning." He doesn't look overly convinced of that. "Maybe."

He starts walking again, and I follow. He points to a door on our left. "Bathroom." We continue to walk until he stops in front of me, and I slam into his back, not paying attention to where I'm going. He lets out a painful grunt and jerks his body away from mine.

"Sorry," I whisper. I step forward and lift his shirt, gasping at the sight of raw, burnt flesh in the shape of my handprints on his back.

"Don't worry about it," he says, shaking his shirt free from my grip and opening the linen cupboard in front of us. He grabs a brand new toothbrush still in its packaging, toothpaste, makeup remover, and wipes.

"This is all kept in a cupboard? Do they have unexpected guests often?"

"Sometimes," is all he says.

"Well, are there any first aid things or antiseptic in there for your back?"

"Don't worry about it. I'll sort it."

"I did it to you, the least I can do is help fix it," I say, pushing him out of the way and looking in the cupboard.

"Really. It's okay. I've dealt with a lot worse."

My eyes narrow as I turn to look at him. "What *is* this place?"

"You'll have plenty of time to discover that yourself," he says with a cryptic half-smile. "Come on, I'll show you to your room."

We're silent as we start heading back up the hallway and turn right down another.

"I'm actually a little surprised she's put you down here with me," he says.

"Why's that?"

"This is the employee's quarters."

"Oh."

"It's probably just for the night. We did kind of ambush her, and it is an ungodly hour. She probably wants to make up a special room for you upstairs with the rest of them, which will take time to set up." I appreciate him trying to rationalise my mother's so-called odd behaviour for me, but it's not necessary.

"She probably just doesn't trust me and that's understandable. Her security team bring in a random, purple-eyed freak off the street in the middle of the night who claims to be her daughter."

Brett laughs before stopping and opening a door on his right. "Here you go. I'm at the end of the hall if you need anything."

"Thanks," I say, taking a tentative step towards the room. As I walk by him, my shoulder and arm lightly brush up against his chest, and a shiver shoots down my spine as my heart beats frantically.

Really? After everything I've gone through with Brett tonight, I still have a crush on him? Ugh.

"Nuka?" he says, grabbing my arm gently and turning me to face him.

"Yeah?" My voice is annoyingly breathy.

"It goes without saying that what happened with us … it can't … I kissed you because I had to. You know that, right?"

Ouch. "You *had* to?"

"I needed to distract you. You were already trying to flake on me. It shouldn't have happened. It can't happen again. Especially now I know who you are. I kind of need this job."

"Right." I nod. "Got it." Crush is officially *crushed.*

"Besides, I don't actually like being used to make another guy jealous. I'm not into high school games."

I gape at him. "At the bar, you said—"

"I needed to get you into the alley where Drake was."

"Oh."

He goes to walk away but quickly turns back. His mouth opens to say something, but he hesitates, his mouth shutting as fast as it opened. "Goodnight, Nuka," he finally says.

"Goodnight."

***

Going to sleep is no easy task. The whole night keeps replaying over and over in my head. The almost kiss or whatever the hell that was between Declan and me, then making out with Brett in the alley, Drake holding me at gunpoint, both of them kidnapping me, and finally meeting the woman who abandoned me as a baby … it's like the night is on a loop. I just can't get it to stop.

When I do finally get to sleep, it only feels like a few minutes before I'm awoken by someone sitting on the end of my bed, staring at me.

"That's a little creepy," I say as I sit up.

"Is it true?" Sasha asks, her golden hair shining in the sunlight filtering through the window. "Are you my sister?"

I smile. "Apparently."

"Why are your eyes purple?"

"*Really*? You too?" I roll my stupid purple eyes. "It's because of my ability. I'm Defective. It caused my eyes to change colour. They used to be hazel like yours, actually."

"My eyes didn't change colour when I got my ability."

"What? You're Defective?"

She nods. "It's why Mum paid for my tattoo to cover up my mark. Of course, she wasn't expecting me to get half a sleeve and my whole shoulder done." She grins as she turns to show me her back—her pale pink pyjama singlet showing off a flower tattoo with pink shaded petals and black outline taking up nearly her entire shoulder blade and green vines reaching out from the flower, with smaller flowers coming out of the vines. It trails down her arm to the inside of her elbow where her Defective tattoo should be, which is covered by another flower. It's so obvious and big that I begin to wonder why I didn't notice last night. "That was fun coming home to her reaction—totally made it worth it."

I laugh. "Well, if it makes you feel any better, she sent me to the Institute. I think I'd rather the tattoo."

"Mum of the year, hey?" Her face casts a sad smile before looking at me with questioning eyes.

"What?" I ask.

"What's your ability?"

"What's yours?" I snap back. Talking about my ability is not something I like to do. Probably has something to do with being forced to go to a normal school.

Sasha smirks, getting off my bed to go stand by the window. The sad-looking, yellow-leafed plant sitting in a pot on the terrace slowly starts turning a healthier shade of green, and the buds slowly grow and begin to open. She turns her focus back to me. "It's not the coolest, I know. Mum always says it's because I used to play in the garden a lot when I was a kid. Pfft." She shakes her head. "Yeah, Mum, *that's* why I developed an ability—because I liked to play outside. I'm like a glorified gardener. It kind of sucks."

"But it certainly explains the tattoo. How old were you when you—"

"Nine … okay, seven. I kept it from Mum for as long as I could. As far as she knows, I was nine. You?"

"Well, I was sent to the Institute when I was one."

"*Damn.*" Sasha whistles.

"Give me your hands."

She comes back over to my bed, sitting opposite me. I heat my hands and place them on top of hers.

"Whoa. That's cool, so much better than my lame ability. Anyway," she says, suddenly switching topics, "Mum and Jonas are going to be out all day today. You and I are meant to do something together. I was thinking breakfast and some shopping."

"Oh," I say, clearly disappointed. "I thought … maybe …"

"Mum's not exactly the 'bonding' kind of Mum. I hardly ever see her."

"Maybe I should just go home," I say.

"No! I *want* to spend today with you. I want to get to know the sister I never knew I had."

My heart sinks. "You didn't know about me?"

Sasha gives me a sympathetic, tight-lipped smile. "To be fair, I didn't even know Mum was married before my dad. That makes Jonas number three, I'm guessing."

"What was your dad like?"

She shrugs. "I don't remember him. I don't even know his name."

I'm sensing a common theme with this family. "I didn't know my mother's name until a few years ago."

"What about your dad? Where's he?"

"He died when I was six. I have adoptive parents, but I don't really talk to them anymore."

"Why not?"

"Long story, but basically they refused to tell me about you, about my bio family."

"Are you sure they even knew about us?"

"They knew … maybe not about *you*, but they at least had the power to find out. My adoptive mum is Allira Daniels."

"*The* Allira Daniels?"

I nod.

"Oh. I don't think Mum and Jonas will be too pleased to hear that."

"Oh?"

"They aren't exactly—"

Brett knocks on my door. "Be ready in twenty," he says before turning on his heel and heading back down the hall towards his room.

"Does he do that a lot?"

"Interrupt? All the damn time. Especially if I'm with a guy. They're like annoyingly big brotherly then."

"Is that part of their job? To keep boys away?"

"If it is, they suck at it," she says, laughing.

Looking at my little sister, who's five years younger than I am, I get the distinct impression she's more experienced than I am with guys. *That's depressing.*

"How are we going to go shopping? Shouldn't you be at school today?" I ask.

"Uh … It's Sunday."

"Oh. Duh. I'm a day ahead of myself."

"Besides, I don't go to school."

My brow furrows. "Isn't that like a requirement for a sixteen-year-old?"

"I'm home schooled."

"Cade home schools you?"

"Pfft," she scoffs. "I home school myself."

"Wow. That's pretty impressive."

She shrugs. "It's all pretty straightforward."

"Really? I barely made it through high school, and I dropped out of uni."

"Clearly I just got all the smart genes in the family." She winks.

I smile at her, but it doesn't reach my eyes. I hate that we didn't get to grow up together like proper sisters should.

"You don't seem as spoiled as they say," I say, nudging her with my foot.

She turns to me, her mouth falling open in shock, "Who said I was spoiled? Brett and Drake? Well, they're so serious *all the time,* it's easy to make them squirm … and it's kind of fun."

"So it's all an act?" I can already tell she's not the same girl from last night.

"Shh," she says, placing her finger to her lips.

"Were you even out last night?"

She giggles.

"I think you're the only girl in history to sneak out, only to sneak immediately back in just so she can get caught."

She shrugs. "I have to show them they don't own me

somehow. They can throw as many bodyguards at me as they want, but the bottom line is, they can't keep me if I don't want to be kept."

"Why do you need bodyguards anyway? I don't get it."

Brett appears in the doorway again. "I don't see you getting ready, Sasha."

She grabs my pillow off my bed and throws it at him. "Go away. We're bonding here."

He laughs and then leaves for a second time.

"I should probably call Declan before we go out, just to let him know I'm okay. We kind of got split up last night."

"Who's Declan?"

"I'm sort of staying with him at the moment. It's just temporary until I can find my own apartment."

"Is he hot?" she asks, a coy smile finding her face.

"Yes, but he's twenty-one—that's too old for you."

"Playing the big sister role already, huh?" She laughs. "I don't mind an older guy. Drake's a pretty good kisser."

"Drake? He's a lot older than you."

"He's only twenty-two."

"Oh. Still too old you. Are you and him … together?"

"God no, nothing like that. We've made out a couple of times, but it's pretty clear it was only out of sheer boredom from being stuck together a lot. He freaks out after every time it happens, too. Says it can't happen again."

"That's understandable. The impression I get is Mummy dearest won't be too pleased if the help is helping themselves to her sixteen-year-old daughter."

"Please, she'd be more upset over losing the employee or being sued or something."

"It just surprises me that Drake's crossed that line. After Brett kissed me last night, Drake kept—"

"Wait, you made out with Brett? Like 'life is not a game, I'm so serious all the time' Brett?"

I feel myself blush. "Yeah. Right before Drake held a gun to my head." I laugh. Sasha looks shocked.

I tell her all the events of the last two days—the PI, the house, the coffee shop, the club, everything. She's in hysterics by the end of my story.

"That's so not fair. I miss out on all the fun."

"I can tell you that being cornered by two guys in a dark alley was not fun. You might do well to learn from that lesson—don't impulsively agree to go home with a guy you meet in a bar."

"I'll keep that in mind," she says with a smile. "Come on, let's get up and go out for breakfast. Mum said you probably need some clothes, so I've bought a heap of my old stuff down for you."

"Thanks."

"I'm just going to run upstairs and get dressed, and I'll meet you out front in ten," she says, rushing out the door.

It's only taken me fifteen minutes and one conversation to fall in love with my sister.

***

After dressing, I go to the bathroom to brush my teeth. Only, when I reach the bathroom, my new toothbrush is missing. I'm sure I left it in here. *Am I in the right bathroom?* The toothpaste and the makeup remover are still in here. *Where did my toothbrush go?*

I look on the floor, in the bathroom cabinet, everywhere, but I can't find it. Maybe I took it back with me to my room? Maybe I was drunker than I thought.

Outside of the bathroom, Brett's waiting for me. His presence makes me jump.

"I'm not that scary, am I?" he says, smirking.

"Why are you waiting for me outside my bathroom?

"Like I told you last night. You're one of them now. Drake and I are going to be stuck to you like glue."

"Great," I mumble.

Brett just laughs and shakes his head. "Great, two Sashas."

"Hey, umm, can I use a phone before we go? I need to call my friend, tell him where I am."

"Come use mine," he says, leading me to the end of the hallway to his room.

He steps aside so I can walk in. I shuffle into his room, the size of it bringing me to pause. It's much larger than mine. His gigantic bed makes my single one look even smaller, and his wide screen TV is an addition I don't even have in my room. French doors open out to the pool area, giving Brett an awesome view of the perfectly maintained grounds.

"Nice room," I state coolly.

"It's not bad," he says with a shrug.

I glare at him. "You've been working here too long if you think this room is only okay. You've seen the room you put me in, right?"

He smiles. "I was joking. I know I have the best room in this wing. The head of home security usually does."

"So you're like Drake's boss?"

He runs his hand through his hair. "Something like that."

"Oh," I say, walking over and sitting on the edge of his bed.

"Uh, didn't you need the phone?" he asks, pointing over to an old, wooden desk in the corner of the room.

"Oh, yeah. Thanks." I make my way over to the desk, picking up the phone. "Is it okay if I'm left alone for this?"

He tilts his head to the side and gives me a derisive look. "You know I'd be able to hear you no matter where I go in the house, right?"

"Then don't listen in."

"Who are you calling?" he asks, his voice laced with suspicion.

"Declan. Who else would I be calling?"

He shrugs. "I dunno. It could be anyone. It's my job to know what goes on in this house." It's clear he's not going to let me have a private conversation.

"Fine, listen in. Whatever," I say inarticulately.

Dialling Declan's house, I feel self-conscious talking to him in front of Brett, who's standing there with his arms crossed just watching me. Declan picks up on the first ring.

"Hello?" he says with a certain tone of urgency.

"Hey, it's m—"

"Nuka? Oh, thank God. Where the hell did you disappear to? Why didn't you come home? What the hell happened last night? Are you okay?"

"Calm down. I'm fine. I'm … I found my mother."

"What? Where are you now?"

"At her house."

"Why didn't you call sooner?"

"I was getting to know my sister. Why—"

"You have a sister?" There's a smile in his tone now.

"Yeah, pretty crazy. I meant to call, but everything happened so fast. Why were you all panicky?"

"Are you kidding me? *Why?* Maybe because the last time I saw you, you were talking to some random guy at the bar and then you disappeared for … oh I don't know … eight hours?" He lets out an exasperated sigh. "I didn't know where you were. I was worried. Where are you, Nuke?"

"At my mother's house."

"Yeah, I got that. *Where* is that?"

"I don't actually know the address. Hang on …" I turn and look at Brett.

"He won't be allowed in," he says. "Not approved guest."

"Who was that?" Declan asks.

"Uh, the guy from the bar," I answer absentmindedly while looking at Brett, my facial expression asking him why Declan can't come over.

"What?" Declan screeches.

Breaking eye contact with Brett, I throw my head in my hand. "It's not like that. He works for my mother." There's a long silence, and if I had to guess what he was doing, I'd say he was pacing back and forth, trying to calm down again. "I'm sorry I made you worry. I kind of got carried away with the fact that I have a mother and a sister and … well, I figured you were at Cassia's last night anyway, so I couldn't go back to yours if you weren't there."

"I'm glad you're okay, Nuke," he says calmly. "When I didn't know where you were, I kind of freaked out. I wish I could've been there for you when you met her. And about Cass—"

"I kind of wish that too," I say with a smile. I don't want to hear about Cassia. "It didn't exactly go as well as I was hoping."

"Oh?"

Brett clears his throat behind me.

I grumble. "I should go. I just wanted to let you know where I was."

"Are you coming back here tonight, or?"

"Uh … maybe, but I'm not sure just yet. I'll see how the day pans out and will let you know, okay?"

"When can I see you then?" he asks. "I think we need to talk about … some stuff."

My stomach churns, making me feel queasy. I know what he wants to say. He wants to tell me that he's back with Cassia and we can't be as close anymore. He's such an idiot for going back to her. I may as well get the conversation over with.

"You got uni in the morning?"

"Yeah. Free arvo though."

"Late lunch? Usual spot?"

"Deal."

-6-

SUSPICIONS

From what I've learnt about Sasha so far, she's insanely smart. She's like some kind of mathematical genius child. While I was trying to work out how much discount thirty-five percent off would be on the sales rack, she'd look at the price and spout the answer like it just popped into her head. I'm not talking an approximate guess, she'd tell me right down to the cent. It's no wonder she has the smarts to home school herself.

There's a knock on my door not long after we get home from our long, exhausting day of shopping.

"Your mother has requested your company," Brett says as I open the door.

"Really?" My eyebrows shoot up and I find myself smiling. I tell myself to act cool, but it's not happening.

"Yup, she wants you to meet Jonas and have dinner with you."

"Should I change? Do I look okay?"

He laughs. "You look fine. Come on," he says, leading me back into the hallway and through the maze that is this house.

He leads me to a formal dining room on the other side of the house. Evidently, I'm the first one to arrive, but my mother's right behind me.

"Jonas should be here any minute," she says, taking a seat at the end of the table.

"I'll leave you to it," Brett says, making his exit.

"Sit," my mother says, gesturing to the chair to her left.

When I sit down to join her, a tall, thin, greying man enters and kisses my mother on the cheek. He looks over at me and continues to walk around to my chair. He holds out his hand for me to shake.

"You must be Nuka." His voice and smile is friendly, but his eyes are cold.

All I can bring myself to do is nod in return.

"I'm Jonas Dalton. It's nice to meet you." He lets go of my hand and makes his way to the head of the table. He looks to my mother and gives her a small head nod, as if they're having some telepathic conversation.

"So what are your plans? Do you have any?" my mother asks.

"Plans?" I ask.

"For a job, where to live?" she asks.

"Well … I … uh," I stutter.

"Jonas and I were discussing it, and we would love it if you could stay with us until you figure out what you want to do. We may even have a job for you. If that's what you want?"

"A job? Umm … I don't need—"

"So what is it that you want? Money?" Jonas asks.

"I just want to get to know you," I say quietly.

Jonas scoffs. "And how do you plan on supporting yourself? We can provide you with a bed and food, but you still need a wage to live on."

"But—"

"I want to get to know you too, but Jonas …" She looks at Jonas and then back at me. "Sorry … *we* fear that you're here for another reason."

"You think I'm after your money," I state, not question.

"Well, you have to look at it from our perspective," she continues. "You come from a middle-class, working family. They're upper middle class, but still middle class. They're influential people, yes, but they're not exactly—"

"How do you know who my family are?"

"We had to check your story out," Jonas answers. "Brett got us all the information we needed."

"Brett?"

"He's good at what he does," my mother says. "We had to make sure you were who you said you were. That you really are my Lavender."

My brow furrows. *How did Brett get all of my information?*

"DNA test," Jonas says, as though he could hear what I was thinking.

I'm still confused until I realise … "My toothbrush."

Jonas nods.

Anger starts to build up inside of me. I try to squash it down, but it just sits in my chest, making my breaths heavy.

"I'm not after your money," I say as calmly as I can manage.

Great. Instead of letting the anger take over, tears have come out. I try to subtly wipe them away, but my mother's stare burns into me.

"Could you leave us a minute, Jonas?"

"Sure. Maybe I'll go have dinner with Sasha, wherever that girl is. It'll give you two time to really talk. I'll tell the kitchen we'll be eating separately."

After Jonas leaves, we sit in silence: me staring at the table, my mother staring at me.

"I'm sorry about ambushing you like that," she finally says. "You have to understand our position in this. You literally turn up in the middle of the night claiming you're my daughter, and you have nowhere to go. The daughter I gave up had blue eyes, yours are purple. I thought maybe … that maybe you were here for other reasons. I couldn't even be sure you were mine."

"That's okay," I mumble incoherently.

"When the test confirmed you are mine, I was so happy that I'd found you and that you were here. But then Jonas pointed out that the DNA test didn't mean you weren't after something, and the fact you have nowhere to live … well—"

"I only don't have anywhere to live because I haven't found my own place yet. But don't worry. I'll be out of here tomorrow. I can go back and stay with my friend—where I was before last night."

"That's not necessary, Lavender."

I wince at my birth name.

"Sorry. Nuka. I still can't believe your father named you that."

"Why *did* he change my name?"

"So here come the questions," she says in a playful tone. Her look turns sombre when she sees I'm not entertained. "I assume he did it so I wouldn't be able to find you when you got out."

"But he changed it long before I was out of the Institute."

"He had plans of busting you out of there the moment he found out what I did," she says, hanging her head shamefully.

"Why did you … why …" I can't ask the question.

"Why did I give you up?"

I nod.

"I wish I could say it was because it was the law, because I *had* to. But if I'm being completely honest, I did it for more selfish reasons than that. I saw it as a way of escaping."

"Escaping?"

"I don't have the best track record with men. Starting with your father."

"My father?"

"He isn't the man the media made him out to be."

"Oh."

"I shouldn't really get into this with you," she practically whispers. "He's your father and he achieved amazing things for this country and your kind before he died, that much is true."

"But?"

She gives a reluctant sigh, knowing I'm not going to let this go. "But he wasn't a nice man, Nuka."

"Did he … hit you?"

Her face relaxes into a half-smile. "No. He wasn't physically abusive. But there are many forms of abuse."

"Why didn't you come find me when he died, or even after I was released from the Institute?"

"After I gave you up, he threatened to kill me if I ever came near you again."

"But you just said he wasn't the violent type?"

"He would've found a way. Staged an 'accident.' He wouldn't have been stupid enough to come right out and murder me. He was smart, manipulative, and he always got what he wanted."

My stomach churns. That's when I realise. "That's why you changed your name. I went to the Institute when I was one. You changed your name around the same time."

She nods. "I was scared he'd do it anyway because he'd lost you. I'm not proud of my cowardice. And that's what giving you up was. It was cowardly. So was not coming for you when your father died. At the time, I'd just left Sasha's father. He *was* the physical type. I had an almost one-year-old, no money, nowhere to go. I knew I couldn't have taken you on as well, even though you were my responsibility. I saw in the news that Paxton was marrying that Defective woman. I thought she'd be able to take care of you better than I could. She could also understand you better than I could. I have no idea what it's like to be Defective."

I nod as I contemplate what she's telling me. "So you knew

where I was and didn't even try to find me," I mumble.

"Sorry, what was that?"

I shake my head. "Sorry, nothing."

"Oh," is all she says, and then, "Perfect timing."

The kitchen staff enters, carrying plates of food.

"I was beginning to think you'd forgotten about us," she half-jokes, but it's the kind of joke that holds truth behind it. I think the staff knows that too because they're quick to apologise and disappear again.

Realising our conversation is over, I start eating the food that looks more like art than something edible. It may look weird, but as soon as the food hits my mouth, I don't care what it looks like. I've never tasted anything like it, or anything as good.

"So about the job." She starts talking halfway through the meal.

"I don't exactly need a job, but I'd love to work for you if it means I get to spend time with you, get to know you more."

"Do you already have a job? How are you able to pay for things?"

"My dad left me a trust fund. It's not much, certainly nothing compared to what you have, but it's enough for me to live off for a long time, probably forever. It's also the reason I'm not here for your money. I don't need your money."

"Oh." Her face brightens a little, making me realise she still doesn't completely believe I'm not here for her other reasons. "Well, it's up to you. You can keep your trust fund in savings and work for us, if you like. We kind of got excited when you turned up last night. We've already got pretty big plans for you."

"You do?"

"I'll explain everything as we go. You want to come tomorrow and see what we have to offer?"

"Sure." *But lunch with Declan.* "How long will we be? I'm meeting a friend for lunch, but I can cancel if you want?"

"Oh, we won't be getting started until tomorrow evening.

We'll show you around, explain what we do."

"What *do* you do?"

She smiles. "All in good time. I'm going to head to bed," she says, even though her food has barely been touched. "Goodnight, Nuka."

"Goodnight … umm …"

She grins. "You can call me Cade until you feel comfortable enough to call me Mum," she says reassuringly.

"Goodnight, Cade." I like how her name rolls off my tongue when I say it.

She pauses in the doorway. "One more thing." She waits until I'm looking at her to continue. "It's probably best we don't tell Jonas about your little trust fund. He's always looking for investors, and while most of his ideas are inspired, it can be risky to invest with him—financially speaking. We'll tell him that you have a little money left over from a previous job, but it's not much and you're willing to work for us to earn your keep. Okay?"

"O … kay," I say, a little confused.

"I just wouldn't want you to lose the money your father put aside for you."

I nod to her and she leaves.

"I hear you're one of us now?" Brett says, catching up to me as I walk down the hallway to my room.

"One of you?"

"Maybe you were placed in the employee section of the house

on purpose after all."

"So, you know where my missing toothbrush is, I hear?" I ask, changing the subject.

He winces. "I had to," he says quietly.

"Well, can I get another one? Brushing my teeth with my finger is sure to cause some cavities."

He smiles and looks a little relieved that I'm not pissed off at him. "I'll go get you one," he says, turning and walking the other way.

Grabbing some new pyjamas from my shopping bags in my room, I start to head to the bathroom. Brett meets me in the hallway with a brand new toothbrush, still in its packaging.

"Going to steal this one too?" I ask, reaching for it.

"Not unless they ask me to."

"They could've just asked *me*. It's not like I don't understand their concern. It may have upset me, but it's not as bad as finding out they went behind my back."

"They still would've checked you out, no matter what you told them. You know that, right? People like your parents—"

"Mother," I correct him. Jonas is no father of mine.

"People like your mother and Jonas," he rephrases, "have to watch their backs. They have a lot to lose."

"A lot of money, you mean."

"To some people, that's everything."

"Is it everything to you? Is that why you do this job?"

"I'm just trying to keep my head above water. Being Defective doesn't exactly open doors for great careers. We do what we have to just to survive."

"That's bullcrap."

He raises his eyebrows at me.

"Look at my adoptive family. Nearly all of them are Defective. They're doctors, politicians, directors, police officers. They don't let their abilities hold them back."

"Must be nice living with that sort of privilege available to you," he mumbles.

"It's available to all of us. You just have to want it bad enough to chase it."

"You have no idea what it's really like out there for us, do you? Have you seen what it's like in the Estates?"

"My uncle runs the Institute. He took us once when we were kids. I got to hang out with other kids who were just like me, which growing up in the world I did, I didn't get to do a lot."

Brett scoffs. "You wouldn't say they're fun if you saw them now."

"I don't believe you."

"I'm sure you don't. You know what they say, 'Ignorance is bliss.'"

He stalks away from me, my mouth left agape.

***

"Is Brett always such an ass?" I ask Sasha.

She invited me for a swim in the pool this morning, and I thought it'd be a good wakeup after a restless night's sleep. Brett's voice kept repeating in my head, calling me ignorant. I don't even know why it's getting to me so much. No matter how hard I tried to forget what he said, nothing worked, and I spent the night tossing and turning.

"Yep," is all she answers with.

"Thanks for the clarification."

"You do know he's probably listening in right now, yeah? His bedroom's right there," she says, pointing to the French doors I was looking out of yesterday when I used his phone.

I shrug before sinking into the pool and dipping my head

under the cool, refreshing water.

"I get the feeling he'll be listening in all the time with me," I say.

Sasha sits on the side of the pool in a tiny bikini, her feet dangling in the water. "Arrogant much?" she says, kicking water in my direction.

"Hardly. I mean because it's clear I can't be trusted."

I pull myself out of the water to sit next to her, and she looks at me sceptically. "Is that what that ridiculous fuss over dinner was about last night? Why I had to have dinner with Jonas? Thanks for that by the way." She shudders. "What'd Mum say?"

"I don't really want to get into it. She offered me a job at least, so I'll be going to work with them tonight."

"Me too. I have to earn my keep … according to Jonas anyway."

"That's what your mum said about me going to work there."

"Yeah. They don't let me do any of the fun stuff, though. I only bartend."

"So that's it? They run a *bar*?" Why couldn't they just tell me that? "But more importantly, they let a sixteen-year-old bartend? Last time I checked, legal drinking age was eighteen."

"Well, it's not like I *drink* the alcohol," she says with a liar's smile on her face. "Did they not tell you about Litmus?"

"Litmus? What the hell is Litmus?"

She smiles. "It's where you find out what you're made of."

She jumps into the water and starts doing laps. Is she really going to end our conversation like that? *'It's where you find out what you're made of.'* That's all I get?

After a gazillion laps, she comes back over to the side of the pool and climbs out, grabbing her towel off the ground. "I'm going to head inside, you coming?"

"Uh, I guess so," I stammer, fumbling for my clothes and towel before following her in. I catch up to her in the hall. "So that's really all you're going to give me?"

She smiles. "You'll find out more tonight."

"Why the big secret?"

She stops walking and turns to face me. "It's not exactly … legal. That's all I can say." She leaves and starts heading upstairs.

As I turn down the hall to go to my room to get ready for my lunch with Declan, I can't help thinking I've heard the term Litmus before.

"Litmus," I mutter aloud, trying to jog my memory. *High school science, maybe?*

Next thing I know, Brett throws his door open and trudges down the hall towards me. I raise an eyebrow at him, which only makes him look angrier. He grabs my arms and slams me into the wall next to my bedroom door, pinning me with his forearm against my chest, crushing me under his weight. I drop my towel and pile of clothes, and they hit the ground with a thud.

"What do you know about Litmus?" he growls.

"Wh—"

"Who told you?" The rage in his eyes is similar to what I saw when he pegged me up against the wall of the nightclub a few nights ago, only this time it's even more intimidating. And I don't even have a gun to my head this time.

"Sasha. Who else?"

"What did she tell you?"

My lip trembles, my body beginning to ache from being held in this position.

"Nothing. Just that she bartends and that it's some kind of test. Whatever that means."

He takes a step back, releasing me from his grip, but not looking any happier.

"I don't exactly know what just happened, but next time you want to know something—just ask me." My tone is quiet and mousy, not exactly how I was hoping for it to come out.

"When did Sasha tell you?" It's obvious he's trying to stay

calm, though he's talking through gritted teeth.

"Just before—at the pool. Weren't you listening?"

"I tuned you out as soon as you called me an ass," he says, managing a small smile. "You weren't meant to be told about Litmus until tonight. You'll go through all the security and confidentiality briefings there. When you muttered 'Litmus'... I thought ..." He struggles to talk. "I thought you might be here for other reasons."

"What other reasons would there be?"

"We know who your adoptive family is."

"You think *they* sent me? I've barely spoken to them for three years. You really think I'd be working for them? And what's Litmus anyway? Why can't you just tell me now instead of tonight?"

"You'll find out tonight. Just stay at the house this afternoon, okay? At least then you can't screw up."

"What about my lunch with Declan?"

"Security risk."

"But I'm not going to—"

"Cancel it."

-7-

LITMUS

"*That's* what you're wearing?" Sasha asks as she enters my room without knocking.

"What's wrong with jeans and a T-shirt?" I ask, looking down at my comfortable clothes. "Is there some kind of dress code?" It's only then do I really take notice of what my sister is wearing, and it's basically nothing. "Or is practical nudity a requirement?"

She assesses herself, turning in a circle as she shows off her cowlick halter-top that barely covers her boobs and exposes her midriff. Her barely there skirt—or is it a head scarf? I can't tell—doesn't leave much to the imagination, but that's okay because her fishnet stockings cover her legs … just. I can't help giving a disapproving stare.

She looks back up at me after inspecting herself and shrugs. "I didn't pick it out."

"Sorry, what?"

"Jonas picks what I wear when I work at the club."

"And Cade is okay with you wearing … that?"

"You can call her Mum, you know."

"I … I don't think I'm there yet," I stammer.

There's a knock at my door before Brett walks in. "I brought your clothes for you," he says, handing me a plastic garment bag.

"My clothes?"

"For tonight. Cade's orders, probably passed down from Jonas."

My heart starts thumping in my chest. Oh God … I'm going to have to dress like Sasha. I glance over at her, suddenly terrified of where exactly I'm going tonight and what I'll be expected to do. *What kind of place is this?*

I slowly unzip the garment bag, silently relieved when I see a pair of black pleather pants. *At least I won't be wearing Sasha's skirt.* My muscles tense when I see I have a top matching hers though.

"I …"

"It's not negotiable, so don't even try. See you both there," Brett says walking out.

"There? You mean he's not going to be hanging off us the whole time like the leech that he is?" I ask Sasha, making her giggle.

"He's doing a showcase tonight, so he'll meet us there. We'll be tailed by the other leech tonight."

"Well, I already like Drake better than Brett."

"I like him better than Brett too, but I still wouldn't say that I like him."

"You've made out with him!"

"Because I was bored. And even making out with him was pretty boring. Maybe you should go for him," she says casually, as if what she just said isn't offensive.

"Gee, thanks. First for implying that I'm boring, and secondly, I'm not really into sharing guys with my sister."

"Well, better get dressed—we'll be leaving soon." She leaves the room and I'm left pondering my outfit for a second time.

I'm not prudish when it comes to my wardrobe, but I'm not exactly this extreme. Slipping the pants on over my thighs, it's like they meld to my legs. I'm surprised to find them comfortable and flexible.

The top, however, is harder to put on. It has a built-in bra and crossover straps at the back. Actually, the more I examine it, the more I realise it *is* a bra. It has a longer piece of material sewn into the stitching that covers my boobs, upper abdomen, and basically nothing else. *I'm going out in public in a bra.*

"I feel naked," I say when I open the door to find Sasha out there waiting for me.

"I heard you swearing a bit in there." If she's trying to hide her smile, she's failing.

I cross my arms over my stomach, reflex I guess.

"Don't cover up your sexy body," Sasha says, making me cringe.

"Don't ever say that sentence to your older sister again." I try to say it seriously, but I can't stop the laughter bubbling out of me.

"She's right though," a deep voice comes from behind us. We turn to see Drake walking towards us. "It is pretty sexy."

"Please don't call me sexy," I say, bringing my eyes up to meet his.

"But we'll still have the same problem no matter what I call you."

"What problem is that?"

"The insane amount of sexual tension between us."

Both Drake and Sasha are laughing now.

I roll my eyes. "I'll try to keep it in my pants. Are we going?"

"Right this way, milady."

"Don't call me that, either."

He laughs again and wraps his arms around Sasha and me.

"Messing with you is fun."

***

The loud thumping of the bass is no match for the heartbeat drumming in my ears. Drake has taken us to a nondescript nightclub, just like every other one I've been to in the city.

The flashing strobe lights trying to blind me? Check. Stocked bar with a huge line of waiting customers? Check. Dancefloor with people gyrating against one another? Check. Sticky floor? Double check. *Eww.*

As Drake walks us through the club, nearly all eyes are on him. I'm guessing it has something to do with the fact he has a skanky blonde on each arm. I realise I just called myself skanky looking, but it's hard not to when I'm only wearing a bra and skin-tight pants. Not to mention the six-inch heels Sasha handed me before we left.

Drake takes us to a cordoned-off VIP area, similar to the one Declan hired for my birthday, but this one is a long and narrow room with comfortable-looking couches lining the sides and a private bar at the back.

We're the only ones in here. I'm about to ask why when Drake keeps leading us through, past the bar and to an unmarked back door.

He opens it to a set of stairs leading down into a black hole.

"What the—?"

"Welcome to Litmus," Drake leans in over the loud music to yell in my ear.

Sasha goes first, and Drake gestures for me to follow.

My eyes need time to adjust to the poor lighting as I step down into the abyss. The music begins to fade as we start walking along the walls of the long, narrow tunnel before us. Soon the only sound to fill my ears is my still skyrocketing heartbeat and the gentle hum of some sort of generator, perhaps from the pipes and cables that run along the roof.

"Is this how everyone gets to Litmus? Or is this like a special entry?" I ask.

"This is a staff entry and emergency exit. There are four ways to get to the arena, but you'll most likely always use this one," Drake says. "It's closest to the house."

"Arena?"

Drake and Sasha share a glance. "Yeah. You'll see what I mean," Drake says.

"I'm getting really sick of this secretive thing," I mutter.

"Just a little bit farther and we'll be there."

As we go along, the narrow tunnel begins to widen, the lights become brighter, and then we're suddenly walking on slick tiling instead of hard concrete. Double doors are up ahead, but before we reach them, we get to a hallway leading left and right, doors lining the corridor until the ends where there are more double doors like the ones in front of us.

"This way," Drake says, directing us to the left corridor.

We wander down to the double doors at the end where Drake puts a passcode into a keypad in a wall and holds the door open for us.

We come to a set of stairs leading up to the floor above us. We take to the stairs and reach another corridor. I count three doors as we pass them on our left, ending at the last one. Drake opens the door, stepping aside to let Sasha and me in.

"Ah. Welcome." Jonas' voice carries across the room as we enter.

There are people standing around, dressed to the nines, sipping colourful drinks in champagne flutes and seemingly enjoying themselves. Everyone has either a blue drink or a red drink that seems to be glowing in the dim light.

Floor-to-ceiling glass windows line the far wall overlooking the area downstairs, but I can't see what's down there from where we stand. There are waitresses and waiters floating around with trays of fine finger foods and more drinks, plus a barman at the end of the room behind a fully stocked bar.

Jonas walks over to us, gently taking my arm. "Welcome to the corporate box," he says.

"Uh, thanks … I guess." *What the frick is a corporate box?*

"Come, we'll talk business and then I'll introduce you around."

"Okay."

He guides me by my elbow, taking me away from Drake and Sasha and through the small gathering of people. I notice Brett's in the group, dressed in black jeans and a tight dark grey T-shirt. He's much more casual looking than the rest of the party goers. He's shaking the hands of men in suits, with a bright smile on his face. He nods to me as we continue past him but doesn't leave his spot.

I'm taken to an adjacent room, much smaller than the corporate box. The small office has the same floor-to-ceiling windows on my right, a plain wooden desk in front of me with a plush pleather business chair behind it, and two less-comfortable-looking seats in front of it.

"Take a seat. Your mother should be here any minute."

"I'm right here," Cade says, entering the room and closing the door behind her. She sits in one of the chairs, and I take my cue, sitting in the chair next to her.

"Okay. First things first. Contracts," Jonas says, sitting behind the desk and reaching into his drawer to pull out a manila folder.

I begin reading as soon as he hands them to me.

"You don't really need to read it in depth. It's a standard employment contract. Even Sasha's signed it. The one you do need to pay great detail to is the confidentiality agreement."

As I begin reading the confidentiality agreement, I get lost in a sea of legal jargon.

"It is understood and agreed to that the below identified discloser of confidential information may provide certain information that is and must be kept confidential. To ensure the protection of such information, and to preserve any confidentiality necessary under patent and/or trade secret laws, it is agreed that ... "

Blah, blah, blah. Okay, I get it. No talking about Litmus to anyone who doesn't know about it. Safer yet, just don't talk about it at all.

I sign the agreement, pushing the form over to Jonas' side of the table.

"And the contracts?" he says, gesturing to the pile of paperwork still in front of me.

Hesitantly, I sign the two identical documents. One states that it's the employer copy, and the other says it's the employee copy. I pick mine up to carry it with me so I can read it later, but Cade takes it from me and puts it back on the desk.

"You can read that another time. Let's show you around," she says, standing.

"O … okay."

Cade links her arm with mine and leads me over to the window.

The scene below is one I can't comprehend. A well-lit square platform sits raised in the middle of the crowded room, stadium seats are positioned against the opposite wall, and there's a standing section directly below us with a long L-shaped bar taking up the other two walls. In the dim light of the crowd, all I can see is more glowing drinks. Blue and red. The bass of the music vibrates through the place, and I can see shadowy figures dancing throughout the entire venue.

Corporate boxes fill the entire upper level where we are. At least, I assume they're more corporate boxes. I can't see into the other windows.

"What *is* this?" I ask in awe.

"Have you ever heard of Litmus paper?" Jonas asks, joining us by the window.

"I don't think so. Litmus sounds familiar, but I'm having trouble placing it."

"It was once used to check the pH levels in something. The more acidic something is, the redder the paper becomes. Alkaline turns the paper blue."

"This doesn't exactly look like a science lab," I say as I start having flashbacks of high school science class.

Jonas laughs. "You're right about that. It's all metaphoric, of course; a gimmick. Are you strong or are you weak?"

"But doesn't alkali neutralise acid, and vice versa? So how is one weaker than the other? Neither of them are weak or strong, they're opposites."

Jonas touches his nose. "Did well in science at school, did you?"

"Not really."

"Sometimes you don't need to be strong to neutralise your opponent. Take Brett for instance. To look at him, he's a total Red. He's built like a brick house. But his ability is extra-sensitive hearing, totally making him a Blue. That doesn't help him in the arena at all. He could easily be taken out by someone of smaller stature with a powerful ability. Nobody knows if you're a Blue or a Red until you reveal what you can do."

"Well, that's just bad science. It doesn't make sense."

"It's a *gimmick,*" Jonas emphasises.

"What did you mean by taken out?" I ask.

"Just watch," Cade says, pointing to the square platform below us.

A deafening roar loud enough to fill the room pierces my ears, even though we're a floor above the noise. Spotlights start flashing, and a rumbling of stomping feet vibrates through the entire place. More screams, more shouts.

The crowd parts as Brett makes his way through, flanked by two guys in black T-shirts that read "security" along the back. He makes his way into the square, stripping off his shirt, and making the screaming louder … I can definitely hear more girls hollering anyway. A shy-guy grin crosses his face, but I can see the cocky smirk he's hiding underneath. *Ugh.*

Someone else takes the path he just made, joining him on the stage. Another muscly guy, smaller than Brett, but still pretty big. His ultra-white hair glows under the lights, giving him an angelic halo effect. He makes his way over to Brett, and he too removes his shirt.

What is this? Some kind of stripping contest? Are they going to lose the jeans next?

"It's Taser. I thought Chi was on tonight?" Cade says. "Brett hasn't faced him for a long time." She sounds a little bit worried.

"Don't you worry about Brett, love. It's only an exhibition fight. Both of them will know to take it easy. Save the real stuff for the real thing."

Exhibition fight? Taser, Chi?

A third person joins the stage, but he refrains from taking his clothes off. He's wearing a plain dark T-shirt, ripped skinny man jeans, and sneakers.

"Welcome to Litmus!" the man yells into his microphone, his voice booming throughout the entire venue. "We'll have an interesting fight tonight. No one's getting out of here unscathed, folks. In the Deakin corner, we have Brawn." Brett steps forward and the crowd starts screaming again. "In Holt, we have Taser." More screams bellow as the other guy steps forward. "Two of the biggest, toughest, meanest competitors go head to head in an ultimate battle of strength."

"You're pitting Defectives against each other?" I ask, my face screwed up in disgust.

"It's not like that, Nuka," Cade says. "It's a sport. It's

entertainment."

"It's a gold mine is what it is," Jonas says with a proud scoff.

"It's disgusting," I say. "How do you call this sport? It's sick, it's demeaning. You all just sit around and watch people beat the hell out of each other?"

A loud dinging sound echoes and Brett starts attacking Taser … or whatever his name is. Taser doesn't get a chance to go on the offensive. He's too busy trying to avoid Brett's fists. Unsuccessfully, too. Brett lands a powerful right hook, and even from this distance, I see the blood fly from Taser's mouth.

They're not wearing headgear, gloves … they've got nothing to protect themselves. This is insane.

Brett's already gotten a few good hits in, but Taser manages to escape Brett's onslaught. Managing to jab Brett in his ribs, Taser drops Brett to his knees. I don't know how Taser brought him down with a single punch, but Brett looks like he's spasming uncontrollably. Almost like he's being …

"They're using their abilities on each other?" I exclaim.

"I thought you said he would take it easy?" Cade scolds Jonas, successfully ignoring me. "Brett's never gone down that quick."

"He'll get back up," Jonas assures.

Brett turns quickly on his knees, punching his opponent so hard in his hip that his entire right leg falls out from underneath him.

I suck in a loud breath and find myself torn. Surprisingly, I'm glad Brett's gotten back on his feet, but I can't help judging him for doing this in the first place. It's degrading, it encourages the divide between normals and us.

As I watch over the crowd from my window, I'm the only one who seems to feel this way. Everyone else is cheering and going nuts. Chanting for Brett … well, Brawn. *Nice nickname, wanker.*

"This is so wrong," I say as Brett sends a left hook into

Taser's face, making him fall to the ground completely.

"So I take it that's a no to going into the arena?" Jonas asks.

"You … you want *me* to go in there? Are you insane?"

"Brett told us how you almost got away from him and Drake the other night. You should've been a simple snatch-and-grab job. But you knocked Drake on his ass and burnt Brett's back to a crisp. It still hasn't healed," Cade says, pointing down to the arena.

She's right. He still has red hand prints etched in his back.

"We need more girls," Jonas says.

"More women," Cade clarifies.

Yeah, because calling us girls would be demeaning. "I … I can't do … *that,*" I say, pointing to the ring where Brett is still beating the hell out of Taser.

"We'll train you, of course. But something tells me you won't need much," Jonas says. "Where'd you learn to fight?"

"Uh … my adoptive mother," I say shyly, trying my best to avoid eye contact with Cade. "She made me and my siblings learn self-defence growing up."

"How long have you been doing it?" Jonas asks.

"I trained two to three times a week for about ten years until I turned eighteen and moved out."

Cade and Jonas look at each other, their smiles scaring the hell out of me.

"We're not going to pressure you to do this, of course," Cade says in a soothing voice. Jonas clears his throat, but Cade ignores him. "Just take a look around tonight, see that this is actually a good thing, and have a think about it. You could be the face of our entire brand."

"You're certainly better looking than Brett," Jonas says with a laugh.

"Your brand?"

"There are five owners, each with four or five players. We're one of the most successful teams. A lot of people would kill for what we're offering you. You could be famous, be in the spotlight, earn more money than you ever could in the real world," Jonas boasts.

"And get killed in the process? All in the name of 'sport'?" I say using air quotes.

"No one's died in years," Jonas says.

"But it *has* happened?" I ask.

"Do accidents happen? Of course. They happen in the real world, too. No one sets out for it to happen, no one wants to lose on their investment."

I shake my head. "You're talking about human beings. And why do you keep referring to outside of Litmus as 'the real world'?"

"We're an escape in here. People come here to forget about out there, if only for a few hours. They come, make a few bets, watch some fighting, they drink, have fun, and go home happy."

"So that's how you make money? By betting?"

"Each of the owners takes a share of the profit on everything. Entry fees, alcohol, sponsorships, and yes, betting. We all have individual bookies working for us."

"And that's why everything's so secretive. Betting on something like this is bound to be illegal."

"That's not the only reason. The secrecy gives the club an element of exclusivity. It's exciting, it's glamorous."

I just shake my head, still disgusted by what I'm seeing.

"You'll find we're not much different to when they used to have professional boxing. Did you find that appalling, too?"

"They weren't being exploited for their abilities," I mumble.

"Just their talent to fight. How is that different here?"

"Then why only Defective people? Why can't normals fight?"

"Well, that would just be unfair. Hell, Brett wouldn't even be in there if he didn't have those damn muscles and his surprisingly strong threshold for pain."

"He's out," Cade says.

While Jonas and I have been debating, we didn't notice Brett going down for the count.

"He's out cold," Cade says.

"What the hell is Taser playing at?" Jonas mumbles. "It's exhibition."

"What's the difference between exhibition and actual fighting?"

"This is all for show. To bring in new sponsors, entice new owners to invest, make people want to become a fighter. It's not real … it's not meant to be real," Jonas says.

"Taser's probably trying to get back at you for rejecting him from our team," Cade says.

"Why did you reject him?" I ask. "Clearly he's the type of fighter you're looking for."

"He wanted a higher cut. Yes, he's a good fighter, but he's greedy. He wanted more than twenty percent."

"They only get twenty percent? They're the ones putting their lives on the line and you give them *twenty percent*? Are you kidding me?"

"To them, twenty percent is still more than what they could earn on the outside."

"*Them*? As in people like *us.*" I shake my head. "I can't hear anymore." People start walking towards the stage with a stretcher and a medical bag. "Take me to Brett. I want to make sure he's okay." My words surprise even myself. *Why do I even care?*

Under Jonas's permission, Cade takes me down to the main floor and the amount of people down here is frightening. The music is deafening—it was loud upstairs, but now it feels like the bass is giving me heart palpitations. For a supposedly exclusive club, it's certainly a packed house. I almost lose Cade numerous times on the way to the bar until she ends up grabbing my hand to lead me.

Drake is standing by the bar, seemingly not paying attention to the commotion on the floor where Brett is now in the stretcher and being taken off stage. I follow Drake's gaze and notice he's not taking his eyes off Sasha who's serving behind the bar.

"Can you take Nuka to the infirmary?" Cade yells at Drake over the noise. "I'll take Sasha back upstairs." She motions for Sasha to join her.

Drake nods and takes my arm, leading me into a side door, entering another backstage corridor.

"How was this place built without anyone's knowledge?" I ask.

"Signed the contract, I'm guessing?"

"Yeah."

Drake sighs. "Please tell me you read it first?"

"They didn't exactly give me time."

Drake shakes his head. "I thought you were going to be one of the smart ones. Make sure you read it."

"What do—"

"So, answering your question, we're currently in the very first subway station this country ever had. They've modified it, obviously, but it was originally going to become a big thing—the underground rail. There was going to be a station in every suburb, this one being central, it was going to be the biggest and best. It ended up being the *only* one. Ever since they perfected solar energy, the idea of a subway line was scrapped. Too expensive and not able to take advantage of the solar. So it was left here to rot."

"Well, thanks for the history lesson."

"You asked."

"It still would've been hard to restore a place like this—turn it into what it is."

"Not if the construction company hired to make the place structurally sound was on the Litmus payroll," Drake says with a smile.

"How long has this been here?"

"The building has been here for a long time, but the actual competition has only been going for three. It took a few years to get everything organised and up to standard, to get enough investors, then there was recruiting."

"How long have you worked for Jonas and Cade?"

"Almost two years. I was hired not long after this place caught on and started operating to its fullest. I don't think they were expecting it to be so successful so quickly."

"You don't find it ..."

"Morally wrong?" he asks, as if he could read my mind.

"Exactly."

"I'm more leaning towards it being a grey area. Do I think the concept of Immunes fighting for entertainment is wrong? Maybe. But it's kind of true that they get paid more and live better lives than most I've seen."

"But—"

"We're here," he says, putting a code into another keypad on the wall. A double door in front of us clicks and he opens the left side, leading me into a room that looks like a treatment room of a doctor's clinic. "He's over there," he says, pointing to Brett, who's being treated by doctors, across the room. "I have to get back to Sasha. Don't leave here without Brett or myself. Got it?"

"Got it." Drake leaves as I start making my way over to Brett. As I walk past Taser sitting on the edge of a bed with someone checking over him, his hand reaches out, grabbing my butt. I stop in my tracks and turn slowly to face Taser who has a cocky grin on his swollen face.

He waves off his doctor and stands up, taking a step closer to me. "You couldn't possibly be going to see Brawn, now could you?" His voice is weaselly and not at all deep like I was expecting.

"Why not?"

"Because he didn't win. He's not allowed a prize," he says,

taking another step forward, almost closing the small gap between us.

"Back off, Brayden," Brett says groggily.

"Ooh, possessive much? I was just having a little fun." His eyes lock with mine. "You must be pretty special if he won't even let me talk to you."

"Nuka, what are you doing down here?" Brett asks, while attempting to sit up in bed. The doctors assist him but then take a step back at Brett's orders.

"Nuka? Your name's Nuka?" Taser's eyes narrow.

"Uh … yeah, why?"

"Rare name. That's all," he says with a shrug. "Catch ya later, Brett." He turns on his heel and walks towards the doors. "I would apologise for kicking your ass … but you know that's not my style," he adds over his shoulder before leaving.

"He seems …"

"Like a dick?" Brett says.

"That's putting it nicely. So, how are you?"

Brett laughs. "You came down here to see how I am?"

"Well, like Taser said, he did just kick your ass."

"Call him Brayden. Taser's a stupid name."

"Oh, okay, *Brawn*."

"Yeah, I'm not a fan of that one, either."

"Why do you do it?" I ask quietly.

"Do what?"

"Don't act dumb. You know what I'm asking."

"Keeping my head above water, Nuke."

"I don't get it."

"Of course, you don't," he says with a sigh. "I knew you'd get like this. I told them you wouldn't be interested."

"Then explain it to me."

"Come out with me tomorrow."

"Wha … what?" My mouth goes dry for some stupid reason.

He rolls his eyes. "Not on a date. I want to show you

something."

I raise an eyebrow.

"Not a date," he repeats himself.

The door opens and Drake pops his head in. "Nuka, I've been ordered to take you and Sasha home."

"I'll pick you up in the morning," Brett says.

"Uh, we live in the same house."

"Exactly. I won't have to go far," he says with a smile before wincing in pain.

"Rough go, bro," Drake says, approaching us. "Glad to see he didn't ruin your pretty face."

"Piss off, Drake," Brett retorts before facing me. "See you in the morning, Nuke."

-8-

NOT A DATE

"So where are we going?" I ask, getting into Brett's car.

"Nowhere fun, so don't sound so excited," he says, sliding into the driver's seat ever so cautiously, trying not to wince.

"So is this what you meant by you've dealt with worse than when I burnt you?"

"All part of the job."

"Okay, so what *is* your job? You're head of home security and then moonlight as an illegal street fighter?"

"Jonas and Cade are my owners. If—"

"*Owners?*"

"It's their word. They're more like my managers. You know how professional athletes have managers and agents and all that? They do that for me. If I do a good job for them, they pay me well. Once I get rid of my debts, I can stop and then do something I enjoy."

"What debts do you have?"

"That's a bit of a personal question, isn't it?" When I don't respond, he sighs and continues. "This car, some student loans"—he shrugs—"living expenses."

"Student loans? You went to uni?" I ask, a little surprised.

"Yes. Muscle man read good," he replies in a caveman voice.

"I didn't mean it like that. I just … the way you talk about Defectives—"

"You know where a business degree gets you when you're Defective? Absolutely nowhere. No one would hire me. So now I'm in debt *and* I'm an undesirable employee. Cade and Jonas took me in, offered me the security job if I'd fight for them. It was an offer I couldn't refuse. I get two wages and the work is easy. It's just …"

"You don't enjoy it."

"I should only need to do this a little longer and then I'll be free."

"What living expenses? Cade and Jonas give you everything."

"Are you going to be asking me questions all day? Don't make me regret bringing you."

"Bringing me *where?*" I ask as we start heading out of the city.

"We're going to my house. My real house."

"In one of the housing Estates?"

Brett scoffs. "You make it sound like a country club. I can assure you, it's not."

Sensing that our conversation is over, I remain quiet. Until I can't anymore. "Okay, so why *this* car. I don't get it. It's a million years old. It still runs on petrol. Surely, this car is worth a lot? You could sell it and be debt free. There'd be a heap of people interested who collect those sorts of things. Doesn't the petrol alone cost an arm and a leg? Didn't we practically run out of that stuff decades ago? Why don't you have an electric car like everyone else?"

"Yup. Regretting this." Sighing again, he glances at me and then looks back at the road. "This car belonged to my dad. He died almost five years ago now, and I don't have the heart to sell it. It doesn't actually run on petrol, Dad spent the money converting it to electric … well, he borrowed the money to convert it. It's been in our family for generations, so even when he got sick, he still refused to sell it—even though that money could've paid for his treatment. He didn't like that all the new cars are the same shape, but it was more than that. He loved this two-door coupe more than me and my sister combined, probably. I can't get rid of it to pay off my debts, just because I wanted to get a degree."

"Oh … sorry. If I had something of my dad's, I'd want to keep it, too."

"Paxton James, right? It sucks what happened to him. He really wanted to do right by us."

"Or so everyone thinks," I mumble.

"What do you mean?"

"Cade says he wasn't the guy everyone thought he was, that he was mean. And my adoptive mother would never talk about him. She'd clam up anytime he was mentioned. It wasn't obvious to me at first, but when I found out about who I truly was, that's when I noticed how anxious she got whenever he was mentioned. I thought she was just purposefully being a bitch and not telling me because she knew I was going to leave them. Then, one night, I overheard my adoptive dad consoling her that she did the right thing by hiding the truth from me. That they were protecting me."

"Did you ask them what they meant?"

"What do you think?"

"I think you ran."

My lack of reply is answer enough.

"Well, you'll never know unless you ask them."

"Thanks for stating the obvious, but that would involve

talking to them."

"You're really stubborn, aren't you?"

"Yeah, I've been told that. I wonder if I get it from my dad … oh wait, I wouldn't know."

"I'm sensing some pretty deep daddy issues here."

"Please. I have so many daddy issues it's surprising I'm not working a stripper pole. Although, what they made me wear at Litmus last night came pretty close."

Brett laughs, and I can't help chuckling with him.

The laughter and smiles fade when we pull into a suburb. On each side of the street, houses are boarded up. The remnants of a burnt car sit in one of the front yards. On the other side, a few doors down, is the remains of what was once a home, now only a burnt shell.

"Not the glamorous country club you were expecting?" Brett asks.

I swallow hard. "No."

As we move farther into the Estate, the more together the houses seem to be. More people fill the footpaths, each of them staring us down as we drive by them.

"Isn't it dangerous bringing this car here? Won't it … you know … get stolen or something?"

"Because every poor person must be a criminal, right?"

"I didn't mean it like that. It's just … everyone's staring."

"I haven't been home in a while. They're probably just surprised to see me."

"So these are your friends?"

"No. Just neighbours."

We're driving slowly through the narrow, cracked street, and as we continue to drive, I have to force myself to ignore my instincts and refrain from locking my door. It's probably politically incorrect—like Brett said, they're just poor, they aren't criminals. I don't want to offend Brett, but I'm more scared right now than when I squatted for a night.

Will never do that again. Declan was with Cassia, so I couldn't stay at his. I had refused to go home to Lia and Jayce's, and the shelter I occasionally crashed at was full. That was the longest, scariest night of my life. Yeah, I know self-defence, but that whole night I sat curled up in the corner of the abandoned apartment, just watching the unlocked door and waiting for someone to come in with a gun or a weapon. I wouldn't have been able to defend myself against that. Ever since then, when I was really stuck for a place, I'd cave and go back home for the night.

There hasn't been a legitimate reason for me to be scared—just a burnt house and car and then dodgy-looking people on the street, but even though nothing has happened, the uneasy feeling doesn't leave me. I tell myself it's because I lived a sheltered childhood and I just haven't been around poor people. *Wow, could I be any more of a snob?*

We turn into another street on our right, a short cul-de-sac. Brett pulls the car into a driveway on our left, in front of an older-looking house. Unlike the others in this area, this house is well kept.

"I apologise in advance for everything you're about to endure." His tone implies he's joking, but given the neighbourhood, I begin to get a little nervous.

Getting out of the car and taking my hand, Brett leads me to the front door where he proceeds to unlock three of the six deadbolts and opens the door. He smiles at my questioning glare.

"Six locks—if you only lock three, unless a burglar knows which three you've locked, they'll never get in."

"Smart," I say in awe.

"Nanna, I'm home," he calls out.

Nanna?

"Brett?" A woman's voice travels down the hallway.

Brett gestures to the couch in the small living room. I shake my head, surprisingly unwilling to leave his side. An older woman wipes her hands on a dishtowel in the kitchen before making her way down the hall to meet us.

The small woman barrels towards Brett, throwing her frail arms around his masculine frame.

"Why didn't you tell me you were coming home?" She glances at me. "And bringing someone with you?" She extends her hand to me, and I give it a light shake. "He's never brought a girl home before, you know," she says with a wink.

"Uh … I—"

"It's not like that, Nanna. It's my job to protect her. Nanna, this is Nuka. Nuka, this is Silver Finley."

"Silver? Like the metal?" I ask.

"My parents liked expensive things," she says. "Come into the kitchen, I'll make tea."

She leads us into the dining room, and I take a seat at the small table while Brett helps his nanna in the kitchen. It's so cute.

She wraps her arms around him again and whispers, "I'm so happy to see you."

I don't know if she didn't want me to hear or not, but I can't help letting out a little "aww" noise. Brett rolls his eyes at me.

Carrying our cups of tea and a plate of shortbread, Silver joins me at the table and meets my eyes with a smile. "You're really pretty, you know."

"Uh …"

"Nanna, stop."

"I can't be excited that I'm meeting your lady friend?"

Brett's face breaks out in a small blush, and I have to hold back a giggle. "It's not like that, Nanna. She's just a job."

Ouch.

"Nonsense. You wouldn't have brought her to me if you didn't at least like her."

"As a *friend,*" Brett says, really emphasising "friend."

"Of course. That's what I meant," Silver says with a sly grin.

"Besides, I'm trying to make a point. She doesn't know what it's like out here. I had to show her."

Silver looks at me with piercing grey eyes. "You're not Immune, love?"

Clearing my throat, I meet her gaze. "I am. I just … I grew up in the city suburbs. I haven't been out to the Estates since I was a little kid."

Silver purses her lips. "Well, they certainly aren't what they used to be. We moved into this house when they were first setting the Estates up about fourteen … no, fifteen years ago now. It was a good idea, but it didn't take long for things to change and go south. We're so far out of the city. It's hard for people to get jobs and to keep them. There's not a lot of work in these parts, so to get an honest job, residents here have to travel for up to an hour and a half to two hours away. There needs to be more infrastructure and more projects to build on, but no one wants to build new communities or businesses when the old ones are falling apart and have the crime rate we do."

Taking a sip of my tea, I try to think of something to say, but I don't have words. I wonder if Uncle Drew knows how bad things are out here. He's the one who created these communities.

"So, you grew up in the city, huh? I could tell just by looking at you that you're a brave soul."

"Nanna," Brett whines.

Silver laughs. "I'm just telling it like I see it. Tell me, what was it like going to school in the city?"

I shrug. "I never went to a Defecti—Immune school to begin with, so I didn't know if I was missing out on anything. It was weird not knowing any other Immunes at school. Well, there were some, but we all made it a point to not hang around each other. Just in case."

"In case what?" Brett asks.

"In case they thought we were congregating or planning something."

"So it seems it wasn't all privilege and easy going for you there, either," Silver says with a pointed glare at Brett.

"Where's Paddy?" Brett asks, changing the subject.

"Working," she replies.

"Who's Paddy?"

"He's my nephew," Brett answers me before turning back to his nanna. "Where is he working? *Why* is he working? He's thirteen years old." Now he just seems angry. "Am I not giving you enough money? I can scrape together some more."

"He's strong-willed. I wonder where he gets that from," she replies in a snarky tone. "I've tried to stop him, but now he's in too deep. He's just trying to provide for his family, like his uncle does."

Brett closes his eyes and pinches the bridge of his nose. "What's he doing?"

"He's running with the southern crew," she practically whispers.

"I'll fix it," he says with determination. I haven't known him long, but from what I can tell, if he wants something, he gets it.

"You can't. I've tried."

"I'm going to do everything I can to fix this. I just need a little time. I'll buy his way out."

"You're already doing so much. I can't ask you to take Paddy on, too."

"I promised her I would take care of him. You're both my responsibility. Sorry to cut this short, but I need to get back," he says, standing. "Maybe I can sort something out with my owners."

Silver nods, a single tear falling from her ageing eye. She wipes it away before turning to me. "It was nice meeting you, Nuka. Please keep my boy in check." She manages a smile, and I force myself to return it. I don't exactly know what's going on, but I have fairly good idea, and I know it's nothing good.

"Come on, Nuke, let's go," Brett says.

"That was a quick visit," I say as we walk outside and back to the car.

"Sorry, but Paddy—" He stops short when another car pulls up to the curb outside the house. "Speak of the devil."

"Uncle Brett," Paddy yells as he gets out of the car and runs over to us. Paddy looks a hell of a lot like his uncle, and his dark hair is cropped short, styled into a faux Mohawk.

"Hey, squirt," Brett replies, but his tone is pretty flat. "We'll catch up another time. I've got things to do, okay?"

"Okay," Paddy says with a sad smile. "She told you, didn't she?"

"Even if she didn't, I would've figured it out with the company you're keeping," Brett says, nodding in the direction of the car.

The driver gets out and starts making his way over to us. He's tall and broad but nowhere near as big as Brett. His brooding stare makes me think he's trying to act tougher than what he is. Not surprising if he's coming to confront Brett.

"Get inside, Paddy," Brett orders. Paddy starts running with no question. "Get in the car, Nuke."

"What's—"

"Now's not the time to act like Sasha. Get. In. The. Car."

I do as he says but don't shut the door the whole way so I can listen in. I can't help myself.

"Been a long time, Brett," a deep voice says.

"It has, Shane." I see them shake hands out of the corner of my eye.

"You know, Paddy's come in quite handy."

"So what's it going to take to get him out of this?"

Shane laughs. "Of course. Mister 'I'm too good for you' thinks he can buy his way out. Paddy isn't for sale. He belongs to us."

"I never said I was too good, just that I wanted more than this life. Isn't that what you want? You have a daughter now, don't you? Don't you want a better life for her?"

"You know I do. But not all of us are given that chance. Not all of us have the opportunity to go to uni, let alone be hired by someone like Dalton. Your nephew came to me. Maybe you should be looking after your own, instead of someone else."

"Don't push me, Shane," Brett says. He's trying to hide his anger, but it's clear in his voice. "How much?"

I'm a little shocked at the figure Shane gives. It would be a considerable chunk of my trust fund, it would be peanuts to Jonas and Cade, but to someone who lives out here? I don't see how Paddy could make Shane that much money in his lifetime.

"Give me a month. If you cut Paddy loose for the entire month while you wait, I'll add five percent. And he's done. He doesn't work for you anymore. Got it?"

"Got it, boss. Consider his employment terminated effective immediately. Of course, if you're late with payment, I may have to reinstate him. Work him double as hard to make up for a lost month of his earnings."

"I'll have the money," Brett says, shaking Shane's hand.

"Pleasure doing business with you again, Brett."

I can't believe he just agreed to that.

Brett climbs in the driver's seat and slams his door shut. Gripping the steering wheel, his knuckles are white. He looks straight ahead, trying to gain control over his erratic breathing.

"Is everything okay?"

"Peachy," comes a flat retort.

"How are you going to get that much—"

"Close your door. We're leaving."

I shut my door and Brett immediately pulls out of the driveway and onto the street. His driving is all over the place. Just like his moods. I don't know which Brett I'm going to be dealing with next. The sweet, caring, responsible guy who looks after his nanna and nephew? Or the moody, quick to react, violent street fighter.

Brett sighs as he calms down and glances at me. "Don't worry about the money. I'll ask Cade and Jonas for an advance to cover it all, but I have some of it in savings."

"I understand why you fight now. You're an amazing person to be sacrificing your life for your family."

He scoffs. "I'm not sacrificing anything. It's true what Shane said. I'm lucky Cade and Jonas hired me. I'm one of the fortunate ones who got out. Not everyone's so lucky. And if I can't get Paddy out, then I've failed. Before my sister died, I swore I'd protect him from the kind of life she had. But being away, living with Cade, protecting Sasha and now you … Shane's right. I haven't been looking after my own."

"He's not right. You're doing your very best to provide for your family. I don't know what happened to your sister, but the fact you've taken on more responsibility than what's yours goes to show how great a guy you really are." I put my hand on his arm to try to soothe him.

He closes his eyes for a brief moment before focussing them back on the road. They're glassing over with tears.

"Great guys still do bad things to get what they want, Nuka. I want you to remember that. Take Shane for instance. We were best friends growing up. Now he's willing to screw over anyone and everyone, just to survive. He was pissed at me for being accepted to uni. He hated that I refused to join his crew. My sister was part of them, and she didn't make it out alive. I'm not going to let that happen to her kid. And I will do *anything* to make sure nothing ever happens to him. Do you understand what I'm saying?"

I nod and take my hand back. We sit in silence all the way home, giving me plenty of time to think.

I was given everything growing up, and it wasn't until today that I realised how lucky I've been. The people out in the Estates have next to nothing, and they're doing anything and everything they can to survive. Brett is putting his whole life on hold, just so he can support his family and keep a roof over their head, and thirteen-year-old Paddy feels like he needs to do the same.

There are hundreds, probably even thousands, of families just like Brett's who don't have the means or the opportunity to fix their situation.

I skated through my childhood and school, completely oblivious to what it's like for others like me. Growing up with Lia, I heard many stories of discrimination and how hard it was for us, but I guess I always thought they were exaggerated—borderline propaganda even. Turning a blind eye to something you never see is easy, but to continue to live with tunnel vision when your blinders have been taken off is next to impossible.

By the time we reach the mansion, I've made a decision.

If I can make a difference in this world, I'm going to do everything I can to make that happen. I have an idea, but I just have to get Cade and Jonas to agree to it.

"Brett?" I stop him as he goes to climb out of the car.

"Yeah?"

"Will you teach me how to fight?"

-9-

THE DEAKIN FUND

I swallow the lump forming in my throat. “I want to run something by you … if that’s okay?”

Jonas, Cade, and Sasha lift their heads from their dinner plates to glare at me. When none of them responds, I take that as my opening.

“I’ve been thinking a lot about Litmus, and what you want of me.”

“You don’t have to do it, sweetheart,” Cade says. “Jonas and I talked it over, and we understand where you’re coming from. You can work the bar like Sasha if you really want.”

I shake my head. “It’s not that. I actually am interested.”

“You are?” Jonas asks.

“Well … I have a few conditions.”

A knowing smile crosses Jonas’s face. “Another Taser.”

“No. I’m not being greedy, but I do want more money.”

Jonas scoffs.

"If you agree to keep on housing me and feeding me, I only want a ten-percent cut."

Jonas's brow furrows. "That's *less* money."

"On top of," I continue, "the twenty percent you usually give. But I want that money to go into a trust. I want to set up a charitable donation fund to contribute to the Institute's Estate programme."

"What's brought this on?" Cade asks.

"Brett," I answer simply.

"Ooh, someone's got it baaaaad," Sasha teases.

I give her my best "shut up" look, but she just laughs at me.

"You can donate half of your twenty percent," Jonas states.

"Don't be so hasty, Jonas. Think about this for a minute," Cade says. "It would be great publicity for us, having a contender donate her entire wage to charity. We can give her ten percent as sort of an unofficial allowance. Under the table, so no one else would know."

"Well, there's more," I say. "Because of who my dad was, and of who my adoptive mother is, I don't want to be associated with them and their campaigns. If it was to get out that it was me who organised it … well … I just don't want to be compared to them. I was hoping to set the fund up as part of the Deakin team. I don't want the recognition, I just want to help."

"Looks like the apple doesn't fall far from the adopted tree," Sasha says.

Both Cade and I glare at her. As much as I don't want to be compared to Lia, I think deep down I know this has stemmed from her influence—I just don't want to admit that aloud.

"It would do wonders for our image, Jonas," Cade says after she finishes giving Sasha a harsh stare down.

Jonas looks pensive for a moment before meeting my eyes. "And you'll be the face of our brand? You'll go into the arena?"

"If I'm completely honest, the idea of going in the arena scares the hell out of me. But Brett's offered to train me. I know self-defence, but I never learnt to be the aggressive one, so I don't know how to attack—not at a competitive level anyway. It might be some time before I'm ready to fight in the arena, but if you agree to give me the thirty percent I'm asking for, I'll try my hardest to get there as soon as I can."

This brings a smile to Jonas's face. "I think you have a deal, little lady. Thirty percent. Ten to you, twenty to your Defective trust, and to start you off, we'll only have you for introductory fights and Wild Card nights. We'll ease you in slowly."

"Wild Card?"

"We generally run them once a week. It's where anyone on the night can volunteer to enter the arena," Cade explains. "If they can beat the assigned fighter, the owners can go into a bidding war over the entrant and they can earn a spot in the competition. It hardly ever happens, they generally always lose. It's usually people out for a fun night. Guys sign up their friend on his bachelor night, teenagers wanting to boast to their friends that they fought at Litmus, things like that. Anyone who's serious about joining the competition come straight to the owners or are recruited. Starting you off on Wild Card nights is an easy way to train you without putting you in too much danger. Of course, we'll have Brett training you on the side, too."

"How long do I have to train?" I ask, nervous they're not going to give me long to get ready.

"How about we see how you're going in a month?" Jonas suggests.

"But if you need more time, we'll give it to you," Cade adds. "We don't want you to feel pressured."

"So you're really going to do it?" Sasha asks, her eyes wide.

"Looks that way."

"What's your stage name going to be?" Sasha asks.

"Stage name?"

"Well, yeah, everyone has one. They all reflect their abilities. Taser can use his hands like a Taser gun. Brett … well, it's not his ability, but he's freakishly strong, so they call him Brawn." The more Sasha talks, the more animated and excited she's getting. "There's also Inferno, he throws a wicked fireball. Psych literally psyches you out—he gets in your mind and makes you feel pain without physically hurting you. There's Chi, she sucks in the energy all around her and uses it to create blasts, knocking her opponent out. And then there's—"

"Sasha, stop overwhelming the poor girl," Cade says. My face must look as distraught as I suddenly feel.

"All I'm saying is she needs the perfect name."

"Well, we have a month to figure one out," Cade says.

"Better go get some rest, Nuka," Jonas says. "You start training tomorrow."

***

"Here. Put this on your eye," Brett says, handing me an icepack.

Touching it to my face, I gasp and wince in pain. "Didn't your mother ever teach you not to hit girls?"

"You think the others in the arena are going to care you're a girl? You're going to have to get used to being hit. A lot of those other guys you'll meet will do way worse than what I've done to you."

Holding the icepack to my left eye, I look up at Brett towering over me and try to give him my best scowl face. He's breathing heavy from our training session, sweat gleaming off his naked abs. I shake my head at my where my thoughts are headed. *Who cares about his stupid abs?*

Each training session is more brutal than the last. Brett doesn't only have me fighting him, but he's making me do weights as well to build up my non-existent muscles. All I've been doing is breathing, eating, sleeping, and training.

Declan keeps calling on Brett's line for me to catch up with him. I haven't seen him since I first came here almost two weeks ago. This is the longest I've gone without seeing him, and I'm running out of excuses as to why I can't. Turning up in bruises isn't an option. He'll assume all the wrong things, and I can't tell him the truth.

But damn, I miss him.

The reality of what I'm doing comes crashing down on me. "At this rate, I don't think I'll ever be ready for the arena."

"You will be. You just need to build up some tolerance."

"To pain?"

"Exactly. How else do you think I survive in there? I don't exactly have an ability that helps me in that department. I just endure it. You're doing really great so far, you're great at self-defence, and I can hardly get a shot in. But when I do, you go down like a ton of bricks. The other problem we're facing is your offensive tactics are shocking, and you don't have the endurance to wear your opponent out before striking. What exactly is your ability? I mean … I know you can heat things, and burn the crap out of me," he smiles, "but how does it work?"

"I convert electromagnetic energy into microwaves and manipulate it into various effects like heat, light, and radiation."

"In English, please."

"I thought you said you were smart?" I say, wincing in pain again. It feels like my cheek is on fire. Ignoring his smirk, I begin to explain. "I really am like a walking microwave. I can heat anything with any part of my body, even my mind. Although it takes a lot longer without touching something. The night you grabbed me and I burnt you, that was me focusing all of my energy on just my hands. I contemplated trying to burn you all over with my body, but the more surface I have to heat, the longer it takes."

"But you don't have to be touching your opponent?"

"No. But I don't think you understand just how long we're talking. I can cook eggs, and heat small things with relative ease, but people? We're talking … I don't know how long, I've never actually tried, but it'd be hours, I'm guessing. Not to mention deadly … probably."

"Doesn't mean we can't try and find a way to use it to our advantage." He holds out his hand to help me up. "Come on. Break's over."

"Ugh, really?" I say, pointing to my face.

"Push through it, Nuke. You've only got a few weeks before they test you in that arena. You need to be ready … or at least strong enough not to get killed."

"No pressure," I mumble.

I get to my feet just as Sasha bursts through the doors to our training room, which is Brett's very own personal gym. Perks of the job, I suppose.

"The Girl on Fire!" Sasha screams.

Brett matches my disgusted face. "No," we say in unison.

"Thought that was a long shot," she replies, exiting the room with her head held low.

"They're getting worse," I say to Brett. "That one doesn't even make sense. My ability has nothing to do with fire."

So far, we have rejected Lava Girl, The Heat, Scorcher and Hot Stuff. That last one was Drake's suggestion—not surprisingly.

"But you could set things on fire if you heated them enough, right?" Brett asks.

I shrug. "I can create sparks with metal and stuff. I once blew up a car battery … but that was with the help of someone who amplified my ability."

Brett scratches his head. "What about Emme?"

"Emme?"

"For a name. Electromagnetic Microwaveable Energy. E-M-M-E."

I shrug. "It's not the worst. But it doesn't really have much … pizazz. Brawn vs. Emme. Gee, I'd wonder who'd win that fight."

"Well, definitely Brawn if you don't stop stalling and actually do some training," he says with a smile, dragging me onto the soft training mats.

"Why do I need a nickname anyway? Nuka matches my ability perfectly."

"And if Litmus was to be discovered and the *new face* of Deakin was using her real name? It wouldn't be hard to track you down. Especially with a name like Nuka."

"Naw, is the *old* face of Deakin upset about being replaced?" I ask, picking up on his emphasis of "new face."

"Pfft. Hardly. I'm only in it for the money, not the fame." He takes a step closer to me, confiscating my icepack. "Besides, with a face like yours, they're making the right choice. So long as we can keep said beautiful face intact."

"You think I'm beautiful?"

He rolls his eyes. "You know you're beautiful."

A blush starts at the base of my neck, making its way up to my face, but before it has a chance to take over me, Brett's swinging an open palm towards me.

We fight and train using many forms and techniques from different areas of martial arts, boxing, and self-defence. It's exhausting.

I duck out of the way, his hand just missing my head. I lunge forwards, pushing him as hard as I can in his stomach. He stumbles back but is on me again within seconds.

My hands fly up in defence, blocking him.

"Hit me, Nuka," he growls at me.

"I'm trying, you asshat." I raise my fist only to have it caught by Brett in his hand.

"Not hard enough."

I'm suddenly reminded of a time, only a few years ago, when I was training with my little brother, Will.

"Hit me, Nuka. Hit me. You can't, can you? Nope, I'm too quick for you!" he teased, shuffling around and bouncing back and forth on the balls of his feet, as if he was doing some fight dance.

I wasn't in the mood. The sun was hot on my back, my mouth was dry, and I felt like retching all over the green grass of our backyard. Having gone out the night before with friends from school, I was fighting a major hangover. I couldn't tell Will that, though. I was only seventeen, and he'd rat me out to Mum and Dad.

"Just because you went through a sudden growth spurt and are now taller than me, that doesn't mean I can't kick your butt, little boy."

"I'd like to see you try," he taunted.

I wanted to wipe that look off the eleven-year-old's face. His ego needed to be taken down a notch.

While he was showboating about, I was heating my right hand. By the time he stopped mucking around and started our sparring routine, it only took one hit. I punched him in the face, hard.

"Argh! Son-of-a ... That's cheating, Nuka," he wailed, holding his cheek.

"Come on, you can take it. I thought you were too fast for me anyway?" I smirked.

Rage filled his eyes. Throwing out the detailed routine Lia had made for us to practise, he lunged for me and we got in our first real fight.

There was yelling, and screaming, and fists being thrown haphazardly. He tackled me, and on our way crashing to the ground, I used my leg to kick him in his gut. Using his weight against him and the momentum from my foot to lift him in the air, I flipped him over my head.

He landed on his back with a loud thud.

Lia came rushing outside. "What's going on out here?"

"Training," I said innocently, sitting up and shrugging.

"It doesn't look like your set programme to me," she accused.

I knew Will was going to tell on me; of course, he would.

"We just got bored of doing the same thing over and over again, Mum," Will said. "We were just mucking around."

"What happened to your face?" Lia asked with motherly concern.

"Oh, Nuka got me good. I let my guard down and she taught me a lesson," Will said with a smile on his face, one I could tell was painful from the burn.

I sat there, shocked. He didn't sell me out. Why?

"Just stick to the programme, okay, guys? It's there for a reason. I don't want either of you getting hurt."

We both nodded and she went back inside.

"Screw the programme," Will said, whisper-yelling. "That was so much fun."

I laughed. "Me kicking your butt was fun? Wanna go again?"

"It's on, bitch."

I'm brought out of my reverie by Brett landing a punch to my jaw. That cracking sound can't be good. A brand new kind of pain takes over my whole head.

My anger flares, and all I see is red. I'm angry at Brett for getting to me. I'm angry at myself for letting him. I hate that I'm beginning to miss my family. It's ridiculous—I've spent the last three years avoiding them. Why now? Deep down, I begin to wonder if it's because I'm realising they were right, but I shake those thoughts away. Cade wants me in her life. She said so.

A surge of energy fills my hands, setting my fingertips burning with heat.

"Are you okay?" Brett asks, breathlessly.

Even though my jaw feels swollen and tight, not to mention aching, I push through it. There's so much energy building up, along with tension in my arms, neck, and back. I have to release it. Stepping forward, I go on the offensive and start hitting back.

Surprising myself, I actually make him wince in pain when my fist connects with his neck. I step back in surprise, but I don't get the chance to do a happy dance before Brett is attacking me again. Throwing my arms up in defence, I try to channel the anger inside of me to my fingertips again. When they start to tingle with heat, I aim for his bare stomach and his beautiful abs … *No, not beautiful. Get your head in the game, Nuka.*

He stumbles backwards when I push him as hard as I can, doubling over in pain from the burns on his stomach. While he's hunched over, I take advantage, stepping forward and knocking him to the ground with an elbow to the back of his neck.

"Ah, shit," he mutters. I go to hit him again, but he rolls over onto his back and throws his hands up in surrender. "It's okay. You got it. You got me," he says, his tone implying he's in a lot more pain than he looks.

"Really?" My eyes light up.

He nods and then takes a moment to catch his breath and regain some composure. I turn to grab my bottle of water, but before I can take a step, Brett pulls me down on top of him. He wraps his arm around my waist and cradles my face with the other hand. "You did it, baby," he says before completely taking me off guard, pulling my head towards his and touching our lips together.

I should pull away, but the excitement over beating him and the enjoyment from his tongue as I open my mouth to him—holy crap, that tongue—I give into it. It fills a void I didn't even know was there.

He pulls me in tight before rolling us over so he hovers above me. He pulls his mouth away for a brief moment, staring into my eyes with a questioning glare. My lips rise into a half-smile, making him grin before taking my mouth with his again.

"What about … whoa." Sasha's voice comes from the doorway, making Brett scramble off me. He's on his feet in less than a second, and I'm left lying on the floor.

I lift my head to look behind me at Sasha standing in the doorway, a smug grin plastered on her face.

"Training seems a lot more fun this afternoon," she says, trying to hold back a laugh.

Sitting up, I turn to face her. "You wanted something?"

"Uh … never mind," she says, rushing back out the door.

Now that she's gone, I suddenly wish she hadn't left. Now I'm alone with Brett again, I don't know what to say. "Umm …"

"I guess that's enough for today," Brett says, not looking at me.

"Oh … okay. I guess I'll hit the shower," I say, climbing to my feet.

"Yup. We'll pick it back up tomorrow. Uh … the training, that is … not the …" he sighs, "I'll just see you tomorrow, 'kay?"

I nod, turning to leave, but I pause in the doorway. "Do we need to talk about this … or?" I ask, looking over my shoulder.

"Nah, I'm good. You good?" He's still refusing to look me in the eye.

"Got it. I'll forget it ever happened."

The look of relief filling his face is telling enough. This was a mistake.

-10-

MY FIRST TEST

"I'm going with you, and that's final."

"Why can't Drake come instead? I need to talk to Declan, and I don't want you listening in."

Declan's been getting impatient the last few times I've spoken to him on the phone. He's worried about me, and I need to show him I'm okay. Not to mention, I'm missing him like crazy.

All I want is an afternoon without Brett. I haven't had a break from him since we started training three weeks ago, and things haven't been the same since we kissed. Anytime I mention it, he pushes me harder in training to try to get me to shut up. And it works.

"Drake has taken Sasha to … something. I don't know, I wasn't listening," he says dismissively.

"Aren't you *always* listening?"

"With this ability? If I did that, I'd go insane."

"Will you tune out Declan's and my conversation if you come?"

"No."

"Why not?" I whine loudly.

He places a finger in his ear. "Can you not go so high pitched, please?"

"Why can't I have a private conversation with my best friend?" I ask in a more rational, low tone.

"Security risk. Plus, you shouldn't be seeing him at all. You're still kind of bruised," he says, cradling my face and running his thumb over my poorly makeup-covered cheek.

"Well, whose fault is that?"

He drops his hand and glares at me. "Yours, because you're still letting me get a shot in. You do realise you have a test fight tomorrow with one of the other team members? You do realise they're going to flatten you, right? We should be training, not going to see your boyfriend."

I roll my eyes before giving him a pointed stare. "First of all—he's not my boyfriend. Second of all, how will one more training session prepare me for something that's happening tomorrow? Besides, I've managed to defeat you a few times now, you know." *None of which were rewarded quite like that first time, though.* "All I want is to have a break, to hang out with my best friend. By myself."

"Look, I'd let you go by yourself if they"—he points upstairs—"approved it. But until they give me the all clear, I have to be on you twenty-four-seven."

"This *sucks.*" *Real mature, Nuka.*

"Okay, Sasha."

"I. Am. Not. Sasha."

"Then. Stop. Acting. Like. Her."

"Argh. You're so impossible."

***

We pull into the parking lot of the small shopping complex where Declan's and my usual lunch place is. Declan's already sitting at a table outside, drinking coffee. I've been so pissed off at Brett and his attitude that I've been too distracted to get nervous about this little chat Declan and I are supposed to be having.

He's back with Cassia, I just know it, and I don't want to hear it. I've prompted him on the phone to just tell me what he needs to talk about, but he says he wants to do it in person. This only fills me with dread. *Please don't let them be engaged, or having a baby, or something equally as stupid.*

"Are you going to get out of the car?" Brett asks. "Or just sit here all day and stare at him?"

"Fine," I mumble, opening the door. Brett opens his too and goes to step out when I pull him back in the car. "Where are you going?"

"I'm coming with you."

"I can't even talk to him alone? You could still eavesdrop from here, why do you have to come in?"

"I don't have to, but I want to. I want coffee."

"Oh … Just don't sit with us, okay?"

"Aww, you don't want me to meet your boyfriend? I'm crushed," he says sarcastically. The frustration growing between us is palpable until he suddenly smiles at me. "You're really nervous, aren't you? Why should you be nervous if he's 'just your friend'?"

Ignoring his question, I get out of the car and walk ahead without waiting for Brett. He catches up easily and slings his arm around my shoulder.

"What are you doing?" I nudge him with my elbow, trying to break free of his grip.

He smiles down at me, seemingly no longer angry. "You make this so easy."

"Make what so easy?"

"Drake's right—messing with you *is* fun."

"You are such an ass."

"So I've heard."

"I guess I do call you that a lot," I mumble.

He finally pulls away from me and heads inside, completely chuffed with himself. He even nods to Declan as he walks by. I want to wipe that arrogant look off his face.

I make my way over to Declan who's looking at me with horrible puppy eyes and a confused expression.

Suddenly my anger towards Brett dissipates, and it's just me and Dec. He stands as I run up to him and throw my arms around him. We don't even need words.

Damn, he smells good. He smells like home, like innocent childhoods and playgrounds and school, when everything was perfect. We stay locked in an embrace for a lot longer than necessary, but I don't care.

He finally pulls away and gestures for us to sit but then looks inside at Brett standing in line and then back at me.

"Don't even ask," I say, sitting down across from him.

"Okay." He drags out the word. "Did you want anything to drink? Eat?"

"I'll get it in a minute. I don't want to go inside while *he's* still in there."

"Who *is* he?" he asks, taking a sip of his coffee.

"He's kind of my bodyguard."

Declan sprays some of his drink while trying not to choke. I think I even see some come out his nose, which brings a smile to my face.

"Bodyguard? Why do you need a bodyguard?"

I shake my head. "Long story. Bottom line is bio mum is rich, meaning both my sister and I are guarded all the time."

"You seem like you already know him pretty well," he says, peering at me over the top of his coffee cup. "Just the way you interact," he adds.

"Yeah. I certainly know he's a dick."

Declan chuckles at that, and Brett turns around from inside to glare at me. I shrug at him.

"I already know him better than my mum anyway. I see more of him than I do of her. Apart from our family dinners that only happen a few times a week, I barely see her."

"Not going well, then?"

I shrug. "She didn't even believe who I was at first. She didn't believe I was hers until a DNA test confirmed it. A DNA test she didn't even consult me about."

Declan winces. "Ouch."

"It just hasn't been how I imagined it would be. I guess I always thought I'd either be welcomed with open arms or shunned completely. This in between business is weird. It's not too bad. I just … I started working for them, thinking that I'd get to spend more time with her, but it hasn't really panned out that way."

"You're working for them? What are you doing?"

Brett, who's just getting to his seat a few tables away, shoots me a warning look.

"Just, bar stuff."

"You work at a bar? Which one?"

My hand reaches for my hair, flattening it across my forehead. "Oh … umm … you know, doing behind the scenes stuff. You wouldn't be able to come visit or anything. I'm in the office a lot." *Wow. I suck at lying, and I think Declan knows I'm not telling the truth.*

"Okay. So what's your sister like?"

"Amazing. But I'll tell you all about her after I order some food," I say, getting up to head inside. "You want anything?"

"Just another coffee. I'll just steal some of your food." He grins.

"So the usual, then?" I always make it a point to order extra fries wherever we eat. Dec is constantly stealing off my plate.

After ordering, I sit back at the table and talk to Declan about Sasha and how we're spending all our spare time together. I don't mention that I don't get a lot of spare time these days because I'm locked in a room with Brett for the most part, trying to not have the crap beaten out of me.

I feel myself light up when talking about Sasha and the house I'm living in. I tell him everything I'm able to without crossing *that* line.

"You look happy," he says. "I haven't seen that smile for a few years."

"I guess I've been feeling pretty lost since I found out the truth about my parents, and I kind of feel like I'm doing something about it now. And while I still don't know Cade all that well, I'm just thankful that I'm getting the chance to know her. She's taken me in, and I think I at least owe it to myself to see where it could go, even if she hasn't been the friendliest so far. Sasha just says that's her." I shrug. "From what I can tell, we're completely different people, so that doesn't help. I have her hair, so does Sasha, but apart from that, we don't have much in common. Cade's very business focussed. You know me—not much can keep my attention for long."

"So you're not going to mention how you got the black eye?"

My eyes dart to his. *Damn it.* I thought he hadn't noticed seeing as he didn't bring it up when he first saw me or in the time we've been sitting here. "Oh, that," I say with a dismissive laugh. "I was just mucking around with Sasha. You know how Will and I used to get."

Declan nods but I'm unsure if he's buying it. "Look, if

anything's going on—"

"There's not. I swear." I swallow the lump in my throat.

Declan goes to say something else when we're interrupted by our food being delivered. After the waiter leaves, Declan starts chowing down. I'm glad I decided to get him his own plate. I'm starving. All this training has almost doubled my appetite.

"I've missed you," I say with my mouth full.

The corner of his mouth tips up into a smile. "You know what I've missed?"

I look at him expectantly.

"Not having you in my bed every night," he whispers, leaning forward and reaching for my hand on the table.

As innocent as he means it, I can't stop the heat from flooding my cheeks. I ignore it, hoping he doesn't notice it.

"It's been weird not having your stinky breath waking me up." I say, expertly making a joke to cover the fact I'm uncomfortable.

"Oh really? Stinky breath, hey?" he asks letting go of my hand and leaning back in his chair.

I want to say, *"No, not really. I miss your morning breath,"* but that would be crossing a line. A line we can't cross. Not to mention it sounds a little creepy … okay, a lot creepy.

Declan glances over his shoulder at Brett. "At least he's decent enough to give us some privacy."

I scoff. "Sorry, not a chance with him nearby. He has like super hearing, and it's super annoying. I haven't had a private conversation in weeks, and from what he's told me, it'll be a while before I will."

"Well, that makes what I want to say a little bit more difficult to get out."

My heart starts thumping in my chest. "Oh?"

Here it comes. The thing I've been avoiding asking him about all arvo, and the thing he has wanted to tell me for weeks.

Declan swallows, goes to open his mouth to say something,

but freezes. Slowly turning in his chair, he glances over at Brett again. Brett's looking the other way, drinking his coffee and pretending he's not listening. I know better.

"What exactly is your mother involved in?" Declan asks, turning back to me. "I get she has money, but constant twenty-four-hour surveillance? It's a bit extreme, isn't it?"

"It is. But they have *a lot* of money. They're worried about me or Sasha being kidnapped, or something. I never quite figured it out myself."

"But—"

"Can we just get to what we're here to talk about?" I ask quietly.

Declan takes my hand again. "The morning of your birthday party, I was offered a job. Sort of an internship now that I'm so close to graduating."

"That's great. Why were you so worried about telling me that?"

"It's in criminology."

"Okay? And?"

"It's in Special Ops on the police force."

My hand pulls away from his when I realise what he's telling me. "I thought you were planning on becoming a lawyer, not a cop. Why *that* department? *Why?*"

"Do you really think a rookie could go straight into an internship like this without the help of someone on the inside? I haven't even done my basic training yet, and there are guys who've been on the force for years who don't get this opportunity. The department had an opening and your mother pushed for them to offer it to me. I can't turn it down. I leave for recruitment training in a few weeks."

"She's not my mother," I say through gritted teeth.

"But the woman you're currently living with is? Really? The woman who gives you a bodyguard yet clearly has no problems with the fact that you're bruised? Yeah, looks like you've found yourself a real winner there in the parent department. Can't you see that Lia did nothing but protect you all these years? And how do you repay her? Running off the minute you could afford to?"

"Why are you suddenly defending her? Because she's giving you a job?"

Declan shakes his head. "I knew you'd get like this. I've never told you what I really think because I knew you'd pull away from me, just like you did to them. I can't handle the thought of losing you, Nuke, but I'm worried I already have."

"Because I haven't needed you the last month? Because I haven't ran to your side for every little thing? Because I realised I was so dependent on you that I needed to do something for myself for once?"

"You won't even tell me what you've been up to lately. You're being evasive and you know it. I realise you have this new family and new life, and you need time to get to know them … but, I miss you. I don't want to lose you. And you're not exactly being forthcoming with the truth, are you? What's with the eye, Nuke? Where are you actually working? Are you going to answer any of my questions truthfully?"

"I can't," I whisper.

Suddenly Brett's at our table, interrupting us. "Hey, we need to get back," he says to me, not even bothering to acknowledge Declan.

"Who are you, her bodyguard or her father?" Declan sneers.

"While she's living in Cade's house, I'm responsible for her."

I can tell Declan's pissed off, but I also know he's not usually one to pick a fight. Not to mention Brett's twice his size. Declan's strong, but Brett…

"We have to go, Nuke. Right now."

Declan glowers at Brett. I'm guessing because he called me Nuke. Until Brett, only Declan called me that. It didn't occur to me to tell Brett to stop. It's almost been a comfort, still hearing it.

"Okay. Fine," I say, getting up out of my chair.

Declan stands and steps forwards for a hug.

I wrap my arms around him. Breathing in his scent, I nuzzle my face into his neck. When I pull back and look into his piercing blue eyes, they beg me to let him in, to tell him the truth. But that's just something I can't do. Especially now. *My best friend is becoming a cop.*

Brett gently grabs my arm to pull me away. As we start walking towards the car, I can't resist a glimpse back at Declan. He waves with one hand while placing the other in the front pocket of his jeans. It makes him look innocent and sweet. *I wish I could tell you everything,* I think as I tear my eyes away from him.

"You need to learn to lie better," Brett says as we get in the car.

"I've never kept a secret from him. I don't know how to lie to him."

"You're gonna have to learn if you want to keep seeing him. You know the rules."

"Yeah, I know." I sigh. "How do you do it? How do you keep it from your nanna, from Paddy?"

"I'm pretty sure Paddy knows. Litmus is kind of well-known in the Estates. But he also knows not to bring it up or ask about it. With Nanna, it helps I don't see her all that often." His voice is laced with guilt. "She knows Cade and Jonas are my owners, but she doesn't know what they have me do. She thinks they're just my bosses and I run their security."

"I still find the term 'owners' weird," I mumble more to myself than him. "How's the Paddy situation going? Did you get the money?"

"It's all sorted. I'm just scared Paddy's going to go right back to them as soon as he can. Or find a different crew." He lets out a shaky breath. "I just want to get him out of there."

There's a lengthy silence, each minute passing casting even

more doubt over what I'm trying to do.

"I'm doing the right thing … right?"

Brett shrugs. "I know I wouldn't be doing it if I had a healthy trust fund to take care of me. But I admire you for what you're wanting to do with the money."

"Am I stupid to think I can actually do this?"

"Wanna go home and train some more?"

I nod. "Definitely. Kicking your ass will make me feel a whole lot better," I say with feigned optimism.

Brett actually manages to smile at me. A real, genuine smile. That hasn't happened in weeks.

***

"Are you ready to go?" Brett asks, standing at my bedroom door.

They offered me a different room a few weeks ago, but I've strangely become accustomed to my small and simple room. It's comfortable. Sasha's room upstairs is ridiculously big … and bright pink. I'm surprised she doesn't get a headache from being surrounded by so much brightness. It looks like a fairy threw up in there. But my room has a certain charm to it, so I decided to stay down here.

"Nuka? Are you ready?" Brett asks again, snapping me out of my trance.

"Uh … yeah. I guess."

"Nervous?" he asks with a sympathetic smile.

"You could say that. I mean, it's kind of hard to get excited about getting beaten up."

"Nah. You'll do great. Besides, it's only one of the other team members today. I'll tell them to go easy."

"Well that's not really the point of this test, right? Isn't it to see if I'm really ready to go into the arena?"

"Yeah, but for your first real fight, you'll be facing a less experienced fighter. You'll probably have to go easy on *them.* We don't want people to be too scared of volunteering."

We start making our way to the garage and to his car.

"Why do they do the whole volunteering thing, anyway?"

"People *love* to root for an underdog. It usually brings in big bets, and they nearly always lose. It's money making. And not to mention highly entertaining. No one really knows what they're getting themselves into until it's too late, and the looks on their faces are priceless."

"But they do sometimes win?" I ask, dumping my bag in the back of his car and getting in the passenger seat.

"It happens occasionally. I sometimes wonder if it's rigged, though. Not many of the winners stick around for too long afterwards. None of the current fighters are Wild Card winners." He shrugs as he starts the car. "I dunno. I've never been asked to throw a Wild Card fight, but that doesn't mean it's not happening. And if you think about it, if no one's qualifying, people would give up trying."

"So it doesn't matter if I lose?"

"You won't lose. You're ready."

"Well you've certainly changed your tune since yesterday."

"Yeah, because you beat the crap out of me last night."

He sounds annoyed but when I look over at his face, he's smirking like he's proud.

We pull up fifteen minutes later to the industrial area of the city.

"Why are we here?"

"Showing you another entry," Brett says, getting out of the car. "Drake told you there were four, right?"

"Yeah, but he didn't tell me why."

"Simple really. If we were ever to be found out, there are three other escape routes to use so we don't get arrested," he says, unlocking a door to a naked warehouse. There's no sign on the outside, no markings, just a plain white warehouse. He closes the door behind us as we head inside.

"I guess that makes sense. Does everyone know about the four entries?"

"Just employees."

"So what you're saying is: everyone who attends Litmus only knows of one entry, meaning if we were to be raided, the cops would most likely find them and not us." My tone is accusatory, even though I didn't mean it to be … okay, maybe I did a little.

Brett shakes his head with a huff. "I wish I could've grown up in the world you did."

"What's that supposed to mean?" I ask, following him into an old, rickety elevator at the far end of the warehouse.

"In the real world, where everyone else lives, it's all about survival. Everyone's in it for themselves. You take what you can get, and you don't give anything away for free. Should I feel bad if people—who are betting on me getting my ass beaten—get arrested while I take the chance to escape? No. And you shouldn't either. I can guarantee that not *one person* in there will do anything to help you if that situation was to arise. Remember that, 'kay? No matter what, get yourself out."

"What about Cade? You don't think she would at least care what happens to me?"

Brett rubs his temple. "Believe me when I say, she's the worst of them all. Self-survival, Nuke. You need to learn it."

Before I can question him further, the elevator doors open to one of the backstage corridors of Litmus.

"So we're right under the industrial area of the city?"

"Pretty much. There are two nightclubs in the city with underground tunnel entries that bring you to the other side of Litmus. Then there's the warehouse, and the last entry is what the patrons use, which is in the old train yards—the only remaining entrance to the old underground rail."

He leads me to a door labelled "Deakin Fighters" and punches in a code, opening the door to a waft of body odour and man scent.

Eww, gross.

"Code is eight-zero-zero-eight-five, by the way," he says leading me in.

Watching the numbers light up on the keypad, I can't help laughing. "Boobs? Really?"

"Five numbers is hard for a bunch of guys to remember," he says with a shrug. "We made it easier."

I hear laughter coming from a group of four guys waiting for us as we enter the locker room.

"Okay, guys," Brett says. "Meet our newest. Everyone this is Nuka, Nuka—everyone."

I shyly lift my hand and give a little wave, which is met with head nods and quiet hellos.

One of the guys, a tall, lean, redhead, steps forward to shake my hand. "Nuka, hey? That's a pretty cool stage name. What—"

"Uh … it's my actual name. But … thanks. I guess."

"Sorry, I just assumed. I'm Palmer, so I know what it's like to have a weird name. Stage name's Inferno."

"Oh, fireballs, right?"

Palmer looks to Brett, "Been talking about me? I didn't know you were so sweet on me," he says, winking.

"It was Sasha, actually," I say.

"Oh. Damn. She's not exactly my type."

Another guy steps forward. He's scrawny compared to the others and shorter than I am. *How is he a fighter?* "I'm Ryker, also known as Psych," he says, shaking my hand.

"Ah, that explains it," I say, realising he's the one who can hurt you without even touching you.

"Explains what?" he snaps, scowling at me.

"That you're a short-ass with no muscles and you're a fighter," Brett answers, playfully punching him in the arm before turning to me. "But trust me, you'll be thankful he's on our team. He's almost undefeated."

"Damn straight," Ryker says.

"'Sup. I'm Colton," a guy with jet-black hair and who's almost as big as Brett steps forward, also shaking my hand.

"He's like me. Crap ability, great fighter," Brett informs me.

"What's your ability?" I ask.

He lifts his arms out to his side and floats off the ground a couple of feet. "I can't go very high, but it does give me an advantage over my opponents. I can attack from a high position, and defying gravity kind of helps pull off some difficult manoeuvres."

"Cool. What's your stage name?"

Colton laughs nervously. "Uh … Archangel. It's sucky, I know. Most people have started calling me Archie."

I chuckle. "It's not too bad. We're struggling to come up with one for me. They all sound lame."

"What's your ability?" Colton asks.

"I can—"

"Why don't you wait and find out?" Brett cuts me off. "Which one of you four is going to fight her today, anyway? Any volunteers?"

None of them says anything.

"Come on, you can't be scared of a girl this size, can you?" Brett taunts, wrapping his arm around my shoulder. "Going to be pretty embarrassing if she can kick on your asses in front of the other teams, right?"

"Wait. Other teams? I thought it was just going to be us?" I ask.

Brett shrugs. "At some point or another throughout the day, we're all here practicing. Most of the others are great, they'll even spar with you and help you out. Most of them … but not all."

"Like Taser?" I ask.

"Don't ask Taser for favours," Colton says with conviction.

"So …" Brett says looking back to the group. "Who's it going to be?"

"I'll do it," says the guy sitting on the bench beside the lockers. The only one who didn't stand to meet me.

"Thought you might, Steve."

Steve disappears out of sight, and a few moments later, there's a tap on my shoulder. I turn to see who did it, but no one's there.

"Call me Ghost," Steve whispers as he reappears next to me. "This is going to be fun. Don't worry, I'll go easy on ya," he says with a playful grin, walking out of the locker room.

Turning to Brett, my eyes go wide. "You expect me to fight an invisible dude?"

He puts his hands on my shoulders. "You'll be fine. The only thing he has is his invisibility. A lot of defensive moves are done by touch anyway. You'll be able to feel him, where his stance is. Just make sure those hands of yours are warmed up and ready to go."

Brett indicates for the others to leave. When they walk out the door, he remains with me. "You'll be fine."

I nod. "They all seem nice."

"They are. They're all pretty great guys, actually. You've probably just adopted four big brothers. Ryker can be moody, but it's only because people are constantly underestimating him for his size."

"I guess I'll have to get used to that, too, being the only girl. Didn't Sasha say there was another girl? Chi … or something?"

"She's on Taser's team—Holt team. There's actually a couple of girls. We were the only team without one, until you."

"Oh. So that's the real reason Cade and Jonas wanted me? For their image?"

"Pretty much. But isn't that also the reason they agreed to give you more money than the rest of us?"

Fair point.

"Get ready," he orders before leaving.

I'm already in my full-length tights, so all I have to do to get ready is tie my hair back and strip off my shirt. The black sports bra Cade gave me to fight in is insanely tight but supportive. *Yup. I'm wearing a bra in public again.*

I was relieved when they decided my "costume" should be simple, not gimmicky. There'd be nothing worse than wearing lame angel wings or fake flames or something.

Cade said once I get sponsorship, I'll have to change my uniform; it'll need the sponsor company's name on it, but she's also hoping to pull something with a logo instead of words so I still look professional ... and hot. Having your mother encourage you to dress so provocatively in public to pull in more money seems wrong somehow. *Welcome to Deakin.*

Taking a few deep breaths, I try to prepare myself for what's about to happen.

If I'm this nervous over a practice fight, what am I going to be like when I face someone for real?

Brett is waiting for me just outside the locker room when I exit.

"Ready?"

"Uh-huh," I say, wiping my sweaty palms on my thighs. "I think so."

He lets out a small laugh. "You really are cu …"

"What?"

"I can just tell you're really nervous. You look like you did the night you met your mother."

When he called me cute, I realise. He was about to do it again, but he stopped himself.

We lock eyes and I can't bring myself to look away until I hear footsteps coming towards us.

"Ready, Nuka?" Colton asks.

Taking some deep breaths, I attempt to pull myself together. My hands already feel tingly from the tension between Brett and me, the nerves building in my stomach, and the adrenaline that's running through me.

Walking out to the floor feels like the longest thirty seconds of my life.

There are two girls fighting on the stage when we reach the others who are standing around watching. Other groups are watching too, and I can only assume we're all separated into our teams.

"Slider versus Ice?" Brett says, and Ryker nods. "This should be interesting."

"They've been at it for a few minutes now. Neither of them has used their ability yet."

"Are they on the same team, too?" I ask.

"They are—Fadden team," Colton says, standing on the other side of me to Brett. "Uh-oh, better step out of the way," he says, grabbing my arm and pulling me back and to his side.

"Why—" I ask before something solid and white flies by my head, smashing on the ground behind us. "Ice? She can throw *ice*?"

"Yeah. With your ability, you may want to try and avoid fighting her in the future," Brett says. "Not to mention she's batshit crazy."

"How do people in the audience not get killed?" I ask.

"One of the emcees' ability is to create large force fields. He puts an invisible enclosure over the ring during a fight for those who have the really active abilities like Inferno and Ice," Colton explains.

"Who wins when those two fight?"

Colton laughs. "Ice usually has the upper hand, but Palmer's won a few times against her. It just depends on the night. We're all on a pretty level playing field, apart from Ryker. But even he knows to put on a good show before kicking butt."

Watching the girls go at it on the stage, it's obvious they're both incredibly strong. I can almost feel each punch as if it were happening to me. Ice is brutal. I'm definitely going to have to up my weights routine before I can face either of them. I'm suddenly not so confident about this fight today.

"What does Slider do?" Just as I ask, she disappears, reappearing on the other side of the arena, trying to catch her breath. "She's invisible like Steve?"

"Not quite," Brett says. "She blinks … it's kind of like teleporting, but on a much smaller scale. I don't think she could blink out of this building, her ability isn't that strong. But it works well for the arena—she can't go outside of the square without being disqualified, so she doesn't need to go big."

I've been distracted by my convo with Brett and Colton, I don't realise when the girls stop fighting. Only when I hear, "Who's the newbie?" being yelled from the stage do I turn myself back to look at them.

"Get off the stage and find out," Brett yells.

They start making their way off the platform, sweaty and wiping themselves down with a towel.

"Looks like we're up," Steve says as he passes me, making his way onto the raised platform.

I think my heart just stopped.

He takes his shirt off and stands with his arms folded across his chest, making him look intimidating as hell. He too, just like Brett and Colton, has massive biceps. He's smaller than Brett and Colton, but not by much.

Every set of eyes on the floor stares at me as Brett leads me up to the stage.

Silently, I tell my hands to stop shaking, but they just quiver more.

Steve approaches, his face soft and suddenly not looking so fierce anymore. "Hey, it's okay. We'll just have a play. Don't worry about the others watching, just treat this as another training session, okay? Brett's told us how good you are, so I'm excited to see for myself."

"I'm just nervous, I guess."

"Fair enough," he says, punching my shoulder lightly. "Look at that. Punch number one's already been thrown," he says with a smile on his face. It makes the nerves dissipate some.

"You've got this," Brett says, gripping my shoulders and turning me to him.

I nod and look into his eyes.

"How are your hands?" he asks, taking them in his. "They're freezing. What are you doing?"

"I … I think I'm too nervous." All the tension fuelling me from the locker room has left me and only terrified doubt remains.

"What'll make you get fired up again?"

I shrug. "It doesn't really help that Steve seems nice. It'd be a lot easier if he was a sleazebag like Taser."

"Well, I seem to piss you off pretty good, and you need to get angry. You always beat me when that happens. So how can I help?"

I laugh. "I don't think it works if you're purposefully trying."

"How about if I do this," he says, cupping my face with both hands and slamming his lips on mine. The kiss is quick, not even long enough for me to react properly, but it's intense. Laughter and hooting surround us, and when he pulls away, he walks off, leaving me stunned.

"Well, that worked," I mutter, turning to face Steve whose eyebrows have shot up so high they're almost disappearing into his hairline.

"How can I beat you up now I know you're his girl?" Steve says.

I roll my eyes, anger growing inside me. I focus on sending it to my hands. "Is that what he was trying to accomplish? Getting you to go easy on me? Because I can assure you, I'm no one's girl, and he clearly underestimates my ability if he thinks he needs to do *that* to give me the upper hand."

Steve laughs. "Okay then. Good to know. I'll be with you in a moment," he says, disappearing.

Confusion and fear don't even have time to set in completely when I'm grabbed from behind and being held in a chokehold. It's tight, making any possible manoeuvre restricted.

Using a simple self-defence move, I jab my elbow backwards and into his side. His grip falters a little, but he doesn't let me go. Then I stomp on the instep of his foot, but being invisible, I miss him and get his ankle instead. It works though, and he releases me.

"Pretty impressive." His voice startles me. I don't know where it came from.

I must look like the biggest idiot, fighting someone who's invisible. I twist around, but he's not giving any indication of where he is.

He reappears right in front of me before landing a punch to my face. My head suddenly snaps back from the momentum, but I've been hit in the face so often these last few weeks, it didn't hurt much. Either that, or he didn't hit me very hard.

My hands are itching to be released of heat.

I take my chance to go on the offensive while he's still visible.

Stepping forward, I throw a jab, but he's quick like Brett, catching it in his palm. It only connects with his hand for a second before he's flinching in pain from the burn.

"Oh, shit," he says, backing up when he realises what my ability is.

Smirking, I take advantage of his disorientation, getting in a few more heated punches and an open-palmed slap to the face, burning his skin. Landing a punch to his stomach and one to the side of his rib cage, I then take an upper cut to his chin. He barely composes himself enough to disappear, but then he's gone again.

Hoping he hasn't moved from his hunched position, I advance on him, throwing in another punch to what I hope is his face and a knee to the gut for good measure.

An "oomph" leaves him, and I think I've winded him.

I back up a couple of steps to give him a breather when I hear his strained laughter.

"Don't back off now. You could've had me," he grunts.

Stepping forward, I punch again, connecting with something, but I have no idea what. He lets out a tiny groan. I punch again but hit air, and then I'm suddenly knocked off my feet, tackled to the ground in a frontal assault.

Falling backwards, I land on my back with a loud thud, hitting my head on the ground as I fall.

He reappears above me, on his knees in between my legs. He raises a fist to hit me, but I roll my head to the side, and he punches the floor beside me.

Lifting one of my legs, I kick him hard in the chest. He wavers slightly, but he's anchored his feet on the ground under his legs, making him like one of those dolls I had as a kid where I'd knock it down, only to have it spring back up again.

My other foot comes up and over in a roundhouse kick to the side of his head. He falls sideways onto the ground and disappears again.

Flipping myself up onto my feet in a single move—something Will and I used to practice so we could look "cool"—I'm on my feet in less than a second, poised for another attack.

I have no idea where he is, and I have no idea what angle he's going to come at me from. I can't really do anything but wait for him to attack.

It's eerily quiet. My head moves from left to right, my ears straining to hear something—*anything* to indicate where he is. Brett's ability would come in handy right now, as I try to listen for Steve's breathing.

My hands are scorching hot and ready.

He teases me, appearing on my left and then blinking invisible again. I lunge to the left and twist, hoping to catch him before he's moved, but he's too quick. He pushes me from behind, and I stumble onto one knee. Assuming he's still behind me, I lean back and elbow him. Where, I don't know, but I turn and attack with my scalding hot hands.

I swear I can almost hear the hissing noise as my sizzling hands burn away layers of skin.

The pressure under my hands moves away as Steve manages to get out of my grasp.

Moving into a standing position, I'm swiftly punched with brutal force on the right side of my face. I'm repeatedly hit from what feels like a million different angles, making it impossible to determine exactly where he is.

Steve must've been holding back until now.

Pain shoots down my left side as he punches me in my ribs. I try to guard it, but then he just punches me in the head.

His moves are fast and deliberate, and I don't have time to right myself before I'm being hit again. I've got a split lip and spit some blood, only to take another punch to the face.

Becoming dizzy, I'm wobbly on my feet. I must be hunching over, as the blows seem to be coming from above me now.

I'm only saved by a voice calling out from the side of the arena. "Time's up."

Stopping immediately, Steve reappears right in front of me. He's breathless and puffing. I join him in taking large, panting breaths as I try to stand up straight.

He towers over me. "Seriously impressed," he says, offering up his hand for me to fist bump.

As I return the gesture, we're met with applause and cheering from those watching.

Steve puts his arm around my shoulders, nodding and waving

to the crowd. We're both in relatively good shape considering we just bashed the crap out of each other. My left side is tender, and I can tell my face will be bruised again. My lip is still bleeding and my head is pounding, but I look at the bright side—I didn't pass out.

"Uh, you can let me go now. I'm not going to fall or anything," I tell Steve.

He laughs. "What makes you think I'm trying to hold *you* up?"

"Oh." I laugh back.

"Good job," Brett says, joining us on stage.

"You've trained her well," Steve says to Brett before looking at me. "And next time, I won't go so easy." He kisses the top of my head, leaves the stage, and starts heading towards the locker rooms.

"That was going easy?" I ask, completely mortified.

"He was joking. Are you okay? Did you want medical to check you over?"

I wave him off. "Nah, I'm good. I'm getting used to being used as a punching bag."

"So … you didn't win, but you came close, and we weren't really expecting you to actually beat him on your first go. You could have, though, but you let your nerves get the better of you."

"I know," I say, still trying to catch my breath.

"However, you did just survive fifteen minutes in the ring. Think you're ready for the real thing?"

"That was only fifteen minutes?" *Felt like an hour.*

"On fight nights, you'll be expected to fight three rounds, but they're only five minutes each. So basically what you just did but with breaks in between. Do you think you'll be able to handle that?"

After catching my breath a bit more, I nod. "I think so. It was actually … kinda fun." *I can't believe I just admitted that.*

"Then we need to celebrate," he says, facing the crowd of fighters below us.

There are low murmurs around the room, everyone staring at me but looking away when I catch them glaring.

"Everyone, shut up!" Brett yells, getting everyone's attention. "As you can see, Deakin is going through some changes. I'm no longer the prettiest of the group." Everyone laughs, and I even hear a wolf-whistle from somewhere. "So, let me all introduce you properly to the soon-to-be new face of Deakin." Brett gestures to the crowd in front of us. "Nuka, meet your new family."

-11-

WE CAN'T BE TOGETHER

I stare down at my "new family" who are clapping and cheering, and they soon start making their way to the stage to meet me.

Everyone seems nice and encouraging, fist bumping me and telling me how impressed they are.

"What's with the fist bumping anyway?" I whisper to Brett. "Doesn't anyone shake hands here?"

Brett smiles a charming half-smile at me. "It's a sign of respect. You've impressed them."

They're doubly impressed when Brett tells them I've only been training for a few weeks. People push their way closer to me to introduce themselves, and Brett leaves me to mingle. He doesn't go far though, and I constantly keep finding his gaze. He smiles every time our eyes meet, and he seems to be booming with pride. I'm guessing he's probably taking all of the credit for my fighting ability.

"At least we'll be off Wild Card nights for a while then," a guy says, slapping me on the back as he approaches. "They tell me you're starting off small."

"Why is that good for you?" I ask him.

"Wild Card nights suck. It's okay money, but trust me, you'll be bored after the first month and itching to get in the arena against me," he says, charm oozing out of him. "They're frustrating because you can't go all out. You have to make sure you don't do too much damage to the contestants."

"Well, after facing Steve, I'll be relieved to face a less experienced fighter."

"You did really well. Surprisingly well, for a newbie," what's-his-face says.

"Thanks … uh … what was your name again? Sorry. I've met a gazillion people in the last five minutes."

He returns my smile. "I'm Flynn. Barton team. Also known as Blaze."

"Oh, so you're like Palmer?"

"Yeah, sorta. We're both fire-starters, but where he throws fireballs, my flames kind of stick to me but only burn my opponent. I guess my ability is more similar to yours, only with flames instead of just heat. It'll be interesting to see if our abilities cancel each other out seeing as we don't burn."

"I look forward to finding out."

My gaze finds Brett's again, only he's now scowling at me.

Great. What have I done now?

"So, what's the deal with you and him anyway?" Flynn asks, nodding in Brett's direction.

I shrug one shoulder. "Who knows," I mutter. "Nothing, really."

"Are you saying him kis—"

"How about we take this party to the bar?" Steve yells from the floor. He's dressed now, fresh from a shower by the look of it.

People start descending the stairs and heading to the bar for an impromptu welcome.

"Drink?" Flynn asks.

"Yeah. I might go shower and change first. I feel kinda gross."

"Yeah, that's understandable. I'll see you at the bar then," he says, walking off.

I start limping my way down the stairs. *When did Steve hit me in the leg? Maybe he kicked me? Maybe I got my ass kicked worse than I originally thought.*

"Need a hand?" Brett asks, holding out his arm for me to take.

"I'll be fine, thanks," I reply.

He rolls his eyes and takes my arm gently. "Don't be stubborn, just let me help you."

"Fine," I concede as I reach for his arm and then gasp in pain.

He grimaces at my reaction in sympathy but doesn't say anything until we get to the Deakin locker room. "Are you sure you don't want to go to medical?"

"I'm fine," I say, holding my left side.

"At least let me look."

He removes my hand from my ribs, lightly pressing along my rib cage. I wince and bite the inside of my cheek to stop from screaming out. Looking down, I see my whole left side is already black and blue. Not badly, but it's definitely tender.

"It looks like it's only bruised," he says, moving his hand away. "But keep an eye on it and make sure if it gets worse that you see someone. I've cracked ribs before, and it looked a lot worse than that. But the fact it's bruised so quickly is a bit disconcerting. You should have a hot shower. Loosen your muscles."

"Okay. Thanks. I'll see you back out there?"

"Uh … umm … yeah," he says, running his hand through his hair.

"Were you wanting something else?"

"No. It's nothing. Don't worry about it." He turns to walk away but stops, looking at me over his shoulder. "Be wary of Flynn. He's only after one thing."

He doesn't give me a chance to respond before he walks out, and the door clicks shut behind him.

Really? He's acting all jealous now?

A long grunt of frustration leaves me before I grab my bag and head for the showers on the other side of the locker room.

Relief washes over me when I find two individual stalls, each with a shower and a large dressing area. I was wondering how sharing a locker room with five guys was going to work.

Getting out of my sports bra isn't as easy as I thought it would be. I can barely lift my left arm because of the bruising on my side.

Okay. What are my options? Thinking through what I could do, I come to the conclusion I'm on my own and just have to bear the pain to get the top off. I can't ask Brett or any of the other team members to help because they're all guys and I don't want them seeing me topless. One of the other girls could help, but I've barely just met them, and asking them to help undress me might be a tad inappropriate. Sasha could help … if she was here.

Sucking in repeated short breaths, I take the bra off as fast as I can, thinking it would be like a Band-Aid and I just need to get it over with. I'm so wrong. My scream is so loud I'm sure they'd be able to hear it from the main floor.

The locker room door clicks open. "Nuka, you okay?" Brett's voice calls out with a hint of urgency.

"I'm fine," I yell, but my voice sounds strained and wrong.

"What happened?" he asks, his voice suddenly soft and right outside the stall.

"I just had some trouble getting undressed, but it's all good now. The pain's subsiding. I'll be"—I wince—"fine."

"I'll just wait for you on the bench until I know you're okay."

"Ugh. Why do you even care?"

"Nuk—"

"No, don't answer that. I'm just in pain and cranky. Also hungry. I've been so nervous all day, I didn't eat lunch in case I upchucked all over the arena."

He laughs. "You shower. I'll go organise you some food."

I shower quickly and Brett was right, the heat on my skin feels amazing. Getting dressed is a lot easier than getting undressed. I still struggle, but it's manageable.

Not expecting a welcoming party, I only brought jeans and an off-the-shoulder baggy top to go home in. It's not exactly something I'd normally wear out with friends.

Friends. Is that what I'm doing here? Making friends? Is that part of the plan? Do I even have a plan at this point? I guess if I'm going to be doing this for the foreseeable future, I should at least try.

When I leave the stall, Brett's exactly where he said he would be—sitting on the bench next to the lockers.

"You didn't have to wait for me," I say, refusing to look at him.

"I know." He holds out his arm and I take it in mine.

At the bar, the music has started pumping, and there are more people here than before.

"Who are all these people?" I ask.

"Friends, friends of friends. It doesn't take long for word to spread when the bar opens early in here." Brett leads me to the side corner of the bar where he hands me a beer and a plate of pastry-covered meat on sticks. "It was the best I could do on short notice."

"Doesn't matter, I'm starving," I reply, shoving one in my mouth and grabbing another to shove in after it. "Fanks," I say with a full mouth.

"I'll be back in a minute," he says in my ear, planting his hand on the small of my back.

I nod. "Okay."

Just as he leaves me, I'm joined by the feisty blonde who was in the ring just before me.

"Ice," I say, nodding to her.

"Holly. Please."

"Nuka."

"I know. So … you and Brett."

I shove another pastry thing in my mouth so I don't have to answer.

She chuckles. "Just wanted to give you a heads-up is all. I don't exactly know how you managed to get him to mark you in such a public display, but that still doesn't mean he won't have his fun then be done with you within a few weeks."

"Uh …"

"Oh. It's nothing against you or anything. That's just how he is."

"Sounds like you're talking from experience." I take a sip of my beer to try to hide my uncomfortableness of this conversation.

She shakes her head. "It was a long time ago now. And I'm not the only one. I just wanted to warn you. Most of the guys at Litmus are the same. They have girls hanging off them constantly. But us? Guys are intimidated by girls who can fight. It sucks."

"Sounds like Litmus is kind of twentieth century. Women are less than men, and men are revered for their muscles and ability to protect their women."

She laughs. "That pretty much explains it."

Brett's talking to a girl in my peripheral vision, smiling and flirting. He touches his hand to her arm as he leaves to heads my way.

I clear my throat, letting Holly know he's coming back.

She leans in and whispers, "When this all fizzles out, come find me. We'll go find real men who love strong women."

I smile and nod politely.

"Holly," Brett says curtly, wrapping his arm around my waist.

"Dickhead," she replies before walking off.

I stifle a laugh.

"I guess she told you about us, then?"

I shrug out of his grip. "Yeah. She did."

"It was a long—"

"It's cool. You're not mine, so it's none of my business." Walking away, I go to find the rest of my teammates to get to know them more, and to stay away from Brett.

He's hot on me one minute and then standoffish the next. He's kissed me … three times now, once in front of all of his friends.

What is he playing at?

Shaking my head, I tell myself to forget about Brett and his confusing behaviour. Finding Ryker at the other end of the bar, I sit on the stool next to him.

"Hey."

"Uh … hi?" He seems shocked that I'm talking to him.

"Umm … how are you?" *Okay, totally didn't think it would be this awkward. Way to make friends, Nuka.*

"Shouldn't you be over there with Brett?" he asks, indicating where Brett is talking with the flirty girl from earlier.

"He seems plenty entertained to me."

"So he was just being a dick earlier when he marked you?"

"Marked me?" That's the second time someone has said that. "What does it even mean?"

"It's an unspoken thing. Kissing someone in the arena is like marking your territory. It's this sacred thing. He basically told every other fighter today that you're his."

I laugh. "Are you serious?"

He nods.

"Then yes, he was just being a dick because there's nothing going on between us."

"Nothing? Are you sure about that?" Ryker quirks his eyebrow at me.

I swallow hard.

"Thought so," he says cockily.

"Why do you do it?"

"Do what?"

"Fight."

"The same reason any of us fight. Money, fame … girls," he says with a shy smile. "Not that any of these girls even glance my way. Even if I am the best fighter."

"Why not?"

"Even though we all have abilities, pretty much everyone else still fights. It's like they use their abilities as theatrics, but the real sport is in the punching and kicking. I'm not a bad fighter—if I met someone on the street, I could beat them, but here? I'm seen as the scrawny cheater who *needs* to use his ability to win. So the other fighters don't really see me as top dog, even though I am."

"So they make you feel like an outsider? That kinda sucks. Have you ever thought of …" I don't know if it'd be offensive or not to suggest he train more.

"Thought of …? What, training more?"

I nod.

"Brett offered, once. It never came about, though."

"What if we trained together? You saw me get my ass kicked today, so I'm sure you can't be any worse than me."

He half-smiles. "You were pretty awesome today, even if you did lose. But if you're serious about the training, I'm in."

As we smile at each other, his face suddenly drops at whomever I suddenly sense behind me.

"How about that drink?" Flynn says in my ear.

Ryker nods his head, telling me to go with Flynn. "Go, mingle and meet everyone. I think you'll like it here. And I already like you more than I do the others." He gives a pointed glare at Flynn as he says this.

Nodding a farewell to Ryker, I follow Flynn to the middle of the bar where I didn't notice Sasha serving until now.

"Hey," I yell at Sasha to get her attention.

"Hey!" She practically jumps the counter to wrap me in a hug.

"Ouch …" I grind out.

"Oh, sorry. I heard you did really well today," she says with a big smile. "I tried to get Drake to bring me earlier so I could watch, but I just missed it. Apparently got here just in time to serve you all though," she says exasperatedly.

"Are Cade and Jonas here, too?"

"Yeah, but they're upstairs in a meeting with the other owners about something."

"How do you two know each other?" Flynn asks.

"Isn't it obvious?" I say, putting my face up next to Sasha's.

"No?"

"She's my sister from another mister," I say. "Cade's my mum, too."

"S-sisters?" Flynn stutters.

I nod, but looking at Sasha, she doesn't seem all that happy to see Flynn.

"Uh … hey … I just remembered I had to … uh … do something. Tonight. Like, right now," Flynn says before going to walk off.

"Oh. Okay—" I say, but I don't think he heard. He's already gone. "What was that all about?" I ask Sasha.

"He's not a nice guy, Nuka."

"Did you two …"

"He was my first. I was head over heels, of course. Turns out the feeling wasn't mutual."

I guess it wasn't jealousy. Brett was right about him after all. "I'll be sure to kick his butt when my time comes in the arena with him."

She smiles at me. "I have no doubt you'll do that."

"Hey," Drake comes up beside me. "Congrats."

"Thanks."

"Are you going to stick around for the fight tonight?" he asks.

"Who's fighting? Actually, it doesn't matter. I'm kinda beat. No pun intended. Where's Brett? I was hoping he'd take me home."

"I don't think he'll be driving anywhere anytime soon," Drake says, pointing to him across the room.

He's now doing shots with that other girl. I see him down two, only to have her replace them as soon as he's done. I wonder how much he's already had to drink. His arm wraps around her waist as he leans in and whispers in her ear, both of them stumbling a bit before righting themselves. I guess I have my answer—he's clearly too wasted to drive anywhere.

Sighing, I turn to Drake. "Can you take me home?"

"I can't leave Sasha."

"Dammit. So I'm stuck here?"

"Maybe you could convince Brett to give you his car?" Sasha suggests, which makes Drake burst out laughing.

"Even I'm not allowed to drive his pride and joy."

"Maybe I'll call my friend Declan to come pick me up from outside one of the club entrances."

"You have more chance of Brett giving you his car than you do of Cade allowing that," Drake says.

"Yeah, okay, not the best idea," I agree.

Storming off in the direction of Brett and his drinking buddy, I grab his shoulder and turn him to face me. "Give me your car keys."

"What? No way." He shakes my hand from his shoulder.

"Well, I'm going home, and clearly you can't drive, so give me the keys."

"I'm not ready to leave yet."

"I didn't say you were coming with me."

"Nuka—"

"No, no. Please stay here and drink up with your new friend. I really don't care. I just really want to go home because if you've already forgotten, I just got my ass handed to me in a fight."

Brett sighs. "Fine. Let's go." He starts walking off without even saying goodbye to the girl at the bar. Her stunned face is almost comical.

"You don't have to come with me," I say, catching up to Brett.

"I'm not going to let you drive my car without me there."

"But you're gonna let me drive it?" My face lights up at the possibility.

"Yeah," he slurs. "I don't think I should've had those shots."

"I've just gotta get my bag," I say, running towards the locker room.

Brett has his head against the wall with his eyes closed when I come back out.

I can't help laughing. "Just how many shots did you have?"

"I dunno. However many that skank gave me."

"You didn't seem to think she was a *skank* five minutes ago."

Brett laughs as we make our way to the elevator that leads to the warehouse above us. "Sucks to be on that end, doesn't it?"

"What end is that?"

"Jealousy."

We get in the elevator, the air suddenly stale and full of tension. We're silent as we ascend and make our way out of the warehouse. When we finally make it to the car, Brett gets in the passenger seat, slamming the door shut.

"You don't think it sucks for me to see guys fawn all over you?" he snaps as I get in the driver's seat. He's clearly been holding onto that for a while. "Drake, Flynn—"

"Drake's just joking, and I've had *one* conversation with Flynn. About fighting, no less."

"Declan," he continues, not paying attention to me.

"Especially *Declan.* Ugh, he's the worst," he adds, mumbling.

"Is that why you 'marked' me as yours in front of everyone? I guess I should be thankful you didn't pee on me like a dog."

"I did you a favour by doing that—trust me."

"A *favour*? Do you realise how that sounds? That I should be so lucky that a guy like you would even look at a girl like me?"

"That's not what I mean. All of those guys in there would stop at nothing to get to you. At least now, they won't try. Except for maybe Flynn. He didn't seem to care that you're taken."

"But I'm *not* taken." I can't believe how insane he's acting. "You're driving me freaking crazy."

"Don't you get it? You drive me crazy every freaking day because I can't have you."

"You've been avoiding talking about us for weeks, what's suddenly changed?"

"Dutch courage," he says, burping at the same time.

"Charming. And if I recall correctly, I've kissed you back—every single time! So, why do you think you can't have me?"

"Well, for one, Cade—she'd never allow it. Two, I don't like coming in second. And three, I'm leaving. Don't you get that? As soon as I can afford it, my family and I are out of here. I'm not coming back. I have responsibilities that I can't turn my back on, just for a pretty blonde girl who gets under my skin."

I know I should be semi-flattered by what he's saying, but his words are just pissing me off.

"Well, first of all, you're right. We shouldn't be together if Cade scares you enough not to fight for me. Don't even get me started on the whole leaving thing—avoiding potential happiness because of something that may or may not happen sometime in the near or distant future. And I have no idea what you're talking about with coming in second."

"Declan," he says but doesn't elaborate.

"Declan and I are just—"

"If you say friends, I swear I'm going to lose it."

"We are!"

"You're in love with him, Nuke. Everyone can see it except for you. That Cassia girl could see it. I saw it yesterday."

"You don't know what you're talking about. And even if I did have feelings for Dec, it doesn't matter anyway because he's with Cassia."

Brett lets out a loud sigh. "He's not with Cassia," he says, but it's barely audible.

"What?"

"The night we took you. He wasn't going home with her like I'd said. He'd just told her that she was right." Brett throws his head back on the headrest. "He told her he was in love with you, then he offered to walk her out. He didn't leave with her."

"He told her *what*? Why did you tell me that he ... oh. You needed to get me outside."

"I tried to tell you later that night … but … I was kinda awestruck by you, by our kiss in the alley. Even though I knew it couldn't, shouldn't, wouldn't, happen again, I didn't want to lose the possibility. And I knew I would the minute I told you about Declan."

Sitting here, listening to Brett finally open up to me, I don't know what to say.

After some awkward silence where I think he may even float in and out of consciousness, I have a chance to process everything he's just said.

"I should get you drunk more often. I'm actually getting answers for once." My attempt to lighten the mood is not quite successful, but he does crack a smile.

"Yeah, yeah. Just start driving home already."

I hesitate before asking what I really want to ask. Brett has just basically poured his heart out to me, and I'm pretty sure what I have to say will crush it. But I need to sort this Declan thing out. I need to see him. "Umm … is it okay … can we …"

"Can we detour to Declan's house? Is that what you were going to ask?" When I don't answer, he nods his head once, trying to hide his disappointment, but it radiates from him. "I figured that was going to be your reaction to finding out he's single." He sighs, looking dejected. "Let's go then."

I start driving and it doesn't take long for Brett to start snoring in the passenger seat. That's fine by me because my internal monologue is going into overdrive, and I'm sure I wouldn't be able to focus on anything he'd be saying anyway.

Is Declan really in love with me?

Declan and I have always been in some weird limbo state between friendship and together. Everyone has always said we belong together, but we've always maintained we're just friends. And we are. But ... I don't know. What if we're meant to be more than friends?

But if that's the case, then why did I push Declan completely aside when I met Brett? Was it because he was with Cassia, and I felt I couldn't compete with that? Brett was there as a fill-in for the one I truly want?

But if I really analyse my behaviour in the past month, it's not exactly like I've been pining for Declan. I miss him, yes. I've wanted to see him, yes. But I haven't needed him.

Am I only interested in Brett because I thought I couldn't have Declan? Is Brett right? Would he always come second?

Am I even interested in Brett at all, or is it because we've been forced to spend so much time together that I just think I'm interested? His mood swings drive me crazy, he's not exactly affectionate, in fact, he's downright shitty most of the time. And as soon as I found out Declan is available, I'm running to his side. But there's definitely something there—I can't deny that.

Assessing them, Brett's supportive ... in his own unconventional way. Not to mention hot. Not that that's something to base a relationship on. And Declan, he's my best friend. I don't see myself ever picking anyone else over him.

He's my family, my soulma...

Holy crap.

I'm relieved when I pull up to his house and his parents' car isn't in the driveway, but the house lights are on. That means he's home alone. There's a sinking part of me, though, that was kind of hoping they'd be home so I could have an excuse to chicken out.

Sitting outside his home for I don't know how long, I just can't bring myself to go in.

Am I crazy for going for this?

What about Litmus? I can't tell him. It will forever be this big secret between us. Maybe he could find it on his own through some manipulative hints left here and there ... I shake my head. *He's becoming a cop. He can't find out about Litmus.*

Which means ... I can't do this.

We're halfway home when Brett finally wakes up. My eyes are streaked with tears, and I've barely been holding it together enough to drive.

Discreetly trying to wipe my tears away, I'm clearly not discreet enough.

"Hey, what's wrong?"

"Nothing."

"We're not going to play that game, are we? I'm pretty sure my hangover is starting to kick in and my head is too sore for lying. Weren't we going to Declan's?"

"We did. You were asleep."

"I was asleep?" he asks, confused. He straightens himself up, sitting upright instead of slouching. "How long was I asleep for?"

"About an hour."

"Oh. So what happened?"

I shake my head. "Nothing."

"There we go with the lying again. Was I wrong about him? Is he *not* in love with you?"

"I didn't even see him, I couldn't bring myself to get out of the car."

"Oh?" Brett's face lights up a little, even though he tries to hide it.

"You don't have to look so happy about it. It has nothing to do with you and me."

"Oh."

"And can you stop saying 'oh' to everything? It's getting really annoying."

"Oh." He smiles before going serious when I don't return it. "So what really happened?"

I glance at him before looking back to the road. "He's joining the police force and going to work for my adoptive mother."

"I know."

"I could never tell him about Litmus."

"Meaning you'd have to lie to him every day."

"Yup. And I can't do it. I can't tell him how I feel because it'll never work."

"I'm sorry, Nuke."

I shrug, trying not to burst into tears again. "I am kinda pissed that you pointed out how I feel about him, though. Thanks for that." I try to make it sound like I'm joking, but I don't think I pull it off.

"Hey, turn left up here," he says.

I do as he says, even though I'm confused as to what we're doing. "Why?"

"We're right near the headland on the coast. We can climb it and look out over the city."

"Climbing doesn't sound fun right now."

He rolls his eyes. "It's not actual climbing. There's a path and everything. And if I can do it with my headache, you can do it with your bruising."

We park the car and as we get out, he comes over, wrapping his arm around my shoulder.

"Why are we here?" I ask, as we start walking to the main entrance and up the small incline that leads to the top.

"Dunno. A break from training, a break from Litmus. A break from everything that's running through your head right now. It just seemed like a good idea."

"A break sounds good."

We spend the rest of the walk in silence, but he never once lets go of me. When we finally reach the top of the small headland, I'm breathless and sweaty. Letting go of Brett, I take a seat on rough benches carved out of the boulders that surround the pathways.

The ocean below us makes crashing sounds as waves hit the rocks. In the distance, the city lights dance. The air smells of salt and the breeze whips at my hair.

"It's so beautiful out here," I say, stating the obvious.

Brett sits next to me. "I used to run here when I was at uni. It was a great escape from everything."

"Thank you for bringing me here," I say, looking into his eyes. He holds my gaze as I put my hand around his neck and bring his head down to mine, kissing him gently.

He's apprehensive at first but slowly gives into it, wrapping his arms around me and holding me tighter. But then he pulls away abruptly.

"We can't," he says, not looking me in the eye.

I nod once, removing my arms from around him.

"Just because you've decided you don't want to be with

Declan, that doesn't mean you don't love him. It doesn't mean I won't always be a consolation prize. You proved that tonight the minute you found out he was single. To be fair, that's how I thought you'd respond, but … I guess there was a small part of me hoping you wouldn't."

"What I realised tonight, after we left Declan's and you were asleep in the car, is that even if Declan wasn't joining the police force, my new life is so different to what it was a month ago. Even if we could get around the confidentiality, he wouldn't understand. If I hadn't just joined Litmus, I think things would be different. But I chose this, and he's chosen his path. And even though I've only just realised my true feelings for him, it friggin' hurts knowing that I have to forget about it … about him. I'm not just losing a possible future with him, I'm losing our entire friendship."

"You need to focus on getting over him, and I don't want to be some rebound. Not with you. If you ever look at me the way you look at him … hell, even the way your face lights up when you talk about him, Cade will probably fire me. Or have me buried. But just so you know …" He leans in closer and whispers, "I'd welcome the punishment."

My face warms, and I try to conceal it with a cough. "Why do you think Cade would object to us being together anyway?"

He shrugs. "My best guess is she didn't like seeing Sasha get hurt by Flynn and doesn't want to have to see that again. Sasha was in a pretty bad way when he dumped her not long after they'd gotten together. You should've seen the way she was with him." He shakes his head. "Poor naïve girl didn't see it coming. And she kind of hasn't settled down since. She doesn't let herself get feelings for any of them now."

"I'm sorry I didn't believe you about him."

"You didn't?"

"I thought you were just being jealous."

"That might've had something to do with it," he admits.

"And I'm also sorry I kissed you just now. It was unfair of me to use you as a distraction. It just seemed like a good idea," I say, smirking as I recycle what he just said about coming up here. "We're going to be okay, yeah? You and me? All of this making out isn't going to make things weirder is it? By my count, you've kissed me three times now, and I've kissed you once. So technically, you're still two up on me. Any awkwardness is your fault."

He half-smiles. "We're all good," he says, nudging me with his elbow.

"Holy crap, did we just become … you know … friends?"

He winces. "Ugh. I think so."

-12-

THE DEAKIN IMAGE

My left side is extra tender this morning. Any kind of movement and I'm wincing in pain. Yet here I am, in another pair of tights, a sports bra, and baggy T-shirt, heading for the training room.

"Where you off to?" Brett's voice calls from behind me as I make my way down the hall.

"Uh … training?"

"You're dedicated, I'll give you that. But you need to heal. There's a difference between just training and an actual fight. You need a day off." He lifts my shirt, running his fingers down my rib cage and over my bruise. "It doesn't look as bad today, but I'm assuming it's painful."

"That's an understatement."

"We'll see how you are tomorrow."

"Now that I've passed my test, shouldn't I be preparing to go into the arena?"

"I think you proved yesterday that you're prepared."

"For Wild Card nights. How long are they going to let me do that for before I need to face one of the others? Speaking of which, shouldn't you be fighting soon? You've been so busy training me, you haven't gone into the ring at all the last few weeks."

He shrugs. "They're paying me to train you. I'll be back on the schedule soon."

"How many fights do you normally do a week?"

"There's five teams, two to three fights a night on busy nights, so one team member does one fight night per week, unless someone is sick or on holidays or whatever. The other nights are usually the gimmicky nights like Wild Card night or showcases—something to try to bring in a bigger crowd. Now that we have six on our team, we'll only do two nights once every six weeks or so. One of the guys might decide to trade to a different team or leave, though."

"Why would they trade?"

"Well, with you joining the team, we're the biggest now. And the more fights you have, the more money you make. We get twenty percent of the team takings on the nights we fight. You get thirty, though. Obviously fighting on a Friday, Saturday, or Sunday night will give you a bigger income than any of the weeknights, as we're quieter. If one of us is offered a permanent weekend fight, or a bigger cut of the profits, we'd probably choose to jump ship."

"So I'm technically taking someone's spot?"

"Yeah. But the guys don't seem too bothered by it."

I'm less than convinced.

"I swear. They're cool."

"Okay."

"Ah, crap. They know," Brett says cryptically.

"Huh?"

Brett gestures to the end of the hallway. Nothing's there.

"Umm—"

"Just wait."

Cade comes gliding towards us from the entryway moments later.

"They know about last night," he whispers.

"Here you two are." Cade's voice travels down the hall. "We need a meeting. Now." She stands with her hands on her hips, waiting for us to come to her. "Both of you."

"O-okay," I stutter, forcing my feet to move in her direction.

Brett and I follow in silence as she takes us into a wing of the mansion I've never been before—her and Jonas's quarters. Whenever we've had a meeting to discuss my involvement in Litmus, it's been at the dinner table over a meal.

Today she brings me to their office. *We're in big trouble.*

"So," she says, closing the door behind us and gesturing for us to sit.

Jonas sits behind the massive mahogany desk, his elbows resting on it, his hands steepled under his chin.

We take the two seats in front of him as Cade sits on the edge of the desk, facing us.

"Going to tell us why you two were making out in the arena last night?" she asks, cutting to the chase.

"Training technique?" I say, but my voice goes up at the end, as if I'm asking a question. Clearing my throat, I clarify, "He needed me to get angry. I was too nervous, so he kissed me to undermine me in front of the others to make me look weak, knowing full well it would anger me enough for my ability to kick in."

Cade just smiles in return.

Wait ... she's smiling?

"How did you find out?" Brett asks.

"Please. You didn't think we heard about it the minute we got there yesterday? If we'd been running on time like we should've been, we wouldn't have missed the fight at all and would've seen it ourselves." She looks over at me. "From what we hear, you did really well." Her smile turns into a look of pride. I think it's the first time I've seen that expression from her.

"It's a brilliant marketing strategy," Jonas says.

Brett and I glance at each other, confused. "Huh?" I ask.

"In the Litmus world, the fighters are like celebrities," Cade begins to explain. "And while we generally like to stay scandal free, something like this would draw crowds to your fight nights. Anything to get a glimpse of the happy couple."

"But … we're not a couple," I say.

She shrugs. "That's unfortunate, it'd be so much easier if you were. But the truth of the matter is, everyone now thinks you are. We're not saying you have to be a couple, you just need to act like it at Litmus."

"Have to? As in you're ordering us to do this?" I ask. This is not what we expected. In fact, we were sure the opposite would happen.

"We're asking you nicely," Jonas says in a less than nice tone. "But if we had to, we could order it. It's in your contract that we handle your marketing."

It's at this moment that I realise I still haven't read my contract.

Brett doesn't seem too happy about this. I'm not thrilled about it either, but if it brings in more money, I guess it's not a horrible idea. We basically already live in each other's pockets—spending entire days training together. It wouldn't be much different to what we're doing now. Our faces must show our scepticism though.

"We're not saying you have to be together," Cade says. "Just be ringside for each other's fights, hold hands when you're in public, and mingle with the sponsors as a couple. If anyone asks about your relationship, just tell them that it's going well and change the subject. You don't need to be all over each other for people to believe it. You don't see me hanging off of Jonas when we're out and about, do you?"

"And I'm thankful for that," I say with a smile. "But speaking of contracts, am I able to—"

"That reminds me," Cade interrupts. "We have the entire team scheduled for a photo shoot tomorrow for the promotional side of things at the two nightclubs and Litmus itself. And we're going to need a name."

"They all suck."

Cade laughs, and Jonas glares at me. "I know," Cade says. "But you're the new focus of our brand. We're introducing you to the world, and it needs to be good. I have a list here of pre-approved names." She hands me a sheet of paper and I begin reading.

"No to Purple Heat. It sounds like a bad superhero. Not to mention, I hate drawing attention to my stupid eye colour. No to Burn, it sounds like an STD symptom." Sighing, I continue down the list. "No to Sun Blazer, because … no. Just no." I shake my head.

"Nuka, just pick one," Cade says exasperatedly.

"I guess this one's not horrible," I say, putting the form on the desk and pointing.

Jonas actually smiles at me for once. "Welcome to the team, Heatwave."

***

"So … not exactly what you were expecting," I say to Brett as we start making our way back to our rooms.

"Yeah," he says quietly.

"What's wrong?" I choke on the words. I don't think I really want to know the answer.

He shakes his head. "It's hard enough being around you as it is. Now I have to …" he sighs. "Never mind. Nothing's wrong. If this'll bring in more money, the sooner I'll be able to get out of here." He walks faster, leaving me as I continue to dawdle back to my room.

Before I get there, my sister's voice travels after me. "Heatwave. Yo, Heatwave!" she yells.

Starting to regret that name already.

"Yes? Flower Girl?"

She screws up her face as she catches up to me. "Flower Girl? Really? That's the best you can come up with?"

"On spur of the moment? Yes. What's up?"

"You have the day off."

"Yeah? So?"

"So, ever since you've started training, I never see you. We need to go shopping."

"Really? We *need* to?"

"Uh-huh. Plus, you have a photo shoot tomorrow so we really must do something about that hair."

"What's wrong with my hair? Did Cade put you up to this?"

"We need more blonde. Maybe some highlights. Definitely need some sort of treatment conditioner," she says, playing with the craggy strands of my hair. "And no. Mum did not put me up to this. Okay, she *may* have mentioned the hair thing, but I want to spend time with my sister. Plus, it won't hurt to have a bit of pampering myself."

"And what are the chances of me getting out of this?"

She quirks her eyebrow at me but doesn't answer.

"Yup. Thought so. I'll just go get changed." I pause at the entrance of my room. "Brett's not on babysitting duty, is he?"

She shakes her head. "Drake."

"Good." I wince the second I say it and mutter an apology to Brett who's probably listening. Just when we thought we could make our way to having some sort of friendship, it had to get all awkward and stupid again.

"Sick of your boyfriend already?"

"Oh great, so it's already spreading."

"I don't understand why you're only pretending anyway after what I walked in on a few weeks ago."

Trying to hide the blush working its way to my face, I avoid looking at her when I say, "It's complicated."

"Mmhmm," she says, unconvinced.

Ignoring her, I make my way into my room and get dressed achingly slow. I'm beginning to understand the excitement of fighting. I'd love nothing more than to get back in that arena and kick Steve's butt for the pain I'm in right now … but maybe when I'm in less agony.

By the time I get back out, Sasha's waiting for me, giant sunglasses in hand. "Here," she says, shoving them at me. "To cover your bruises."

"Where did you even get these?" I ask as I slip them onto my face. "The rims are giant. I look like a fly."

She shrugs. "You can bring them back into fashion."

"Being the trendsetter that I am," I say sarcastically.

"Just wait. Word is already spreading about your fight with Ghost. Soon everyone will want to be like you."

"What? Bruised?"

Laughing, she shakes her head at me. "Let's just go."

Sasha informs the hair stylist what needs to be done, and while we both have tin foil wrapped in our hair, and we're left alone, Sasha brings her chair closer to me. Drake's outside, somewhere, probably taking advantage of us being busy and contained to one spot.

"Okay. Spill. Why's it so complicated?" she asks.

"Huh?"

"You and Brett."

I avoid eye contact with her as I start. "So it turns out that my friend, you know, the one I was staying with?"

She nods.

"I kinda didn't realise it, but I'm sorta … I think I'm … We've always just been friends. But when Brett told me that Declan was single, not taken like I was led to believe, it kind of hit me like a ton of bricks. Bam, you're in love with your best friend, you dumbass."

"Oh."

"Also, Declan's just told me that he's becoming a cop. Isn't exactly a great match for the 'new face of Deakin.' Not to mention putting the whole place at risk of being shut down."

She whistles. "Damn."

"So even though I like Brett—"

"You admit it! You do like him."

"Yes," I admit. "But at the moment, all I can think about is Declan. And Brett knows that. He's already told me he doesn't want to come in second, and I don't want to string him along. But now …"

"You're forced to," she says resignedly.

"Exactly."

"Dude, that sucks."

"Pretty much."

When we leave the hairdresser's a short time later, my hair's a bright platinum blonde now instead of a golden colour. Walking down the centre strip of the shopping centre, I jump behind Sasha as if I'm using her as a human shield when I see Declan coming the opposite way.

"Just my friggin' luck," I murmur.

"What are you … oh … is that Dec—"

"The one and only. Is he gone yet?"

"He just went into a store."

I stand upright again and turn to face Sasha, only to be met with an overly amused expression.

"You certainly have a type," she snickers.

"What do you mean?"

"You don't see it?"

"See what?"

"Declan is like the smaller, normal-sized version of Brett."

I tilt my head to the side. "Have you been drinking? They're nothing alike. Okay, so they both have dark hair. But that's it."

"They have the same build, except Declan's just smaller. They've got broad shoulders, strong arms. Even their facial features are similar. It's actually kind of freaking me out a little," she says, eyeing something behind me.

"What do you mean?" I ask.

"Nuke?" His voice startles me.

"Sorry. Forgot to tell you he came out of that store pretty quick," Sasha says, an obviously fake innocent smile on her face.

Glaring at her, I reach into my handbag to pull the oversized sunnies back out, slipping them on before turning to Declan. "Hey!" *Wow, so that came out high pitched and wrong.*

"What are you doing here?" he asks. "And what's with the hair?" he says smiling, reaching out and touching it.

"Just shopping with my sister," I say, playfully slapping his hand away. "Oh, yeah, Sasha, this is Declan."

They shake hands, Sasha's knowing smirk appearing as she eyes him up and down.

"No bodyguard today?" he asks.

"Drake is ..." I look around, but I still can't see him anywhere. "Somewhere. He's been good at pretending to be invisible today."

"Nuke?" Declan asks, his tone suddenly low and laced with concern. "Take off your glasses."

"What?"

He reaches forward, quickly but gently taking my glasses off before I can stop him. I hold in a breath as he assesses my face. "It's gotten worse, Nuke."

I look to the ground, unable to meet his eyes.

"Oh that," Sasha says with a wave of her hand. "I sure taught her a lesson, right, Nuka?" She elbows me in the ribs on my left side, smiling cockily. I wince in pain.

"*You* did that to her?" Declan asks.

"She's really good at self-defence," I say, trying to sell the lie.

"Note to self, don't piss off Nuka's sister." Declan smiles and I let out a sigh of relief. At least he's bought it.

"Damn straight," Sasha says, landing a quick jab to my ribs.

I find myself yelping in pain this time. I hold onto my side, tears filling my eyes and heat flooding my face as I try to hold in my scream of agony. I glare at Sasha and only then does she realise what she's done, her hand flying to her mouth in shock, giving me a silent apology.

"Maybe your true ability is brute strength," I grunt out.

"Did it really hurt that bad?" Declan asks, stepping forward to try to take a look.

I step back as he reaches for the hem of my shirt. "It's okay. It's fine, really. See," I say, letting go of my left side, gritting my teeth and breathing through my nose until the pain starts to subside. Once I've calmed down a bit, I visibly relax and I think Declan sees it too. "See. I really am fine."

Nodding, he looks down at the ground, looking more nervous than he was a moment ago. The three of us stand in awkward silence for what seems like forever.

This has never happened before with Declan. I don't know how to act around him anymore. It feels like someone's sitting on my chest and I need a reminder that I actually have to breathe.

"So … I … uh …" Declan starts. He runs his hand over his

hair and down his neck. "I'm leaving next week."

And boom! Just like that, the crashing weight on my chest falls to my stomach.

"For training?" I ask, my voice cracking.

He nods.

"How long for?"

"Six weeks."

"That'll be the longest we've ever gone without …"

"I know," he says, stepping forward and putting his arms around my waist. He leans in, resting his forehead against mine. "It's going to kill me."

The weirdness dissipates at his touch. Tears pool in my eyes, but I refuse to let them spill over. I want to live in this embrace forever. But it doesn't last.

Declan is ripped away from me quicker than I have a chance to react.

"Keep your hands off her, mate," Drake says, grabbing Declan by the shirt.

"Simon?" Declan asks.

Drake lets go of him, stepping back.

"You know Drake?" I ask.

"Drake?" Declan asks.

"Declan, right? From uni?" He turns to me. "I only did one year before I dropped out and came to work for Cade."

"Uh … yeah," Declan says, not taking his eyes off Drake.

"Well, sorry about that, Dec. All I could see was some guy trying to mack on my boss's girl."

My mouth goes dry in sudden panic. Sasha actually facepalms. *Drake, what did you just do?*

"Let me guess. That would be the other bodyguard? The 'dick' as Nuka was calling him two days ago?"

"Ah. So you've met him," Drake says, smirking.

Declan just stares at me, his gaze painful to watch as his expression goes from angry to hurt. "Well, I guess this is goodbye. For at least six weeks, anyway." His words sting. There's no emotion behind them. He looks to Drake. "Is it okay if I give her another hug before I go? I'm leaving to go to recruitment training. For the *police*." He's staring Drake down in a way I can't decipher.

"Of course, bud. Nuka's told me about her best friend, I just didn't realise it was you. Sorry for overreacting and stuff. Come on, Sash, let's give them privacy to say goodbye."

When they're a few feet away from us, I turn to Declan. "What's with the evil stare?"

He steps forward and wraps his arms around me. "What's your family into, Nuke?" he whispers. "Last I heard about Simon was he was going to work for Litmus."

I pull away in shock, but he holds me tighter, making me wince in pain. He lets me go as soon as he realises he's hurting me, looking down at my side and then up to my face, pure shock and realisation in his eyes.

"You're not—"

"I can't," I whisper. "I can't talk about it. How do you even know about …" I look over at Drake and Sasha to see them quickly glance away under my stare, pretending to be interested in the roofing of the undercover shopping strip. Looking back at Declan, I don't need to finish my sentence. *He knows.*

"Everyone at uni knows about Litmus. It's dangerous. You can't …"

"You don't understand, Dec. I can't talk to you about this, you can't talk to anyone else about it. You need to let it go." Fear takes over my voice.

I go to walk away but he pulls on my hand. "I'll get you out of this. I don't know how, but I'll save you. I'm not going to lose you to that place. I'm not losing you."

Making eye contact with him, I squeeze his hand and fake confidence to get through the lies I have to force myself to get out. "I'm not yours to lose, Declan." *Lie. I'm completely, one hundred percent his.* "I'm happy." *Lie. I want him by my side.* "And I don't need saving." *Finally, something that's true.* "I don't want to be your damsel in distress. I want to do this. You may not understand it, but you have to understand that there's nothing you can do about it. It's my choice. They're not forcing me to do anything."

Letting go of his hand, I walk away from the man I love for the second time in two days. Only this time, it's forever. I know that now. Being friends with him won't work. It's messy, and complicated, and now that he knows about Litmus, it puts both of us in danger. I don't want to begin to imagine what would happen if they found out an outsider knew—one that's going to be a cop, no less.

That's it then. No more Declan.

-13-

THE FACE OF DEAKIN

Getting to the photography studio with Brett is about as awkward as I was expecting. The drive over was quiet. He was being civil, which at first freaked me out because it's so unlike him.

The studio is completely decked out in white. White backdrop, white overhead lights. The entire space is crammed with a heap of photography equipment, the only open areas being in the reception and kitchen area we walked through to get in here and space on the floor in front of the camera.

I think I just walked into every girl's dream when I see the other four guys from Deakin, all shirtless except for Ryker who's wearing a tight, fitted, black wife-beater top.

Colton is wearing a pair of black angel wings that span out and stop just under his knee. It's hard for me to contain my giggle as we join them on the studio floor.

"Nice wings," I taunt. Colton shoots me a dirty look. "Sorry, couldn't help it. I had to say something."

"If you weren't Brett's girl, I'd show you just how much of an angel I could be," he purrs, waggling his eyebrows up and down.

Laughing, I ask, "Do you actually fight with those things on? They're not a hindrance?"

"Sometimes I do, sometimes I don't. Depends on who I'm fighting. I'm not going to go up against Blaze wearing them, but Slider or Chi I will. My babies are highly flammable," he says, petting one of his wings as if he was stroking a pet.

"Okay!" a high-pitched female voice comes from behind us. "Welcome, Heatwave," she says grabbing hold of my hand and shaking it vigorously, her red-rimmed glasses sliding down her nose from the movement. Her orange hair is in frizzy tight curls and sits in a messy bun atop her head. "I'm Olivia, I'll be running this shoot today." She looks over at the others. "Welcome back, boys. How about we get started with you while we get Heatwave into makeup to cover up some of that bruising. Which fighter managed to do that, anyway?"

"I didn't realise I went so hard," Steve says quietly, looking anywhere but at me.

I shrug. "All good. I *do* want a rematch though."

A collective "oooooh" breaks out. "I'm putting my money on her," Palmer says.

"Me too," Ryker adds.

"Anytime, princess," Steve says now smiling, his cockiness from when I first met him returning once again.

"Are you sure you want to nickname me that? Won't look too good when you get beaten by a princess, now would it?"

"I beat him all the time, and he doesn't seem to care," Palmer says. "Then again, I'm a queen, not a princess," he adds, winking at me.

"Follow me, Heatwave," Olivia cuts into our joking around. She leads me into a small room at the back where there's a tall woman with a ridiculous amount of makeup on and a chair facing a mirror. "Vidia will cover up those horrid bruises, my dear. Anything that can't be covered can be digitally altered later."

Olivia leaves the room, and I hear her shout to the guys, "Okay, boys, let's get you oiled up. Shirt off, Brawn."

"My favourite part," Palmer says, which causes everyone out there to laugh. Even I crack a smile.

"Sounds like you've got some competition for your man," Vidia says as she starts brushing out my hair.

Wow, news travels fast. Maybe she heard Colton call me Brett's girl? Maybe Cade told them ahead of time?

"I'm not worried," I say with a small laugh.

"I guess you'd be used to everyone wanting him. What everyone else wants to know is how you managed to get him to commit. Many girls have tried and failed."

Easy, just get his owners to put it in a contract. I don't answer her aloud and give her a tight-lipped smile.

"Okay, so we're going with a grungy street fighter look today," she says, quickly changing the topic to business talk. "Thick smoky makeup—we'll need something pretty heavy to cover your bruises. Then we'll add extensions to you hair and then cover your hair in a gel that'll give your hair a sexy wet look."

Vidia's hands are magically fast, and I'm ready to get in front of the camera in only thirty minutes.

Walking out to the studio floor, I take my shirt off to reveal my plain black fighting outfit Cade told me to wear. Olivia gasps when she sees the bruise down my left side.

"Oh, shit," Steve says.

"I'm fine, I swear. It barely even hurts anymore."

Olivia grimaces. "I guess I'll have to polish up on my digital editing skills. Never mind, I'm sure I can fix that later. So, Heatwave, can I have you front and centre, please?" She starts ordering us around, putting us in our places, and physically forces me to put my hands where she wants them.

The first few takes have all of us standing with our hands on our hips. Brett's behind me and slightly to my right, and the others flank either side of us, going backwards into a V-shape.

"Heatwave, we need you to really smile in these ones. You own these boys, they'll fight anyone for you. And guys, I need you to look cocky and arrogant. Not that you lot will have to try hard to accomplish that."

This makes me genuinely smile and Olivia quickly takes a quick few snaps, muttering things like, "Awesome. Great job. Hot."

We're put in a few more positions, everything professional and straight forward. There's no real banter or goofing around like I thought there would be. I guess the guys have done this enough times to know that the quicker you get it done, the sooner you get out of here.

"Okay, last group shot. We'll have you back in the same V-shape you were in before, but this time you four face the back, and Brawn and Heatwave take a step closer to the camera. Brawn, I need you behind her, your hands on her hips." We all get into position. "Now I need your hands on his," she instructs me, placing my hands on top of Brett's. "We need your hair out of his face," she says, bringing my hair around to hang over my left shoulder. Brett's hands feel stiff and unnatural under mine, as if he's purposefully tensing them. "I need your head in her neck," she says to Brett, and I swear I can feel his eyes roll. But a second later, his head is there in the cleft of my neck, his breath on my skin, making me shiver.

"Sorry," he mutters. It's the first word he's said to me since we first got here this morning.

"It's okay," I whisper back. "You just breathed on a funny spot is all."

Olivia makes her way back behind her camera and starts taking shots. "Heatwave, I need you to be more … arrogant. I mean, look at the guy you've got by your side. Smirk like every girl he's ever been with is right here in this room and you're taunting them. You've won. He's yours."

"I don't know if that many girls would fit in here," I say, and the whole room bursts out laughing. I even feel Brett chuckle against my neck.

"Not my point," Olivia says. "You need to gloat about your relationship. Brawn, I need you even closer, actually kiss her neck if you have to, wrap your arms around her tighter. Hold her like if you let her go, you'll lose her forever."

"That won't be hard," he whispers low enough that only I can hear. Then he places his lips gently on my shoulder, making his way up to my neck. His hands embrace me around my front, his hands caressing my stomach.

It's not hard for me to find my arrogant smirk.

"That's great, Brawn. Heatwave, you've got the smirk, now I just need you to open your eyes."

Heat floods my cheeks as I open my eyes, not realising I'd closed them, savouring the moment. The guys behind us laugh again, only making my blushing worse.

Telling myself to calm down, I focus all my energy on looking arrogant. Olivia's words repeat through my head. I've won. Brett's mine. Even though I know it's not actually true, the smile finds my face immediately at the thought.

Olivia takes a few more shots and then tells everyone else they're wrapped. Brett and I apparently have more work to do.

She takes single photos of me in numerous poses; a lot of which I doubt will be usable because I feel so awkward, I'm sure it shows on my face. While we're doing this, Brett stands off to the side, and out of the corner of my eye, I see movement in the form of a tall blonde. *Vidia.*

She sashays her way over to Brett, her hand landing on his arm.

"Heatwave. Yo, Heatwave!"

Oh, that's me. "What?"

"Eyes over here," Olivia says, snapping me out of my trance.

"Sorry," I say, shaking my head, trying to refocus myself. It doesn't take me long to glance back over their way, though.

"Okay, Brawn. I think she's missing you. Get back in here," Olivia orders.

Brett nods his head to Vidia before walking over and wrapping his arm around my waist. The camera flash goes off a few times before Brett leans in and whispers, "Thank you," in my ear.

"For?" I whisper back.

"Getting me away from her."

I tilt my head to look up at him. "Another Holly?"

"Uh … yeah, sorta."

"Anyone you haven't slept with?"

"In this room? Just the one," he says, winking.

Even though there's a tiny part of me that is irked by that, I still find myself smiling.

"Well, that's tempting," I say, my voice laced with sarcasm.

We find ourselves laughing, the tension between us over the last few days dissipating with each shared smile.

"Stop looking so happy," Olivia yells. "You're supposed to be badass street fighters."

This only makes us laugh more, making Olivia give up. "I guess I've got what we need. That's a wrap."

Throwing our shirts back on, Brett and I make our way out to the car.

"So Holly, Vidia, *and* Olivia, hey?" I ask once we're on the road.

"Not Olivia. I was only joking about that. If you didn't notice, she was more interested in checking you out than me."

"Is anyone else going to be approaching me, telling me this'll be over in a few weeks? Or asking me how I got you to 'settle down'?"

He lets out a small laugh. "Just tell them you can't help being perfect."

"Pfft, I'm far from perfect."

"That doesn't mean it's not a good comeback."

"Oh sure, because it won't earn a slap to the face or anything."

"You're forgetting you're Heatwave now. Everyone's going to be scared of you."

"I'm actually going to have to beat someone for *that* to happen."

"You've only had one fight, and you almost won it. You'll get there with a bit more training."

"What *is* the plan for training? I'm kind of thinking we need to up our game. I also might've mentioned to Ryker about possibly training with him."

"Really? Ryker?" Brett asks, rubbing his hand over his chin. "I guess …"

"He said he wants to learn how to fight."

Brett laughs. "He's number one. Why would he need to learn to fight?"

"Because you guys make him feel like crap for using his ability more than everyone else does. He wants to make it a fair fight."

Brett's obviously sceptical, but he nods his head in agreement. "We could probably use him to up your pain threshold."

"That doesn't sound like it'll be much fun."

"It won't be. How are your ribs feeling?"

"Still a little tender, but we really need to train tonight. It's the second day we haven't."

"You need to heal, though. If you go doing more damage while you're still hurt, you could be out for a lot longer than a couple of days. We'll do a weights session tonight and get back into training tomorrow."

"But—"

"No buts."

"You're a butt."

"Real mature."

I'm hoping our playful banter means the awkwardness is really gone.

***

Pain, so much pain. "Holy mother f—"

"Nuka, breathe." Brett's soothing voice is doing nothing to ease the drill that's attacking my body.

"It hurts!" I scream, hunching over.

"I know. You just have to breathe through it. Block it out. Ryker, will you ease up a bit?"

Training with Ryker is more brutal than I was expecting. He stands in front of me, arms across his chest and a giant smirk on his face.

"You're enjoying this, aren't you?" I grind out.

"Come on, Nuka. If you can get through this kind of pain, you'll find the arena easy to survive."

He finally releases his invisible hold on me, and I collapse to the ground, breathing heavily and welcoming the serenity of painlessness.

"Shouldn't you be training, too? Why's it pick on Nuka day?" I whine.

"Because we've been training with Ryker for two weeks now, and you haven't been able to overcome his ability," Brett answers for him.

"Are you saying you can?"

Brett nods to Ryker, and then his whole body tenses. His jaw is set, and his fists are clenched. Taking rigid movements towards Ryker, he raises a fist and punches him in the jaw, making him fall to the ground.

Brett visibly relaxes. "Now your turn," he says to me.

"Are you sure you don't have a double ability and have some supernatural high pain threshold?"

"Overcoming pain is not a physical thing. It's all mental."

"Oh, okay, Zen master."

Between upping my weights routine and pushing training sessions to the limits, my body is starting to protest. And now they're attacking my mind.

Jonas and Cade haven't said any more about going into the arena yet, just that it'll be soon and to keep training to make sure I'm ready when the time comes. Brett's gone back to fighting, and I haven't been introduced officially to the fighting world yet, so I haven't had to be at Brett's fights for publicity. So I'm at home doing weights and cardio morning and night, and we spar in the middle of the day—unless it's fight night or the day after, then Ryker has stepped in. Today, they're both ganging up on me.

Ryker wasn't lying when he said he's not bad at fighting, but his reflex to use his ability responds too quickly when someone gets the upper hand.

"It's all mind over matter," Ryker encourages. "You can beat it, or at least hold it off from consuming you. Ready to go again?"

Nodding and getting to my feet, the pain slowly starts in my brain, making its way down into my neck before consuming my entire head. Sweat drips off my brow as I try fighting it. I grunt from the energy of refusing to give into it, refusing to collapse. *Come on, Nuka. Keep concentrating.*

"Try to think of something … anything to distract you from

the pain. A memory, a funny story someone told you. Anything," Brett says.

The first thing that comes to mind is Declan. I have years of fun memories with him. Surely, I can conjure up something distracting enough.

Walking through the dauntingly long corridor of my brand new school, I told myself to ignore the blatant stares, the judging looks, and the tiny hint of fear in some of my classmate's eyes. I stared straight ahead and kept walking towards my goal—my classroom.

Starting a new school in the middle of the year would be nerve wracking under normal circumstances, but I wasn't normal. I've never been normal.

"Hey! Skate park girl!" I heard a voice yelling from down the hallway. Turning around, I was met with the face of an angel. Okay, maybe not an angel, but definitely my saviour. His bright blue eyes were almost covered by his shaggy dark hair.

"Hi," I said nervously.

"First day?"

"Uh ... yeah."

"I'm Declan."

"Nuka."

"Welcome to Howard Academy." He gave a confident smile, one I could only match.

"Nuka … Nuka?" Brett's voice brings me out of my daze.

"What?"

"You did it."

It's only now I remember where I *actually* am and what we're doing. "I did it?"

Looking at Ryker and Brett with their astounded expressions, I realise I'm not in pain. Until I snap out of my trance and realise that I am. *So much pain.*

Grabbing my head and letting out a loud scream, I beg Ryker to stop.

"Sorry," he says before mentally releasing me.

"What were you thinking about?" Brett asks. "You completely tuned out. It was like you weren't even here."

"Uh … nothing in particular. Just school …" My hand itches to play with my hair, but I force myself to keep my hands by my side.

Brett knows I'm lying, though, his face falling in disappointment. "Right. So whenever you feel you can't go on, just think about *him* and you'll be fine. I think that'll be enough for today." He stalks out of the room. The door slams behind him, and I flinch.

"That was weird," Ryker says.

"Nah. That was just Brett."

Reaching for my water bottle, I take a seat on the floor and take a sip. Ryker sits next to me.

"Can I ask you something?" he asks.

"What?"

"You and Brett. You don't exactly … I mean … you don't act like a couple behind closed doors. I thought I was going to have to put up with mushy lovey-dovey stuff during our training sessions, but I haven't. I don't feel like the third wheel at all."

"I don't hear a question in all of that."

"Are you two …"

"It's just really complicated. There are some trust issues. My best friend's a guy, so Brett's not too happy about that. And he has a history with nearly everyone from Litmus."

I don't know why I'm not telling Ryker the truth—that there's nothing really going on between Brett and me. For some unknown reason, the words just aren't coming.

"He was a bit of a manwhore before you," Ryker says. "You want to keep training while he sulks about whatever he's sulking about?"

"Sure. But it's my turn to cause you pain."

***

Sitting down to our family dinner, I'm surprised to see an extra place setting next to mine.

"Who's—"

"Hey," Brett says, walking in and taking the spare chair.

"Oh. Never mind."

"We have some good news," Cade exclaims.

"Oh?" I ask.

"We're all set. Your first fight is in a week."

"A week?" I sputter. "Great." I drag out the word. On the inside, I'm cringing. *What if I stuff it all up? What if I lose?*

"You're ready, Nuke," Brett says.

"And are *you* ready?" I ask him. "To take this"—I gesture between the two of us—"public?"

"All part of my job, sweetheart."

Yeah, would've been more convincing if the "sweetheart" didn't come out so sullen.

"You'll need to cease with the training," Cade says. "At least where you're getting hit in the face. Vidia can only do so much with her makeup brush."

Ugh. Vidia.

"We'll be revealing your promo posters on that night. It's what we've been waiting for. We needed to know they'd be ready before we committed to a fight date."

Jonas, who's been quiet as usual, letting Cade do all of the talking for him, hands over an envelope.

Inside are all the photos from the shoot.

"That one," Cade says, "is the new team banner."

Brett looks over my shoulder as I lift it closer to me. It's breathtaking, intimidating, and fierce all at the same time.

My purple eyes bore into the camera lens, glowing with radioactivity. Brett's lips are on my shoulder, his face obscured. His arms protectively surround me, supporting my bruised side, which isn't digitally covered like Olivia said it would be, but it gives it attitude. With just his hands, he's warning vengeance on anyone who hurts me.

Beside me, facing the opposite direction, is Steve, his back muscles tense and rigid, his whole body almost a translucent glow. Colton's on the other side of him, only one of his black wings visible as it falls at his side like it's an extension of himself, another limb. On the other side of Brett, Palmer stands with a hand behind his back, a superimposed fireball in his hand. Lastly, Ryker's on the end, smaller than the rest but glancing over his shoulder, his side profile giving a knowing smirk. His attitude oozes *"I'm number one."*

"It's perfect," I say in awe. We look like a team, and Brett and I look like a couple.

"Except you can't see my face," Brett says.

"You can't see any of the other's faces either," I point out.

"No one needs to see your pretty face now, anyway. You're taken." Sasha's voice comes from the doorway, as she arrives late—something I have grown accustomed to when it comes to family dinners. "Give me a look." She walks around the dining table and sorts through more of the photos from the envelope. "Whoa," she says, picking one up. "You look insanely hot, Nuka."

She hands me the photo, and it takes less than a second for me to work out when the photo was taken. Brett's chest is barely visible behind me, but my face is angry, full of rage. It was the first photo taken after Brett re-joined my side when Vidia cornered him. I look like the grungy street fighter they wanted me to be, but I know better. The look of contempt on my face is one of competition, of my desire to fight; only my intended victim is not a fellow fighter, but a makeup-brush wielding ex-girlfriend. It's a look of pure jealousy.

Cade looks to me, a proud smile on her face. "You are the new face of Deakin."

-14-

MY FIRST FIGHT

"Ready?" Ryker asks me, bouncing on his heels in front of me as I sit in the locker room with my head in my hands.

"Do I look ready?" I snap.

"No need to bite my head off," he says, holding his hands up in surrender.

"Sorry. I just need a reminder of why I'm doing this. This is stupid. It's demeaning, it's—"

"Fun, exciting … you'll get lots of money."

To be more specific, my charity *will get lots of money.*

I stand and hug Ryker, hoping it will somehow calm my nerves. "Thank you."

"No problem. You're going to do great."

The door clicks open and the rest of the team enters, Brett bringing up the rear.

"What are you guys doing?" I ask as they start stripping off their shirts.

"We're escorting you out there," Colton says. "No one's going to mess with our girl."

"Ugh. Cade and Jonas's idea?"

"We're 'revealing our new brand,'" Steve says with a roll of his eyes.

"Come on, we'll be announced any minute," Brett orders.

We head out as a group and wait behind the double doors that will lead us straight to the floor.

"Up front, Nuka," Brett says.

I stand by the doors, feeling nauseated and a little bit ridiculous in full hair and makeup. My hair has been curled, styled, and left down, by orders of Cade. *"Image is everything,"* she said. Apparently, girls have to look like pin-up models to fight. I at least convinced them to forgo the fake eyelashes, stating how hard it would be for me to see.

I am worried about the hair though. I've been training with my hair up—having it down is just inviting my opponent to pull on it.

The announcer, force field guy—Felix as Brett calls him—starts amping up the audience. "Welcome to Wild Card night!" he yells. "You're going to be introduced to a brand new fighter tonight. She's young, she's hot—in more ways than one. She's joining the Deakin ranks. She is, Heatwave!"

The crowd goes ballistic, and the rumbling of their cheers and stomping feet vibrates the air.

"Let's do this," Brett says, opening the door for me.

Telling myself to not pay attention to the faces surrounding me, I look ahead at the arena and keep my eyes trained on Felix. I concentrate on putting one foot in front of the other and try my hardest not to smile. I'm meant to appear fierce.

Brett and Colton flank me on each side, trailed by the others behind us. The crowd parts for us, making a clear path to the arena. It almost feels like I'm gliding, as we head towards the stage.

Above the bar behind the ring, our new banner hangs. I barely have enough time to appreciate it before we reach the steps to the platform. Brett grabs my hand, walking me up to the stage, and the rest of the team waits at the bottom of the steps. Girls practically swarm the guys, trying to get close to them.

Brett turns to me, his hand cradling my face. "This doesn't go on my tally, it's an order," he says with a smile as he leans in and kisses me feverishly, pulling my body into his.

"You'll do great," he whispers when he pulls away. He leaves me, my legs weak at the knees. When he reaches the bottom of the steps, he stays ringside.

I turn slowly, facing the crowd—a sea of screaming bodies. Felix joins my side as I try to regain my composure.

"Oh! *Oh!* Did *that* just happen?" Felix yells. "I bet there are a lot of broken hearts out there right now. Brawn … in *love?* You must be one tough girl," he says, nudging me with his elbow.

I continue to stand as still as a statue, keeping up my fierce charade as my heart beats wildly in my chest.

"Before we get started, and before all you women out there start signing up to take this girl down for stealing the man of your hearts," he starts bantering again, "I'd like to tell you a story."

What is he doing? I glance down at Brett at the bottom of the steps, looking for an answer, but he looks as confused as I feel. He doesn't know what's going on either. Felix was meant to do a quick, simple introduction.

"A long time ago, there was a man. He was no ordinary man." Felix is getting animated and walking around the arena, making sure everyone in the crowd gets a glimpse of him. "He was born to be a leader, born to stand out in a crowd, born with one purpose: to become president." The crowd screams, but Felix just yells louder into the microphone. "To rid our world of discrimination and give us Immunes a chance at life."

He's not talking about ... I close my eyes for a brief second and tell myself this isn't happening.

"Unfortunately, before he could accomplish that goal, he was gunned down by anti-Immune activists."

The crowd lets out a collective "boo."

No, no, no, no, no, no.

"You're probably wondering what this has to do with this lovely, fine specimen before you," Felix says gesturing to me. "Not many know that he had a daughter. Well, ladies and gentlemen, that daughter is here, and she's *all* grown up. She's here fighting for vengeance for her father, fighting for her right to be noticed, and … as we've just seen, fighting for the man by her side."

Angry, so very angry. My hands explode with tingling heat, itching to get some action. The urge to run off this stage right now is so strong I'm surprised my feet aren't moving yet.

"Who will try to defy her honour? Who wants to knock her back in her place? Step forward, *now.*"

Even though the crowd is screaming and yelling and getting riled up, all I hear is crickets. No one is stepping forwards. It's like I'm back at school, asking to join a group assignment, only to be met with frightened stares.

"Don't tell me this little lady is too intimidating for you?" Felix taunts. Still no one steps forwards. "Well, no wonder you were able to steal Brawn away from these ladies who are clearly too *chicken* to fight for his attention." Felix wraps his arm around me. "How about any men? Any men out there wanting some action in the arena with *her*? I can't guarantee Brawn won't break your neck for it later … but—"

I grab the mike, holding it up to my mouth. "I'm pretty sure I could take care of that myself, Felix," I say, my voice laced with cockiness, ready for a fight. Right now, I want to punch Jonas and Cade out, but I'll settle for punching someone else instead.

"Ooh, did you hear that? Someone's just begging to be taken

down a notch."

"I'll do it," comes a deep, slurring voice near the front of the stage. A group of rowdy males are pushing a guy towards the steps.

Felix leans in, whispering into my ear, "Might need to go easy on this one. He already looks a little wasted."

"Yeah. Just a tad."

"Are you any good, anyway? I heard you almost beat Ghost. That's pretty impressive," he says, still speaking quietly in my ear so now one else can hear.

"You'll just have to wait and find out," I say with an arrogant smile.

Even though I'm pissed as hell Felix said all that stuff about me being Paxton James's daughter, I know it wasn't him. No, this has Jonas and Cade written all over it.

He nods to me and I go to my corner. The average-sized drunk takes to the stage, waving to the crowd as if he's on a float in a parade.

"Only a few minutes before bets close, people. Who's going to win? This guy … uh … what's your name?" Felix leans in to the guy.

"Uh … umm … Knox," he stammers.

"Well, there's a fake name if I ever heard one. Who's going to win? Heatwave or … *Knox*," he says his name in a dismissive, mocking tone. "The newbie fighter or the drunk man. Then again, no one has seen Heatwave in action yet. She might suck at fighting. Knox here though, he looks pretty sturdy … maybe."

Felix reaches over and tries to push Knox over in a playful manner. Knox wasn't expecting it, and being a little drunk, he stumbles a bit, but not far.

"Yeah. You'll do," Felix says.

I was told this would happen. Felix is stalling for time. Betting is open before an opponent is chosen, but hardly anyone will take it because it's risky—they don't know what the challenger looks like or what their ability is.

As soon as an opponent is chosen, the bookies' jobs get frantic. People only have a few minutes to sort their bets. Experienced punters will know which bookies to approach—who gives the better odds, who favours men versus women. I was told that because I'm a woman, unless another woman challenged me, the odds would most likely go in the challenger's favour. Even with the drunkenness. Especially with the drunkenness, actually. Having a few drinks numbs the senses; they generally can't tell when they're in pain so they keep going, even if their coordination is a little off.

Sasha's tried to explain the maths of it all, how odds are worked out, how much gets paid out and each cut. I lost her pretty quickly, and I still don't understand most of it.

Felix takes Knox to his corner, still bantering with the audience, playing up the fight.

"What about this ability of yours? Want to show us what Heatwave's up against?"

"Uh … okay." Knox starts to take his shirt off.

"Whoa, getting naked is your ability?"

"Just wait," Knox says, right before flexing his bicep. Without warning, his chest grows from average to almost double its size. His arms follow suit and then the rest of him, and suddenly I'm looking at someone who'll give Brett a run for his money in the muscle department.

Oh, crap!

"Might want to adjust those odds," Felix mutters to the crowd, no doubt giving the bookies an order.

I stand patiently in my corner, trying to regain some of my confidence that just took a major blow.

"Nuka," I hear a yell from the ground below.

Brett's on the side of the arena at my feet. I kneel down so I can hear him over the crowd.

"What?"

"Are you okay?" he asks.

"I'm ready. He's not that much bigger than you. I can take him." *I think.*

"I know. But are you *okay?* I seriously didn't know he was going to bring up the dad thing."

"Oh, that. I'll be fine. Just make sure you get me to Cade and Jonas as soon as this fight's over."

"Done."

"Okay, lovebirds," Felix says into the microphone. "Geez, turn my back for two seconds and she's already trying to escape into the arms of her boyfriend."

Exaggeratedly, I roll my eyes at him with my hands on my hips.

"Bets are now closing, fighters take your stance."

We meet in the middle of the arena, and it looks as though Knox is sweating bullets.

"Scared?" I ask, my tone mocking.

"Of you?" he scoffs.

"Oh, so you usually sweat this much?"

"It's hot in here, okay?" he slurs.

After a couple more minutes of waiting around for the bets to close, there's a loud ding of the bell that indicates the clock is ticking. When Knox doesn't make a move, I wave for him to come closer. "Come on. Time to hit me."

This whole cocky act is kind of fun. When Cade told me I had to be confident and arrogant in the ring, I wasn't sure if I could pull it off. *"Fake it 'til you make it,"* she said. Whether it's the crowd chanting "Heatwave" over and over again, the fact that my giant opponent looks terrified of me, or maybe it's just the adrenaline giving me arrogance I need, I feel ready for this fight.

About a full minute goes by where we walk circles around each other, trying to suss each other out.

Knox finally charges towards me, but I'm too quick and easily step out of his way. I think his intention was to knock me on my ass. He quickly turns and tries to attack me from behind, but I elbow him in the face before he reaches me.

Stumbling backwards, he grabs hold of his nose and swears under his breath.

It takes about another minute for him to gain his composure back. He advances on me again, but I dodge his fist by ducking to my left and kicking out my right leg to meet his stomach.

It's clear he has the muscles, but he doesn't have the training.

While he's still hunched over, I turn and land a heated left hook to his cheek and then a quick jab with my right hand into his throat.

At this moment, he decides he needs to grow again. He's grabbing for his throat and trying to breathe, but suddenly he's even bigger than he just was. He's well over seven foot tall and wider than a friggin' doorway.

Stumbling back in awe, I'm briefly overcome by fear. The crowd, which I'd basically blocked out until now, distracts me with their screams just long enough to not see the burly fist coming.

My body slams into the ground as an excruciating pain takes over my jaw and neck, but I know I need to get back up or this fight is over.

Rolling out of the way, I scramble into a crouched position before swinging my leg out, kicking Knox's legs out from under him. He loses his balance and falls backwards as I get to my feet completely.

I know I should kick him while he's down—it's what they'd want me to do, but I just can't bring myself to do it.

Being so big, he struggles to get back up. By the time he does, the buzzer dings.

"Saved by the bell," I mutter.

Round one down. Two more to go.

We each go to our respective corners for a breather, and I notice Knox has reduced himself to regular size. He's still trying to catch his breath, and he even looks a bit wobbly on his feet. He's pale, and I start to wonder if he's going to be okay.

Brett hands me a bottle of water from below. As I take a sip, my jaw locks and feels tight, pain radiating down the left side of my neck from where he punched me. The rest of me is still raring to go, so much so, the plastic bottle I'm holding begins to melt under my heat.

"Oops," I say, dropping it to the ground.

I know I won that round, but I need to make sure I'm not distracted again in these other two. If one punch could hurt me this badly, I can't let him get another one in.

The two-minute break feels like it's only thirty seconds. There's another ding, and we're up again.

Knox is struggling. He's back to gigantor size, but it's obvious by the look on his face that he's straining to maintain it. I can use this to my advantage.

Round two moves swiftly and without much of a challenge. I get in a few great punches before Knox even has the chance to retaliate. His movements are slowed down now he's a giant, and I'm pretty quick on my feet, so I manage to duck, weave, and escape most of his attempts. When he does finally connect, the laws of gravity seem to disappear as I go flying across the arena. I land with a thud, but I get back on my feet, albeit struggling a bit.

Knox starts transitioning down a notch. He's back to Brett's size and really isn't looking too good. He's wobbly, a little disoriented, and looks like he could pass out … or vomit. I think I can knock him out if I get a good punch in. A little voice in my head tells me to go easy. They don't want us knocking out volunteer challengers.

When the bell rings, ending the second round, I walk to my corner. When I turn around, Knox is on his knees in the middle of the arena, grabbing at his chest and shrinking back to his everyday size.

Rushing over to him, I help him to lie down.

"Are you okay?" I ask.

He nods. "Yeah. It just takes a lot out of me. I … I don't think I can transition again, and there's no way I can beat you as I am. I didn't think a girl could hit so hard." He laughs and then starts coughing.

"Take a breather, and we'll see how you are in a few minutes."

Standing, I make my way over to Felix who jumps up onto the platform. "He's not sure he can go on," I tell him.

Felix goes to talk to Knox and is then suddenly announcing my win.

"Ladies and gentlemen, we have just experienced history here tonight. In just two rounds, Heatwave has managed to wipe her opponent out. Knox, my boy, you fought hard, but it seems we have a feisty new Litmus fighter on our hands. *Heatwave!*"

Really? Just like that, it's over? I won?

The crowd cheers as medics rush the stage to tend to Knox. Brett jumps in the arena, quick to come to my side to hold my hand up, victorious.

He lets me have my time in the spotlight before dragging me off the stage where we're escorted by security back to the employee quarters. When we get into the outer corridors, Brett lets go of my hand. "Look at you! I knew you could do it. And you barely broke a sweat," he says, slapping me on my shoulder. His excitement is a little overwhelming.

"You're exaggerating, because I feel gross. I'm covered in sweat, and I'm not entirely sure it's all mine." *Eww.*

"Want to have a shower before I take you upstairs?"

"Nope. I want to rip Cade and Jonas apart right now."

He stops walking and turns to face me. "You have every right to be angry, but you may want to tread carefully with them."

"I just won them a lot of money, they can hear what I have to say."

He doesn't say any more, just leads me upstairs to the corporate box. When we walk in, all heads turn to us. There's people smiling at me all round, raising their drinks and congratulating me as we make our way through the crowd. Jonas and Cade are by the windows that overlook the arena. Locking eyes with them, I nod my head in the direction of their office, and they follow us, letting us in.

"You really should have showered before coming up here, Nuka," my mother chides.

"Well, you shouldn't have told everyone who I am."

"We probably should've asked you firs—"

"No, we shouldn't have," Jonas says, cutting her off. "It's part of her image, her brand. The daughter of Paxton James has come to the dark side to seek vengeance. You can't make this stuff up!"

"But it is made up. He's not the reason I'm here. *She* is," I say, pointing at Cade. "I didn't want anything to do with the political world. I grew up in it, remember? It's why I'm setting my charity up in *your* name. I don't want to be associated with them. Not to mention I had to come up with a stupid stage name to protect my identity, and you just go and throw it in everyone's faces."

"No one knows your real name," Cade says. "The only information made public is that Paxton had a daughter, your name was kept out of it. We made sure of it. I didn't even know your name and I'm your mother."

"It wouldn't be too hard for someone to do some digging," I say through gritted teeth.

"This isn't a big deal, Nuka," Jonas says.

"Maybe not for you. My whole life I've been the daughter of assassinated presidential candidate Paxton James. I wanted to come here and be someone else, be my own person. Why aren't I known for being Cade's daughter? The daughter of Deakin?"

"It doesn't have the same ring to it," Jonas says simply.

"I don't friggin' care. I don't want my dad to be part of my marketing strategy."

"Nuke," Brett interrupts. "You've said your piece. How about I take you down to get showered."

When I turn to give Brett a death stare, he looks sheepish, boyish even. How can someone so tough be so weak when it comes to Jonas and Cade?

"Brett's right. You've said your piece, we'll take it into consideration, but you can't come up here demanding things, young lady. We've been more than fair—"

"We'll give it some thought," Cade says, interrupting Jonas in a more calming tone than his. "You did well tonight. You should go celebrate after you've showered and filled your promotional commitments up here. Just forget about the business side of things. We'll handle it, okay?"

Knowing that this conversation is over—at least from their side—I storm out of the room but not before I get one last warning from Jonas. "We know what's best. Remember that."

-15-

HEATWAVE

"Get showered, then we'll head back upstairs to talk to the important people," Brett says.

"You can tell the 'important people' to go f—"

"Nuke, it's part of your job."

I tense my jaw and let out a huff. "Fine."

Showering as slowly as I can to put off the inevitable, I eventually get out and change into skinny jeans, sparkly top, and my leather jacket. Brett's waiting for me by the door when I get out of the locker room. "If you're a good girl, I'll take you to the after party with the rest of the fighters."

"Why are you so scared of them?"

"Of who?" he asks.

"Cade and Jonas."

"Do I really have to tell you about needing this job, again? I'm starting to sound like a broken record."

"I just don't understand why you won't stand up for what you want. It's not like you're defying them by telling them you don't want to do something."

He shakes his head. "I can't risk it, Nuke. I have nothing to fall back on."

"I'm sure they wouldn't cut you loose because you state your opinion. And I'm sure you could get back on your feet if they did."

"How, by joining Shane's crew? Breaking into people's homes and selling whatever I can get my hands on?"

"Have you even tried to do anything with your degree? You could—"

He stops walking and puts up his hands. "Just stop. You have no idea what you're talking about, and I don't want to get into this with you. *Again.* Let's just go, pretend to like each other, mingle, and then I don't know about you, but I could do with a drink."

"*Pretend?* Ouch."

Brett sighs. "You know what I mean."

Brett leads me into Deakin's corporate box, placing his hand on the small of my back as any good fake boyfriend would do. He proceeds to drag me around, introducing me to stiff people in formal attire who congratulate me on both my win and for my relationship with Brawn. I have to bite my tongue to keep from sarcastically saying, *"Yes, it's a full-time job trying to hold down a man."* Ugh.

After twenty minutes of schmoozing, everyone starts congregating by the windows. Another fight has started. My face finally drops from the forced effort of having to smile.

"Now's your chance to escape—they're distracted with Taser and Slider," Brett whispers in my ear. His arm's still around me, even though the crowd has moved away from us.

"Then let's get that drink."

We sneak out, Cade catching my eye as we reach the door. She looks alarmed, but then half-smiles and gives a subtle nod, turning Jonas's arm towards her so his back is to us and he can't see us leaving.

With our obligations fulfilled … kind of … Brett walks me around the upstairs area to the opposite side of the arena, arriving at another door.

"The fighter's box," he says, opening the door.

The interior is nothing like the Deakin corporate box. It looks more like a seedy nightclub in here than a high-class lounge. Under a giant black light, everything glows in pastel. There's an unmanned bar to our right and bathrooms to our left. As we move farther into the room, there are couches strewn around the small area and a group of people huddled by the windows. At least that's the same as in Deakin—everyone's all interested in the fight.

Brett pours red drinks into glasses at the bar, offering me one.

"Are you sure you don't want me to stay sober so I can drive your drunk ass home again? How will we get there if we're both drunk?"

"I'll only have a couple."

Shrugging, I take the glowing drink from him. As I put the glass to my lips, the scent of pure alcohol fills my nostrils, making me shiver—and not in the good way.

"What is this?" I ask, wrinkling my face. "It smells like cleaning solvent."

"It's *your* drink. You proved tonight that you're a Red."

"Don't even get me started on the really poor science gimmick."

He shrugs and half-smiles. "I dunno, you seem pretty acidic to me."

Pursing my lips, I try not to smile back. "What's actually *in* the drink?"

"Vodka."

"Is there any beer?"

He laughs. "Sure."

Swapping my glass out for a bottle of beer, Brett downs my discarded drink in one go and then brings his with us as we make our way over to the window where the others are.

"Nuka!"

Brett immediately retreats to the couches a few feet away at the sound of Holly's voice. She runs from the other side of the room and throws her arms around me. Everyone else takes their eyes off the fight, and suddenly I'm surrounded by the rest of Deakin and others I'm sure I've already met, but I can't remember their names.

They're all congratulatory, patting me on the back and fist bumping me.

"You were awesome tonight," Holly says when the crowd goes back to watching the fight.

"Thanks."

The fight round ends with a loud ding, and murmurs break out amongst the fighters.

"Who won?" I ask.

"Dunno. It was close," Steve says, not taking his eyes off the arena.

"That close, huh?"

"It was one round each until that last one, and they're both still standing. I reckon it'll go to Taser, though. He got more hits in."

"So I see you've still got a hold of him," Holly says, distracting me from what's happening in the arena.

"Huh?" I ask, turning to face her.

She nods to Brett who's now joined on the couch by Ryker and Colton.

"Oh. Yeah, I guess."

"You must be really good in bed."

Did she really just say that? Out loud? "Uh … we … uh …" *No, I don't have to tell her anything.*

"Wait, what?" she exclaims. "You haven't …"

“Not like that,” I try to say, but even I don’t know what I mean.

“Not like what?”

Glancing over at Brett, my eyes scream for him to come save me. He shakes his head, slowly and firmly. I swear I can almost hear his thoughts, *“I’m not dealing with crazy tonight.”*

Sighing, I turn back to Holly. “Well, if you must know, Brett has some issues in that area. Maybe it was from whoring around all those years, but he can no longer … you know—”

“Nuke,” his voice interrupts me as he reaches my side. He looks at Holly. “She’s joking.”

Holly’s staring at us wide-eyed, and she’s clearly trying not to laugh.

“Excuse us,” Brett says, grabbing my arm and dragging me away.

“Was that hard? No pun intended.”

He shakes his head. “You’re going to be the death of me, I swear.” He tries not to smile, but his lips curve up at the edges.

“Well, if you’d just saved me when I wanted you to.”

“I’m getting another drink,” he says, walking to the little bar area.

A few more fighters approach me, Flynn being the only one I recognise. His light skin and golden hair are in complete contrast to the two guys he’s with who are both tanned with dark hair.

“Hey. These are two of my teammates. They wanted to meet you. Seb, Tao, this is Nuka … sorry, *Heatwave*,” he says mockingly.

They both offer their fists for me to bump.

“It was the best of a bad bunch of names they let me pick from.”

The three of them laugh. “Don’t worry. We all know what that’s like,” Seb says.

“Oh? What are your stage names?”

“I’m Titanium,” Seb says.

"Gemini," Tao says.

"So I'm guessing you're like some sort of man of steel type thing, and you're …?"

Flynn laughs, slapping Tao on the back. "When you go into the arena with him, you have to fight two of him."

"Note to self, avoid fighting Tao for as long as I can," I say.

"Good plan," Flynn says.

"I dunno," Ryker interrupts, joining us with Colton at his side. "I've been training with her. I reckon she could take Gemini," he says with a proud smile.

"Whoa, don't let Brett catch you flirting. That one belongs to him." We all turn towards Taser's voice. "Yes, everyone, I'm here! Victorious again."

I want to wipe the cocky smirk off his face.

Stepping forwards, he joins our little group. "I'd say we can share in the win, but it's not like the drunk you fought put up much of a fight, did he?"

"Back off, Brayden," Colton says.

"Not to mention you showed weakness by showing concern for your opponent. Have they taught you nothing?"

"Showing compassion is not a weakness." Ryker beats me to the punch. "It shows she's not heartless."

Taser leans closer to me. "I don't know how a little bitch like you has so many guys waiting in line to defend you."

I flinch at his words, not because they're hateful, and untrue—which they are—but because they've come out of nowhere. Narrowing my eyes, I glare at him. "Maybe it has nothing to do with me, and everything to do with the fact that you're a dick."

Taser chuckles as the others let out a collective "oooh." "I can't wait to get in the arena with you, little girl. They're going to need a body bag when I'm done."

Brett's gruff voice cuts through the air. "That's enough, Brayden. Go be an ass somewhere else."

"Why are you so whipped?" Taser asks Brett but doesn't take his eyes off me. "She doesn't seem all that special," he adds, roaming over me with his eyes.

"Nuke, let's just go," Brett says.

"Yeah, run away. Until next time," Taser taunts.

Brett starts dragging me away.

"What the hell is his problem?" I ask, as we start to make our way downstairs and back into the crowd.

Brett showed me the fourth entry tonight, so we have to exit through the opposite side of the building.

"I don't know. He's always been painful, but I have no idea what his deal is with you."

He holds my hand as we make our way across the main floor and through the busy bar area when a high-pitched screeching voice calls after me. "Heatwave. Heatwave!" Ignoring it, we continue on. "Nuka!"

Stopping dead in my tracks, I turn towards the voice. Only the fighters and staff are supposed to know my real name.

Has it got out already?

I'm almost knocked off my feet when I see who the voice belongs to.

"Gabby?" *Gabby from high school, Gabby?* "Last time I saw you, we were kind of wasted on a dancefloor at my birthday," I say as she hugs me. "What are you doing at Litmus?"

"Me? You're asking what *I'm* doing here? *Heatwave?*"

"That's a bit of a long story, actually."

A warm hand wraps around me from behind. "Nuke, we going?" Brett asks.

Gabby's face lights up. "Brawn!" She looks star-struck.

"Who's this?" Brett asks with a polite smile.

"Gabby. We went to school together," I tell him, not taking my eyes off her. "I still don't know why you're here … how you're here? You're …" I stop myself before saying the word "normal."

"My dad's an investor. Sometimes he lets me come. You have no idea how much I freaked out when I saw you take the stage. I tried following you backstage, but they wouldn't let me. Oh my God, this is insane." She starts jumping up and down excitedly. "And you and Brawn … Oh my God, you're so lucky. This is so awesome."

"Okay, okay, calm down, geez," I say, her smile becoming contagious.

"I never pegged you as someone who hung out with the cheerleader, peppy type," Brett says in my ear.

I nudge him with my elbow. "Shut up."

He turns to Gabby. "Is it okay if I take my girl home?"

I swear Gabby's blushing. "Uh … sure. Of course. Nuka, we'll definitely have to catch up." She leans in for another hug. "And *soon.*"

"It was good seeing you," I say politely, before turning to head out.

We make it through the rest of the crowd, getting a few more stares and people wanting to shake both our hands along the way.

"That's the only downside to parking at this club," Brett says as we get into the hallway. "We have to walk through the crowd to get out."

We make our way down the darkened hallway that leads to a tunnel, similar to the other club entrance.

I climb up the narrow stairs leading to the VIP area of Alchemy, the bar in the city. Brett follows close behind me.

"Damn," he says under his breath, but I hear it.

Stopping mid-step, I turn and look down at him below me. "What?"

He shakes his head. "I was wrong—you're not going to be the death of me, those jeans are," he says with a cheeky smile.

Continuing up the stairs, he grabs my hand as we make our way into the club.

"Want to hang out here for a bit before heading home? Get a drink without being harassed by egotistical fighters or cheerleading high school friends?"

I laugh. "Sure. But you do realise, *we're* egotistical fighters, right?"

"You maybe. I'm as down to earth as they come."

"Ha! Okay, Brawn."

"Sure thing, Heatwave."

***

"Meeting, now," Brett says, standing in the doorway to my room.

"Huh? What time is it?" I croak, rolling over in bed.

"Eight. Cade was very enthusiastic that you must be upstairs in five minutes."

I groan. "I don't wanna. What have I done wrong this time?"

"Don't know, but you don't want to piss her off by turning up late."

"Ugh," I say, my voice still coming out hoarse.

We got in late last night after staying at the bar for a few more drinks. Finding a quiet corner to hang out, we spent most of the time talking. I can't even remember what we talked about; it was one of those drivel-fuelled conversations that meant nothing but also meant everything. We weren't our misconceived perceptions of each other, we were real. He wasn't a guy from the Estates, and I wasn't a girl from a privileged childhood. We weren't Litmus fighters. We were Brett and Nuka—two people who grew up so differently and yet, as it turns out, have so much in common.

"Come on," he says, entering my room and flicking off my bed covers. "Up."

"Fine. But I'm taking this meeting in my jammies."

We head up to Cade and Jonas's office, where our last serious meeting happened. Where Brett and I became "a couple."

Walking in, I immediately regret my wardrobe choice.

"Gabby?" I ask, staring at my friend I ran into last night.

"Nice PJs," she says, laughing.

She sits next to a man I've never met, and Jonas and Cade are behind the desk.

The man stands up, reaching out his hand to shake. "Heatwave."

"Please," Cade says, "you can call her Nuka." Her smile is a little over exaggerated and is freaking me out a little.

"Nuka, I'm here to talk a deal with you," the man says.

"Deal?"

"My daughter thinks you're worth backing, and after what I saw last night, I agree with her."

"Your new sponsor," Cade says.

Gabby's dad gives me a broad smile. "So, let's talk about the Heatwave brand."

-16-

SUMMONED

Falling into a routine becomes easy. My life is simple—fight, socialise, train, repeat. The weeks fly by, and before I know it, I have six fights and six victories under my belt.

Right now, they have me fighting on a Friday night, and Brett on a Saturday. We have Sundays off to rest, and we've taken up the habit of visiting Brett's family.

Brett's been feeling guilty about letting Paddy get in too deep with Shane, and so he's promised to invest more of himself in their lives again. He thinks by visiting them weekly, Paddy will stay in line. Paddy is a pretty awesome kid for someone who's been through a lot in his short life.

I know I don't have to go with him, but it's either that or stay at home as Drake has Sundays off and I can't go anywhere without one of them by my side. Sasha's usually studying so I don't have anything else to do. Not to mention Brett's nanna is adorable, and it doesn't hurt to remind myself what I'm fighting for. *Literally.*

We train Mondays through Wednesdays and have Thursdays off to rest up for the weekend.

I'm improving with my training. Ryker and Brett are harsh, but their techniques work. I'm so far undefeated, but to be fair, nearly all my opponents have been drunk.

Tonight though, lying in medical as they check me over and bandage my injuries, I realise how close I came to my first loss.

My opponent was a girl who had friggin' claw hands. She almost scratched my damn eyes out. I closed my eyes and just hoped for the best as I blindly beat the hell out of her.

"Now you know how my back felt," Brett says with a smirk as the last cut is bandaged.

"Oh, so I can thank you for that challenger, can I? Another ex?"

The doctor clears me to be released, and I climb off the bed, taking a step closer to Brett.

He laughs. "How much of a manwhore do you really think I am? I'm joking! Geez."

"Are you though?"

He wraps his arms around me, bringing me closer to him. "I'll let you in on a little secret. I can count the amount of women I've been with on one hand. And you already know two of them. It's all an image."

"Why don't I believe you?"

"Because Brawn's image won't let you. Come on, let's go home."

He releases me from his hold and takes my hand as we walk out of Litmus and to his car, just like we do every week.

The line between us is blurring, but I can't bring myself to stop it. We find ourselves showing affection even when others aren't around. We haven't kissed in private—only for show in the arena—but we've picked up our own little habits, like just now, him wrapping his arms around me when no one's watching.

But Declan's always in the back of my mind, and I'm sure he's in Brett's too. I still haven't seen him since our run-in at the shops, and with each passing day, it's getting easier, but I still think about him.

When we arrive home, there are messages on my voicemail. Brett arranged a landline to be put in my room with my own number a while ago so I'd stop using his, but it's more of a pain in the butt than anything. I liked it better when no one could reach me.

Kicking off my shoes, I lie down on the bed and hit play on my voicemail. The first one is from Gabby, apologising for missing my fight tonight. Ever since we reconnected at Litmus, she's been to all my fights, and we've even started hanging out again like we used to in high school. She, Sasha, and I generally spend our Thursdays together shopping or hanging out here. Gabby was put on the approved list of visitors because of the whole sponsorship thing.

Declan still isn't on that list. Not that I'd invite him over, even if he were. And just as the thought of him enters my mind once more, so does his voice. On my voicemail. *How did he get my private number?*

"*Hey Nuke ...*" he sighed into the phone. "*Please don't be mad at Gabby for giving me your private number. We really need to talk. I've been trying to get a hold of you ever since I got back from the academy, but your boyfriend isn't passing on my messages.*" He has, I've just been ignoring them. "*Your uncle's looking for you. My house was your last known address, and they've been sending meeting requests for weeks now. If you keep avoiding the director of the Institute, you'll be arrested. I don't think it matters that you're his niece. Just call me back, okay? I miss you.*"

My gut clenches. I don't know if it's because of the sound of his voice that I miss so much or because my uncle has summoned me. They only do that if Immunes have been reported for suspicious activity.

Immunes used to have to go to the Institute for monthly counselling sessions. Now they're voluntary, *only* mandatory if there's some sort of issue.

Why does Uncle Drew want to see me?

"Did I just hear what I think I heard?" Brett says, coming in my room without even knocking.

Quickly sitting up, I rub my eyes as if I'm tired, trying to conceal the fact they've started to tear.

Brett stiffens, and I realise I wasn't discreet enough.

"Yeah. My uncle's requesting to see me."

"Why?" he asks defensively.

"How should I know?" I match his accusing tone.

"Call him," Brett demands.

"Right now? It's Friday night, and one o'clock AM. He's not at work."

"He's your uncle, right? Call his house in the morning, but wait for me, I need to listen in."

"Is this Brett talking? Or Cade and Jonas's lackey, head of security?"

"There's a difference?" he asks, his brows knitting together in confusion.

"There is. I like Brett. I'm not a fan of the lackey."

He tilts his head. "What if I'm being both?" He moves farther into the room, sitting across from me on my bed. "I'm concerned as to why the director of the Institute wants to see you."

"Concerned for me or for them?" I ask, pointing upstairs.

"Both." He reaches for my face, his thumb caressing my cheek. "They're not going to like this. *I* don't like it."

"Do we have to …"

"What?" He removes his hand from my face.

I shake my head. "Nothing. It was a stupid question I already know the answer to."

As I meet his gaze, his face softens. "Maybe we'll see what

he wants first before we tell them."

"Really?" I ask.

"We'll call him in the morning. You can explain that you're not avoiding him and that you've been staying at your new boyfriend's house." He winks.

"And you won't tell Jonas and Cade?"

"Not until there's something to tell them." He leans forwards, kissing my forehead and then gets up to leave. He turns as he reaches the door. "No matter what it's about, we'll work out how to get you out of it. I promise. Get some sleep."

I doubt that'll happen, but I lie back down anyway and at least try.

Yup. Not happening.

I wish I could replay the voicemail again, just to hear Declan's voice, but I don't want to hurt Brett like that.

I've been so wrapped up in Litmus lately, I've barely had time to think about Dec, and until I heard his voice tonight, I was sure I was moving on—albeit really slowly. I thought I was at least making progress.

With the exclusion of training when I'm fighting Ryker, I don't allow myself to think about him, but clearly it's not working.

Why can't I just forget about him? I shake my head at myself. Of course, I'm not going to forget about the guy who's been there for me for more than half of my life.

Then I think of Brett and how great he's been lately, and I feel terrible for even thinking about Declan like that. It feels like I'm cheating, even though I'm actually with neither of them. *How do people deal with the guilt of actual cheating?*

I highly doubt I'm going to get much sleep at all tonight.

***

Morning doesn't come fast enough, and with the lack of sleep, I think I'm going to be a walking zombie at Litmus tonight for Brett's fight.

Brett knocks on my door. "Ready to do this?"

I nod. He sits next to me on my bed as I reach for the phone.

"Hello?" a young boy's voice says.

"Hey, Micky."

"I'm Andy," he says.

I took a shot. They are twins after all. "Sorry, Andy. It's your cousin, Nuka. Do you remember me?" The twins are six, but I haven't seen them regularly since they were three.

"Umm ..." he answers. I'm guessing he's forgotten who I am.

"Is your daddy there?"

"Hang on." There's a muffling noise, and a faded "Dad," in the background.

"Drew Jacobs," my uncle says, picking up the phone.

"Hey, Uncle Drew. It's Nuka."

"So you *are* alive," he says in a playful tone.

"Of course, I'm alive. Who said I wasn't?"

"No one. It's just no one's heard from you for a while. Are you okay?"

"Is that why you're summoning me to the Institute? You thought I was missing?"

"Not missing. We're all just worried about you. You haven't spoken to your mother in five months."

"I'm twenty-one, I don't need to check-in every day."

Brett whispers in my ear, "You need to stay on his good side, Nuke. Tone down the attitude."

"Sorry, Uncle Drew. You know I'm still mad at Lia."

"I think you get your stubbornness from her."

"I'm not like h—"

"So, I need a meeting with you."

My heart beats harder in my chest at his words. "Why? I'm fine."

"I know. But I haven't seen you in a while, and I just want to make sure you're okay. In person. Where have you been staying? You really need to inform the Institute of your whereabouts, you know."

"That's the only reason you want to see me?"

"We can even do it here if you like. You don't need to make the trek to one of the Institute offices. This is purely an overprotective uncle, wanting to check on his niece—the niece he hasn't seen in a really long time."

Turning my head to face Brett, he nods.

"Okay. What time?"

"How about you come for lunch?"

Brett whispers again, "Don't forget Drake or I will have to go with you, so be polite and ask."

"Uh, can I bring my boyfriend with me?"

He's silent for a moment. "Uh, I guess. If that's what it takes to get you here, then yeah, bring him along. I for one am interested in meeting the man who stole you away from Dec …" he starts coughing. "Sorry, got something stuck in my throat. See you at lunch."

Hanging up the phone, I turn to Brett. "Do you think we have to tell Cade and Jonas?"

"Maybe after the lunch. It sounds like he genuinely just wants to know you're okay. I don't think it's an official meeting—it's at his house."

"Are you going to come with me? I know you have a fight tonight … but … I'd kind of like it if you came instead of Drake."

Brett huffs a tiny laugh. "You're certainly singing a different tune from a couple of months ago when you were begging Sasha to have Drake babysit you."

I nudge him with my elbow. "Maybe you've grown on me. Also, I just told Uncle Drew that I was bringing my boyfriend, and one fake boyfriend is all I can handle right now."

"Fake relationships are hard work. Guess we have a lunch to get ready for."

***

Walking into Uncle Drew's apartment building, I freeze up. Maybe coming here wasn't a great idea after all.

I used to live in this apartment with my father. After he died, I lived here with Lia, Jayce, and William.

Memories of growing up here flood my mind. They're all happy, and it makes me wonder how we got to how we are today—not talking to each other, keeping secrets, despising each other—then I realise, for the most part, that's all been on me.

I lead Brett to the security reception desk, giving our names to be let upstairs. Getting on the elevator, I reflexively reach for Brett's hand. He takes it and rubs it soothingly.

"It'll be okay," he whispers.

The elevator doors open to the small foyer of the giant penthouse apartment.

The twins are chasing each other around the living room, but Uncle Drew and Aunt Jenna are nowhere to be seen.

The twins are fascinating. Micky has dark brown hair like my uncle but blue eyes like my aunt, and Andy has the opposite—blond hair like Jenna but green eyes like Drew.

I often wonder how Aunt Jenna handles the twins, but then again, she'd probably know how to handle twins more than anyone because she's Jayce's twin sister.

"Hello?" I call out.

The boys stop dead in their tracks, their smiles wiped from their faces, suddenly shy and timid. Aunt Jenna walks out of the kitchen area, holding out her arms for a hug. She's giant, over six feet, so my head is basically buried in her chest when she embraces me.

"It's been too long, Nuka," she says soothingly.

"I know."

She turns to Brett. "And this is the boyfriend?" she asks, biting her lip and offering her hand.

"Yeah. This is Brett. Brett, Aunt Jenna."

She leans in and whispers in my ear. "Damn. He's super-hot."

Brett laughs, and I swear he even blushes a little.

Just like Lia, Jenna's only in her thirties and doesn't look older than twenty-five. She's also on the police force with Lia, and they were partners for a long time.

Uncle Drew finally makes an appearance. It's so weird not seeing him in a suit and tie. Wearing a hoodie and dark jeans, he looks like he's ten years younger than what he is.

It's sad when you reach an age where your aunts and uncles could pass as your friends.

"Nuka," he says, hugging me. "What happened to your neck?" he asks, pulling back a bit.

Crap! The scratches from last night. "Oh, you know, clumsy me. Walked into one of those prickly trees. I wasn't watching where I was going and it cut me up everywhere—all over my arms and everything."

"She says clumsy, but she really means drunk," Brett says with a charming smile.

Nudging him, I grit my teeth and play along. "My aunt and uncle don't want to know about that," I say, laughing.

"By all means, please fill us in on what you've been up to. Do you go out drinking often?" Uncle Drew asks.

"Has the inquisition already started? We're still standing in the entryway."

Uncle Drew grabs my hand and leads me to the couch in the living room. "Sit."

I slump down on the couch and Brett sits next to me.

"So what's this really about?" I ask as Uncle Drew sits on the opposite couch.

"I'll take the boys to the rooftop to play," Aunt Jenna says. "Give you guys the privacy you need. Brett, how good are you at playing catch? Maybe you could help me."

Brett looks to me, silently asking me what I want him to do. I nod gently and gesture for him to go upstairs. He'll still be able to hear everything we say anyway.

Brett stands, following Aunt Jenna and the twins outside.

"So?" I ask.

"The whole family is worried about you, Nuka."

"Why? I've been gone for three years, why's it any different now?"

"Because we've always known where you were. You've always been with Declan. He said you've been covered in bruises the last two times he's seen you."

Everything's suddenly clear in my mind. Declan's behind this meeting.

"This isn't an official meeting, is it? Declan put you up to this. Where is he?" I ask, glancing around me, expecting him to walk in here any minute. Butterflies fill my stomach, while my mind fills with dread. I should've brought Drake instead of Brett. I don't want him to hear this.

"He's not here," Uncle Drew says. "I told him it wasn't a good idea for him to be here when I spoke to you. He's just worried about you, we all are. He said some … alarming things."

"He's just jealous of my relationship with Brett," I try to cover.

"So you know that boy loves you more than anything in this world, and you're with Brett anyway? *Really*?" The disappointment in his tone is hard to miss.

"It's complicated. I know I haven't been the best friend I should've been these past few months, but I have a lot going on right now. I'm trying to get to know my real family. My mother, sister—"

"We're not your *real* family? The people who accepted you and raised you as our own?"

He changes from disappointed to angry in the blink of an eye.

"I don't mean it like that," I say, sheepishly.

"Do you realise how much your mother has done for you? Lia always protected you. She kept you out of the media, she protected you from the monster that was your father. She …" he stops talking, realising he's said something he shouldn't have.

"Monster?" I ask, my voice breaking.

"Oooh, she's going to kill me," he mutters, his leg jumping up and down with nerves. "But, no, you need to know who your father really was." He sighs. "He wasn't a good person, Nuka."

"So I've heard."

"Your bio mum tell you that?"

"And if she did?"

"It's just rich, coming from her," he mumbles. "Look, your dad did great things for this world, but he did them by doing unspeakable things. He embezzled money from the Institute to fund his lifestyle, conning the government into giving the Institute funding for his Immune workers, only to pocket the money himself. He starved and tortured your uncle Tate to manipulate your mother into doing his dirty work."

"I don't understand."

"Lives were lost because of what he made us do."

"*Us*?"

"A long time ago, your mother and I were agents for the Institute. When your dad took over as director, it was because we put him in that position. We led a takeover, basically stealing the Institute for ourselves. Will's dad died during the struggle, along with eight others. We thought your dad was doing it to free you and the rest of us who were forced to live at the Institute. It became pretty clear that he did it to gain political advantage. He didn't even care that lives were lost. He got what he wanted."

"But he took over the Institute for the right reasons—to free everyone." I try to justify. "Good people can do bad things to get what they want." I half-smile at the words that Brett once told me.

"His selfish motivations may have been disguised as selfless deeds, but his intentions were less than moral."

"I don't really understand why you're telling me this."

"Your dad wasn't killed by an activist group. He was killed by one of our own. Because of his manipulative ways, he ruined so many lives. People lost their family, their friends, all because of your father's needs to take over the Institute and begin his political career. He practically forced Lia into almost marrying him. He took advantage of the fact she'd lost Will's dad and made her believe he was the only one who supported her. All the while shutting the rest of us and the family out of her life. She was trying to work out how to escape from him, when he …"

"Died?" I croak.

"Did Lia ever tell you that your dad was a bad person? Did she ever try and persuade you to hate him like your bio mum obviously has?"

I shake my head slowly.

"No. She took you in despite your dad being responsible for her losing Will's father. Do you *understand* that? He was responsible for her partner's death, and she never once told you about it. Because she loves you. She never wants to see you upset, and she would never intentionally hurt you. Ever. And you've turned your back on her, on Jayce, on your brother and sister. They may not be your blood, but they're your family. I don't exactly know what's going on with you, why you're bruised all the time, or what those scratches are about, but if it has anything to do with that new boyfriend of yours, I need to know."

"It has nothing to do with him," I answer quickly. *Maybe a little too quickly.* I want to explain, but I can't. In desperation, I lean forward and grab one of the twin's colouring pens off the coffee table. "You know how Lia used to teach us self-defence, and Will and I would get out of hand …" I start rambling the same story I told Declan, while scribbling a note on a piece of paper. "Well, I started it up again, but with my biological sister. And she's frickin' brutal. Declan saw me after we'd sparred, that's all."

I hold up the note to him, which reads:

Whatever Declan told you, I can't talk about it. Brett is my bodyguard, and he has super-sensitive hearing and is listening in, but this is not a cry for help. I'm happy. But I CAN'T talk about it. There will be consequences if I do. Please understand that this is what I want. They're not forcing me to do anything I haven't volunteered myself for. Please drop this. I'm happy!!!

That last part is underlined and I added a few exclamation points.

"You realise as the director of the Institute …" he starts.

My eyes widen more, and my head starts shaking frantically.

"That any suspicious behaviour needs to be monitored, right?"

"What suspicious behaviour?" My voice trembles.

"You're shutting people out who've been there for you for nearly your whole life. We don't have your new contact information, we can't get a hold of you. It's like you've dropped off the face of the planet. It's suspicious behaviour for an Immune. All we're really asking is to be kept in the loop."

Nodding, I let out a small sigh of relief.

"You're not in any trouble. Not at all. Just … think of this as a warning. Okay?"

"Okay, Uncle Drew."

"So you'll need to give me your new contact information

before you leave this arvo, okay?" he says, as he scribbles down a note on the same piece of paper I did. He passes it to me and it reads:

This isn't over. I'm going to call you in for another meeting—an official one. Bring a different bodyguard.

"Understood."

"Now that's out of the way," he says, standing. "Lunch."

Lunch goes smoothly, and I think Brett has even won over my uncle by the end of the meal. They get into a heated discussion over the Estates and what they've become, but Uncle Drew is open to hearing Brett's opinion and even asks Brett what he thinks should be done about it. Drew says he wants to help change the way things are, but it's difficult with the funding and political side of everything. It doesn't feel like he's making excuses. He seems genuinely unsure of how to fix things.

"So …" Brett says as we get back in the car to go home.

"So," I reply.

"Your uncle is pretty cool."

"Yeah, he is."

"Your dad kind of sounded like he was a sociopath, though."

"I'm kind of not surprised after what Cade told me."

"And you're okay with that?"

I shrug. "No, but I don't know what I can do about it. He's gone, and for the better it seems. It does make me wonder though …"

"Wonder what?"

I throw my head back on the headrest of my seat. "There's things I know I should feel guilty about, but I don't. All those things Uncle Drew said to me? I know abandoning my younger brother and sister was wrong, but I did it anyway. And the scary part is, I don't feel all that bad about it. I miss them, but I don't feel guilty. I feel a little bad, but it's not like I've made the effort to go and see them, even though I've wanted to. Maybe my dad's lack of conscience is hereditary. I'm certainly not going to learn any moral values from Cade. She encourages her own daughters to dress skanky so they can earn more money for her."

"You're out of your mind if you think you're anything like either of them. You're giving the majority of your wage to charity."

"Yes, and I earn that money by physically hurting other people. Something else I should probably feel bad about."

"We're not forced to do it, Nuke. Everyone is there for a different reason, but we're all there voluntarily. We know what we signed up for."

"Are you all there voluntarily, though?"

He stiffens in his seat, his jaw tightening.

"Like you said, the only other option you have is to join Shane."

"But it's another option. We all have choices, and you didn't have to choose to give away the money you earn, but you did it anyway, and for no other reason than you want to help people. I'd say growing up with Allira Daniels did that. Just because your biological parents aren't exactly winners, that doesn't mean you're destined to turn out like them. In fact, you can make the choice to make sure you don't."

"You make it sound so easy."

"It's really that easy, Nuke. You just have to decide to be different."

-17-

KNOCKED OUT

"Word on the street is if you knock out your volunteer tonight, Cade and Jonas are planning on graduating you from the little fish pond," Colton says, wrapping his arm around my shoulders.

"And get fed to you sharks? Dunno if I'm ready for that yet. And who says 'word on the street,' nowadays? You weirdo."

"Who says 'nowadays'? You know what they say—you are who you hang with."

"Yeah, but they pay me to hang out with you, so what does that make me?"

"The luckiest girl in the world?" He kisses my head and then shakes his butt, dancing his way out of the locker room.

Shaking my head at him, I can't help smiling. I haven't been fighting for long, but the team has seriously made me feel welcomed.

Ryker's awesome and the one I spend the most time with—other than Brett. Colton and Steve are a laugh, and we're always goofing off. Palmer's the only one I haven't really spent much time with. A part of me thinks he actually believes I stole Brett off him. That boy is one delusional puppy.

"Hey." Brett's voice comes from the doorway.

"Hey," I say, trying to act cool, but my voice comes out breathy, and my face reflexively lights up. *Traitorous face.* "Is it true? Jonas and Cade want me to knock my opponent out tonight? I thought they didn't like that with volunteers."

"Minus your debut fight, you've gone three rounds with all of your challengers. It's time they get taught a lesson." The cocky smile that looks so perfect on him appears.

"I can try …"

He closes the gap between us and puts his hands on my shoulders. "Do this last test, and you're truly one of us. Welcome to the big leagues."

"Gee, way to make a girl feel nervous."

"I have faith." He moves his head teasingly close to mine. All I want him to do is move that little bit closer and touch his lips to mine. "Let's go," he whispers.

"Uh-huh."

Neither of us makes a move.

He raises one of his hands to cradle my face, his eyes boring into mine. They seem unsure, but I know my eyes are begging for him to kiss me.

The door swings open. "You're up, buttercup," Colton yells.

We pull away quickly from each other, and Brett grabs my hand and walks me out, both of us pretending like something didn't just nearly happen.

I shake my head. It's so ridiculous. We've made out so many times now. We're about to make out again—it's become a ritual, a good luck kiss before a fight—and yet, I'm getting flustered about being close to him in the locker room? *Really?*

The whole team hasn't escorted me to the stage since that first night, but at least two of them do every time I fight. Then they're flanked by security guards. I know it should make me feel stupid, needing an escort to an arena where the main objective is to fight, but the escort makes me feel powerful and confident.

As I walk up to the stage, my stomach flutters with anticipation. I don't know what's come over me tonight, but I'm excited to kiss Brett for the thousandth time.

Our bodies draw in close, and he cradles my face in his hands, the anticipation building. My breath hitches in my throat. He leans in and his lips touch … my forehead.

What the?

He bounds down the stairs and out of sight before I even have a chance to start breathing again.

Felix joins me on stage, but it's all a blur. Staring straight ahead, I wait numbly in confusion for my opponent to volunteer.

Forget Brett, I tell myself, but there's a louder nagging voice in the back of my head asking, *Why didn't he kiss me?*

I try to focus on this impending fight, reminding myself I need my head in the game. If I can prove myself this one last time, I'll be earning more money and making my way up. I'll finally get this charity off the ground. We decided to have some backing before announcing it to everyone.

A man of average build, probably in his late thirties, steps forward to take his place in the volunteer corner. Felix talks to him, but it's always the same bantering, same recycled jokes, and I don't listen anymore.

I do take notice when he rips his shirt off, tearing the material like it were paper, making his bulging muscles now visible.

Ah, shit.

"And what else do you have in store for us?" Felix asks. "Apart from your impressive muscles."

"I'd like to keep that a secret, thanks."

Can he do that?

"Whoa, a blind match, ladies and gentlemen. This hasn't

happened in years!"

I recall Brett briefly mentioning something about blind matches once, but he said it was so rare I wouldn't have to worry about it.

From what I remember of the conversation, if a volunteer refuses to show their ability before the fight, the odds will go in their favour because it generally means they have an extreme advantage they don't want giving away too soon.

"Heatwave, do you accept this challenge?"

Brett also told me the Litmus fighter assigned to the Wild Card night has the right to refuse a blind match, allowing another willing fighter to take their spot.

But I have to do this. I'm so close to getting what I want—more fights, and money for my charity.

"I accept," I say, raising my hand for a fist bump from my challenger.

He folds his arms across his chest, staring down at my hand with disgust.

"Oooh," Felix says into the mike. "Disrespect in the arena here tonight! Should make for an interesting fight. What has Heatwave gotten herself into?"

What, indeed.

The first round starts, and we dance around for a bit, trying to feel each other out. There's no doubt in my mind that I'm facing an experienced fighter. I can tell by the way he moves, the way he's assessing me.

As much as I'm psyching myself out right now, I have to take on this challenge. If I can't beat this average-looking guy, how am I going to go up against any of the other Litmus fighters? I just need one knockout to qualify.

Advancing on my opponent—I didn't pay attention to his name—he's ready for every one of my moves. Blocking, ducking, weaving, he's anticipating everything.

He hasn't tried to hit me yet, but he's looking at me like I'm his dinner. He's ready to attack, he's just waiting for the perfect time.

The look in his eye is a little crazed, and it's freaking me out.

Where the hell did this guy come from?

The clock's running down, and neither of us have really got any hits in. I've thrown a few, but he's blocked them all.

Finally, he starts advancing. His fists are fast. Insanely fast. Blocking his first two approaches, I'm unable to go for a third. He connects with my jaw, a loud crack reverberating through the whole venue.

Did my bones seriously just make that noise?

Ignoring the pain, I go low, attempting to attack his abdomen and chest, but an uppercut flies at me, knocking me backwards.

As I stumble, he's on me again within a millisecond. He grabs me around my throat, slamming me onto my back on the ground.

Landing with a loud thud, I let out a shrill scream as he climbs on top of me. One of his knees grinds my right forearm into the ground, his other knee crashing into my ribs. With his hand still on my throat, I focus on burning him, making him release me.

I roll him off me and press my burning hands into his neck and chest.

The buzzer dings seconds after I regain control, making me curse under my breath.

Struggling to my corner, I'm terrified this guy might have me beat. At least in that round.

I sit on the ground in my corner of the ring as Brett reaches my side on the main floor, passing me up a water bottle.

"Are you okay?" he yells.

I nod and wince at the same time.

"Something's not right. He's … he knows you."

"What do you mean?" My voice is breathless. I lean towards him to hear better.

"You have a tell. You're a person of routine. I could anticipate what moves you'd make after fighting with you for a few weeks," he says, talking super-fast. "He's studied you. He knows your moves. How does he know your moves?" Now it seems like he's talking more to himself.

"What do I do?"

"There's nothing you can do. Apart from breaking your routine. Your strategy."

"So, get all random on his ass."

Brett smiles. "One way of putting it."

"Got it."

"Nuke, be careful. I have a bad feeling about—"

The second round buzzer dings.

Standing, I take my stance across from my adversary. Using Brett's advice, I try to swing randomly, use different techniques and go out of order of what I normally would. But I'm a creature of habit, and throwing my routine off is throwing off my balance.

Keeping my guard up, I'm doing everything I can to try to keep him off my face which he seems so fond of messing up right now.

When he finally moves on from there, pain shoots down my left side. When he kneeled on my ribs during round one, I think he did some damage. Now he's targeting that area, like he knows it's the place to hit.

He takes a step back, and I finally think he's easing up on me when he takes a good, square hit to my gut and then another to my jaw.

And now I'm coughing up blood.

I freak out for a second, thinking he's caused internal bleeding. I'm relieved to find out it's coming from my mouth, but he's friggin' knocked a tooth out. *Bastard!*

Motivated by revenge, and remembering to go random, I throw myself at him with precision and determination.

But his fists don't give a damn about my determination as they beat me into submission with each blow.

The buzzer for the second round dings, and I struggle to even limp my way to my corner.

This time, Brett jumps into the ring.

"Nuke," he says getting in my face.

My vision's blurry, my head wobbling. "What?" I whine.

"Nuke, Look at me," he says, holding my head in his hands.

"I am."

"Shit. Nuke, you're not going to make it another round."

"Oh, I'll make it," I slur.

He purses his lips. "You're in a bad way."

"Yup," I agree, putting extra emphasis on the "P" sound. I'm thinking now would be a great time for a nap.

"No! Stay awake. Baby, I need you to stay awake."

I smile. "You called me baby."

"Yeah … I did."

"You don't do that nearly enough."

He half-smiles but shakes his head. "Nuke—"

"Baby," I correct him.

"You need to end this. The next time he punches you, hit the deck, and stay down."

I grimace. "I can't do that. That's like … cheating, giving up."

"Nuke …"

"Nah-uh."

He rolls his eyes. "Baby. You need to, or he'll end you. Do you understand?"

"I'm not taking a dive," I say, determined to make it through this next round.

As the bell dings and I make my way back into the arena, it doesn't matter what I want to do because my body doesn't cooperate.

After a quick, swift punch to my head, I succumb to darkness anyway.

***

My breathing is staggered, my lip trembling as I try to take in stilted breaths. Attempting to roll to my side, a sharp pain shoots throughout my entire left side, and I scream out in agony.

"Nuka," Brett's soft voice distracts me.

Opening my eyes, I'm blinded by the overhead lights of the infirmary at Litmus. My head pounds, an ache forming behind my left eye.

I lift my right hand to my forehead; it's covered in plaster.

"Wha—" my voice is hoarse and gravelly, my throat dry and painful.

Brett grabs hold of my left hand. "Nuka, do you know where you are?"

"I may be broken everywhere else, but my brain still works," I choke out.

He laughs. "Glad to see he didn't beat the attitude out of you."

"Nuka," a sobbing girly voice says.

My eyes meet Sasha's as she stands at the end of my bed.

"I'm fine. Really." *Okay, even I know I'm lying.* "So what happened? I mean … I remember the guy, and losing … Dammit, he knocked me out, didn't he?"

"And broke your wrist, cracked two of your ribs … and …" Brett grabs a mirror and holds it up. My left eye is a little swollen, but it has been worse before. The most damage is a bruised jaw and neck. "It probably hurts to talk. He almost … he tried to …"

"Kill me? Is that what you're trying to say?"

He nods.

"A bit extreme, but isn't that the point of the game? So he won. He'll become one of us, right?"

Brett purses his lips. "Yeah, that's happening. But something's not right. He knew to attack your left side. He knows you were injured there a few weeks ago. I don't know what's going on, but I'm going to find out. The way he knew you—"

"He's probably just been to my fights before. Hell, our banner has a photo of me with a giant bruise down my left side. It was clear he was an experienced fighter. Maybe he just saw this as an easy way in, instead of trying out or negotiating with the owners."

"Maybe."

"Nuka," Sasha says again.

"What?"

"Are you going to be okay?"

"I'm fine, Sash. My ego's a little bruised, though," I laugh … well, cough. "I really thought I was going to get my first knockout tonight."

"Well, you did, in a way," she says with a small smile.

"So, broken wrist and ribs, hey? That sounds painful—"

"You're on some pretty awesome painkillers," Brett answers.

"When do I fight again?"

"Six weeks," he says.

"Six?" I throw my head back on the pillow … slowly. "That sucks." I was hoping to move up tonight, not take a step back. "When can I go home?"

Brett and Sasha share a look. "How are you feeling?" he asks.

"Is that a trick question? It feels like I got the crap kicked outta me."

"Brett wanted to take you to the hospital," Sasha says softly.

"Mum and Jonas wouldn't allow it. We'd feel better if you at least stayed here with one of the onsite doctors."

Rolling my eyes before my body screams at me not to, I just shake my head. "Just take me home."

They both reluctantly agree and help me up, the bed paper crinkling underneath me and falling to the floor. The walk to the door of the infirmary is slow going. My ribs on my left side are broken so I lean on Brett on my right, my whole left side hanging limp. Colton and Ryker are waiting outside the door when we get out into the corridor.

"Holy shit, Nuka," Colton says, covering his mouth with his hand.

Ryker's staring at me with narrowed eyes. "You weren't focusing."

I half-laugh. "Already with the lecturing? You don't think you could wait until I was at least able to train again?"

He throws his hands up in surrender.

Movement behind him catches my eye. Taser's coming down the hallway, dressed casually in jeans and a tight T-shirt. "Aww, someone get a little hurt?" he asks, his condescending tone hitting me like another punch in the face.

"What are you doing here, Brayden? It's not your fight night," Brett says.

"I can't come support my team? Chi's fighting tonight, you know." He has a weird smirk on his face, and his words are laced with menace.

"Colt," Brett says, gesturing to take his place next to me, holding me up. Taking a step towards Taser, Brett crosses his arms over his chest. "No. You can't. Well, you can, but you never do. What are you doing here, Brayden?"

"You set this up," I accuse, realising what Brett's implying.

"Now, now, no one likes a sore loser."

Brett grabs Taser by the shirt, pushing him sideways, crushing him into the wall. "What are you playing at?" he spits at him.

"Save it for the arena, *Brawn.* I'm not saying the little bitch didn't get what she deserved, but you can't prove anything. You can't touch me. Jonas and Cade wouldn't like that very much, would they?"

Brett lets Taser go, taking a few steps backwards.

Taser tsks, "No, we wouldn't want to upset them." He straightens his shirt, standing up straighter. "See you tomorrow night, Brett. Looking forward to it." He walks off, leaving the rest of us standing there not really knowing what to do with ourselves.

"Tomorrow night?" I ask when Taser's out of sight.

"I'm scheduled to fight him," Brett answers. "Come on. Let's get you home."

-18-

RECOVERY

"Sash, help Nuka into my room," Brett orders, as we walk painfully slow down the hall.

"Where are you going to sleep?" I ask, confused.

"I'm not leaving you tonight. You might have a concussion, you might pass out again, the list of 'mights' is endless. You're stuck with me, okay?"

"If this is your way of trying to get into my pants, I have to say, your timing isn't great. I'm a little too sore for that."

Sasha laughs, and Brett just shakes his head at me. We get to his room, and Sasha helps me over to the bed.

"Can I take a shower?" I ask.

"Yeah, but you can't get your arm wet. I'll help you," Sasha volunteers.

"I'm pretty sure I can do it myself."

"Lift your arm to shoulder height," she orders.

I lift my right arm easily.

"Other one, smartass."

Yeah, okay, she has me there. It hurts to lift my arm with my cracked ribs. "Fine. Just go get me some pyjamas and bring them in here." Sasha leaves to fetch me my clothes, and Brett looks about as horrible as I feel. "I can sleep in my own room. You don't have to—"

"He did this because of me," he says, not making eye contact.

"What?"

"It's my fault you're in pain."

His eyes meet mine just as Sasha comes back in with clothes and a plastic bag. Averting my gaze from Brett, I struggle to stand as Sasha helps me into the bathroom. She starts wrapping my cast in the plastic, making sure it's as airtight as it can get, before turning the shower on for me.

After awkwardly showering, with my sister helping me the whole time—undressing me and washing me in places no sister should ever have to—she dresses me and takes me back to Brett's bedroom, laying me down on his bed.

"I'll come by in the morning to help you, okay?"

"I'll be fine by then, I'm sure of it." I let out a sad laugh. "I almost got that out with a straight face."

As soon as Sasha's out the door, I'm glaring at Brett.

He takes his shoes off, removes his shirt, climbs into bed next to me, removes his jeans under the covers, and chucks them on the floor.

"Okay, spill … wait … are you nak—"

"Calm down, I'm wearing boxers." He rolls on his side to face me.

"You just didn't want me to see your scrawny legs?"

"I *do not* have scrawny legs."

"Why did you say he did this because of you?" I ask, the conversation suddenly serious.

His smile fades. "That fight. The first night you came to watch us … It was only an exhibition fight. Flat rate, no betting, no percentage, just basic flat-rate pay. I thought it was weird that he asked me to …" He sucks on his top lip, biting down so hard I wonder if he's breaking skin.

"Asked you to what?"

"I threw the fight," he practically whispers.

"What? Why?"

"Brayden offered me more money, and I needed it. At the time, I thought it was weird, too good to be true, but I was too focussed on getting my family out of the Estates. It wasn't a proper fight. Betters weren't going to miss out on money if I took a dive. I couldn't see the catch. But now …"

"He wants you to do it again? For real this time?"

"Yup. And he's threatening to tell everyone what I've already done. By getting me to agree to the exhibition fight, he backed me into a corner. I think tonight was a warning for what'll happen if I screw him over."

"Maybe," I ponder, pursing my lips.

"You don't think so?"

"Well, I guess it makes sense. But you also have to remember that he can't expose you without exposing himself, right? So if he hired that guy to fight me tonight, it was just a scare tactic. He'd have to be bluffing, because if you go down, he'll go down."

"I'm sorry you're in pain because of me."

"You didn't do this, Brett. Who knows, Taser might've had nothing to do with this. Maybe it was just a coincidence."

"If he wasn't there tonight, I'd be inclined to agree with you, but he *never* comes to fight night unless he's on."

Starting to get uncomfortable in the position I'm in, I try to roll onto my side, but I can't move without gasping in pain.

Brett sits up and leans over me. "Are you okay?"

"Yeah, just trying to get comfortable."

"Did you want more painkillers?"

"There's more? Gimme!"

He laughs, reaching over to his side table, and then hands over a glass of water and two pills.

Swallowing them down, I hand back the water and wait for them to kick in. “Thank you for staying with me.”

“Anything for you, baby.”

“Baby?” I laugh.

“Oh, so you only like to be called that when you’re out of it and about to pass out from pain?” He smirks.

I laugh even more remembering our conversation on the side of the ring. “Oh, yeah. I forgot about that.”

“You were pretty out of it. Now make sure you stay over on your side of the bed.”

“Of course, because right now it’d be so easy for me to jump you. Considering I can’t even roll on my side, I think you’re safe.”

“I’m more worried about what *I’d* do if you came near me,” he mutters, rolling over and putting his back to me.

Even though I’m in an enormous amount of pain, I can’t wipe the smile off my face.

***

“Kill me,” I grunt. “So. Much. Pain.”

Brett sits up, handing me more water and more pills.

“Thanks.”

“Is there anything I can do?” he asks, taking the water from me and lying back down beside me.

“Yeah, win.”

“What?”

"Tonight, against Taser. Put that bastard in a coma."

He smiles. "I would, but I'm not going in tonight. I called Ryker this morning, asked him to take my spot."

"Good. Ryker can put him in a coma then."

"So you're thinking it *is* Taser's fault now?"

"Maybe. Okay, yeah, it probably is. But why's Ryker really taking your place? It's not because of me, is it? You don't have to stay here, I'll be fine on my own."

"It *is* because of you, but not because of the reason you're thinking. I decided I need to call his bluff. Plus, I put it to Cade and Jonas that it would look insensitive of me to fight when my girlfriend's at home, injured."

He's called me his girlfriend a thousand times, but this time when he said it, it sounded natural. *Real.*

"So you're just going to babysit me all weekend?"

"How is that any different to what I already do?"

"Hmm, true."

There's a knock at the door, followed by Cade entering the room. Brett sits up, moving away from me. She takes one look at me, her face ashen. "Oh, Nuka, honey. You look …"

"Terrible? I know. I don't feel too great, either."

"Is there anything I can do for you?" she asks.

"I think Brett has it sorted." I throw him a smile. He, however, is scowling at Cade.

"Well, I just thought I'd come down here and let you know … that man, the one you fought, he was all set to sign with Holt—"

"Taser's team? Really?" I shoot Brett a knowing glance.

"But it turns out, he's not Immune."

"What?" Brett asks.

"He's normal? What is he, some kind of fighting robot? Please tell me he's not human."

"I'm sorry. But the good news is he's no longer with us," Cade says.

My brow furrows. "They killed him?"

Cade starts laughing. "No, dear. He's banned from fighting, and from Litmus."

"Oh, sorry. I think these painkillers are making my brain fuzzy."

"Sure they are, dear."

Was she just being condescending?

"Make sure you rest up, okay?" she says before leaving.

"He was normal?" I say more to myself than to Brett.

"Probably just adding insult to the injury. Your badass rep will be tainted now by the fact you were beaten by someone who's normal."

"How could he have been normal? He was a frickin' machine."

"If I had to guess, I'd say Brayden sought him out for his talents. He did it on purpose."

"But we can't prove it?"

Brett shakes his head. "No. We can't."

***

After four days of lying in this bed, I'm now able to move around and shower by myself—slowly and carefully. Sasha's been a saint, and Brett even more so. Cade came to check on me that first day, and that's all. It really pisses me off that she doesn't seem to care I'm majorly injured, but I guess I can't say I'm surprised.

Climbing into bed after a shower, I'm shivering. It's freezing in here, and I couldn't even get the water hot enough to warm me. I know something's wrong.

"Brett," I whisper. I don't know where he's gone, but I know he's still on the grounds somewhere. "Brett," I say a little louder, doubling the blanket over me and curling into a ball.

"I'm here," he says, entering the room. "What's wrong?"

"So cold," I say, my teeth chattering.

"Cold?" He approaches me, feeling my forehead with the back of his hand. A sizzling noise fills my ears as Brett snatches his hand away, shaking it off as if I've burnt him. "You're burning up. Literally. You just almost set my hand on fire."

"I'm sick? I don't feel like I have a flu or anything."

"You probably have an infection. We need to take you to the hospital and get a proper diagnosis." He pulls the blanket off my shivering body, lifting my shirt to expose my ribs. "Shit!" He walks around to his side of the bed, frantically grabbing his shoes and putting them on.

I'm wondering what has him so freaked out until I look down at my side. It's practically black.

"You need a doctor, Nuke. You need one, like, yesterday." He rushes over to the phone, picking it up and dialling a single number, I guess to phone upstairs to Cade's room. "She's got an infection. I'm taking her to the hospital … No, I'm taking her … You're not listening to me. She has a fever, her entire side is black, she could have internal bleeding … Fine." He slams down the phone. "Your mum's on her way down."

She arrives a few minutes later. "Nuka, how are you feeling?"

My lips are trembling from the cold. "Freezing."

She looks at Brett. "Give her some meds, wait for the fever to come down, and see how she is then."

"Cade—"

"Do as you're told."

He storms into the bathroom, and a few seconds later, there's a loud slam of the cabinet doors.

"You'll be fine," Cade says in a soothing voice. "He's just overreacting because he's worried about you. He really cares about you, you know."

"Uh …" I don't know what to say to that.

Brett re-enters the room, handing me different pills than the painkillers he's been giving me. "I've got it from here," he says to Cade.

"Let me know if anything else develops," she says, making her way back to the door.

Brett checks my fever again as she leaves.

"They're not going to work that quickly," I say, swatting his hand away.

He lies down next to me, gently pulling me into him. "I'll keep you warm."

"Don't. I'll burn you."

"I don't care."

With his arm draped over me, I succumb to sleep quickly.

After what feels like a couple of minutes later, he's shaking me awake.

"Nuke, let's go," Brett says.

"What?" I grumble, not opening my eyes.

"It's been an hour and your fever hasn't dropped. It's time to go to the hospital. *Now.*"

"Have you told Cade?" I ask groggily, slowly cracking my eyes open.

"Nope. And I'm not going to this time. Let's go."

"Can I at least get dressed first?"

"What you're wearing is fine. We need to go now while Jonas and Cade are … busy."

I screw up my face. "Eww. Did you just say my mum is upstairs having s—"

"Yes, so we don't have long. Let's go."

"Eww again," I say, rubbing my head and putting on my slippers.

Before walking out the door, I grab a spare small blanket off the bed, which I'm guessing Brett put there while I was sleeping.

Wrapping it around me, we quietly sneak out of the house. We probably should tell Cade, but I'm in no position to argue—I feel like crap.

Sitting in the car makes me woozy. I'm dizzy, freezing, and in pain. Not a great combination to be riding in this stupid sports car.

Lowering the seat backwards into a slight reclined position, I try to go back to sleep, but Brett's driving is erratic. If this infection doesn't kill me first, I'm sure his driving will.

He speeds right up to the emergency department, parking diagonally across a pathway. He's out of his door and at mine in impossible time.

A security guard approaches us looking all high and mighty for someone with a plastic badge. "You can't park here, mate."

"Please, just until I get her inside," Brett says frantically, opening my door.

The guard takes one look at me before his face turns ashen. He helps Brett lift me out of the car and into the ER. "What happened?"

"Biking accident," Brett says.

Okay, I guess I've been in a biking accident.

They lead me to an uncomfortable chair in the waiting room, where I sit wrapped in my blanket while Brett goes to the administration booth.

When he comes back with forms to fill out, the guard asks him to move the car. He hands me the forms and promises to be right back. The guard follows him outside, probably to make sure he actually moves the car.

Left alone, I try to fill in the forms, but I'm shaking and my vision is a blur.

Brett takes ages, and by the time he comes back, he finds me rocking back and forth.

"I'm really not feeling good," I say.

He laughs a little. "Thanks for the update, Captain Obvious."

"Shut up."

He sits in the chair next to me, pulling me in to him so my head rests on his shoulder.

"I couldn't fill in the paperwork," I say, gesturing to the clipboard beside me.

Brett reaches over me and takes it in his hand.

"What happened to your arms?" I ask, pointing to the reddened skin on his forearms.

"You have a really high fever, Nuke. Which for you …"

"I burnt you?"

"Totally worth it. I felt you up while you were asleep as a consolation for the burns."

"Liar."

He laughs. "Seriously though, I'm fine. You just worry about yourself right now." He starts filling in the forms with all my information, not even needing to ask me for the details.

"How do you know so much about me?" I ask, watching him write, my head still in the nook of his shoulder.

"I had to do a background check when you first came to us, remember?"

"Oh. And you remembered it all?"

"You going to be okay while I go give them these?" he asks, ignoring my question.

Nodding, I sit up straighter and wrap the blanket around me tighter as he goes to hand the forms in.

He comes back super-fast. "They said it shouldn't be too long."

They lie. The minutes tick by, and each sixty seconds seems to get longer and longer.

"I think my fever's finally breaking," I say after half an hour of waiting. I throw the blanket off me, suddenly feeling warm. I'm too warm now. My hair is wet with sweat and sticks to my neck and back, only making me feel hotter.

Brett feels my sweaty forehead with the back of his hand.

"You're cold and clammy."

"I think I'm going to be sick," I say as bile rises in my throat. "Can you help me to the bathroom?"

He wraps his arm around me, helping me to stand. As soon as I'm on my feet, I know I'm not going to make it. I lose the contents of my stomach, also bringing up some blood. I'm wobbly as my eyes fill with black spots and the darkness pulls me towards it.

"Well, I'm sure that'll get their attention," I hear Brett mutter as I pass out.

***

Coming to, I'm vaguely aware of being in a hospital bed. I have a thingy-ma-bob attached to my finger, my wrist has a new cast—a bright blue one—and my left side, while still painful, is no longer in agony.

"Hey." Brett's soothing tone calms the erratic beeping coming from the machine that's monitoring my heart.

"What happened?"

"A whole lot of medical jargon that I couldn't follow. You ended up in surgery. You almost died."

"Died? Like dead, like no longer here?"

He laughs. "Yes, like no longer living, dead."

"From a fever?"

"It wasn't just a fever," a voice comes from the doorway. A man in scrubs and a lab coat walks in, grabbing my chart off the end of my bed. "Your fiancé tells me that you were in a biking accident a few days ago?"

My brow furrows at the fiancé comment.

"That's not what happened?" the doctor asks.

"No, it is. I came off my bicycle."

The doctor's eyes narrow, and Brett hangs his head.

"Motorcycle. Sorry. I don't know why bicycle came out of my mouth. Maybe I hit my head, too. Did you check that out?" *Great covering, dumbass.*

"The family doctor said she cracked a rib and broke her wrist, but said she'd be fine," Brett says.

"Well, the ribs are broken, not cracked. A fragment of broken rib punctured your spleen, and you've been bleeding internally since the accident. We operated, we did everything we could, but in the end, there was too much damage and too much time had passed. We had to remove your spleen completely."

"I have no spleen? Don't I need one of those?"

"It shouldn't affect you too much. However, the spleen plays an important role in fighting off bacteria. Your immune system may suffer, and you may be prone to infections from now on, but that's worst-case scenario."

I nod but am silent. What does this mean for a person who is constantly injured?

"Could you, uh, give us a minute?" the doctor asks Brett, gesturing for him to leave the room.

"Sure," Brett says with uncertainty in his tone. He doesn't fight it, though. He'll still hear everything.

Once he's outside, the doctor turns on me. "How did you really get your injuries?"

I swallow, hard. "Bike accident."

"Maybe if you had broken your left wrist, I'd believe you. But if you came off your bike, falling on your left side, why is your right wrist broken? Also, who did the original cast? It wasn't … *wrong*, but it wasn't exactly neat."

"I don't know what you're getting at." I try to force myself to keep eye contact with him, but it's impossible under his fierce scrutiny.

"If your fiancé had anything to do with your injuries, you can tell us. You'll be safe here. We can get the police—"

"No," I say a little too quickly. "I mean, you're wrong about him. It was my mother who told me not to come to the hospital because she thought I really was fine. Our family doctor said so. My fiancé didn't do this." Fiancé sounds weird rolling off my tongue. "When I was thrown from the bike, I slid a pretty long way, and I ended up slamming into a car on the side of the road. I put my arm up to stop the impact, but that was stupid, because it was crushed when it rammed into the car."

He looks at me sceptically, but I think he buys it. "You'll need to stay at least a couple of days to recover, plus you'll need a few weeks rest once you're discharged."

I nod. "Can't do much with a broken wrist anyway, right?"

"I'll come and check on you on my rounds tomorrow," he says before turning on his heel and walking out.

"Thank you," I call after him.

A smile finds my face when Brett reappears in the doorway. "Why does everybody assume I'm the one beating you up?" He returns my smile as he approaches, kissing my forehead before sitting in the chair next to my bed.

"Why does the doctor think you're my fiancé?"

"They wouldn't tell me anything otherwise."

"Oh. Does Cade know yet?"

"Uh … yeah."

"Are we in trouble?"

"That's what you're worried about? You almost died, and you're worried about what she thinks?"

I shrug and then scold myself as pain shoots through me.

"Once I told her that you definitely would've died had I not brought you in, she kind of went silent. She knows I made the right call."

"But she didn't get in her car and come see if I was okay," I say more to myself than Brett.

"She's not that kind of mother, Nuke. You should know that by now."

"Yeah, I know. What about Sasha?"

"I only spoke to Cade, but I'm assuming the fact Sasha isn't here means she wasn't told. She'd be here if she knew. She loves you."

"She does?"

"I overheard her saying to Drake that the only good thing that came from being Cade's daughter was being related to you."

"I kind of feel the same way right now," I mutter, wallowing in self-pity over my failing relationship with my birth mother.

"You still have hope Cade will accept you, don't you? That she will want to bond with you?" He's asking a question, but it comes out more like he's stating a fact.

I shake my head. "I think I realised a while ago that's not going to happen … but … I still want her to be proud of me. Is that stupid?"

"Not stupid at all. Unrealistic maybe, but not stupid," he says, grabbing hold of my hand.

There's a commotion outside the room before we hear, "Where is that silly girl?"

Silver.

"Nanna, I told you not to come," Brett says, getting up to hug her hello in the doorway. Paddy trails in behind her.

"What are you—"

She comes closer to my bed. "You didn't think I'd not come visit you, now did you?" She leans in, kissing my cheek. "What have you done to yourself?"

Brett and I glance at each other. "Just a nasty bike accident," he says to his nanna, the lie thick with guilt. I've noticed he can't lie to her as well as he can to everyone else.

"Right. Bike accident," she says knowingly. I don't think Brett gives her as much credit as she deserves.

"I'll be fine," I say with a weak smile.

"You still look hot, Nuka. Even with the bruising," Paddy says, making my smile grow.

"Patrick Michael Finley, that is no way to talk to a lady," Silver scolds. "But he has a point. You're still gorgeous. Imagine what the kids would look like if you and Brett—"

"Nanna!" Brett yells.

"I know, I know. Just friends," she says, holding her hands up in surrender while winking at me. An uncontrollable giggle escapes me. "Seriously, you'd think he'd be used to my teasing by now."

It's true. Every Sunday we go over to her house for lunch, she always comments about the two of us being good together.

It's taken a while, but I'm finally realising she's completely right. Brett saved my life yesterday. He'd never gone against Cade and Jonas before, but he chose me. He chose to protect me over any consequence they'd throw at him.

"Brett, dear," Silver says. "Could you take Paddy down to the cafeteria? We haven't had the chance to eat today."

Brett narrows his eyes but does as his nanna tells him. "Uh, okay. Come on, Paddy."

"I'm glad you're okay, Nuka," Paddy says before following Brett out the door.

Silver cocks her head to the side and sighs at me.

"What's that look for?" I ask.

"You need to put yourself and Brett out of your damn misery and tell him how you feel."

"W-what?"

"Don't give me that naïve 'I have no idea what you're talking about' pout." She smiles as she waves her finger in my face exaggeratedly.

Yeah, okay, she's got me there. "But you don't know the full story—"

"The best friend, right?"

"Wha—he … how …"

"Brett told me about the other boy, but you can't deny there's something between you two. I've watched you for months now. You've been getting closer every time I see you. Your faces light up around each other. I understand you're confused about what you feel towards this other boy, but where is he while you're lying in this hospital bed?"

"He doesn't know … I can't …"

"You can't tell him because of who your employers are, right?" Silver says in a knowing way.

I nod.

"You and Brett live in the same world. I've never seen Brett this happy and you're not even together. I just know in my heart that you belong with him. Even if you don't know it yet."

I'm speechless.

"I'll leave you to think about what I've said. Rest up, pretty girl." She walks out, leaving me with nothing to do but think about her words.

Brett and I *have* been getting closer lately. I've been aware of it happening but have had no desire to stop it. It's gone way beyond having a crush. It's gone way beyond wanting to date him. I want to *be with* him.

When Brett returns twenty minutes later, he almost looks worried. "Please tell me she didn't give you the same speech she just gave me?"

I giggle. "Probably."

Carefully and slowly so I'm not in too much pain, I scoot over, rolling onto my right side to make room for him on my bed. He raises an eyebrow but gives in relatively easy. He takes his shoes off and lies down beside me, one arm under his head holding it up, the other by his side, careful not to touch me.

"You saved my life."

"Yeah … I did. And I'd do it again, too." He goes to reach for me, but hesitates, taking his hand back and placing it by his side.

"I won't break if you touch me," I whisper.

He moves his hand to my hip, squeezing it gently. Reaching my left hand up to his face, I wince in pain before dropping it to his chest.

He picks my hand up and gently brings my fingers to his lips, kissing them softly.

"I thought I was going to lose you," he says.

In this moment, I have absolutely no reason not to tell him how I feel about him. Not one reason. The words are on the tip of my tongue; all I have to do is say them out loud. *Say them!*

"I'm falling for you." The words come out as barely a whisper, but I say them.

He smiles that half-smile that looks so damn good on him. "I know."

"You know?"

"I hear it. Every time you look at me, your heart starts beating harder." He's smirking now as he places my hand over his chest. "It matches mine."

"Damn your ability," I mutter, pulling back slightly. "Why didn't you say anything?"

"Because your head needed to catch up. I need you to choose me."

"I do. This is me choosing you."

Leaning forward, our lips touch. His hands wrap around me, gentle and cautiously, careful of my injuries. Where his touch is soft, his mouth is firm and certain, claiming me as his. Like so many of our other kisses, it makes me want more, but this time it's not for show. It's for real.

"Tomorrow," Brett says, trailing kisses down my jaw and neck. "It's been three long days, and I can't wait to get you home, and in our bed."

"*Our* bed?" I croak.

"I guess that is a bit presumptuous of me … and I mean, you're probably still sore … and …" He runs his hand through his hair.

His fluster makes me smile. "Tomorrow … if I'm not too sore."

"No pressure, Nuke. Whenever you're ready."

I kiss him with as much fervour as I have, letting him know how much I want him.

A throaty groan escapes him as his hand trails down my side, grasping my hip.

"Ugh." Sasha's voice comes from the doorway. "Is there ever going to be a day where I don't walk in on you two canoodling now that you're together for real?"

We both laugh as Brett pries himself away from me and climbs off my hospital bed.

"Sorry," I apologise to her.

"No you're not!" she shrieks.

"Okay, I'm not. But I'll try to contain myself when you're around."

"I make no such promises," Brett says sitting in the chair next to my bed and smirking arrogantly.

"How are you feeling today?" Sasha asks.

Brett was right about her. The minute she found out I was in here, she forced Drake to bring her here, even though visiting hours were over. She kicked up a stink, made a fuss, and practically forced her way in to see me. She and Brett have barely left my side ever since. Silver and Paddy came by again yesterday, but Cade and Jonas haven't bothered at all. Not that it should surprise me. Although, you'd think they'd be concerned for one of their fighters. Apparently having five others to choose from means they feel fairly comfortable with almost losing one of them.

"I can't wait to get out of here," I say.

"Just one more day, baby," Brett says.

Sasha rolls her eyes and puts a finger down her throat, mock throwing up. "Sickening," she mumbles.

I just laugh at her. "Just wait. One day you'll meet someone, and you'll beg them to call you baby."

"Not likely. They could call me queen, or master, or hey—here's a weird suggestion, they could call me Sasha, you know, *my name*. Treat me as an equal."

"It's just a term of endearment, it's not meant to be demeaning," I say.

"Uh … Nuke," Brett whispers. "I think Flynn used to call her baby."

"Oh, honey," I say, as she starts welling up with tears. Reaching out, I take her hand in mine.

I've never seen her get upset over a guy before. Hell, she uses Drake like a toy. I know she was hurt by Flynn, but I guess I didn't realise just how bad until now.

I open my arms and she climbs onto my bed, snuggling into me.

"He's stupid, you know that?" I say.

"Of course, I know that. He's such a stupid bogan." She starts laughing through her tears. "It sucks what he did, but I've learnt my lesson. I deserve better. I can take what I want from guys, and I'll never fall for anyone again."

"Sounds like a good plan," I lie. That doesn't sound like a good plan at all, but I'll let her wallow in her self-pity. For a little while anyway.

"Why look for Mr. Right when Mr. Right-now is around the corner."

"Hmm … that's probably not the best attitude to have, but I'll let it slide because you're upset."

"Hey, now that you're taken, maybe I could make a pass at Declan."

I know she's joking and I shouldn't react, but my heart's still hooked up to these monitors, and my traitorous body lets the whole room know how much I hate what she just said.

I avoid looking at Brett. I don't want to see his hurt face.

"I've gotta go get ready for my fight tonight," he says, standing.

Damn it. I'm already screwing this up. "You'll be by to pick me up tomorrow?"

"Of course," he says, coming to kiss me on the forehead before walking out.

"Good luck," I yell after him, but he's already gone.

"I'm sorry," Sasha says after a safe enough time for Brett to be out of hearing range. "I didn't think you'd react like that, though. I was only joking."

"I know you were. I don't even know why my body did that."

She grimaces at me as if I just said the dumbest thing ever. "Just because you've decided to be with Brett, that doesn't mean your feelings for Declan are gone."

It's not like I'm pining after Declan, though. I'm happy with Brett and I'm not doubting my decision to be with him. I know he's the one for me, but … part of me will always belong to Declan.

"How can one heart belong to two people?"

She shrugs. "It's probably better for it to belong to two people than to give it wholly to one, only to have him smash it to pieces."

"I'll get Flynn in the arena, I swear I will."

"That's okay. He's not a bad guy, really. And I think that's what I hate the most. He didn't promise me the world, he didn't lead me on. I just wanted more than what he was willing to give, and when he realised that, he was upfront and honest about it. So I can't really hate him. I hate myself more than anything. I think deep down, I knew. I always knew he wasn't that into me."

"So you've just been toying with random guys ever since?"

"I haven't slept with any of them, if that's what you're getting at. I told myself I wouldn't do it again until I was sure."

I huff out a little laugh. "So it really is all an act."

"Yeah, yeah," she says dismissively.

"I love you, Sasha. You know that, right? I'm so happy I get to have you in my life."

"You too," she says awkwardly while looking away.

It makes me wonder how many times she's been told "I love you" growing up. By the way she's reacted, I'm guessing not a lot. Cade definitely doesn't seem like the affectionate kind of mum. It's such a vast difference to the way I was brought up—in a house full of love, encouragement, and support.

"I mean it, Sash. You're in my life forever."

She nods, but I sense she doesn't believe me, and I don't know how to convince her.

***

"Where's that ringing coming from?" I murmur while opening my eyes.

I'm still in the hospital. The lights are all on.

"What time is it?" *How long have I been asleep?*

No one answers—I'm all alone.

The phone on my bedside table is ringing. That's where it's coming from.

"Hello?" I say groggily, picking up the receiver. According to the clock next to the phone, it's just past 10:00 PM.

"Nuka?" a small voice says.

"Who is this?" I ask, confused.

There's sobbing on the other end of the line. "It's … Paddy."

I bolt upright, ignoring the slight twinge in my side. "Paddy? What's wrong?"

He sniffs.

"Is it Brett? Is he okay?"

"I need Uncle Brett, but I can't get a hold of him, and I don't know where Litmus is."

I sigh. "So you know about Litmus."

He sniffs again. "Nuka. I really need him." He's blubbering now.

"Paddy, just tell me what's wrong. I'll work out how to get a message to Brett."

"She's dead."

"What? Who's dead? Paddy, what's going on?"

"Shane killed Nanna."

My gut pinches. *That can't be right.*

Silver's ... dead?

-19-

UNCERTAINTY

"Paddy, calm down. What did you say?" *I had to have heard wrong.*

"Can you just get Uncle Brett, please?"

"Have you called the police?"

"No. And neither can you."

"If something happened—"

"Nuka, you can't. You just … can't, okay? Please, I'm begging you. I trust you because Uncle Brett trusts you."

I think I'm going to vomit. "Where are you?"

"At home."

"Where's…" I swallow hard, "Your nanna?"

"Living room," he says, his voice a quivering whisper. "There's blood everywhere."

Yup. Can definitely taste the bile now. "Stay right there until we come get you, okay?"

"What if Shane comes back?" His shaky voice sends chills

down my spine.

My heart thunders in my chest, and the machines around me start beeping like crazy. I start fumbling to remove all the wires and needles from my skin as I try to process what Paddy's saying.

"You need to hide. Lock yourself in a closet, the bathroom, anywhere safe …" I say, now climbing out of bed in a panic. "If there's nowhere safe, you go to a neighbour you can trust—"

"They won't help me once they find out Shane's involved."

"Can you get anywhere safe?"

"The bathroom has a lock. I … I can hide in there."

"Okay, you hide in there and wait for us, okay? It may take an hour or two to get out there. I have to go get Brett, and then we'll come to you, okay? Don't open the door for anyone else."

"Please hurry. I'm scared."

My heart sinks to my stomach, the churning nausea feeling only getting worse. *This can't actually be happening, right?*

"I'm leaving now," I say, hanging up the phone.

I should call the cops. That's what you do when someone's been murdered, right? Why am I not calling the cops?

Murdered.

Maybe she's not dead. He's overreacting. He's thirteen, what would he know?

"So much blood."

I should call an ambulance.

Just get to Brett, just get to Brett.

I don't know how I got to Litmus. My body must be on autopilot, because I don't recall getting dressed or sneaking out of my room. I don't even remember hailing down a cab on the street.

Yet, here I am, making my way into the old train yards to the main entrance of Litmus. The cabbie was reluctant to drop me off out here in the middle of nowhere, but I don't have a key for the warehouse entrance, and there's no way either of the clubs would let me through while I'm wearing the only pair of shoes I had with me—a pair of fluffy slippers. I may've gotten through if they recognised me as Heatwave, but I figured this would just be easier.

That was before I got here and remembered how long the walk is. My stitches hurt, I still feel queasy—I don't know if it's from the situation or the painkillers I'm on. I try to run, but my shoes, and my body, won't let me.

What am I doing here? I should've ignored Paddy's pleas and called the cops. An ambulance, at least. Someone, anyone!

It was almost 11:00 PM when I got out of the taxi. I really hope the fight starts late tonight, or Brett's going to be in the ring by the time I get in there. I try to pick up my pace, but it only makes me dizzy.

Finally arriving at the Deakin locker room, I'm sweaty and gasping for breath.

I punch eight-zero-zero-eight-five into the keypad and stumble in.

Brett and Ryker look up at me from the bench seats in the middle of the room.

"Nuka?" Brett asks, his face aghast. "What are you doing out of bed … and the hospital?" He rushes to my side, holding me up as I pant for more air. "Baby, what's wrong?"

"Paddy … in trouble," I struggle to get out.

"Paddy?" His eyes widen in fear.

"It's … he said … Shane … your nanna …"

He turns to Ryker. “Ryke—”

“I’ve got you covered. Go,” Ryker says, shooing us out the door.

Brett doesn’t ask questions on the way to the car. He drags me by my hand and I try to keep up. The closer we get to the car, the more urgent his steps become.

“Brett, my stitches,” I remind him as his grip on my arm becomes a bit too tight.

“Sorry,” he says, letting my hand go completely.

“Give me your keys,” I say as we get nearer the car.

“What? No.”

“I have to … there’s something you need to know, and I’m not going to tell you if you insist on driving. But, if you give me the keys, I can explain on the way. Even with my broken wrist, and insanely sore side, it’ll be safer if I drive.”

He stops dead in his tracks, turning to face me, his eyes glistening as he hands over the keys. “She’s dead, isn’t she?”

“H-how did you—”

“It’s how Shane works. Paddy screwed him over, now he’s out for revenge. He doesn’t go after you, he goes after your family first.”

“But Paddy doesn’t work for him anymore, right?”

“We really need to get to him, Nuke. Fast.”

“Okay.”

We don’t talk any more. Brett silently stares out the window as I drive.

I don’t know how to console him. There’s no way to console someone in this type of situation, is there?

I reach over and grab a hold of his hand, gripping it tight. He holds it like it’s a lifeline but doesn’t look in my direction, continuing to stare out the window. Eventually, I have to grip the steering wheel again, so I move his hand to my thigh to give him something to hold onto.

It’s at least half an hour before he finally speaks, his words coming out in sobs. "I told him this would happen. I told him to stop."

"Stop what?"

"The last time we were there having lunch a few weeks ago. He was fidgety, he looked guilty … he wasn't being himself. I confronted him while you were doing the dishes with Nanna in the kitchen."

"He went back to Shane after you paid him off?"

He shakes his head. "Worse. He went out on his own."

"I don't understand."

"He was doing business on Shane's territory," he says through gritted teeth, his sadness suddenly replaced with anger. "I told him!" He removes his hand from my thigh, punching the dashboard and causing a small indent.

I pull the car over to the side of the road and put it in park but leave the engine running.

"What are you doing?"

"Get out," I say, opening my car door.

"We don't have time for this, Nuke." He tries to grab my hand but I pull it away. "What the hell are you doing?" he yells as I climb out of the car.

"Get out of the car, now!" I yell back.

I make my way around to his door. When he refuses to get out, I open it, grab his arm, and practically drag him out.

"What do you want from me?" he screams.

"Get it out. Get all of your anger out now, because when we get to Paddy, it needs to be gone."

"He got her killed!"

"Yes, he did. And he is thirteen years old. He's going to need his uncle to forgive him. He's going to have to live the rest of his life knowing that his actions got his family killed. You can't make it any worse for him."

"Nuke, we need to go. We need to get to him before Shane does."

"Then let it out. Punch the ground if you have to, stomp your feet like a toddler. You need to calm the hell down before I'll take you anywhere near him."

Please let Paddy be safe is all I can think as I stalk back to the car while Brett lets off steam.

He paces back and forth for a while, yelling at an invisible Paddy. I know we need to get going, but I'm right. He needs to get this out.

He's quiet but subdued when he finally gets back in the car. I put the car in drive, speeding off as safely as I can. We need to get to Paddy before it's too late.

"Thank you," Brett mumbles.

The neighbourhood is quiet when we finally reach the Estates. Not really a cause for alarm considering it's almost 1:00 AM, but the stillness is eerie. Pulling into Brett's driveway, I grip the steering wheel tight. My knuckles turn white as I think about what we're going to find when we get inside.

Brett's armed with his gun that he keeps in the centre console and reaches the front door before I'm even out of the car. My heart sinks when he pushes the door wide open. I guess the six-lock trick didn't work this time.

Please let Paddy be safe. This has become my mantra the rest of the drive here.

By the time I get the courage to get out of the car and make my way through the front door, I find Brett sobbing on the ground near a puddle of bright crimson liquid surrounding his nanna.

So much blood.

My hand grasps at my stomach as the other covers my mouth, and I have to turn away.

Tears pool in my eyes, and the urge to run to Brett almost consumes me. But I have to leave Brett where he is on the floor. As much as I want to go to him, I need to find Paddy. I avoid looking at Silver, the way her lifeless body is splayed out on the living room carpet.

With my heart thundering in my chest, I round the corner only to find the bathroom door wide open and the light on.

"Shit!" *I shouldn't have made Brett stop.*

I'm frozen in the hallway, unable to move. Taking in a deep breath, I force my feet to work. My steps are slow, cautiously going in the direction of the bathroom. Terror surges through me like it's adrenaline; I'm visibly shaking by the time I reach the end of the hallway.

He's gone, he's dead. We were too late. I should've called someone.

Letting out a shaky breath and wiping tears from my eyes, I take the last step, making it to the threshold of the bathroom.

The window's open, the room empty.

Still shaking with fear, I make my way to the edge of the bathtub and sit. "Where are you, Paddy?" I mutter to myself.

The cabinet under the sink flies open, and I jump in fright and fall backwards into the tub. My head hits the porcelain edge, sending pain down the back of my neck.

Paddy's squashed into the little cabinet, clambering his way out. I'd find this whole thing humorous if we weren't in this situation. I probably just gave myself a concussion. My stitches aren't faring so great either.

"Are you okay, Nuka?" Paddy's small voice makes me scramble out of the bathtub, reaching for his held-out hand. Finally finding my feet with his help, I wrap him in a massive hug.

"You're okay. What happened? Why wasn't the door locked?" I don't realise how tight I'm squeezing until he lets out a little grunt.

Brett appears in the doorway, reaching out and taking Paddy out of my arms and into his own.

"Shane. He … he came back." Paddy starts sobbing through his words as he's pressed into Brett's chest. I think Brett's holding on just as hard as I was. "He was banging on the bathroom door, and I knew he was going to get in, so I opened the window as loudly as I could, then got in the cabinet hoping he'd think I'd jumped out. Once he got in, he realised I wasn't in here and left. But I was too scared to come out until I knew for sure it was you guys who came in the second time."

"We need to get out of here," I say.

Brett nods. "Let's go." He turns to walk back out of the bathroom when he stops short in the doorway. "Shit, a car just pulled up. Nuka, take Paddy out the window, wait until they come inside, then get Paddy to the car. Now."

"I'm not leaving you."

He turns, grabbing my shoulders. "Now's not the time to be stubborn. I need you to stay with Paddy. Shane isn't exactly the type of person to come on his own. Get Paddy to the car. I'll be out there to join you soon." He kisses my forehead and then pushes me towards the window as he turns and starts walking down the hallway.

Blood whooshes in my ears to the beat of my heart. I don't question him this time, turning to usher Paddy out the window.

The drop is small, easy enough for both of us to handle. He hits the ground with a thud, and I'm close to follow.

"Stick behind me, got it?" I whisper. He nods, his eyes wide in fear.

I grab his hand as we sneak alongside the house, the only sound our footsteps and heavy breathing. Reaching the edge of the house, I peek my head around the corner. Two guys are standing by the front door, talking. They're only a few feet away from us. There's no way we could get to the car without them seeing us.

"What do we do?" Paddy whispers, obviously not quietly enough, because one of the guys snaps his head in our direction, making eye contact with me.

"Run! Run the other way, go around the other side of the house."

We take off at a sprint, and I'm thankful Paddy's fast. The sound of pounding footsteps stalks us. We round the corner at the back of the house, only to come to a skidding halt. There's one guy behind us, and the other in front of us. We start backing up as they begin to get close, but there's nowhere to go. We're being cornered into the back fence.

"I don't suppose Uncle Brett's taught you how to fight?" I ask quietly.

"A little." His voice is shaky and unconfident. Not exactly what I was hoping for.

"I'll take the guy on the left, he's bigger."

"Your stitches," he whispers, but we're out of time. The goons are on us.

Everything happens so fast.

It's clear they're not experienced fighters when my guy goes to attack and I dodge him easily. I struggle with my broken wrist and ribs, plus my operation site, but I'm able to keep my guard up. He's unable to get a hold of me; he can't even hit me, no matter how many times he tries.

I turn and kick him in his happy place, and he hunches over.

A rippling pain shoots down my left side, but I have to push through.

Gritting my teeth, I step forwards and elbow him in the back of the head while he's still hunched over. He collapses to the ground—just where I need him. Turning and kneeing him in the back, hard, I punch the side of his head with my fist, effectively knocking him out.

My first knockout.

I glance around to find Paddy. He's being dragged by the other guy and is almost at the front of the house.

Running after them, I'm quick to tackle them both to the ground, the pain in my side now throbbing.

Paddy and I scramble to get away from our attacker, but all three of us freeze when we hear a gunshot come from inside the house.

"No!" I yell.

Shane's henchman gets off the ground and starts running for the front door. Now's our chance to get to the car, but neither of us can find the strength to move.

"I have to make sure Brett's okay," I say to Paddy. "You get to the car. I'll be there soon, okay? Lock the doors, and don't let anyone in but me or Uncle Brett."

He nods. "Okay," he says, his voice cracking. "Nuka—"

"Everything will be okay," I lie. If I go in there and Brett's … I can't even think about it. I have to have hope that he's okay.

As we get up, I push him in the direction of the car as I start to make my way to the front door.

What if Brett's dead? This makes my feet stop moving. I'm sure less than a minute has gone by since the shot went off, but it feels like hours. Neither Brett nor Shane have come out.

What if Shane comes out… I should go to Paddy. We need to get out of here. *You can't leave Brett.*

I almost collapse when the henchman from before steps out of the door, his eyes boring into mine with hatred and disgust.

"No," I whisper to myself.

Brett's gone.

Tears flood my cheeks, and my breath comes in sobbing gasps.

I'm expecting Shane to follow his man out. Relief consumes

me when he doesn't.

"Brett." As soon as I see him, relief takes over me and I propel myself forwards.

I push the other guy out of the way and grab a hold of Brett as tight as I can, tears flowing freely. "I thought you were gone," I whisper frantically.

"I'm still here," he says, kissing the side of my head. "But we have to go. Now."

It's only then I realise why the other guy's still standing behind me. Brett's arm is stretched out, training his gun on him.

"Is Shane …" I don't want to ask.

"Not dead. I shot him in the leg which is only going to slow him down, not stop him. So start moving."

He doesn't need to tell me twice. We rush to the car, Brett never once taking the gun off the other guy.

Paddy unlocks the car for us, and it only takes a split second before we're speeding off into the night.

-20-

GOODBYE

We've been driving for a while now, all three of us completely silent. My side is aching, and I'm pretty sure one or more of my stitches have either come out or ripped or something. I'm too scared to look down. The pain tells me something's not right, but I can't worry Brett about that now.

"What are we going to do?" I ask.

"I don't know." Brett shakes his head. He looks in the rear-view mirror at a terrified Paddy. "I really don't know," he whispers.

"You have to leave—for good."

"We can't, Nuke. There's no way."

I let out a sigh, as I reach into my back pocket, holding onto my side as I do. I go to hand over my money card, but he eyes me sceptically.

"Take it. Take my trust fund."

His eyes widen. "We can't do that."

"It's your only option."

His jaw clicks as he contemplates it, but he doesn't take the card from me. "Are you going to come with us?"

Dropping my hands to my lap, I shake my head as my eyes start to fill with tears. "I can't," I whisper.

Brett pulls over to the side of the road, coming to a sudden stop. "Stay in the car, Paddy." He gets out and walks around to open my door, holding out his hand for me to take.

As I climb out, he shuts the door behind me, wrapping his arms around my waist. He pushes me against the car door, his body blanketing mine as he takes my mouth with his. Tears streak my face, as I hold onto him like it will be the last time. Because I know it will be. I can't leave, but they can.

He pulls away, breathing heavily, his forehead still pressed to mine, his arms still wrapped around me. He's just as reluctant to let go as I am. "*That* was for offering us the world. But I can't let you do it. If you were going to come—"

"I can't. I can't leave Sasha, I still don't know my mother … I can't turn my back on what I set out to do, which is find out who I really am."

"You're the most amazing person I've ever met." He wipes one of my tears away with his thumb while he cradles my face. "And I'm not going to leave you. If Cade and Jonas were to find out what you did—"

"I can handle them. You have *no* other option, Brett."

He steps away and runs a hand through his hair. "You still have no idea who Cade is, do you?"

"What do you mean?"

"The reason we're paid to follow you and Sasha around? It's so you can't get out. None of us can get out. Cade doesn't care about you, Nuke. Trust me, I know."

"What did she say?"

"She saw you as a target the minute I brought you home."

"A target?"

"Their next money-making venture. They've been fairly good to you so far because you've done all they asked. If they know you're the reason I'm gone … I don't want to think about what they'll do."

"Cade's my mother. She may not be a good one, but she is. Surely there's some mother instinct buried deep inside her that won't let Jonas hurt me."

"Fighters aren't the only ones Jonas owns." His tone is dejected, sad.

"But—"

"Once Jonas has you, you're lost in Litmus forever. I can't take off and leave you, and I especially can't leave with your backup source. It may just buy your way out one day."

"Buy my way out?"

"You still haven't read your contract, have you? They've kept it hidden from you, right?"

I nod.

"It basically states—in a whole lot of confusing legal crap—that you belong to them for as long as they want you to be. The only way out is to pay out your contract, or serve your time. The only other option is running. This is our only chance for both of us to get out."

"If what you're saying is true, isn't Sasha just as trapped? Am I just meant to leave her there? I've already abandoned my other siblings—am I just going to do it again? There's also not enough money in my trust fund for the three of us to live. It'll get us by for a while, probably a few years even, but then what? Like you said—we're undesirable. We'd need jobs. Even with just the two of you, you're going to have to find work."

He shrugs. "I've always had to scrounge for work. It's nothing I'm not used to."

"But it is for me. The string of odd jobs I've had never worked out. I wasn't groomed for hard work. At least Litmus is easy. I can do that."

"I'm not leaving without you, Nuke. If you don't go, we don't go. Simple as that."

"And when Shane comes to kill Paddy, or you? You think I want to lose you that way?"

"You'd rather send me away knowing I could never come back? Have me leave you voluntarily?"

"I'd rather know you're out there somewhere, living the life you deserve, hoping with all hope that you're happy, and that I did the right thing."

"We can protect Paddy. I'll add a few more years to my service, and get Jonas and Cade to take Paddy in. With Nanna gone, there's no one else to look after him. Jonas and Cade have paid off my debts, I just need to finish out my service. If I leave now …"

"How long do you have left?"

"Five years."

"Five?" I screech.

"Well, it was two until I had to take the advance for Shane. And it'll be more now if they take on Paddy, too."

I shake my head. "Not going to happen." I shove my money card at him again. "You and Paddy are leaving. You won't be able to draw money from the actual bank, so you'll have to use ATMs. There's a limit to how much you can take out each day, but it's pretty high. It shouldn't take you more than a week to empty it. You can't use the card forever, they'll be able to track you. Pin number is zero-one-two-nine."

"Nuke—"

"Stop. You're selfless to a fault, and a pain in the ass. You're cocky, arrogant, and piss me off with your erratic behaviour … but you're also someone I will do anything for, because I care about you more than I ever thought possible. I'm giving you your freedom. You deserve it. And if what Uncle Drew said about my dad embezzling this money is true, then it's not mine to begin with."

"I can't—"

"You can, and you will. You told me once that you would do anything to save your family. I'm not going to be the person who stops you from doing that. You tell me I'm stubborn, so you know there's no point in arguing with me."

"You are stubborn. And I will never be more grateful, or thankful, for that. For what you're giving us." He kisses me, his mouth covering mine, his hands embracing me. When he pulls away, his face is wet with tears. "We have to get going. Shane might be right behind us."

He pulls me off the car, but as I go to take a step, I feel lightheaded and almost collapse.

"Are you okay?" Brett asks, before catching a glimpse of my side. "Shit, Nuka. Why didn't you tell me you're hurt?"

"I'll be fine. Let's go." I go to take a step, but Brett stops me, lifting up my bloody shirt. "We have to get you back to the hospital."

"Not until I know you're gone and safe."

He doesn't bother arguing, even though I can tell he wants to. I guess he realises how counter-productive it'd be.

We make our way back into the car, and as soon as Brett puts the car in gear, he starts talking a million miles a minute.

"There's so much to do. We have to go to Drake's."

"Drake's?"

"I have some stuff stashed there. Clothes, things Paddy and I'll need. I've always had it in case we needed to leave suddenly or I finally got enough money to get out. We can't go back to the house, Jonas and Cade will know something's up. Speaking of which, when you get back to the hospital, you have to pretend you never left. No one saw you leave last night, right? No one saw you at Litmus?"

"I … I don't know. They could've."

"Just deny it. You need to convince them you have no idea where I am, you had nothing to do with me leaving, and you can't let them know you funded it."

"Okay."

"I mean it, Nuke. If either of them suspect …"

"What? What will they do?"

He shakes his head. "There's a lot they could do. They could hurt you, punish you, make you fight more than you're able just to make you earn more money for them. Hell, for all I know, they could kill you. Jonas isn't above doing something like that. I think the best you could hope for would be they make you take over my contract. Be promised to them for five years. If they find out you're the reason they lost me … yeah … that's best-case scenario."

"Okay, got it. Don't let them find out."

His left leg starts hammering against the floor. "We shouldn't be doing this."

"Yes, you should be. You need to."

"There has to be another way. What if Shane comes after you?"

"He doesn't even know who I am."

"Yeah, okay. That's true."

"I know you're doubting this, but I'm not. It feels … right." I shrug. "It's hard to explain."

"It feels right that I'm leaving you?" I don't miss the rejection in his voice.

"It feels right that I'm the one to save you. I hate that you're leaving, but everything inside me is telling me that this is what I need to do. I saved two lives today."

He grabs my hand and brings it to his lips.

"Why aren't you coming with us, Nuka?" Paddy asks from the back. He's been so quiet, I almost forgot he was there.

"I'm not done saving people. I'm going to get Sasha out of there."

Brett smiles, but it's a tight-lipped, unsure smile.

***

It's still dark when we arrive at Drake's, but it's nearing 5:00 AM, and the sun will be coming up soon. We all file out of the car, letting ourselves into the house with a key on Brett's keyring.

I head straight for the bathroom, hoping to find some painkillers or something to dull the aches and pains I'm feeling all over. I only need to last a little bit longer, and then I'll be back in the hospital. They can give me the good drugs again then.

Reluctantly, I lift my shirt, revealing a bloody, oozing scar. Two of my stitches are loose, and the wound smells gross.

I'm a mess. I'm dirty from the scuffle on the front lawn, the bags under my eyes suggest I haven't slept for days, and my pale, pasty skin lets me know I'm not in good shape.

I clean my wound as best I can and cover it with a bandage I find in a first aid kit under the sink. It'll do until I get back to the hospital.

Squashing down the temptation to throw up, I gulp some tap water and splash my face with the coolness.

When I leave the bathroom and enter the living room, Drake's out of bed. He's wearing only boxers and is holding a gun.

A small smirk plays on my lips.

"I thought someone was breaking in," he rationalises. "What's going on, guys?"

"Remember how I told you that one day I may have to take off?" Brett says. Drake nods for him to continue. "That day's come."

"But … you're still locked in for—"

"I know, but something's come up. I have to leave this morning. Like right now."

Drake runs his hand over his hair. "Okay. So what's the plan?"

I'm a little surprised Drake's taking this okay.

"I need to leave the car here. We can't take it with us, it'll attract too much attention, and we'll be easily tracked."

"Wait … are you saying …" Drake's eyes light up.

Brett shakes his head. "Don't get too excited. It belongs to Nuka now."

"What?" I ask, stunned.

"It's the least I could do," Brett says. "Maybe you can get some of your money back by selling it."

"If all I had to do was sleep with you to get the car, I would've done it ages ago," Drake says.

I actually find myself giggling despite the situation.

"You need to take the car back to the hospital and leave it in the parking lot. It'll make it look like I went missing from there."

"What do you need me to do?" Drake asks.

"I need to borrow your car, and you'll have to pick it up from the train station later. You also need to make sure she gets to the hospital safely. She's not looking too hot."

"Thanks," I say sarcastically.

"You know what I mean." He looks between Paddy and Drake, his eyes telling them to leave the room without him actually having to ask.

"Come on, Paddy, we'll get all your stuff together to leave," Drake says.

They don't even make it out of the room before my tears start. It takes even less time before Brett has me in his arms.

"I don't want to say goodbye," I whisper. "Do you think … will you ever come back?"

"There'd be a lot of people after me if I did. But if you ever asked me to—"

"I can't do that to you. I care about you too much."

"I'm only going to say this once, and you don't have to say it back. In fact, I'd probably prefer you didn't, or I don't see me walking out that door, ever. But, I—"

"Please don't say it. I won't be able to let you go."

He nods. "This is the hardest thing I've ever had to do."

Wrapping our arms around each other tighter, he kisses me like he never has before.

What we've become … it's something I didn't know could exist outside of me and Declan. Declan may be my soulmate, but I chose a different path and fell in love with someone who's just like me. He's broken, weighted with baggage, and emotionally stunted. But we match.

He pulls back from me. "You need to go, Nuke."

I shake my head. I can't leave, not yet.

"Please. I'm so close to refusing to leave you, I can't stand it."

Sniffing, I wrap him in another hug. "Okay."

"You can trust Drake. He's one of the good guys."

"Thanks, bro," Drake says from the entryway.

"You didn't let me finish." Brett says, before focusing back on me. "He's a good guy, even with his lame come-ons and serious lack of game."

"Is that really called for?" Drake asks.

"It got her smiling, so yeah. It was totally called for." He hugs me for the millionth time before stepping away completely. "You need to go," he says, placing the car keys in my hands.

This is it? This is our end?

With one last look into Brett's chocolate eyes, Drake wraps his arm around my shoulders as he escorts me out of the house and to Brett's … no, *my* car.

"Wait!" I hear Brett's voice as we reach the bottom of the

porch steps.

He bounds down them, almost knocking me over as his mouth connects with mine in some desperate plea for me to change my mind and go with him. It almost works.

"I had to do that one last time." He pulls away, leaving my lips tingling and my heart broken.

I stare after him as he walks back into the house. How can something feel so wrong, yet be so right at the same time? Why is doing the right thing so damn sucky?

I hand the keys to Drake.

"Really? Really, really?" He's so excited, I can't help but smile at the guy.

"I'm not exactly in the best shape to drive."

"Oh my God! I could kiss you."

"Please don't," I say, putting my hand up to stop him coming closer. It just makes him laugh.

We're silent for the short drive back to the hospital. Drake helps me back inside and up to my ward where I try to sneak back into my room. Unsuccessfully.

There are two uniformed cops standing in the entryway talking to one another. I'm grateful that I don't recognise either of them from growing up around cops.

I start shivering. I don't know if my injuries are suddenly worse or I'm nervous the cops are here, but Drake has to physically hold me up.

Surely they haven't found Silver yet?

A nurse rushes to my other side, helping us to get me to my room. We get pretty close before the police notice we're there.

"Miss James?" one of them asks.

I nod and swallow hard.

"I'm Officer George, this is Officer Shay. We were alerted to your missing status after the hospital found your bed empty around ten thirty last night. Could you tell us where you were?"

"Do you mind if I lie back down first? I'm not feeling too

great."

They step aside so the nurse and Drake can help me to the bed. "I'll go find the doctor," the nurse says.

"So where were you? The hospital mentioned worries of an abusive fiancé," Officer George says while giving Drake the evil eye.

I laugh. "He's not my fiancé," I say, pointing at Drake. "He's my brother. I called him and asked for him to take me out. I couldn't sleep, and I was hungry. Hospital food isn't very good, you know." I screw up my face.

"You were gone for a significantly long time, and now you're covered in dirt, you're bleeding, and you're not looking too good."

"Am I in some kind of trouble just because I left the hospital without telling anyone? I went out with my brother, I fell over, my stitches opened up, the car wouldn't start, so we've walked a really long way just to get me back here, okay?" *I'm getting better at this lying thing.*

Officer George is sceptical, but Officer Shay nods his head and says, "We're glad you're okay, Miss James. We'll be in touch if we have any more questions. We're glad this had a happy ending and that you're safe."

"Brother?" Drake asks with a smile when the officers leave.

I shrug. "You've made out with my sister, so ..."

He cringes. "She told you about that?"

"Like the first day I ever met her."

He shakes his head. "She's going to get me killed one day."

"You're not like Flynn, are you? You're not going to hurt her? Because Cade's the last person you'll have to worry about if you do. You'll have to go through me first."

He laughs. "Not possible, my friend. It's not like that between us, and it's never gone further than making out. She's made it perfectly clear where I stand."

"Do you want more with her?"

He shrugs. "That's not important, because it'll never happen. She's too closed off to let anyone in. I'm actually surprised she warmed to you so easily. Growing up with your mother, not knowing her father, then her first boyfriend being a total dick to her … I'm glad—for her sake—that you didn't go with Brett."

"She's the only reason I'm staying."

Drake smiles and takes my hand. "You're pretty awesome. You know that?"

"So are you, when you're not trying to get into my pants." I snatch my hand away, and he laughs.

"You know it's all an act, right? Have I ever once tried to get in your pants while we've been alone?"

I think about all the times he's said inappropriate stuff to me, and he's right—someone has always been there with us.

"Why do you do that? Why can't you be this Drake all the time?"

"We live in a world that's all about image. They expect things, expect you to act a certain way."

"That doesn't mean you have to do it."

"I think you can turn that accusation around on yourself there, missy."

"Wha—"

"*Heatwave.*"

"Yeah, okay. You got me there."

We're interrupted by the doctor coming in. It's the same doctor I had that first night I was brought in.

"Have a fun outing, did we?" His tone drips with condescension. He looks at Drake. "They tell me you're her brother?"

Drake nods.

"You are aware that your sister has had major surgery? She shouldn't be out gallivanting at all hours of the night. She needs rest." He looks to me. "Don't even get me started on you."

Why do I feel like a child being scolded by her father? "Uh

…"

"I'm sorry. That's unprofessional of me. You just … you remind me so much of my own daughter, and if she was here, in your position, I'd … How about I check you over."

I lift up my shirt for him, and his brow furrows as he takes in the sight of my bandaged wound. "Who—"

"I took a fall and the stitches popped open. They were bleeding and this was all I could find to cover them."

He purses his lips, removing the bandage. I know it's bad when he flinches.

"We're going to have to take you for a scan, make sure no internal stitches have also torn. Infection is already setting in, so you'll need a dose of antibiotics. We'll need to redo these stitches, and you'll be stuck here for a few more days I'm afraid."

Sighing, I throw my head back on the pillow. "Dammit."

"No more midnight adventures with your brother, okay? I'll get those tests ordered." He goes to walk out but turns back at the last second. "Your fiancé … is he …"

"He's gone. For good." It's true, and it'll get this weird overprotective doctor out of my hair.

The doctor nods once and walks out.

-21-

REPERCUSSIONS

After another three days in hospital, they're finally letting me go home tomorrow. My internal stitches proved to be intact, so the issue was mainly with my outside ones. My weird overprotective doctor is still weird, but Sasha thinks he's dreamy for an older guy and always gets the giggles when he checks on me while she's here.

I haven't told her about Brett yet. Whenever she's asked where he was, I've lied and said Litmus.

I've been expecting the cops to come. Surely Silver's body has been discovered by now. Really, that should be the last of my worries because from what I can tell, there's no way to trace Silver back to me or Litmus. Brett has a connection, but he's long gone.

I'm terrified of having to lie about Brett's unknown whereabouts to Cade and Jonas. Drake picked his car up from the train station with no problem, so it's confirmed. Brett and

Paddy are gone—where to, I don't know, but it's probably better that way.

When I see Cade making her way towards my hospital room, I start to panic. She shouldn't be here. She hasn't visited me at all since I've been in here. I still had another day to prepare myself. I can't do this right now.

What the hell do I do?

"You're looking better," she says in a motherly tone, entering the room.

"The doctors say I can go home tomorrow." I'm frozen in my bed, my voice sounding stiff.

"I actually came to talk to Brett. I assume he's been with you since he has neglected all of his Litmus obligations and security detail since you've been in here."

"No?" I say with forced uncertainty. "He hasn't been here for days. He told me he was at Litmus." *Am I laying it on thick enough?*

"Are you screwing with me right now?" she yells.

Temper, temper.

"Seriously. Are you joking?" she yells again.

"Why would I be—"

"His car's outside, he must be here somewhere."

"He told me Drake was picking him up and that he was going to leave the car here. I have his keys in my drawer."

She narrows her eyes at me. "You didn't think that was suspicious? Why would he leave his car here? How *dumb* are you?"

"I …"

"I don't want to hear it, Nuka. This is all on you."

"On me? Why? What am I able to do from a hospital bed? I know he was having family issues, maybe he's at his home with them. I don't know, I'm not his keeper."

"Please. That boy would've done anything if you asked. What did you say to him? That you didn't really love him? That your relationship was all still an act? There's no doubt in my mind you did something. You've been stringing him along for months. It's not like you could do any better, you should've just grit your teeth and accepted him."

"Like you do with Jonas?" Yeah, okay, even I know that's a low blow.

She takes two steps towards me, the sting of her backhanding me across the face hitting me before realisation does. Everything everyone has ever said about Cade comes crashing down in crystal clarity.

"You do *not* say shit like that. Jonas has been good to me and good to your sister. He's treated you with more respect than any of his other fighters as a favour to *me*. You do not disrespect him, okay?"

"Okay," I say, completely scorned. I guess Brett was right. They'll be nice until I start pushing the boundaries, something I was already playing with before he left.

"Are you seriously telling me you have no idea where Brett is?"

"I can honestly, one hundred percent, tell you I don't know where he is." *Totally not lying. And that's why he didn't tell me where he was going.*

"Someone's going to pay for this."

Cade walks away, and all I can think to yell after her is, "I'm feeling a lot better. Thanks for asking."

I rub my cheek where she slapped me, muttering to myself about not being strong enough to hit her back. Even if I wasn't in the hospital with all these injuries, I'm not sure I'd have the guts to attack her, and that thought disappoints me.

A high whistling noise comes from the doorway. "She got you good. I swear I heard it from down the hall," Drake says.

Sasha gives me a tight-lipped smile. "Just be glad she didn't hit you with her massive wedding ring."

"Does she do that often?" I ask her.

"Not since I learnt how to avoid pissing her off to breaking point. It's a handy skill to have. You'll probably want to learn it."

"I guess I should stop refusing to obey every little thing she tells me to do."

"That's probably a good idea. At least for a little while," Drake says.

"Okay, guys. Can you please tell me what's going on?" Sasha says. "I haven't seen Brett for days, Nuka's been a mopey sack of potatoes, and you two are suddenly … nice to each other. It's weird and freaking me out. Did Brett break up with you or something?"

"Can potatoes be mopey?" I ask Drake, a smile gracing both our lips.

"Shut up. Just tell me. I won't tell Mum, you know I won't."

Drake and I exchange a glance, and he nods for me to tell her.

"Brett's gone." I manage to keep the tears at bay—barely.

"Gone?"

"Won't be coming back, gone," I clarify.

"Where is he?"

"We honestly don't know. His nephew got into some trouble, and they needed to get somewhere safe."

"But how could he afford … holy shit, you gave him your trust fund, didn't you?"

"Crap. If you worked that out so quickly, we're so screwed when Cade finds out." *This is not good.*

"You knew and didn't tell me?" she asks, pushing Drake in the chest.

"Wasn't my story to tell," he says with a lame shrug.

Sasha's face suddenly turns dark, her mouth dropping open in realisation. "They'll kill you if they find out."

"Which is why they won't find out, right?"

She nods. "Got it."

***

I've been home for two weeks, and so far, Jonas and Cade haven't really asked too many questions. Drake's and my story remains the same, so when they've asked, we've both maintained that neither of us know where Brett is.

My stitches are out and my bruises are healed, but my wrist and ribs are still painful.

I tried going back to my room when I got home from the hospital, but it made me feel disjointed and wrong somehow. It was on the fourth night of tossing and turning that I climbed into Brett's bed and actually got a decent night's sleep. I sometimes expect him to walk through the bedroom door any minute, climb in bed, and cuddle into me, but I know that'll never happen. I've been pretty good at keeping it together around Sasha and Drake, but it's embarrassing that I've ended up crying nearly every night. I just keep telling myself, *I did the right thing, I did the right thing,* over and over again.

As much as I remind myself that I have the right to wallow—at least for a little while—I can't help feeling like one of those lame girls who do nothing but mope because she lost her boyfriend. But it's not like I have something to distract me from thinking about him considering I'm still recovering and can't *do anything.*

Originally, I came looking for Cade because I thought she'd help me find my voice, who I truly am. In a way, I guess she did. She gave me Brett and he made me realise I can do so much in this world. He hasn't had anything handed to him. Until my trust fund, he's had to work for everything his entire life. Me, on the other hand, I had endless opportunities around me, and I rebelled against them, throwing them all away.

I may not be going about helping this world in a conventional way, but I'm doing something I know, something I love, and something I can accomplish. Even if that is beating the crap out of people. I can't wait until I'm completely healed and can get in the arena again to start building my charity.

There's a short knock on the door. "Meeting," Drake says, opening the door just a crack.

"You can come in, I'm decent."

He opens the door wider as I sit up in bed. "We need to get upstairs as soon as possible."

"We?"

"They've called a meeting for the three of us. You, me, and Sasha."

My heart leaps into my throat. "Why?"

He shakes his head, and shrugs. "I don't know, but just stick to the story in case this is about to blow up in our faces. They can't know we had something to do with him leaving."

I get out of bed, which I've only just realised I didn't get out of today—at all. When we start making our way out the door and up to the office, my legs feel like jelly.

Sasha's already in Cade and Jonas's office when we arrive. The lighting is dim in the early evening light, and it's kind of eerie. I want to ask them to turn a light on, but the looks on their faces tells me I should tread carefully. Cade and Jonas look furious. Sasha looks terrified. Her eyes are wide, and her bottom lip's trembling.

"So, would you two like to tell us again about not knowing what happened to Brett?" Jonas says with a startling calmness to his tone.

"We don't—"

"Cut the crap," Cade snaps.

Glancing at Sasha out the corner of my eye, I begin to wonder if she betrayed us. Tears have pooled in her eyes, and she's giving me the most apologetic expressive I've ever seen on her.

As if she could sense my accusation, she subtly shakes her head before lowering her eyes, looking at the ground.

Jonas is glaring at Drake with a bemused expression. "Where's Brett?" His voice comes out deep and gruff.

"We don't—"

Drake's cut off by Jonas swivelling the computer screen on his desk to face us. On it, there's security footage of the hospital parking lot. It shows Drake and I getting out of Brett's car. He rushes to my side, holding me up as he assists me inside the hospital.

"Still sticking with your story?" Jonas asks.

Trying to be quick on my toes, I say the first response that pops into my head. "Brett had left his car there, like I said. Drake and I went out for a bit. I was feeling claustrophobic being stuck in that hospital room." *Pretty good for an off-the-cuff response.*

"You're forgetting one thing," Cade chimes in. "Brett left with his car hours earlier. We have that on tape too."

Shit.

"You all need to stop lying to us," Jonas says.

"We're not lying," Drake says. "We honestly don't know where he is … but … we know why he left."

"And why didn't you tell us this sooner?" Cade asks.

"We thought you'd blame us. And … he asked us not to say anything. His nephew … he got into some trouble," Drake says, his usual confident voice shaking.

"We know," Cade says. "We gave him the money to get him out of it."

"Only, Paddy didn't get completely out of trouble," I say. "Brett needed to take his family away from everything. Start fresh. There was no stopping him."

"How would he have been able to afford something like that? You can't just pick up and leave if you have no money. And we know Brett's finances; we know all of our fighter's finances. Brett couldn't have done it," Jonas says.

"You don't know everyone's finances," Cade says, glaring at me. "Nuka, how much is left in your trust fund?"

I swallow, hard. "Uh …" *Shit.*

"Why was I not alerted to this trust fund?" Jonas snaps.

"It's really not that much, Jonas," Cade starts, suddenly getting flustered. I guess she didn't think through blurting that out. "It was to supplement her income from us, seeing as she's only receiving ten percent for herself."

"That's a lie," Sasha says. "Mum didn't want you to know because she planned on taking it for herself."

Cade's eyes—and I'm sure mine too—go wide.

"What?" I ask.

Cade rounds the desk and is on Sasha quicker than my mind can register what's happening. She raises her hand, giving Sasha a backhanded slap, not unlike she did to me in the hospital.

"You're really choosing her over me?" Cade yells. She goes to raise her hand again, but I'm quicker to react this time, catching it before it connects with Sasha's face.

"Don't fucking touch her," I hear myself saying, immediately regretting it because I know what's coming, but also proud of myself for standing up to Cade.

She tries to use her other hand to punch me. I'm able to get my guard up and push her hard, making her stumble backwards and trip. Her butt hits the ground with a thud.

The fast movements and sudden scuffle have severely hurt my side.

Cade looks up at me, her face scrunched in anger, her eyes trying to glare a hole in me.

I stand over her, holding onto my left side. "What did Sasha mean, you were going to take my trust fund?"

"Yes, Cade. I'd like to know as well," Jonas says coming around to stand behind her.

A long shiny piece of metal in his hand catches my attention.

"Why do you have a gun?" I ask, my voice coming out jittery.

Sasha starts backing up a few steps and away from our mother.

Cade doesn't say anything and Jonas doesn't answer me. Cade lowers her head, staring at the carpet in front of her.

"Planning on leaving me?" Jonas asks, using the muzzle of the gun to push a strand of Cade's blonde hair behind her ear. It's unsuccessful as the barrel is too thick, but it's certainly successful in being scary as hell.

"Of course not. I would never—"

"Don't lie to me," he growls.

I find myself holding my breath. Sasha reaches for my hand, squeezing it like if she lets it go, she'll fall to the ground. Drake is quiet behind me, and I don't want to turn around to give him eye contact. I can't take my eyes off that gun. The silvery steel glints off the fading light from the sun setting outside.

"I don't need you, you know," Jonas says. "There would be plenty of women who'd be lining up to replace you. Do you want that? Because I can give you your out. Right now. Just say the word." He holds the gun to her head now, right against her temple.

"You know I want to be with you," she says, her voice quivering.

"Until I can believe you again, I'm revoking all of your access to my money. Got it? You will need to provide all receipts for the things I give you money for. There will be no more 'shopping trips,' no more outings. That goes for you too, Sasha."

Cade nods, tears falling freely down her face.

He takes the gun away and then offers his hand to help her off the ground. "Now that we have that sorted," he says as Cade gets to her feet, "back to the original issue."

The gun now faces me. My heart, which was already racing,

now beats impossibly fast.

"You lost us our best fighter," he says.

I want to argue with him that Ryker is his best fighter, but I don't think a "who's number one" debate is on Jonas's agenda right now.

"No. He was gone anyway. Nothing—not even lack of money—would've stopped him from saving Paddy." I can hear the pleading edge in my voice.

"You," he addresses Drake, "You didn't think to stop him? Did neither of you think to stop him? Did you know, Sasha?"

"She had nothing to do with it. She didn't even know until …" *Stop talking.*

"Until?" Jonas pushes.

"I found out a few days after he left," Sasha admits. I shake my head at her. She doesn't need to be involving herself in this.

Jonas rubs his head with the back of his hand that's holding the gun like he's in thought. The fact he's so calm with waving that thing around makes me even more anxious, reminding me that Brett said Jonas isn't above killing.

It's taking everything inside me not to break down, not to sink to the floor in a puddle of nervous tears.

We're all silent as we watch Jonas make his way back to his desk. He takes a seat, placing the gun on the wooden surface.

Cade stands visibly shaken, obviously put in her place. Her eyes still haven't left the floor. It's the first time I've actually seen her show any weakness. She's always so composed.

"You've betrayed us—all three of you," Jonas says. "There will be punishments, of course. Sasha, as I've already said, no more shopping trips on my dime. You want something? You'll have to pull more shifts at Litmus. Perhaps as something other than a bartender."

She nods but remains silent.

"Nuka. I guess now that you're officially single, we can use that to our advantage."

"Advantage?" my voice croaks.

"There'd be plenty of punters who'd pay a lot for you."

"No," Drake says as he stands a little straighter.

"What do you mean, they'd pay for me?" I ask.

"For your *company*, of course."

"She won't be doing that," Drake says.

"Well, this isn't up to you," Jonas says. "In fact, you're no longer needed at all."

I go to step in to beg for Drake's job, thinking that's what Jonas means. But I'm wrong. *So very wrong.*

The gunshot explodes in my ear as Drake's blood spatters, and I feel the spray on my skin. Arms wrap around me, holding me back as I try to get to Drake, to help him, to save him. Sasha's grip is too tight, though, and I don't have the strength, mentally or physically, to break free. Instead, I turn in to her, sobbing into her shoulder as we hold onto each other. She whimpers as she starts to shake. It doesn't take long for the roles to reverse and I'm soon consoling her. She was closer to Drake than I was. They were more than a bodyguard and his assignment, they were friends. Sometimes more than just friends.

There's no way he could survive a shot at such close range, and I can't do anything but stand here, holding onto my sister, rubbing her back like it'll make everything better. I shake my head at myself. *Nothing will make this better.*

A metallic taste fills my mouth, and at first I think some of his blood spattered in my mouth, but then I realise I'm biting on my cheek so hard, it's bleeding. Bile rises in my throat, and I fear I won't be able to squash it back down.

"Now," Jonas says, standing.

Sasha and I unwrap our arms from each other but our feet remain planted to our spots on the floor.

Jonas makes his way around the table, stepping over Drake's lifeless body like it's not even there. "As you can see, I'm severely hurt by your betrayal. I didn't want to do that, but he was no longer trustworthy, and I have no means of making money out of him. You, on the other hand, will be able to make it up to me, beg me for forgiveness, and earn back my trust."

I don't know how to answer him. Surely yelling "no!" will result in a bullet in my head.

"I'll take over Brett's contract. Five years, right? I'll do it," I stammer.

Jonas laughs. "Oh, my dear girl, that will just be the beginning. You think you're in the same league as Brawn? *Really?*"

"I'll train harder, I'll get better. Ryker can take over my training."

"Who's Ryker?" he asks.

"Psych," Cade answers.

Wow, he doesn't even know his fighter's real names.

"Seven years. Minimum. That'll take you close to fighting retirement age. You can retain your ten-percent cut, but you can kiss your charity goodbye."

"But—"

"This isn't a negotiation," he yells.

I nod, shrinking back into myself.

"If you're not performing to the standard expected of you, you *will* be earning money for me through other means. Got it? As I said, I could earn a lot from you. 'A night with Heatwave' has a certain ring to it."

"Jonas, please," Cade says.

Really? Now she's going to play mother? I guess it's good to know that even Cade has her limits. I can dress provocatively to earn her money, but taking it further than that isn't acceptable.

"Don't you start, woman. You've already got enough to make up for."

"I'll take on more responsibilities," Sasha says. "I'll become a bookie now instead of later like we discussed. I'll give you a bigger cut than the others. Anything. Just don't make Nuka do

… that."

Jonas cracks a small smile, knowing he owns us all now. "I'll give you one more week to recover before your training will start up again. Cade, you can organise that with Psych. And bring up two guys from Litmus security. They'll guard the girls until we can hire someone permanently. Someone who's not going to let them get away with anything and isn't going to screw us over. Someone who won't want to get into their pants, clouding their judgement. They're under lock and key from now on, okay? They're our greatest possessions, and we will not lose them like we lost Brett. Understand?"

Great.

"Yes, Jonas," Cade replies obediently.

"You two are dismissed," he says, waving the gun at Sasha and me. "Cade, clean this up."

"Yes, Jonas."

Sasha starts pulling me towards the door, and I make the mistake of glancing back. Just once. Drake's eyes are vacant, and he's covered in blood. I'm one hundred percent sure I will never get the image of Cade dragging his lifeless body out of my head.

Sasha and I are both silent as our feet move robotically towards my room.

"Can I stay with you?" she asks, her voice mousy.

"Of course," I say. I wrap my arm around her and lead her into my bedroom.

"Did that really just happen?"

"I wish it didn't."

"What are we going to do?" she whispers.

"I have no friggin' clue."

She sniffs, wiping her nose with the sleeve of her top.

"Was Cade really after my money?" I ask.

Sasha starts sobbing. "She's been trying to get away from Jonas for years. It's why she told you to keep the trust fund a secret. She wanted me to … she …"

"She asked you to get close to me, so you could work out a way to take it?" My tone isn't as angry as it should be. For some reason I know Sasha wouldn't do that to me.

"She said that you stole that money from *her,* that your dad owed it to *her,* and it was unfair that you didn't earn it. I believed her at first, but then I spent five minutes with you and knew she was wrong. I realised within the first day of knowing you that being your sister was way more important than being her daughter. And she was about to throw you under the bus. To Jonas, no less. Please, you *have* to forgive me. I know Mum never will, but I don't even care about that. I just don't want to lose you. Please," she pleads through her tears.

"We'll get out. I promise," I say, taking her into my arms.

How am I ever going to keep that promise?

-22-

NO PLAN

We both have a horrible night's sleep. Just when I start to drift off, Sasha startles and starts crying again. I join her, and by morning I think we're all cried out.

I keep seeing it over and over again. Drake's blood going everywhere and his body dropping to the ground, empty of any life. In my memory, Cade doesn't even flinch. She stands in the corner, looking at the ground, unmoving, like some obedient dog.

Everyone told me to be scared of Cade and Jonas. I just figured they were a team, both as bad as each other. I repeatedly told myself to stay on their good side because I didn't want to encounter their infamous wrath. But it was all him. Cade's attitude, her scariness, it all came from orders passed down by Jonas. He owns her, just as he owns all of us.

I know I should probably feel sorry for Cade, but I don't. It's her job as a mother to protect her daughters from monsters like

Jonas, not sell them to him.

There's a quiet knock at the door before Cade enters, two men trailing behind her—one I recognise from Litmus security, the other I've never seen before. Sasha and I sit up in bed, covering ourselves with the sheet. We're wearing pyjamas, but it's still awkward.

"Your new assignments, gentlemen," Cade says. When she turns her head to face them, bruises on her neck stand out—four circular marks from fingers digging into her throat. I can only assume she's been through a whole night of punishment.

"Uh …" the Litmus bouncer stutters.

"It's only until we can get full-time replacements. It's your job to make sure they don't leave this house unless on an approved outing. You are to escort Nuka to training, and make sure Sasha completes her studies. You're not here to make friends. This is a job, and professionalism is needed. The reason the last two didn't work out is because they got too close. Understand?"

They both nod.

"You do not let them talk you into going out unless I have approved it. Got it?"

"You pull me out of the club so I can babysit spoiled princesses? Really?" the one I don't know says.

"You'll be getting paid double while you're here. If that doesn't interest you, there's the door," she snaps, pointing behind them.

For a moment, I think the one I recognise is about to take an exit, but one look at Cade's face and I realise why he's second-guessing himself and keeping glued to the spot. She has her intimidating face on.

"Right. I'll leave you to it, then. Keep an eye on both of them, but particularly *Nuka*."

"Thanks, *Mum*," I yell after her as she walks out. It's the first time I've ever called her that, and it will definitely be the last.

She briefly freezes at my barb but doesn't bite, continuing down the hallway.

"Are you … is she … I didn't realise she had another daughter, let alone you … you're *freaking Heatwave,*" Litmus dude says.

"I hate that name. Call me Nuka."

He nods once.

"Logan, how did you get roped into doing this?" Sasha asks.

"I have no idea. One minute Cade was asking for a favour, the next minute I'm down here with you." The poor guy looks so nervous.

"And who are you?" Sasha asks the other one.

"Byron. I work at Alchemy."

"Not anymore, you don't," I mutter under my breath.

Alchemy is one of the bars that's attached to the staff tunnels. It's the one Brett and I were drinking at only just a few weeks ago. *Ugh.* I shake that thought from my mind before it threatens to take over me.

"Is it true what they're saying? Brett and Drake are …" Logan asks. *There are rumours already?*

"Gone," I say, stronger than I thought I could.

This just makes Logan look more nervous. He runs his hand over his blond hair and stares up at the ceiling as he rubs his neck. Byron on the other hand stands with his arms folded, his grey eyes glaring at us as the light from outside makes his bald head shine.

"Calm down, Logan. We won't give you any trouble, I swear," Sasha says in her put-on innocent voice. "But can you go outside while we get out of bed and get dressed?" Oh, geez, she's even batting her eyelashes.

"Uh … I don't know, is that allowed?" Logan asks, his voice shaking like he's unsure of himself.

"Well, they're not paying you to watch us undress, you perv," I say, rattling him even more.

"You take the terrace door, I'll take this one," Byron says professionally.

Logan heads towards the door that opens up to the pool area. When they're both gone, and the doors are closed, I start to get out of bed when Sasha stops me. "If we're going to get out, we need to do it while these two imbeciles are watching over us. Before they hire professionals." Her voice is quiet but urgent.

I shake my head. "This needs planning. We can't just wing it."

"What do you suggest we do?" she yells, but still in a whisper.

Throwing my hands up in the air, I shake my head at her. "I don't know," I whisper-yell back.

I put my head in my hands, the hopelessness of our situation almost causing me to break.

"If I could get in contact with my family …"

"Aren't you, like, fighting with them?"

Sighing, I nod. "Yeah, but I also know they'd be there for me if I really needed it. I've always known that."

"That must've been nice, growing up in that type of environment." I don't miss the longing in her voice.

"Yeah," I admit. "It was."

I grew up in the most supportive home anyone could've asked for. I had the stereotypical annoying younger brother, the adoring baby sister, and two parents who gave me love. All they wanted to do was protect me and give me everything I wanted. And I threw it away like it was nothing. Sasha barely had a single parental figure and has grown up on her own. She makes the best of her crappy situation, and mostly without complaint.

In this moment, my respect and admiration for Sasha grows.

***

"Eager to get back to it already?" Ryker says, entering the training room. He throws his gym bag on the ground and takes his shirt off, eager to get back into training.

"Not eager, forced," I reply flatly.

My wrist is still in a cast, my ribs are still broken—and will be for another three weeks according to the doctors—yet, here I am in the training room because Jonas needs me to be ready the minute my cast comes off.

Byron stands at the entrance to the room, his face devoid of any emotion. He's good at his job, never letting me out of his sight and definitely not allowing me any wiggle room. It's only been a week so far, but the guy barely even talks to me, just grunts one-word answers all the time.

"New wall decoration?" Ryker asks.

"Replacement."

"So it's true? Brett's really …"

"Gone." I lean in and whisper, "But not dead like Drake."

Ryker's jaw drops. I nod at him as my eyes fill with tears, but I refuse to let them spill over. That is, until Ryker hugs me. There's no stopping them after that.

"Sasha and I really need your help here," I whisper so quietly I'm unsure if he heard it all.

"So, ready to get to it?" he asks, pulling away from me and acting completely normal as if he didn't hear me.

"Oh … okay."

Byron starts grabbing onto his stomach like he's in pain. He nods to Ryker. "Can you watch her for a minute? Don't let her go anywhere?" His voice is strained. "I just need to go to the bathroom real quick."

"No problem," Ryker says with a casual shrug. Once Byron leaves, Ryker turns to me. "Okay, you've only got a few minutes. Spill."

"Did you just—"

"Yes, and it's only going to take him a few minutes to realise his bowel isn't exploding like I made him think it was going to."

"Nice."

"Nuka, what's going on?"

I explain as quickly and as briefly as I can. I tell him about Brett leaving, Drake dying, my changed contract, and the fact that Sasha and I are now trapped here.

"What do you need me to do?"

"I need to get in contact with my adoptive family on the outside, but I don't know how I can go about it, and I can't get you to do it directly. Drake barely had anything to do with Brett leaving, and it cost him his life, just because they couldn't use him like they can me. They killed *him* to punish *me*. If you get involved ..."

Ryker nods, but I see the Adam's apple in his throat bob nervously. "I'll see what I can do."

"Aren't you two meant to be training?" Byron barks, re-entering the room.

And with that, Ryker starts with the head games, and I go about trying to find a way to block him out.

"Wait," I exclaim. "I need to get ready for it. I'm already in enough pain without adding your imaginary crap to it."

Closing my eyes, I breathe in deep and imagine Declan's face like I have so many other times while fighting Ryker. The only problem is his face keeps morphing into Brett's, and that certainly isn't going to help keep the pain at bay. If anything, it'll make it worse.

"Nuka?" Ryker pulls me out of my failing trance.

"Yeah?" I ask, opening my eyes.

"How about we start with some weights. We'll go slow."

I let out a sigh of relief. "Thank you."

***

"Still nothing?" I ask.

Ryker shakes his head. "Sorry. They're not calling me back."

He's been trying to get a hold of my family for me, but with no luck. He says he's left two messages for them on their phone but hasn't heard back. He can't leave a detailed voicemail, and I'm wondering if Lia and Jayce are ignoring him because they don't know who Ryker is or what he could want. He's too paranoid about mentioning my name over the phone, which is understandable considering where Drake is right now. We can't risk Cade and Jonas finding out—I won't let Ryker put himself in danger like that. It's not worth risking Ryker that way.

"I'm sorry I'm not helping you. Short of going to their house, I've tried. I swear."

I reassuringly place my hand on his shoulder. "It's okay. I knew it'd be a long shot, and I don't want you going to their house in case they have you followed or something. I wouldn't put it past them."

His eyes go wide.

"I'm not saying you *are* being followed … but, it's better to be safe than sorry, right? I'll get to my family another way. My uncle said he was going to call me in for an official Immune assessment, but that was well over a month ago now. We just have to hope that he calls on me soon. It's probably the only chance for Sasha and me to get out of here."

"How's Sasha holding up?"

"Not great."

Drake still haunts us. Sasha and I have taken up Brett's room now, neither one of us comfortable being alone in the house. While I train, she studies to become a bookie, and apart from that, we don't leave each other's sides.

I recently found out it was always Jonas's plan to make Sasha a bookie. He realised when she was younger that she had a high understanding of maths, so he's been grooming her for the position ever since.

She told me she had a deal with Jonas that she could finish high school before becoming his slave. She also told me that she actually finished high school months ago and she's taken up a few uni courses since then—unbeknownst to Cade and Jonas. She's doing it by correspondence, so she's been able to pass off her studying as her home schooling.

But now, because of me, she's just like the rest of us. Owned.

We're not allowed visitors, and the only person I'm permitted to see is Ryker. Cade has shunned Sasha just as much as she has me, and in a way, it's made Sasha and me even closer. But it's affecting Sasha—I can tell, even though she's trying to hide it.

Cade may not be a great mum, but she's the only one Sasha's ever had, and losing Cade has done something to her.

"She seems to be running on survival instincts, almost like she's a robot. She does what they tell her to, but I can tell she's struggling."

"It's got to be hard on her. I know Drake and her were close."

I nod, not really knowing how to explain just how close they were.

Logan comes back into the training room at that moment, resuming his position near the door.

Ryker and I go back to training, and I whisper in his ear, "If you keep giving them bathroom issues every time we need to talk, they'll start getting suspicious."

"Please, they're both too dumb to put two and two together," he whispers back. "Okay," he says louder so Logan can hear. "I've gone pretty easy on you so far. Now you have your cast off, and your first fight is in a few days, this is really our last chance to push you. You ready?"

"Ugh."

"Come on!" he yells enthusiastically. "Gotta keep that sponsor of yours happy."

I stop dead in my tracks. *Of course.* Spinning on my heel to face Ryker, I mouth the words, "Gabby. Tell Gabby." She can get to Dec.

-23-

I'M BACK

Walking back into Litmus sends a chill down my spine. It's my first fight back, and I think I'm even more nervous than I was for my first fight with Steve. Back then they expected me to be crap, now they're hoping for it.

I can hear the taunts now. *"Oh, how the mighty have fallen!"* Okay, so that's a little dramatic. It's not like I almost died … well, okay I did, technically.

The pressure is on me to do well tonight. I can't let my first loss become what I'm known for. *Knocked out by a normal. Ugh.*

Walking into the Deakin locker room, I'm met by Ryker, Colton, Steve, and Palmer. They all hug me, even Palmer, which is surprising.

When Palmer pulls out of the hug, he looks me in the eyes with a sympathetic stare. "Ryker told us what you did for Brett. I'm sorry he's gone."

I nod, willing the tears to stop forming in my eyes. "Me too," I whisper as he steps away.

"Is it just me, or do you look extra tarted up tonight?" Colton asks, stepping forwards to pull on a strand of my curled hair.

I have to laugh. If I don't, I'll cry. "I'm not sure if it was payback from Vidia for Brett leaving, or if she was ordered to 'up the skank.'"

Colton smiles. "I like it."

"Why does that not surprise me?"

"Come on," Steve says. "You've got an ass to kick."

I'm relieved when my entrance is met with screaming and applauding. *Better than booing, anyway.*

I make it to the stage, and Felix welcomes me back with a big hug. He starts bantering with the audience, as usual.

"Heatwave is back! And she is determined to claw, and fight, and beat the crap outta you, just so she can redeem some of her floundering reputation."

A few of the audience members laugh. I manage a weak smile.

"But there's a big misconception out there that certain people from upstairs want me to clarify."

Great, here we go. More blindsiding from Cade and Jonas. What's it going to be this time? I'm actually the daughter of a long-lost royal bloodline?

"Is it true, Heatwave, that Brawn is no longer with us? We've been hearing these rumours for over a month now. He hasn't been here at all while you've been recovering. Come on, you can tell us. We're really good at keeping secrets." Everyone laughs. "What really happened to Brawn?"

I tsk playfully, telling myself to keep calm. "Well now, if I told you, I might just have to kill you, too."

"Oh!" Felix yells taking a few animated steps away from me. "Was that a confession?"

The audience is lapping it up. I was told to keep Brett's

disappearance vague, but Jonas and Cade think playing up the rumour of me killing him would be good for my weak image. Either the audience knows this is all a show, or there are some really screwed-up people in this audience. *Uh, hello, they're betting on you to beat the hell out of someone. Yeah, pretty safe to say—they're pretty screwed up.*

"Perhaps you haven't been out injured at all? Maybe that's just an alibi. Maybe, we should get a challenger up here to find out how rusty you really are."

The crowd goes wild, clapping and cheering, and before I know it, I have three volunteers to choose from.

As they take to the stage, I quietly ask Felix, "Is this normal? I've never had more than one volunteer before."

He leans in and whispers in my ear, "They think you're an easy mark because of your last loss. No pressure, kid, but you're going to have to prove them wrong."

I nod. "I'm ready."

Training with Ryker has been going exceedingly well. Turns out, Brett was a big ol' softy on me, allowing me breaks when I didn't need them. Ryker pushes me way past where I think my boundaries are, but it's effective. He still lets me have a break, but not before we get to breaking point. He knows I need to perform well, so he doesn't hold back. Plus, I secretly think he enjoys causing pain.

"Okay," Felix says. "First up, let's make sure you all qualify. Don't want to make that mistake twice." He turns to the audience with an "oops" expression, making them break into laughter.

The man knows how to entertain, I'll give him that.

Two men and one woman stand before me, each showing off their ability. The woman steps forwards, her limbs stretching like rubber. She does a flip backwards but completely does a full loop before her lower half of her body follows.

"Flexible. Got it," I mumble, moving onto the next person.

He holds his arms out and winces as they turn to some kind of metal or steel. It only goes to his shoulders, though. I wonder if his ability is only local to his arms or if he can do this to his whole body and is just holding back.

I nod. "Interesting."

As I move onto the last guy, he steps forward, creating sparks between his fingers. I'm instantly reminded of Taser and his ability, and my suspicions automatically go into overdrive. *Did Taser send another one?*

I instinctively shake my head. "Number two. In the middle. You're up."

The crowd goes insane with screams as the other two contestants leave the stage.

Felix says into the mike, "Okay, you've got a few minutes to finalise bets." He then leans into me and whispers, "Confident move, going for the biggest contender. Let's hope you can pull this off, hey?"

I nod. "Let's hope."

I decide to not even play with this guy. This needs to end quickly. When the round one buzzer goes off, I don't stall. My hands are quick, and my feet are faster. He can't predict the randomness of my moves—something Ryker and I have been working on. It's been hard with the broken arm and ribs, but we've worked around that.

It turns out my opponent's body armour can protect all of him, but every time I connect, it falters, making him weak.

Heating his armour causes him pain, so I use that to my advantage, making sure my hands are blazing hot at all times.

By the end of round one, he's looking pretty battered. I've barely been touched. My knuckles are bleeding from the hits I've been dishing out, but that's nothing compared to what I've been through lately. I don't ease up in round two, and with a minute still left on the clock, I deliver two extremely hard blows to the side of this guy's head. A right hook, followed by my elbow to his face while his guard is down. He falls to his knees, giving me my opportunity. With a knee to his head, he's down and out. My first *real* knockout.

Quick, simple, done.

I take my victory proudly as the crowd screams my name in a chant.

I'm back.

***

After fulfilling my promotional duty, I'm on my way out of the corporate box when Cade grabs my arm. "Meeting, now," she says in my ear.

Sighing, I follow her into the office where Jonas is behind his desk.

"Great fight tonight," he says.

I almost stumble backwards, surprised by the praise.

"It's a great start to getting you back in the game," he adds.

"Uh … thanks."

"We'll be moving you onto the main roster in two weeks, so you've only got one more Wild Card night left."

"Do you think I'm ready for that?"

"Don't care, really. You'll bring in bigger money fighting the others—especially after that knockout."

"And if I get injured again because I'm *not* ready?"

"You already know what'll happen then."

"A night with Heatwave?" My voice cracks as I swallow the lump in my throat.

"Train hard, Nuka."

***

Jonas would make a great motivational speaker. His words, "Train hard," keep running through my head during training sessions, and Ryker's been pushing me harder and harder. He's had to stop sending my bodyguards to the bathroom every time we needed to talk—Byron's not as dumb as he looks—but he subtly gave me a heads-up a few days ago that he got to Gabby. Now all I really need to do is wait.

I still feel like we're nowhere near getting out of here, but at least now there's hope. Gabs just has to go to Declan, and he will go to my family. *This has to work.*

"You're going to kill it," Ryker says, walking into the locker room at Litmus. "Better get you ready for your last hoorah."

It's my last Wild Card night for a while, and it almost feels like a graduating ceremony.

Walking out and taking centre stage, I go stand in my corner and wait.

"She's been known to kill a man," Felix starts.

Here we go. This rep's probably going to follow me everywhere.

"Heartbroken by our very own Brawn, she killed him in cold blood and is back to finish off any man who may cross her."

All I can do is laugh. It probably makes me seem even more psycho.

It still kills me to hear about Brett, or even think about him, but with my sole focus now on getting Sasha and me out of here, I've barely had time to wallow over him.

I don't cry at night anymore, mainly because I don't want to show how weak I really am in front of Sasha. But the tears are always there, always on the brink. I nearly always make it to the bathroom before I let them spill over.

Felix calls for challengers, and just like my first fight, there's hesitance within the audience. Not surprising since I knocked out my last volunteer, and now Felix is telling everyone I killed a man. I'm under strict instructions to not do that to this volunteer … knock him out, not kill him. Although, I'm sure they meant that too.

When the crowd starts parting to make room for a sole challenger to make their way to the stage, the only thing I can see is the top of his head through the throng of people. But then he speaks.

"Next time you try to kill someone, you better make sure they're really dead."

That voice. It's competing with the one inside my head screaming, *No, no, no, no, no!* He can't be here.

Am I breathing? I'm pretty sure I've stopped breathing. Air? Hello? I need you. Fill my lungs, dammit!

I'm praying to a god I don't believe in that I'm maintaining my composure at seeing *him,* but I can't be sure, because right now all I'm trying to do is remain standing.

Brett walks up the few stairs, taking to the stage.

I remain frozen in panic and confusion. *Why the hell is he standing in front of me?*

The crowd goes ballistic, while Felix stands still with his mouth agape. He snaps his head out of whatever confused trance he was in, yelling into the microphone, "Guess he's not dead after all. Brawn, tell us, where've you been?"

The crowd is still screaming, and Brett waits until they quieten down before answering. "It's true that I left." There's a collective gasp from the audience as if he just said the worst thing imaginable, like him dying was more acceptable than him voluntarily leaving. "I abandoned the one person who gave me everything. It didn't take me long to realise that it was a mistake.

I belong here, with the woman I'm in love with." The crowd's awing fades away as he steps closer to me, suddenly making me feel like we're the only two people in here. "However, by her stunned expression, I'm not entirely sure she wants me back."

"You shouldn't be here," I whisper, surprising myself that I actually get any words to come out at all.

"Sorry, what was that, Heatwave?" Felix asks, putting the microphone in my face.

Brett takes another step, the only thing separating us now is Felix's arm and the microphone. "She said I shouldn't be here."

The crowd boos.

"Why are you here?" I ask.

"I had to come back."

"No," I whisper. I take Felix's mike and shove it out of the way. "They'll kill you. They already—"

"I know," he whispers. "But I've got it covered. Just trust me, okay? Go with whatever I say, and I'll explain everything to you as soon as I can."

I nod.

"First thing, pretend to be more pissed off than stunned, please."

My mouth opens to protest, but I relent and nod again instead.

"Just put on a good show."

Thankfully, Felix pretends he can't hear what we're saying.

Part of me won't stop asking questions. *Why is he here? Where's Paddy? What happened to make him come back? Why is he doing this?* Then there's the other part of me that's making me plant my feet to the spot to save me from throwing myself at him.

Brett takes the microphone from Felix and turns to the audience. "Seems like my little impromptu vacation made my girlfriend a little bitter. So I challenge her to a fight." He looks back at me with a smirk. "If I win, she has to give me another chance. If she wins, I'll let her make her own mind up whether or not she takes me back."

Ah, the dependable audience that we cater for, always up for a bit of male chauvinistic behaviour; their screams are deafening.

I join him at his side, electricity running through my fingertips as they meet his on the microphone. I'm *really* struggling to keep my distance right now.

"I thought this was Wild Card night. Can't really have a Litmus fighter volunteering, right?" I say.

"I'm pretty sure the crowd doesn't mind," he says, sending the audience into even more of a frenzy. "Besides, when I left, I broke my contract. Technically, I'm not a Litmus fighter anymore. You're just scared I'll win."

I raise my eyebrows. "You're going to wish you stayed away."

I take to my corner, crossing my arms as I do, faking confidence that just isn't there right now.

Felix takes the microphone as Brett strips off his shirt.

Don't look at his abs, don't look at his abs. Shit! I looked at his abs.

"We'll give a few moments for you all to finalise your bets. Will Brawn win his girl back, or will Heatwave stand her ground?"

Brett doesn't take his eyes off me and smirks every time I break my gaze with him. I'm scared if I continue to stare at him, I won't be able to hold back. My body is itching to be next to his.

The buzzer for round one seems to take an hour to go off, but when it finally does, Brett doesn't hold back on me.

He advances swiftly and without hesitation. Starting with a few simple jabs, they become quicker and more frequent as I block each one, eventually morphing from closed-hand punches to open-handed strikes.

"Put on a good show, baby," he says, taunting me as he doesn't let up, his hands moving faster than my eyes can keep up with. Somehow my arms manage to keep blocking him.

"If I do that, will you tell me what the hell you're doing here?" I ask, managing to throw my first hit—a solid punch straight to his gut. I turn 180 degrees, sending a knife-hand strike to his ribs with one hand and then attempt a palm strike to the side of his head with the other, but he's too quick. My knife-hand strike hits him, but he dodges my palm.

He straightens up and attempts to send a jab and then a right hook into my jaw, but I dodge and duck, punching him in the ribs under his arm. He swings with his other fist which makes me duck again, but I spin and elbow him in the same spot I just hit.

He lets out a little grunt. "I came back for you. I shouldn't have left in the first place."

"But Paddy," I say, throwing another fist at him which he blocks.

"He's safe, I promise, but you can't tell anyone that. Official story is Shane found us and killed him."

"Huh?"

I go to knee him in the ribs, but he grabs a hold of my thigh, pulls me forward, and pins me to him.

"I can't explain here." He brings his other hand up to my face, caressing my cheek. The crowd screams, and I mentally beg for him to kiss me, but I know that's not allowed. Not yet.

I push him off me and stumble back a few feet. He tries to advance again, but I turn on my side and extend my leg, kicking him in the chest. As his feet falter and he takes the time to correct his balance, I pivot on my left foot and send a roundhouse kick to the side of his head.

He recovers quickly but not before I get the chance to shuffle back so I'm at the edge of the arena. He cocks his head in my direction, confused as to what I'm doing, and that's when I run for him.

My left foot meets his abs, and he does what I'm

anticipating—he grabs hold of my ankle. Using the momentum from charging at him, and him holding me as an anchor, I lift my other foot, kicking him in the jaw as I do a backflip in the air, forcing him to let go of my left ankle. It all happens in a quick, swift move, but it feels like I move in slow motion.

The buzzer dings, signalling the end of round one, just as I land my feet back on the ground. It's not graceful, and I have to crouch down to keep balance, but it doesn't stop the smirk from finding my face. I'm sweaty, panting, and out of breath.

I stand straighter. "Ryker and I have been experimenting with my feet, seeing as I couldn't fight with my hands for a few weeks."

His stunned expression as he rubs his jaw makes me smile even wider.

"Pretty safe to say you're fired as my trainer."

"I want you so friggin' bad right now," he says before taking to his corner for our break.

His words send a tingling to my stomach that I hope never leaves. I don't think I can make it another round without kissing him.

Felix jumps back in the ring, spouting about how amazing the first round was, but I don't hear it. I'm completely tuned to one thing only—Brett.

When round two begins, I can no longer help myself. It's been nearly six weeks without him, and now he's making me hold back when all I want to do is take him in my arms again. I think he feels it too, because he doesn't attack. We slowly approach each other, and then he lifts me so my legs are wrapped around his waist. His hand gently pushes the hair out of my face before taking my mouth with his.

This is what it's meant to be like.

He came back for me.

This is my forever.

-24-

A DEAL

When Brett sets me back down on my feet, Felix is on the microphone. “Did anyone see who caved first? They’re back together, so does that mean Brawn won?” He seems genuinely confused as to how they’re going to call the fight. “Perhaps we’ll have to go to the scoring of round one.” He puts his finger to his ear and nods as he’s given information in his little earpiece. “Which goes to *Heatwave*!”

I’m surprised the audience hasn’t passed out or lost their voices by now from all the screaming. Brett raises my hand in victory before a sea of security guards line our path to backstage.

Brett practically drags me away and through the doors. Once we’re out the back and alone, he proceeds to push me against the wall, taking my mouth with his like he owns it. Which, I really don’t care if he does. He can claim ownership of all of me right now, I really won’t mind.

He pulls back, easing off me just a fraction. “I guess we

should go face them sooner rather than later."

"You haven't seen them yet?" My throat goes dry and my stomach churns.

"I have a plan. You'll see," he says, kissing my nose. "But first, I'm thinking we should shower … because of the fight, of course." He smirks, and I can't help myself—I start dragging him towards the locker room without hesitation.

We stumble in, and he starts kissing me again, moving us towards the showers. His hands trail down my back, making my need for him intensify. He hooks his thumbs into the waistband of my tights, but before he can start to tug them down, a throat clears behind us.

"You're back," Jonas says as Brett and I pull away from each other, startled.

"We were just going to come see you, actually." Brett takes hold of my hand and grips it tight.

"Mm, looks that way," he says, his tone dripping with cynicism.

"We thought you left to protect your family," Cade says.

Brett runs his hand through his hair. "Turns out, I wasn't quite fit for the job. They got to Paddy anyway."

"Why did you come back? You had the money to get out," Cade says.

"They took the money, too."

He lost my trust fund?

"So you only came back because you had to," Jonas says.

"The only reason I left was for Paddy. But now he's gone." Even though Brett told me Paddy's safe, him choking on the words makes me worry about where Paddy really is.

"Why shouldn't we punish you?"

"You're right, I did the wrong thing. I should've come to you first instead of running away, but at the time I thought it was my only option. You won't want to punish me when you hear what I have to offer. I'm here to make a deal."

"Oh?"

"I'll match her contract. Seven years, and ten percent, right?"

"Who told—"

"Ryker. I saw him when I arrived here tonight."

Okay, I know Brett well enough to know that's a lie. Plus, I've been with Ryker all evening, right up until my fight. *Who really told him?*

"We'll take this act as far as you want us to," Brett says. "You saw the crowd out there—they love us. And with Nuka and me together, you wouldn't have to worry about us running off. She's all I ever want, and I don't have my family standing in the way anymore."

I wrap my arm around him and look up into his chocolate eyes. "You're all I want, too." Okay, not quite—I still want us all to be out of here.

"Aww, how sweet," Cade says snidely.

"How are we going to trust you again?" Jonas asks.

"My screwing up had everything to do with my family and nothing to do with Litmus or you. You've both been tremendously generous with me over the years, and I'm sorry I panicked and ran—so incredibly sorry. It's why I'm willing to make it up to you by taking a percentage cut. I want to show you I'm serious about this. Nuka and I have no money and nowhere to go. Pretty simple really, you want to make money, we need a place to sleep and a wage to live on."

Jonas rubs his jaw in thought. "I'm still going to be hiring a new head of security. We've just found someone who seems like he'll be a good fit, and we can't exactly trust you now."

"That's fair," Brett says.

"And add a year each, no more security wage, and then we have a deal."

Cade scoffs, but Brett steps forwards and shakes Jonas's hand. "Eight years. Done."

"We'll let you two get cleaned up, and we'll see you upstairs for your comeback promotional schmoozing." Jonas and Cade go to leave, but he turns back at the last second. "Don't be too long … if you know what I mean."

Brett starts laughing at me as my face goes as bright as a tomato. When Jonas and Cade leave, Brett wraps his arms around me. "Guess the moment's kind of passed now," he says.

"Yeah, finding out we're stuck here for eight years doesn't really do it for me. I mean, really? *That's* your brilliant plan?"

"It's only the beginning."

***

We're welcomed into the corporate box with a round of applause from our investors and sponsors, and any other person Jonas and Cade invited to be schmoozed. Brett refuses to let go of me as we go from person to person and he gives a generic explanation for his whereabouts. "There was a death in my family, and I didn't handle it well. I needed some time off and didn't know when or if I was going to return."

I think everyone was expecting some juicy gossip, but the truth proves to be a good way to shut the conversation down. They're all sympathetic but move on quickly to topics like who we're scheduled to be fighting soon and that our fight tonight was amazing to watch, even if it was only one round.

It seems to be true that everyone is unwilling to talk about the real world in here. That's not what Litmus is about.

After making the rounds, Jonas and Cade tell us to go home. I'm itching for Brett to tell me what's really going on, but Byron and Logan are driving us home. The car is full as Sasha is also with us, so I have to settle for having Brett's arm wrapped around me and no answers. For now. It's a compromise I adjust to easily.

Brett and I don't even acknowledge Byron and Logan's goodbyes, or Sasha's "I'm happy you're back" remark as she makes her way up the stairs to her own room which she hasn't been in in weeks. We're behind the closed door of our bedroom in record time.

"Okay. The truth—now," I demand.

His lips turn up in the corners of his mouth. "Can't we just …" he says, stepping forwards, wrapping his arms around me and kissing my lips softly.

I'm determined to stay strong, even though every second his lips are on mine, my determination slowly declines.

Forcing myself to pull away, I give him my best "I'm unimpressed look," but it only makes him laugh.

"In a few more days, it'll all make sense. I promise."

"Why did you come back? Where's Paddy? What happened to the money? How are we going to get out of here?"

"We're going to get out of here, I promise. But … it might take a while. The money's in an untraceable account, Paddy's safe and staying with a pretty awesome family I recently met, and I came back because I seem to have this habitual compulsion to try to save the people I love."

This time when he kisses me, I don't try to stop him. My lips part, eagerly accepting his as he takes me in his arms. A moan escapes me when he pulls me in closer, his hand running down my back, gripping my hip with just enough force to make me groan embarrassingly.

When we come up for air, I'm completely breathless.

"I love you, Nuke."

No, now I'm completely breathless. "I love you too."

-25-

FIGHT OR FLIGHT

Brett's arm drapes over me, his hand resting on my bare stomach. His deep breathing on my neck is an odd comfort. It reminds me that he's really here, that last night really happened, and that he came back *for me.*

Lifting his arm and the sheet off me, I try to slip out of bed without waking him, but he pulls me back into him, gripping me tighter.

"You're not going anywhere," he mumbles, still half-asleep.

"We should get up, it's late."

"No, we should stay in bed all day. We have lost time to make up for."

"I think we made up for it enough last night." *And he didn't get burnt. Yay!*

I was nervous about taking the next step with Brett after my past and only experience, but after embarrassingly explaining myself to him, I realised there was absolutely no reason to be nervous. It was Brett and I was ready.

Still, we took things slow. We giggled through some minor awkwardness, but my first night with Brett was as close to perfect as I could've asked for.

He kisses my shoulder, making his way up to my neck.

"Or we could just stay in bed," I murmur.

We're interrupted by a knock at the door and Cade walking in. She stops short as she sees the state of undress Brett and I are in, but she doesn't leave to give us time to get up and put clothes on, just moves farther into the room.

"I'm here to introduce our new head of security," she says, simply.

Brett and I sit up, covering ourselves with the sheet. I rub my eyes and yawn, awaiting the new bodyguard.

My heart stops beating when he walks in. Brett puts his arm around my shoulder, giving it a reassuring squeeze.

What the hell is going on?

I don't dare say anything. I don't dare let on that the person standing in front of me has been in my life since I was little. He's overbearing and a pain in the ass, always sticking his nose where it doesn't belong. But his intentions have always been brotherly, even though he's Lia's age and almost old enough to be my father.

"Nuka, Brett, this is Kyle."

Not laughing at the obvious pseudonym for Kai is almost impossible, but I manage. I know how important it is to ensure I don't give away the fact they've hired a special ops cop as the new head of security.

"I'll leave you to lay down the law with these two," Cade says, leaving promptly.

Before the door's even shut, Kai raises his finger to his mouth to silence me. He takes out a device from his back pocket and starts scanning the room with it. I want to ask what he's doing, but the words don't find my mouth.

Brett starts rubbing my back soothingly while Kai makes his way around the room. Once he's done, he gives us a nod.

"I told you the room was clean," Brett says.

"Yeah, but you haven't been here for over a month. Anything could've changed," Kai says.

"How do you two …"

"Okay, confession time," Brett says, running his hand over his head.

"*Confession*? Please don't tell me you're like some undercover cop?"

Brett laughs. "Hardly. After Paddy and I left, we went up north, taking the money out at every ATM we could find, just like you told me to. We made it to a little secluded area on the beach where we hired a cabin for a few days to figure out what we were going to do. Because of all the stops, and not wanting to leave too much of an obvious trail if they got a hold of your financial records, it took us about eight days to get up there.

"It was on the eleventh day that Paddy finally broke. He called me an idiot for choosing him over you and told me I needed to come back. It was in that moment that I realised all I was looking for was permission, an excuse, anything to propel me back here. We were packed and back on the road before Paddy had even stopped yelling at me."

"If you came back after two weeks, what have you been doing for the last four? What took you so long?"

"We didn't know how to go about coming back without being killed, or what to do, how to keep Paddy safe, or how to get you out of here … so …"

"He went to Declan," Kai finishes for him.

"*You* went to Declan? How did that turn out?"

Brett rubs his jaw. "Let's just say, with a bit of training, he'd make a pretty good Litmus fighter."

My hand flies up to my mouth. "He didn't … did he? You didn't kill him, did you?"

Brett and Kai laugh. "I let him have his shot. I deserved it," Brett says quietly. "After I explained everything that happened and why I was there, it was like all the anger, jealousy—or whatever it was between us—just disappeared. He went into saving Nuka mode."

"That still doesn't explain why Kai's here, or—"

"Kyle," Kai corrects me. "You're going to have to get used to that."

"Used to it? You mean you're not here to get us out?"

Brett and Kai share a glance.

"Get dressed. We have a meeting to get to," Kai says.

"A meeting?"

"Just do as I say, okay? You always were a pain in the ass when it came to asking you to do anything." Kai tries to say it with a straight face, but I see the hint of a playful smile underneath the tough exterior. He goes to walk out but stops just before the door. "And seriously, I don't really want to see this"—he gestures to Brett and me in bed with a wave of his hand—"again. I know you're an adult now, but I've known you since you were eight, and this is just wrong. So very wrong. If Brett wasn't such a giant, I'd have beaten him down already."

My face heats and flushes with embarrassment, while Brett just laughs it off as Kai walks out the door.

***

Kyle, Kyle, Kyle, I repeat in my head, trying to get used to it. Kyle and Cade are standing by the front door when we eventually emerge from our room, and we just catch the end of their conversation.

"I've been in this business for fifteen years, and I've learnt that it's best to build a bond with my subjects. If they respect me, they're much more cooperative. I'm just going to take them out for breakfast, woo them a little, and set some small boundaries so we all get along and this goes smoothly. The last thing you want to have to do is find yet another HOS in a few months."

She clears her throat and nods, gesturing to us standing behind Kyle.

He turns to us. "We ready to go?"

"Is Sasha coming?" I ask.

"I'll be talking with her later," Kyle says.

Damn it. I was hoping this was our out.

"We'll be expecting you back for lunch," Cade says. "Not a moment later."

"No problem," Kyle answers. Either he didn't pick up on her suspicious tone or he's ignoring it.

It doesn't take long for us to be on the road and for me to start probing for answers.

"So where are we really going?"

"Do we really need to tell you?" Kyle asks. "I mean … my being here should be clue enough that your mother's involved."

"I'm trying not to get my hopes up here, so I don't want to assume anything."

"So you *want* to see your mother?" Kai … *Kyle, Kyle, Kyle,* asks, raising his eyebrow at me in the rear-view mirror. "The impression I'm under is you want nothing to do with her."

"I may have a lot of apologies to make," I mumble.

With Kyle's reluctance to talk and Brett staring out the window pretending like I'm not here, the trip into the city is a silent one. We pull up to a random parking lot, our final destination still a mystery to me.

It's not until Kyle leads us down a few alleyways, across a few streets, and then backtracks a bit do I realise we're being led to one of the Institute offices. Kyle's just making sure that if we're being followed, we'll lose them. We're walking briskly, so briskly I have to jog a couple of steps every now and then to keep up.

He leads us to a side entrance into the Institute building. Kyle has a key, opening the locked door to let us in. The sound of our feet on the tiled floor is the only thing I can hear, or perhaps it's the only thing I can focus on right now. We walk up a few flights of stairs and open the door to the third-floor offices. Kyle leads us to my uncle's office and knocks, awaiting a response before entering.

My feet freeze in position, unwilling to take me into the room.

"It's okay, Nuke. I promise," Brett says in my ear, giving me an encouraging little push towards the door.

The minute I see her, my eyes fill with tears. "Mummy?" I squeak. It just blurts out of me, and before I can even cringe at myself for being a grown-ass woman calling her mother "mummy," I'm in her arms and sobbing like the child I'm behaving like.

Dad's here too. He joins in, then Uncle Drew, and Aunt Jenna also, making it a group hug.

"Guys," I sniffle. "I'm a little squished."

They all pry themselves off of me, Mum almost in the same state of tears that I am when she pulls away.

"Your friends are here too, but we asked for some time alone first," Uncle Drew says. His tone makes me nervous, and then I realise—while they all look happy to see me, none of them look actually happy.

Mum seems pensive, and Dad just looks like Dad—but he's always had a good poker face; he needs one, being a psychologist and all. Aunt Jenna actually looks a tad angry.

"I'll leave you guys to fill her in, I'll go debrief the others," Kai says.

Uncle Drew gestures for us to take a seat, and we all sit in chairs that have been crammed into this tiny office. Everyone sits except Aunt Jenna who paces back and forth along the window that overlooks the street.

"So," she starts. "Care to tell us how you've ended up in the belly of the biggest illegal syndicate in the country? Fighting, drugs, money laundering, prostitution—it's all there, and you're right in the middle of it."

"Can you not treat my daughter like a suspect?" Mum says. "You're not an inspector right now, you're her aunt."

"Don't start again, you two," Dad warns. I guess there's been a lot of arguing amongst themselves before we arrived.

"It's just sport," I say but then see the disappointment in both Mum and Aunt Jenna's eyes. Even Brett's staring at me with a stunned expression, like he can't believe how naïve I am.

"Have you really not noticed it?" Brett asks quietly.

"Noticed what? I turn up, then fight, make small talk with rich people, mix with the other fighters, and then go home. What's there to notice?"

"It's not just illegal betting and street fighting with no rules and no regard for the fighters," Jenna says. "We've been after Litmus for years now."

"Why don't you just shut it down?"

"Litmus is too big. We're pretty sure it has some of our officers on its payroll, and we're sure Dalton has more connections and resources than we'll ever know. And from what Brett's told us, there's four other Jonas Daltons who each own a piece of Litmus. We could always raid it, sure, but all that will do is shut it down for a while before they take up again somewhere else, or even in the same spot. We need to gather evidence to put them all away for life."

"So that's why you've sent Kai to us? You're not going to get us out?" I ask, the disappointment crashing down on me.

"The couple of agents who've been let in to the inner circle haven't been invited to come back. We've gotten in a few times as patrons, but that gets us nowhere. We need someone who can live in their world, get deep inside. This won't be a quick sting. We need a full undercover operation."

"You agreed to this?" I ask, turning to Brett.

"I told them it's up to you what we do. I've been with your family the last few weeks trying to work out a plan for this whole thing, but then when Gabby went to Declan and told him what happened with Drake, about your contract, I went back to Litmus as soon as I could. I don't know what's going to happen, but no matter what, you and I will be together. Where you go, I go. I'm not leaving you again. Ever."

"Nuka," Mum says, "If you want out, we'll get you out. We can protect you, Brett, and your sister. We'll get you to a safe house, we'll—"

"You know it's not that easy, Lia," Aunt Jenna says.

"It's not?" I ask.

"Do you realise how deep this goes? To get away from someone like Dalton, we're talking full-scale lockdown, witness protection type stuff. No jobs, no life, hidden somewhere remote where you'll be looking over your shoulder every five minutes until we can get him. Which won't happen if we can't even get an agent in there."

"But we're constantly looking over our shoulders now. We saw Jonas shoot someone point-blank. You think he won't hesitate to do the same to me or Sasha … even Brett?"

"You think he won't hunt you down and do it anyway if you leave?" Aunt Jenna yells before forcefully making herself take a breath to calm herself down. "Nuka, do you understand what this would mean for us? You could help us bring the whole system down."

"You're talking like an inspector again," Mum says. "What if this was one of the twins?"

"Nuka," Uncle Drew pitches in, "you have the chance to do

the right thing here. You could help—"

"Not you, too," Mum says, glaring at Drew. He just shrugs at her.

"Kai will protect you," Aunt Jenna says.

"She's not doing it," Mum says more confidently.

Aunt Jenna drags a chair over to sit in front of me. "Look, Nuka. You have every right to want to run, and if you decide to do that, then you will have the full support of us and the rest of the family. But if you escape him, I have no doubt he'll do everything in his power to find you. If you tough it out for a while, you could help put a lot of bad people away and give yourself true freedom."

"My freedom was lost the minute I signed that damned contract," I mutter.

"Nuka," Mum says with her motherly soothing voice. I didn't realise how much I missed it until this very moment. "You don't have to do this," she says again, only this time I think she's pleading.

I throw my head in my hands. "I can't make this decision without Sasha."

"You don't have to give us an answer right away. Take the time to think about it, and if you ever need to get in contact with us, just go through Kai. If you ever need a time for us to pull you out, we'll do it," Aunt Jenna says.

"Perhaps we should give you and Brett some alone time to talk it over some more," Mum says, her brows knitting together in concern.

"You're being hypocritical, Allira," Uncle Drew says.

"What?" she snaps.

"Do you want to discuss what *you* did at Nuka's age?"

"Yeah, people ended up dead because of what I did at her age. I want them to make sure they really think about what they're doing instead of jumping on the bandwagon of some spur of the moment plan, where anything could go wrong and could blow up in their faces."

"Are you talking about when my bio dad—" I start but then see Mum's eyebrows go up in surprise.

"You *told* her?" Mum yells at Uncle Drew.

"She needed to know. And this isn't the same, and you know it. You and Jenna are leading this. Kai loves Nuka like family so you know he's not going to screw this up—he'll do anything to make sure she's safe."

"Lia," Dad says, turning her chair to face him. "You know I hate it when Drew's right." He smirks in Uncle Drew's direction which earns him a middle finger, but Dad just laughs. "And as much as I *hate* this idea …" he sighs, turning serious, "I think this is the best option for everyone to get out safely. It's certainly the only option if we want Nuka back in our lives."

"How is putting their lives in danger doing it safely?" she asks softly.

He kisses her on the forehead and then the nose. Being here with Mum and Dad only makes me realise that if I ever do get out of this, I want them to be in my life. We can't go into witness protection for the rest of our lives, and as long as we can be civil and keep the peace between Jonas and ourselves, he won't hurt us. If we continue to do our jobs, we'll be safer there than anywhere else we could flee.

I realise what needs to be done.

"I'm not saying this as a definite, because I still have to talk to Sasha, but I think I agree with Aunt Jenna. If we ever want any kind of life for our future, we can't be looking over our shoulders the whole time. We need to get out, but we need to finish them when we do."

"You're going to be okay living there for the foreseeable future?" Brett asks me, taking hold of both my hands.

"As long as we're together, I don't care where we live."

He half-smiles as he leans in and gives me a soft, lingering kiss. A throat purposefully clears, and when Brett pulls away,

Dad's standing with his arms crossed and a scowl on his face.

"I'm a little old for the overprotective dad thing, aren't I?" I say.

"Nope. You'll always be my little girl."

His overprotectiveness reminds me of how Brett is with Paddy. "What about Paddy? Where is he?" I ask.

"He's safe," Aunt Jenna says. "He's staying with Uncle Shilah and Tate until we can ensure his safety from Shane and his crew."

"How can you ensure his safety if he's staying with Uncle Tate who's a very public political figure?" I ask.

"Have you ever seen Uncle Shilah in the media?" Mum asks. "It's perfect protection for Paddy because they have people watching over them, but the only one who's ever in the media spotlight is Tate. Perhaps it would change if he was ever to run for president, but for now, it's the safest place for Paddy."

"He's going to testify against Shane. We'll keep him in protection for as long as we need to," Aunt Jenna says.

I turn to Brett. "So he's completely safe?"

"One hundred percent," he says.

"And the money?"

"In an account in Paddy's name. I couldn't open it in just your name, they wouldn't let me. Also, being in his name, it'll be untraceable to Jonas and Cade. It'll be waiting for us when we get out."

"Okay," Uncle Drew interrupts, his eyes looking at the clock on the wall. "I promised your friends they could have some time with you before you had to get back."

"Unfortunately," Aunt Jenna adds, "We can't really risk being in contact after this. If you need us for anything, you need to go through your handler, Kai."

"So … this is goodbye?" I choke out the words.

"Only until we get them," Aunt Jenna says.

"How long will that take?" I ask.

It's almost like the whole room lets out a collective sigh.

"It could be a few months …" Mum says.

"Why do I feel like there's a but coming on?"

"Most likely, it's going to take a few years to get what we need," Aunt Jenna says.

"But just remember," Mum says, "We'll be there to pull you out at any time."

I nod, and wipe my sniffily nose with the sleeve of my shirt.

Aunt Jenna is the first one to hug me, followed by Uncle Drew. Dad hugs me quickly like he's afraid if he holds on too tight, he'll never let go. He whispers in my ear, "Find your way back to us. Please." And by the time Mum's turn comes around, we're both a blubbering mess.

"It's really dusty in here. Your uncle should really clean more," she says, wiping her eye.

"I'm sorry … for everything. I wish the last three years never happened."

"I wish we hadn't kept secrets from you like we did."

"You had your reasons … and I can see why … but …"

"I'm so sorry. All we wanted to do was protect you."

"When can I see Will and Illy?"

Mum looks down at her feet, then back up at me with tears freely flowing now. "Probably not until …"

"Until this is all over?"

She nods. "I can't risk them getting involved … I'm sor—"

"I understand, Mum."

"Be safe, okay?"

"Don't know how safe I can be when it's my job to fight, but I'll try."

"Boy am I regretting forcing those martial arts lessons on you now." She laughs a little. "I love you, Nuka."

"Love you too, Mum."

She turns to leave but pauses in the doorway. "So what was your real name anyway?"

I screw up my face. "Lavender. Eww."

Mum laughs. "It's not so bad." She leaves the room, and it's just Brett and I until I hear his voice.

"It's better than Striker." He stands, leaning on the doorframe with his arms crossed.

"Declan," I whisper.

As if silently asking for permission, I look at Brett with questioning eyes.

"Go. You know you want to," he says.

It's all I need. In a split second, I have my arms wrapped around Declan so hard, I'd be scared of him breaking if he hadn't bulked out since I last saw him.

"Whoa, joining the force certainly agrees with you," I say, grabbing his bicep as I pull out of the hug.

"Kind of part of the job. I guess I could say the same for you." He points to my now toned fighter's body.

He runs his hand through his hair awkwardly. I have no idea what to say to him. But we're saved by a high-pitched screeching.

"Nuka!" If Gabby's voice is even piercing my ears, I'd hate to see what she's doing to Brett.

As expected, he's got his fingers in his ears, I assume to try to stop the ringing of her voice.

She rushes to me, giving me a hug. "You have no idea how worried I've been. Since Psych told me what really happened, I … I've been so scared." She hugs me again.

"I'm fine. Seriously."

"I spoke to Dad about it, and he said he can pull some strings and get you transferred to Reid, or another team, if you want."

"Wait, your dad knows?"

"How else do you think we got Jonas and Cade to hire Kai," Declan says.

"Huh?"

"Have you not noticed how much Jonas and Cade fumble and

fawn all over my dad? Once I told him what was going on, he was going to pull his money from the whole thing. But I told him if he did that, you might get punished for losing your sponsor. So instead, he came with me to talk to Declan and the police. He's cooperating with them by giving them all the information he has in exchange for immunity, plus he'll keep supporting you until you can get out."

"Really?"

"Please, I won't let anything happen to you. Or Sasha. I'm really glad we've become close again—like we were back in high school."

"Me too."

"Uh … I hate to interrupt, but I really should be getting back to the briefing Kai's giving," Declan says.

"Wait … you're on this case?" I ask.

"Yeah. Pretty funny that you're my first real case as a fed, right?"

"I think you guys should talk," Brett says. "Come on, Gabs, I'll buy you a cup of coffee."

"Oooh, Brawn just asked me for coffee," she sing-songs. It's hilarious to me that she still can't call him Brett. "Oh, and before I forget—seriously, any time you need to pass information onto me, please, please, please send Psych." She fans herself with her hand. "That boy can come over *any* time he wants."

I'm still laughing by the time they're out the door and it's just Declan and me left.

"So …" I awkwardly say.

"I really should be getting back."

"We can't just … talk?"

"That's funny, you haven't wanted to do that with me for months."

Groaning, I drag him farther into the room and push him down on one of the chairs, taking the one opposite him for myself.

"What, Nuka?"

I cringe at him using my full name. "Can we not do this right now?"

"You wanted to talk, so talk. Maybe start with how you fell in love with your bodyguard, and then go from there."

"Can we really not do *that* right now, either?"

"We need to."

"Why?"

He sighs, running his hand through his hair again. "Before your birthday, I thought we were … I don't know … going somewhere? And then you met him, and I practically haven't seen you since."

"You joined the academy, I joined Litmus—there was no future …"

"But you wanted one?" he asks, his eyes locking me into place under a surprised stare.

"Yes, no … I don't know. By the time I worked out I had feelings for you, I already had feelings for Brett as well, and he was the easier choice. We were living in the same world, you and I had been living separate lives for months. And then …"

"Then you fell for him."

"I fell *really* hard," I say with a half-smile. "I think he's it for me, Dec." I don't want to hurt Declan, but he needs to know the truth.

He stares at the floor instead of me. "You and I have always had this connection. I don't know what it is or how to explain it. I guess deep down I always thought you and I were going to end up together, but in a weird way, I guess I kind of felt pressured into thinking that way? You know what it's been like for the past eleven years, trying to define our relationship to people. They just don't get it. We've always been there for each other, for each tragic break-up, picking up the pieces for one another like it was what we were made to do."

"Maybe that's what we are. People who'll be there for each

other no matter what."

He nods but doesn't take his eyes off the floor, still refusing to make eye contact with me. "Maybe. All I know is it friggin' hurts not being around you every day. I miss you like crazy."

"Me too."

"But I think this time apart will do us good. Maybe it'll break this unhealthy co-dependency thing we have. I've been going insane just wondering if you were okay or not, but now that I know Brett a little, I can rest easy knowing he'll never let anything hurt you. It's just hard for me, because I know you guys have something special. He's changed you. He brought you home, he made you want to reconnect with your family. That's something I tried to do for three years. He made you realise what you want from life. I was kind of hoping to do all those things for you. Isn't that what best friends are for?"

"You couldn't do all those things, Dec. We're too close, we know each other inside and out. I needed to distance myself so I could find my true self. Brett was just there to help."

"I kind of hate that he's a good guy. It'd be so much easier to hate him if he was a dick."

I laugh. "Did you really punch him? I mean … *really*? He's a professional fighter—are you crazy?"

He laughs. "I must be. I'm letting my best friend risk her life for a stupid underground fight club bust. It just doesn't seem worth it to me."

I pull him up as I stand, taking him into my arms for the last time.

***

Going over the options with Sasha back at the house, I'm shocked to find her pumped for the idea of staying. Brett and *Kyle* seem surprised too.

"Really?" I ask.

"I want to bring those fu—buttheads down," she says, refraining from cussing.

I glance at Kyle and then back at Sasha. "Please, you can swear in front of him. He's heard a lot worse come out of my mouth."

"It's true. She's been swearing like a drunk bogan since she was twelve," Kyle says.

"And who was the grown-up teaching me all the bad words?" I exclaim.

"Yeah, yeah, back to the case at hand, hey?"

"I've lived with Jonas since I was ten years old," Sasha says. "Him and his bastard rich friends found it appropriate to grope my ass from when I was fourteen years old, so yeah, I want to do this."

"You don't want to run?" Brett asks.

"As much as I've fantasized about it, I didn't have high hopes for the plan to begin with. Nuka's aunt's right. Jonas *will* come after us. I'm pretty sure he sent someone after Brett. If we truly want to get away, we have to stay."

"So this is going to be our lives now?" I ask.

"We're going to get 'em," Kyle says reassuringly.

"What do we do until then?"

Brett wraps his arms around me. "You mean apart from act like the shining celebrity couple for our adoring fans, fight, kick butt, and—"

Sasha puts her hand up, stopping him from talking. "If you're going to say something lame like 'make love,' I'm going to puke. Like right now."

Brett laughs. "I wasn't. I was going to say we try to get out of here as soon as we can, but"—he looks at me—"she doesn't have the worst idea." He smirks.

I smile up at him and he lands a kiss on my lips.

Kyle clears his throat.

Sasha groans. "Ugh, I'm so not team Bruka."

-26-

FOUR YEARS LATER

"Three years, three-hundred-forty-two days to go," Brett whispers in my ear.

Rolling over in bed to face him, I run my hand up his chest, wrapping it around his neck. "It sounds so long when you put it like that," I whine.

I love waking up to his hopeful face every morning, but every morning it's the same, and every morning's a struggle to keep positive like him.

"Sooner if they can nail these guys," he says, kissing me on the nose. "We can find a place to live, get married, start a family of our own."

I tense under him at his words but hope he doesn't notice.

The rejection is obvious when he pulls away, sitting up in bed and running his hands through his hair.

"It's not that I don't want those things. You know I do," I say, sitting up and wrapping my arm around him from behind with my chin resting on his shoulder.

He nods his head but still doesn't turn to face me. "I know, Nuke. It's hard for you to think about our future when it's still so far away."

We've been at this game for a little over four years. We're halfway through our contract, and Kyle doesn't seem any closer to bringing this place down.

"It wasn't supposed to take this long," Brett says.

"I know. Things are probably just more complicated than we realise."

Kyle doesn't talk to us about the case, and if I'm completely honest, I don't want him to. I know more agents have managed to infiltrate a few of the teams, but we've all agreed it's best if I don't know who they are. I haven't recognised any one new as Lia's colleagues, but I've also told myself not to look too hard. I'd probably act different around them, and it's easier for me to face everyone if I don't know what they're up to.

Since finding out what really goes on, I've noticed things. Things I don't want to see—drugs passing hands and way too wasted girls being held up by a couple of guys who have a glint of anticipation in their eyes. At first I got Litmus security onto them, but all they'd do is kick them out, ultimately bringing the girl's fate forwards an hour or two. I've tried cornering the girls in the bathroom, but some have insisted they want it, that they're "on the job" and are getting paid to act wasted to make their client's sick fantasy more realistic. But others have been innocents. Drugged and confused, they often don't know where they are. Sasha and I have saved a few girls by sneaking them out back to the infirmary to sleep off the drugs in safety, but it doesn't feel like it's enough.

Cade and Jonas have loosened the tight leashes a little with us, but we're still very much watched twenty-four-seven. Particularly me and Brett. Sasha has a bit more freedom than us, but she's still always guarded when she goes out. Byron signed on as one of our full-time guards, and we still have randoms watching over us too. Logan got out as soon as he could, not wanting to end up like Drake. Pretty smart on his behalf.

"Ready for your fight tonight? It's been a while since you've done a Wild Card night, hasn't it?" Brett asks. I'm thankful for the subject change.

"A few months."

The Heatwave brand is one of the best. I'm right up there with Ryker, Brett … and Brayden. Ugh.

He's still the biggest ass on the planet. Ever since Brett called his bluff and turned the threat of cheating around on him, his attitude has gotten worse. But we're secure in the knowledge he'll never tell, because it will only incriminate himself.

He's beaten me every time in the ring, but I can hold my own against him. He's never knocked me out, but he's come close a couple of times. I've only came close to beating him once.

Since my raging comeback with a knockout four years ago, I've been undefeated on Wild Card nights. Since that fight, I've been fighting with the big guns, and Wild Card nights have gone back into rotation between the others.

The transition was pretty smooth, although it took a good two months before I had an actual win. Flynn was my first, and I still revel in that fact. I think Sasha's hurt motivated me to do well. Once I had the confidence and knowledge that I *could* win, I found winning came easier and the glory is addictive.

Wild card nights are fun, but I now understand what the others mean when they say you get over them. There's no challenge in them. Tonight won't be any different.

Sasha, Brett, and I walk into the Deakin locker room to find Gabby straddling Ryker on the bench seats.

"Guys … I mean, really?" I complain.

Gabby laughs, removing herself from Ryker's lap. "We have something to tell you all," she says, her smile practically blinding me.

"I …" Ryker stutters. "I asked her to marry me."

Sasha's face lights up as she runs over to Gabby, throwing her arms around her.

I, on the other hand, look at Brett. His jaw's set, and he has a fake smile plastered on his face. I know exactly what he's thinking. *It should be us.*

I hug Ryker and then Gabby, congratulating them both with enough enthusiasm as I can muster, just hoping I pull it off. Then I pull Brett away, leading him back into the corridor outside the locker room.

"I love you, you know that, right?" I say.

"Of course, I do, Nuke."

"I promise. As soon as we get out of this mess, it'll be you, me, my insane family, and Paddy, all gathered to join you and me in wedded bliss … or some crap like that."

He narrows his eyes. "Did you just propose to me using the word 'crap'?"

I laugh. "I think I did, yeah." I didn't mean it to come out like a proposal, I kind of just blurted it out, but that doesn't change the fact that I want that life with him. One day.

He kisses me a sweet lingering kiss that makes my lips tingle and my heart dance. "I never meant for you to propose or promise to marry me right away … I just … I needed to know that you think about that stuff. The future, *our* future."

"It's basically *all* I think about."

He runs his hand through his hair, taking a step back from me and letting out a loud sigh.

"What aren't you telling me?"

"I overheard Kyle on the phone the other day. I didn't mean to eavesdrop, and then he made me promise not to say anything … but I can't keep this kind of secret from you."

A lump forms in my throat and I can't seem to swallow it down. "What is it?"

"It's Declan. He's—"

"Oh my God, is he okay? What happened?" My heartrate skyrockets in panic.

He laughs a little, touching his hands to my shoulders. "Calm down, he's fine. He's good. He's actually getting married. In a few weeks, I believe."

My stomach sinks a little, but my heart starts beating at a normal pace again. "You gave me a heart attack. I thought you were going to say he was dead or something."

He pulls his head back, assessing me. "You're not … upset?"

"Why would I be upset?"

Okay, maybe I am a little bit. But not for the reasons he's thinking. I want to be there, I want to see my best friend get married, but I can't. Because I'm still trapped *here*.

Brett shrugs as his eyes fill with uncertainty.

"All I want is for him to be as happy as I am with you. I miss him like crazy, but not like … *that*." My voice drops low to a whisper, "I haven't thought about him like that in a long time."

He steps forwards, wrapping his arms around me and bringing his lips to mine.

Mere seconds later, and way too soon for my liking, he's pulling away from me. "Company."

Colton walks up behind me, wrapping his arm around my shoulder. "Ready?"

"Almost. Hey, you know about the party going on in there?" I nod to the locker room. "Ryker has an announcement."

"He actually did it? I swore he was going to chicken out," Colton says with a grin. "Better get in there and congratulate him." He goes inside and as soon as the door closes, Brett's kissing me again, holding me tight, and reminding me why I chose to be his.

"I love you," he says, pulling back the tiniest bit. "Come on, you've got a fight to get to."

***

As I take to the arena for the second time this week, I drown out the hooting and hollering around me. I've learnt to tune it out over the years … well, that, and I think I'm partially deaf from so many blows to the head over time.

Brett stands off to the side of the arena, just like he does on all my fight nights. I can't imagine my life without him by my side. His support is what's getting me through Litmus life.

I'm still tender from my fight a few nights ago with Steve. He traded to Reid team about two years ago. He's probably one of my favourite opponents to fight. Right now I'm a few wins up on him, but it's a long running tally that has gone back and forth for a while now. I love that guy, but I will own that bastard one day.

Ryker remains faithfully by our side at Deakin, along with Colton. But we've gone through fifths a few times now. Since Palmer up and left, we've been looking to fill his spot, but no one seems to fit with the rest of us, and they've all been pretty crappy fighters. Plus, they haven't been desperate enough to sign over their lives for a few years, and that's what Jonas and Cade want—full control over their fighters. I think we've given up on the idea of a fifth now.

Palmer fell in love with a boy who comes from money. Clarke basically bought Palmer's way out. Palmer didn't owe Jonas and Cade anything, he was smart with his money, but they still made him pay an early exit fee—an exorbitant amount none of us would be able to afford.

Nodding to Felix as I take to the stage, I look out over the crowd, wondering which person I'll be fighting tonight. Sasha should be in there somewhere, taking money, placing bets. It's a step up from working the bar; plus with all her on-the-spot mathematical genius, she's great at making Jonas more money than any other bookie has.

Over the last four years, she's dated a couple of Litmus security guards and a barman, but she has a strict *no fighters* rule since Flynn. None of her boyfriends have ever gotten serious, and she doesn't seem like she's in a rush to settle down. She's only twenty, so there's definitely no need for that anyway. She'll find someone … someday. I just hope he has a heart as big as hers. Someone I could look to as a brother.

And then I see him walking to the stage; my *actual* brother, *William.* His face is aghast, and I'm pretty sure he has no idea what's going on, why I'm here, or if he realises the fact he's just volunteered to fight me.

In my head I'm screaming at him to run. I'm yelling at him for even being here. I haven't seen him for almost … *shit* … has it really been seven years since I moved out of home? He was fifteen the last time I saw him which was about four or five years ago.

It's definitely him. Just … a grown-up him.

Felix holds Will back as he reaches the stage, whispering something in his ear—I assume he's telling him to stay back from me until the fight starts.

This can't be happening. He can't be here. My heart thunders in my chest.

What the hell am I going to do?

There's only one thing I can do. I have to kick his ass so he never comes back.

Approaching him, I leave my expression as blank as I can

manage. I don't give any sign that I've recognised him. No one can find out who he is.

I motion to Felix to get this show on the road. As I get closer to the middle of the ring, I speak loudly into Felix's microphone.

"Come on, little boy. Show us what you've got."

THE END … FOR NOW

******

THANK YOU FOR READING LOSING NUKA!

Protecting William, (Book 2 of the Litmus Series) is set to be released in September, 2016.

Saving Illyana (Book 3 of the Litmus Series) will be close behind, due to be released early 2017. (Actual release date TBA)

Other works by Kayla Howarth:

THE INSTITUTE SERIES

The Institute (Book 1)

Resistance (Book 2)

Defective (Book 3)

Through His Eyes: And Institute Series Novella (Book 4)

ABOUT THE AUTHOR

Obsessed with YA fiction, Kayla Howarth's still a teenager at heart.

Her love of reading and movies inspired her to start something she never dreamed possible: Writing her first novel.

One book turned into two, two turned into three, and there's no sign of slowing down any time soon.

Find her at:

www.kaylahowarth.com

Made in the USA
Lexington, KY
11 March 2018